POKÉMON™

ADVENTURES

RUBY & SAPPHIRE

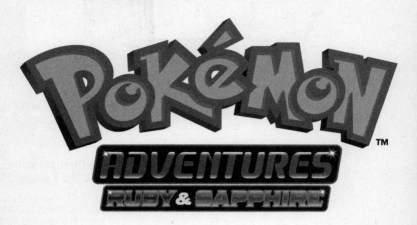

Pokémon ADVENTURES
Ruby and Sapphire
Volume 18
Perfect Square Edition

Story by **HIDENORI KUSAKA**
Art by **SATOSHI YAMAMOTO**

© 2013 Pokémon.
© 1995–2013 Nintendo/Creatures Inc./GAME FREAK inc.
TM, ®, and character names are trademarks of Nintendo.
POCKET MONSTERS SPECIAL Vol. 18
by Hidenori KUSAKA, Satoshi YAMAMOTO
© 1997 Hidenori KUSAKA, Satoshi YAMAMOTO
All rights reserved.
Original Japanese edition published by SHOGAKUKAN.
English translation rights in the United States of America, Canada,
United Kingdom, Ireland, Australia and New Zealand arranged with SHOGAKUKAN.

English Adaptation/Bryant Turnage
Translation/Tetsuichiro Miyaki
Touch-up & Lettering/Annaliese Christman
Design/Shawn Carrico
Editor/Annette Roman

Printed in the U.S.A.

Published by VIZ Media, LLC
P.O. Box 77010
San Francisco, CA 94107

10 9 8 7 6 5 4 3
First printing, September 2013
Third printing, August 2016

POKÉMON™ ADVENTURES

RUBY & SAPPHIRE

18
VOLUME EIGHTEEN

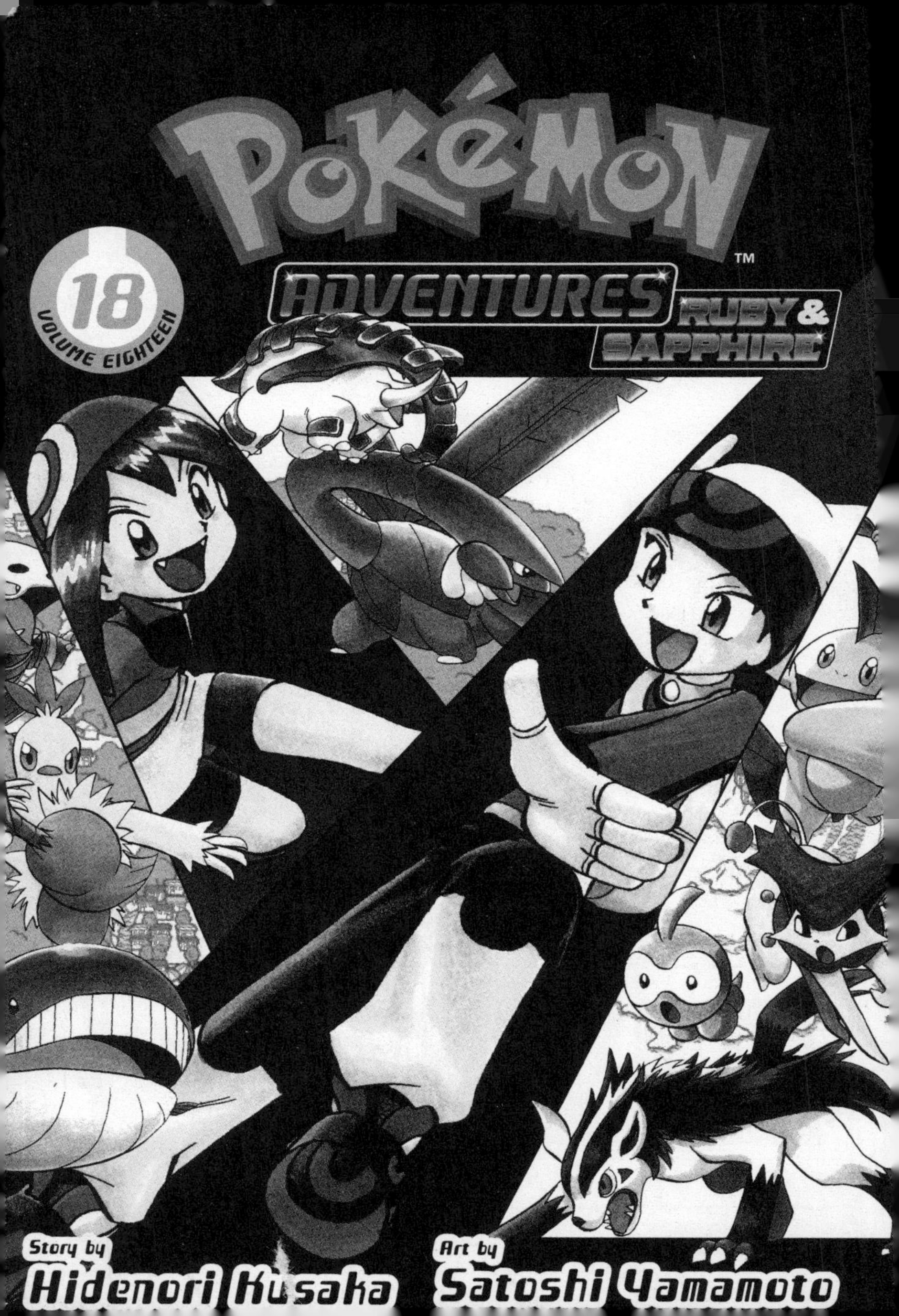

Story by
Hidenori Kusaka

Art by
Satoshi Yamamoto

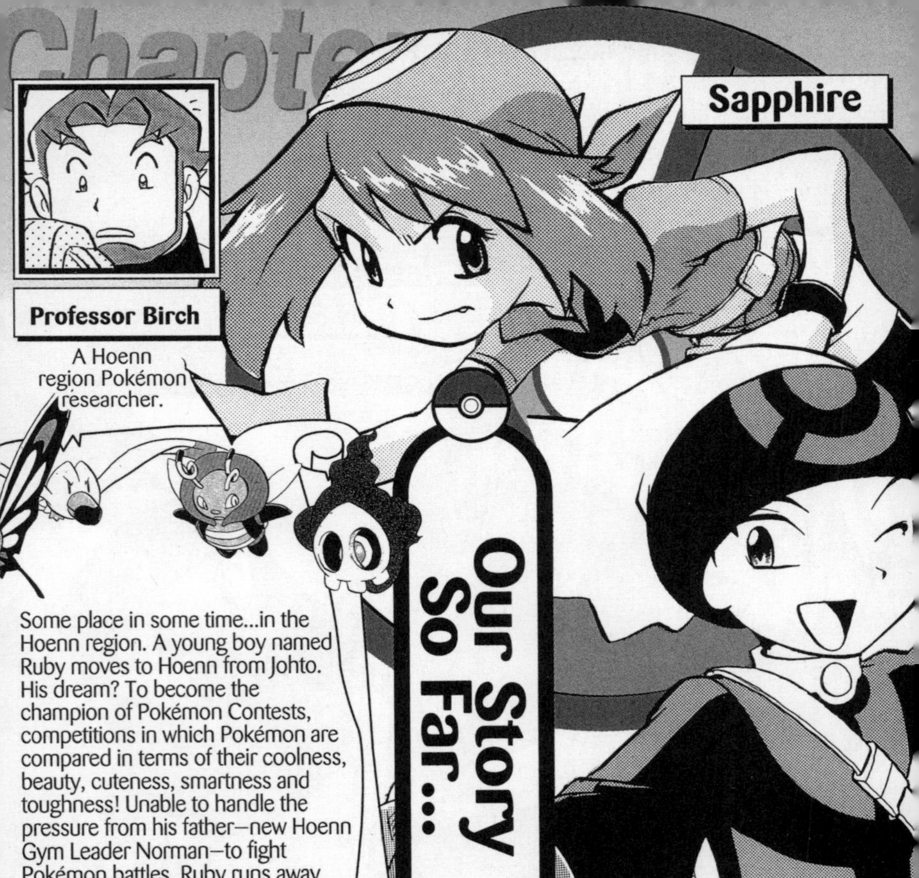
Chapte
Sapphire
Professor Birch
A Hoenn region Pokémon researcher.
Ruby

Our Story So Far...

Some place in some time...in the Hoenn region. A young boy named Ruby moves to Hoenn from Johto. His dream? To become the champion of Pokémon Contests, competitions in which Pokémon are compared in terms of their coolness, beauty, cuteness, smartness and toughness! Unable to handle the pressure from his father—new Hoenn Gym Leader Norman—to fight Pokémon battles, Ruby runs away from home. When Norman catches up to Ruby at the Weather Institute, he is in big trouble...!

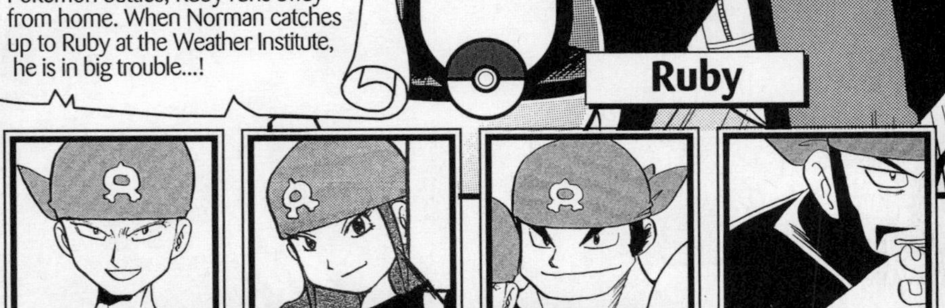
Amber
Archie's most trusted follower. He has a Carvanha.
Shelly
A member of Team Aqua who has a Ludicolo.
Matt
One of three members of the Team Aqua SSS. Muscular and intelligent.
Archie
The leader of mysterious Team Aqua. A ruthless, cold-hearted man.

Story of The Four

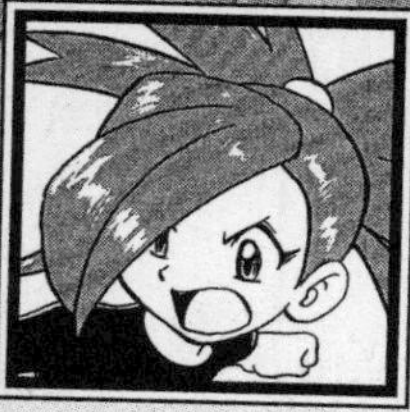

Flannery

The hot-tempered Gym Leader of Lavaridge Town.

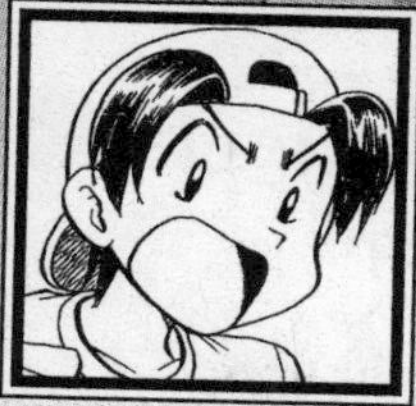

Ty

Gabby's trusty camera operator.

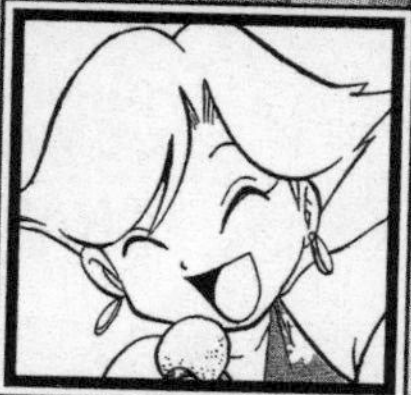

Gabby

A busybody Hoenn TV reporter.

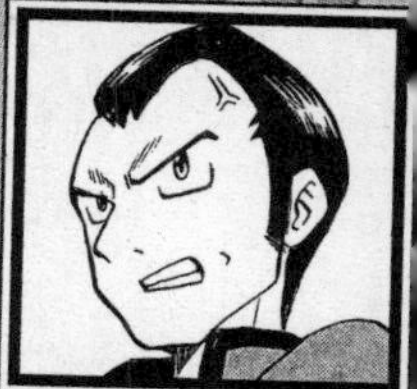

Norman

Ruby's father, the Gym Leader of Petalburg City.

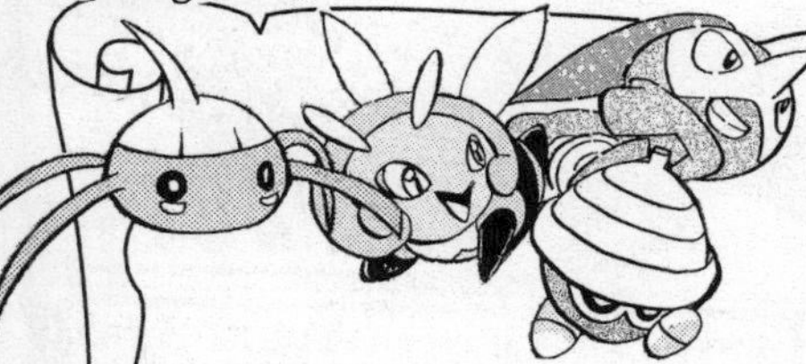

After a fierce battle, Norman finally agrees to accept Ruby's dream to become the champion of Pokémon Contests. Meanwhile, Sapphire, who is competing against Ruby in an 80-day challenge, has already managed to win badges from three Gyms.

When she heads down to Lavaridge Town to earn another, she gets mixed up with evil organization Team Aqua, who are attempting to put a stop to the volcanic activity of Mt. Chimney! Sapphire teams up with Gym Leader Flannery, and together they try to foil Team Aqua's evil scheme...

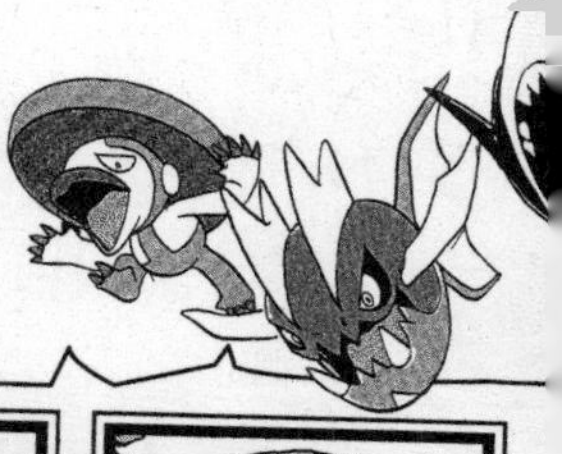

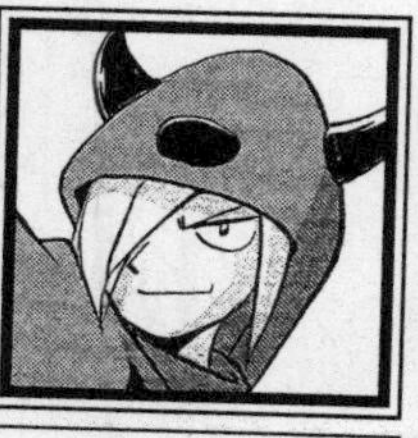

Blaise

One of the Three Fires of Team Magma. Ruby must battle him in Explorer 1.

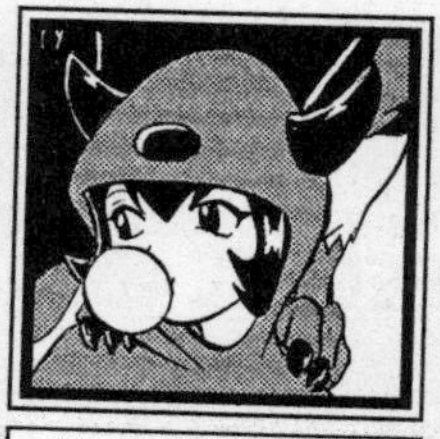

Courtney

The only female of the Three Fires of Team Magma. Fiesty and a skilled tactician.

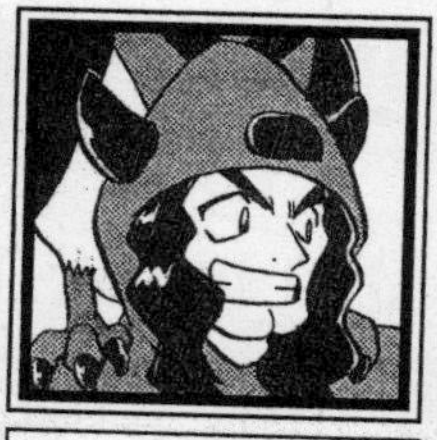

Tabitha

One of the Three Fires of Team Magma. He has a Torkoal.

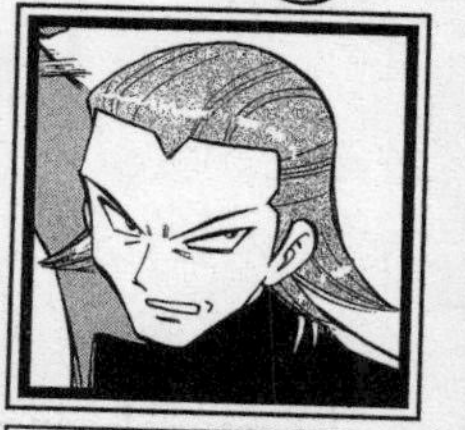

Maxie

The leader of Team Magma.

TRAINERS OF THE FOURTH CHAPTER

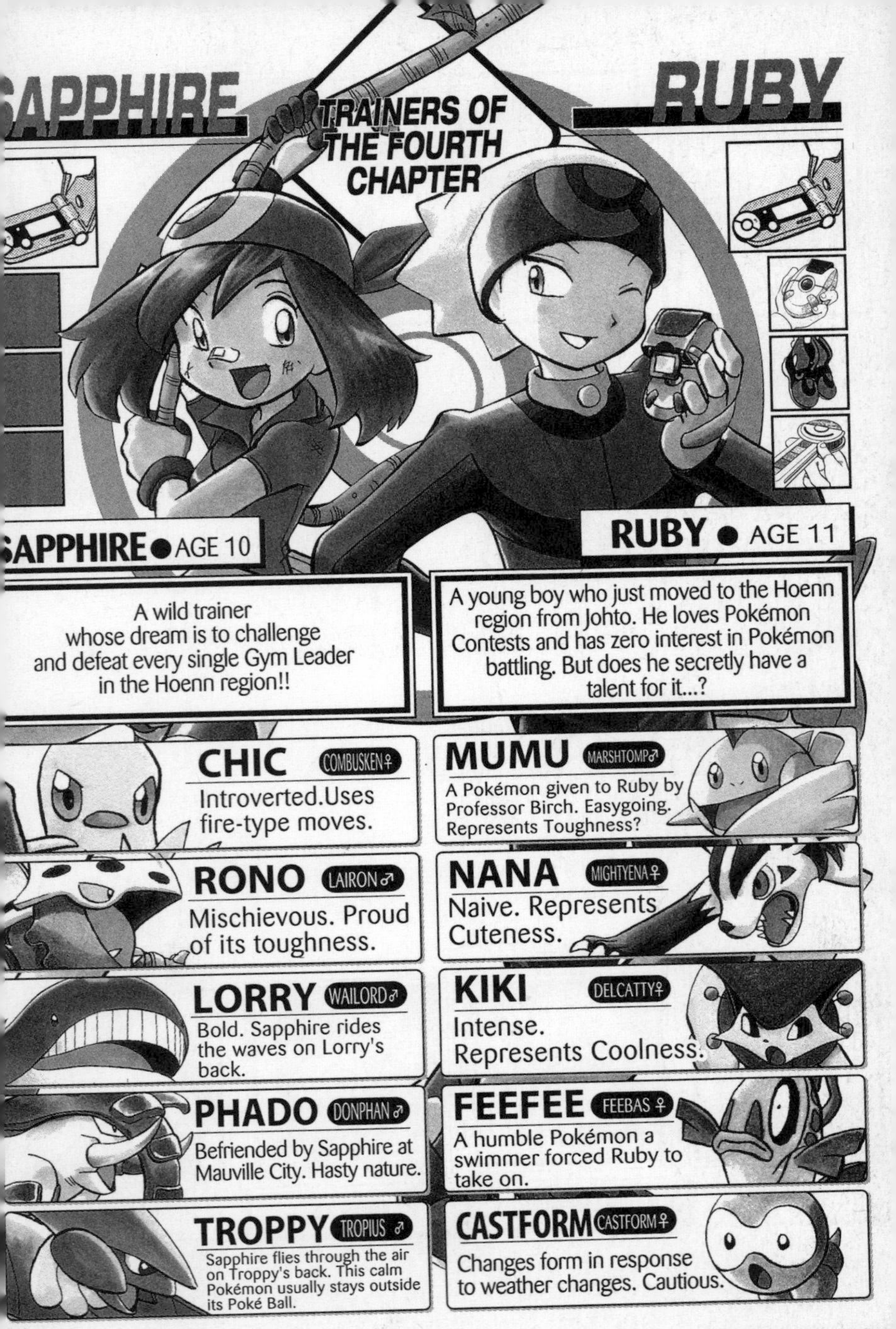

SAPPHIRE

SAPPHIRE ● AGE 10

A wild trainer whose dream is to challenge and defeat every single Gym Leader in the Hoenn region!!

CHIC (COMBUSKEN♀)
Introverted. Uses fire-type moves.

RONO (LAIRON♂)
Mischievous. Proud of its toughness.

LORRY (WAILORD♂)
Bold. Sapphire rides the waves on Lorry's back.

PHADO (DONPHAN♂)
Befriended by Sapphire at Mauville City. Hasty nature.

TROPPY (TROPIUS♂)
Sapphire flies through the air on Troppy's back. This calm Pokémon usually stays outside its Poké Ball.

RUBY

RUBY ● AGE 11

A young boy who just moved to the Hoenn region from Johto. He loves Pokémon Contests and has zero interest in Pokémon battling. But does he secretly have a talent for it...?

MUMU (MARSHTOMP♂)
A Pokémon given to Ruby by Professor Birch. Easygoing. Represents Toughness?

NANA (MIGHTYENA♀)
Naive. Represents Cuteness.

KIKI (DELCATTY♀)
Intense. Represents Coolness.

FEEFEE (FEEBAS♀)
A humble Pokémon a swimmer forced Ruby to take on.

CASTFORM (CASTFORM♀)
Changes form in response to weather changes. Cautious.

Pokémon™

ADVENTURES

RUBY & SAPPHIRE

18

VOLUME EIGHTEEN

CONTENTS

● Chapter 215 ●
Assaulted by Pelipper II

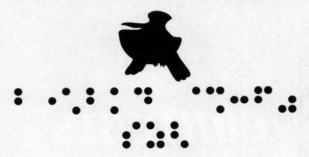

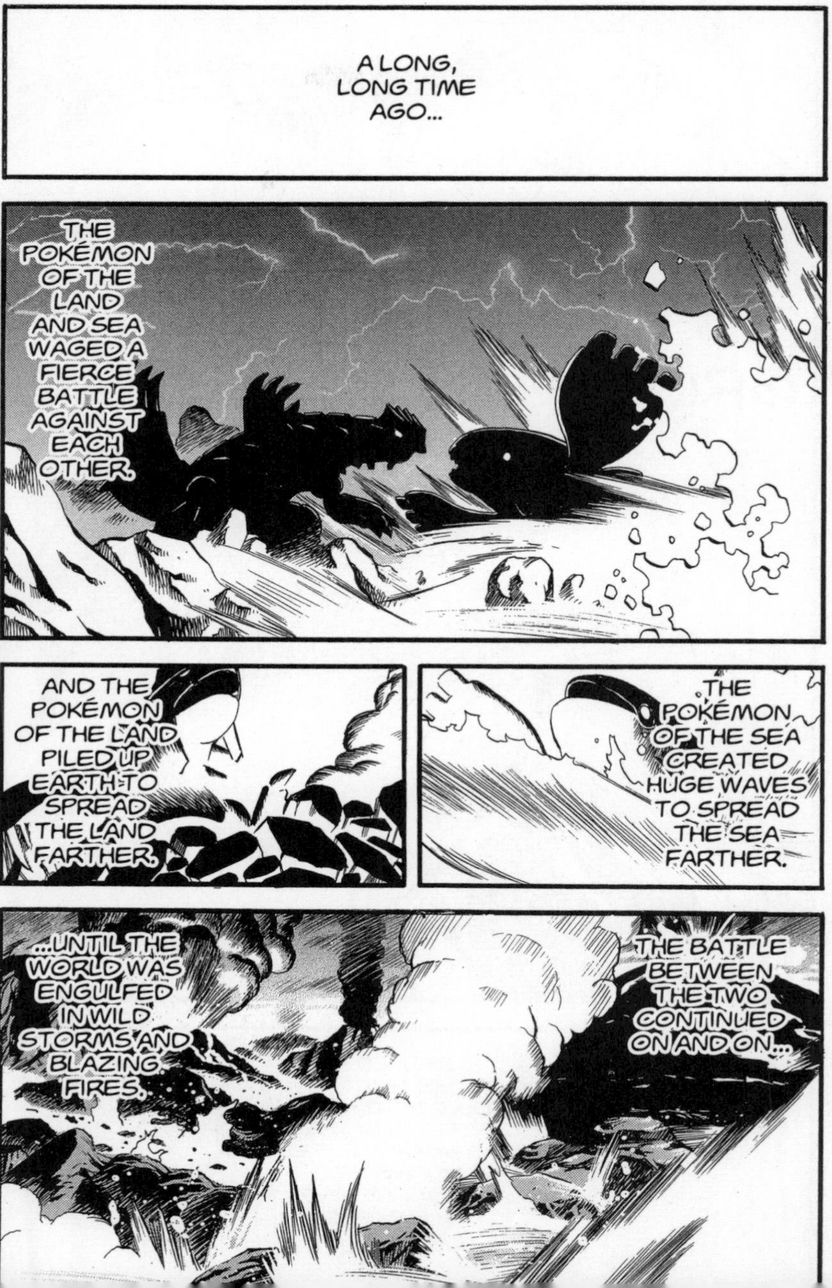
A LONG, LONG TIME AGO...
THE POKÉMON OF THE LAND AND SEA WAGED A FIERCE BATTLE AGAINST EACH OTHER.
THE POKÉMON OF THE SEA CREATED HUGE WAVES TO SPREAD THE SEA FARTHER.
AND THE POKÉMON OF THE LAND PILED UP EARTH TO SPREAD THE LAND FARTHER.
THE BATTLE BETWEEN THE TWO CONTINUED ON AND ON...
...UNTIL THE WORLD WAS ENGULFED IN WILD STORMS AND BLAZING FIRES.

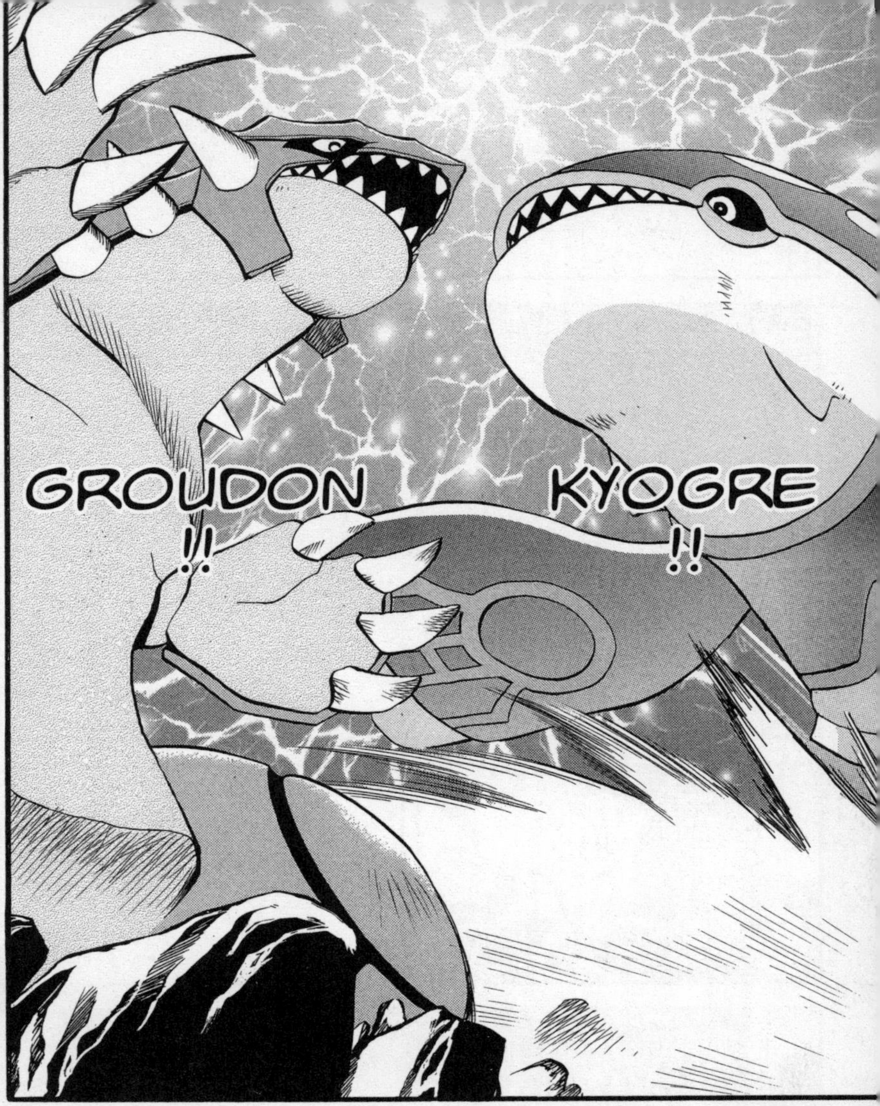
KYOGRE!!
GROUDON!!

IT SEEMED AS IF THEIR BATTLE WOULD NEVER END. BUT FINALLY THE TWO SWAM INTO THE DEPTHS OF THE OCEAN...AND DISAPPEARED.

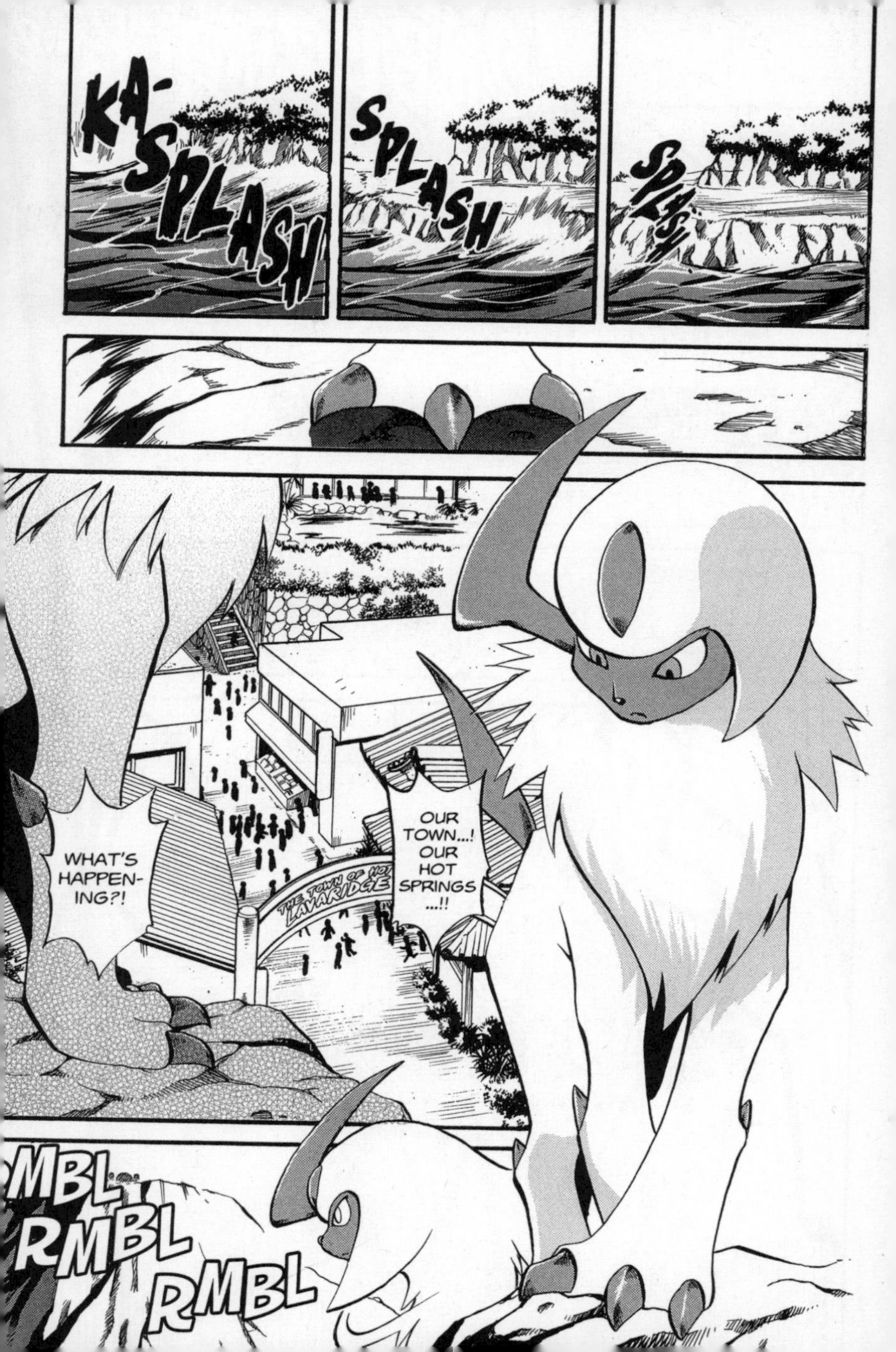
SPLASH
SPLASH
KA-SPLASH
OUR TOWN...! OUR HOT SPRINGS ...!!
THE TOWN OF HOT
LAVARIDGE
WHAT'S HAPPEN-ING?!
MBL
RMBL
RMBL

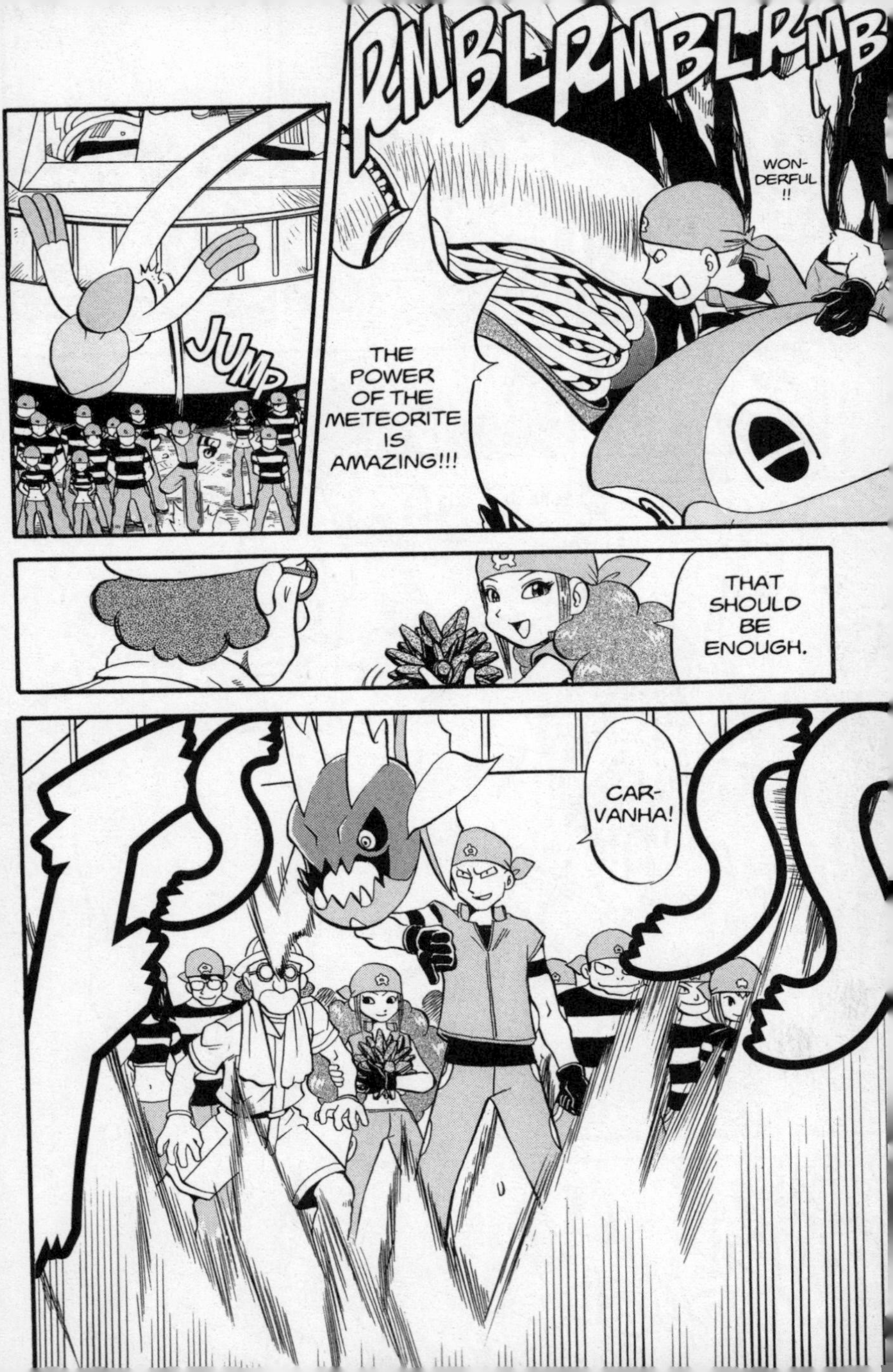
RMBLRMBLRMB
WON-DERFUL!!
THE POWER OF THE METEORITE IS AMAZING!!!
JUMP
THAT SHOULD BE ENOUGH.
CAR-VANHA!

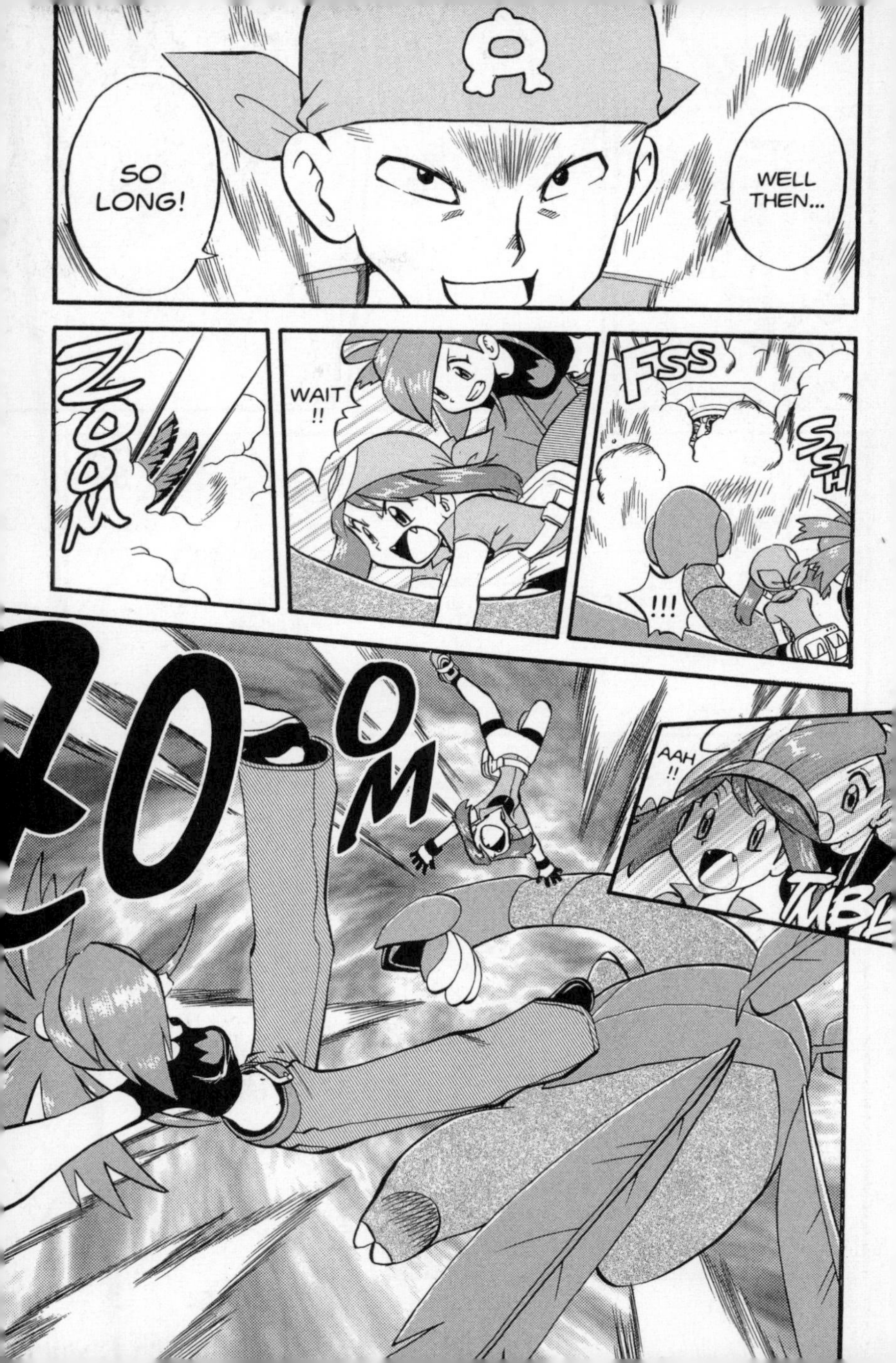
WELL THEN...
SO LONG!
FSS
SSH
!!!
WAIT !!
ZOOM
AAH !!
TMBL

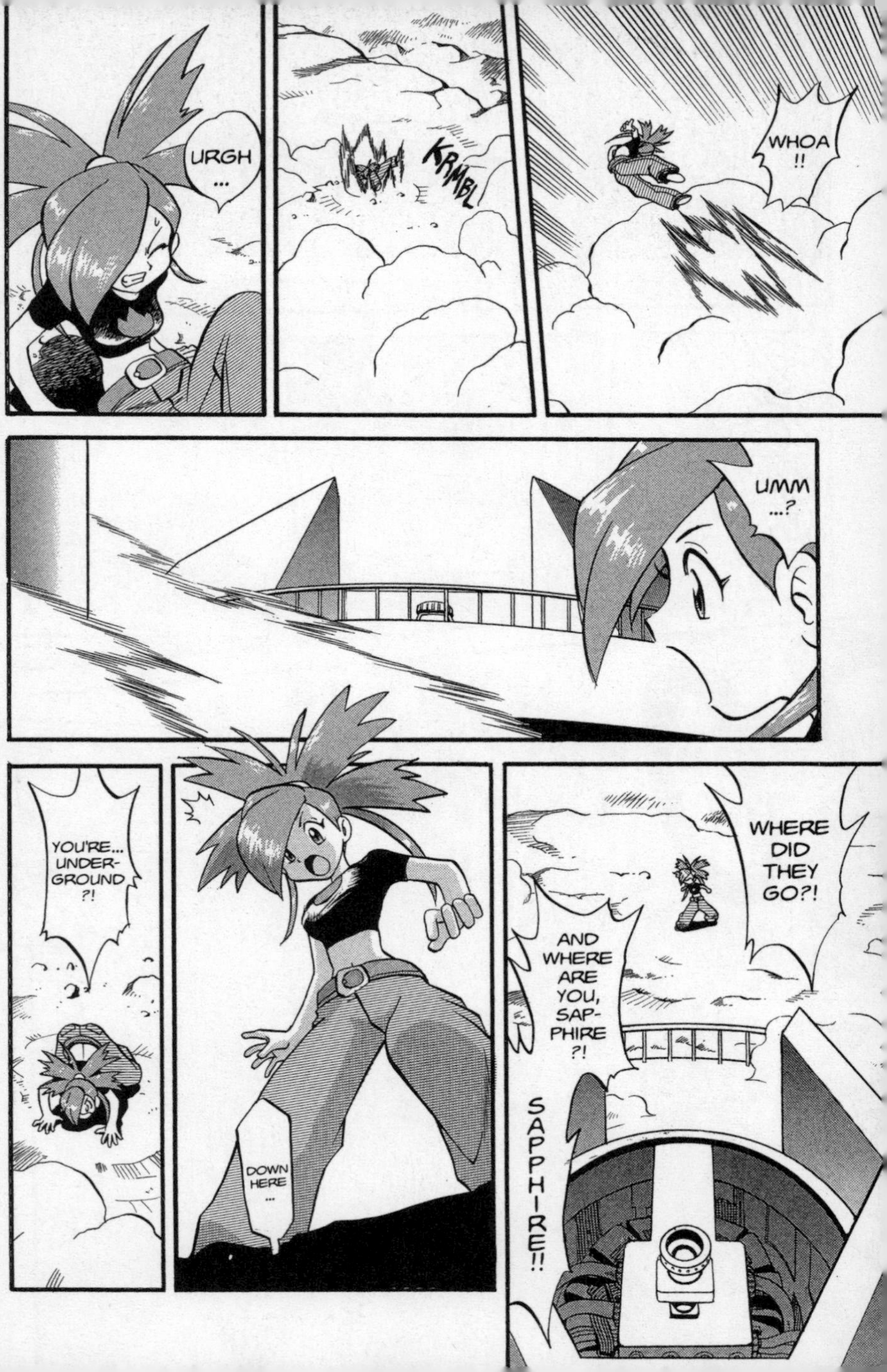
WHOA !!
KRMBL
URGH ...
UMM ...?
WHERE DID THEY GO?!
AND WHERE ARE YOU, SAPPHIRE ?!
SAPPHIRE!!
DOWN HERE ...
YOU'RE... UNDERGROUND ?!

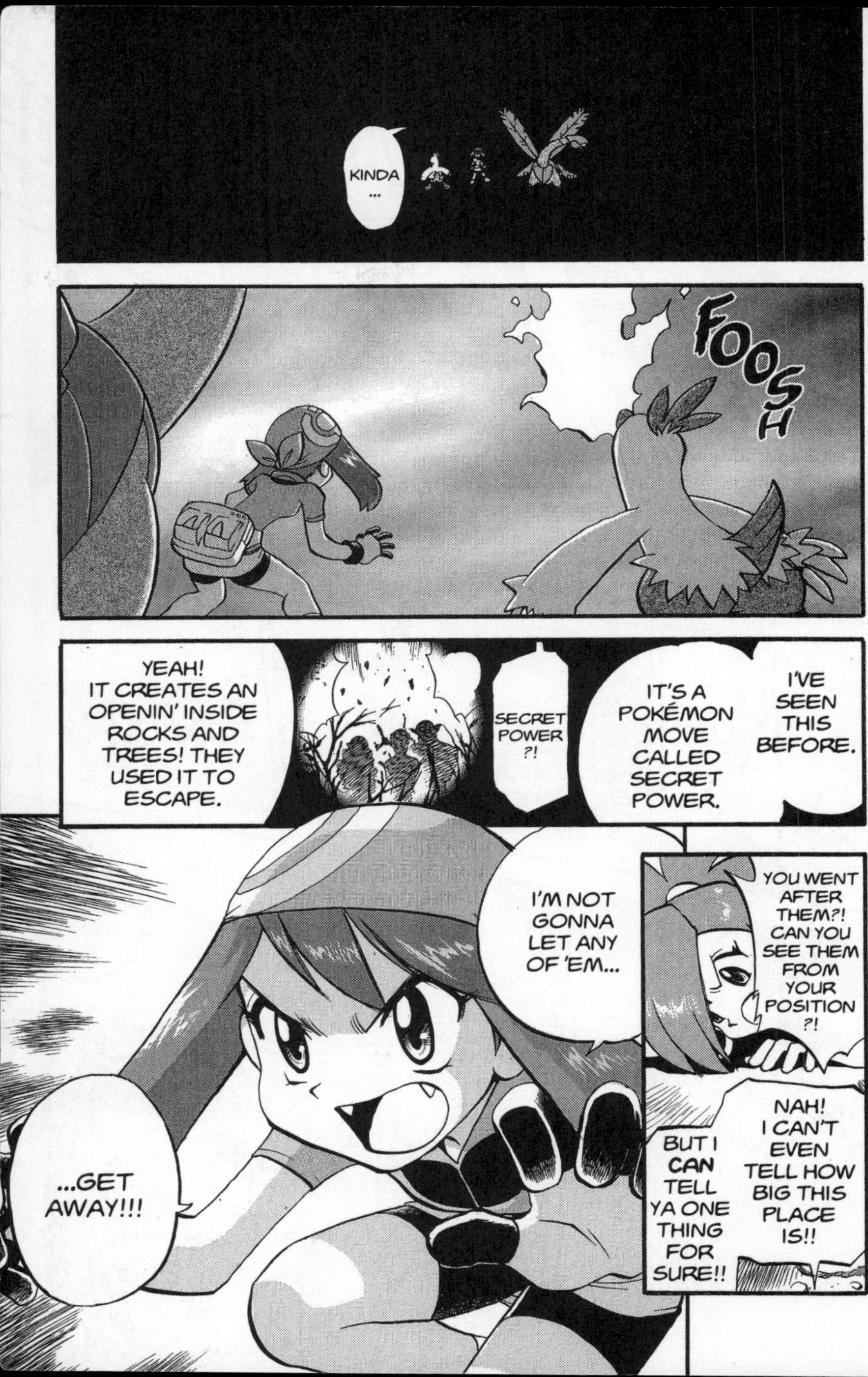
KINDA ...
FOOSH
I'VE SEEN THIS BEFORE.
IT'S A POKÉMON MOVE CALLED SECRET POWER.
SECRET POWER?!
YEAH! IT CREATES AN OPENIN' INSIDE ROCKS AND TREES! THEY USED IT TO ESCAPE.
YOU WENT AFTER THEM?! CAN YOU SEE THEM FROM YOUR POSITION?!
NAH! I CAN'T EVEN TELL HOW BIG THIS PLACE IS!!
BUT I **CAN** TELL YA ONE THING FOR SURE!!
I'M NOT GONNA LET ANY OF 'EM...
...GET AWAY!!!

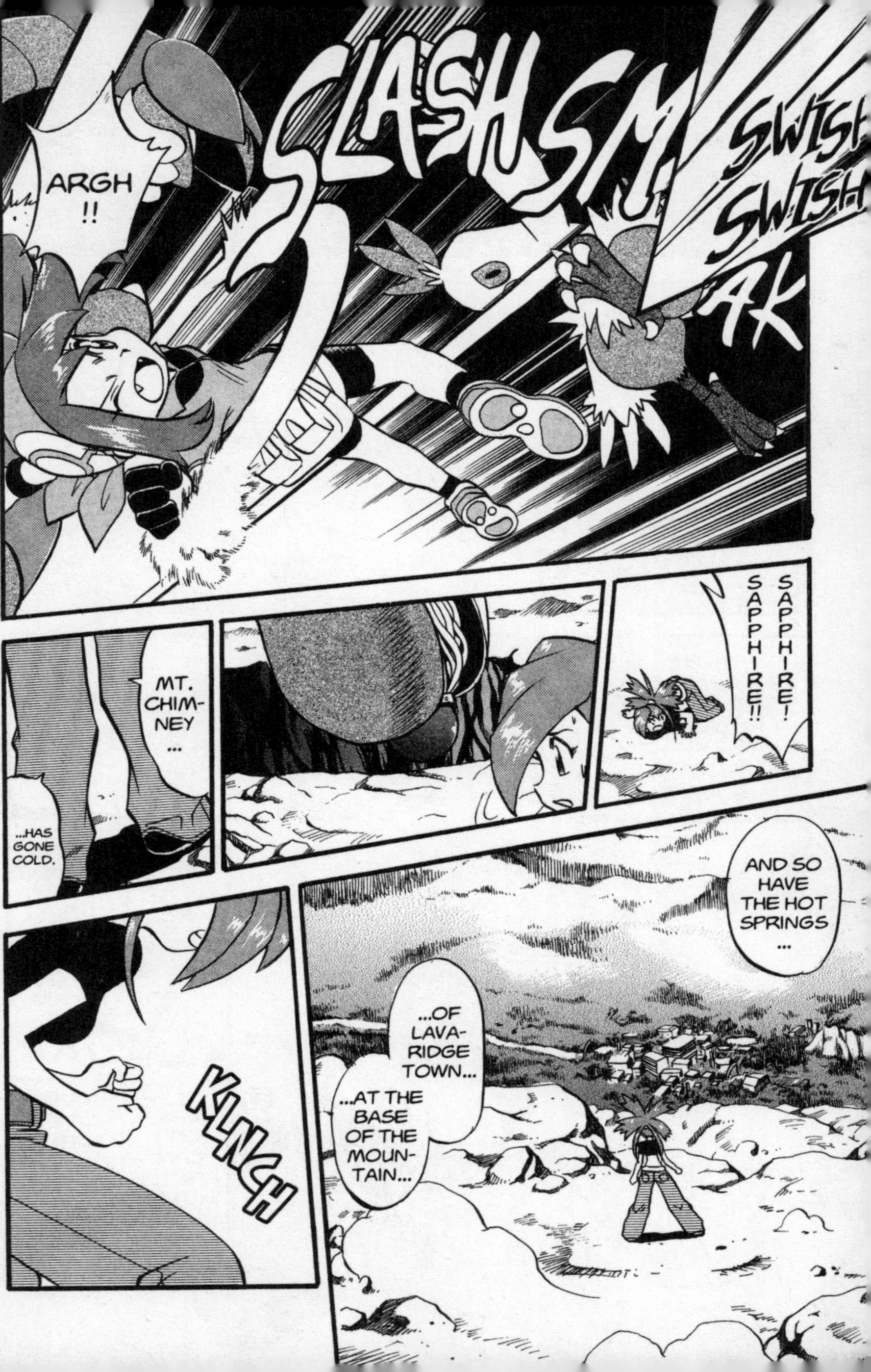
SWISH
SWISH
SLASH
SMAK
ARGH !!
SAPPHIRE!
SAPPHIRE!!
MT. CHIM-NEY ...
...HAS GONE COLD.
AND SO HAVE THE HOT SPRINGS ...
...OF LAVA-RIDGE TOWN...
...AT THE BASE OF THE MOUNTAIN...
KLNCH

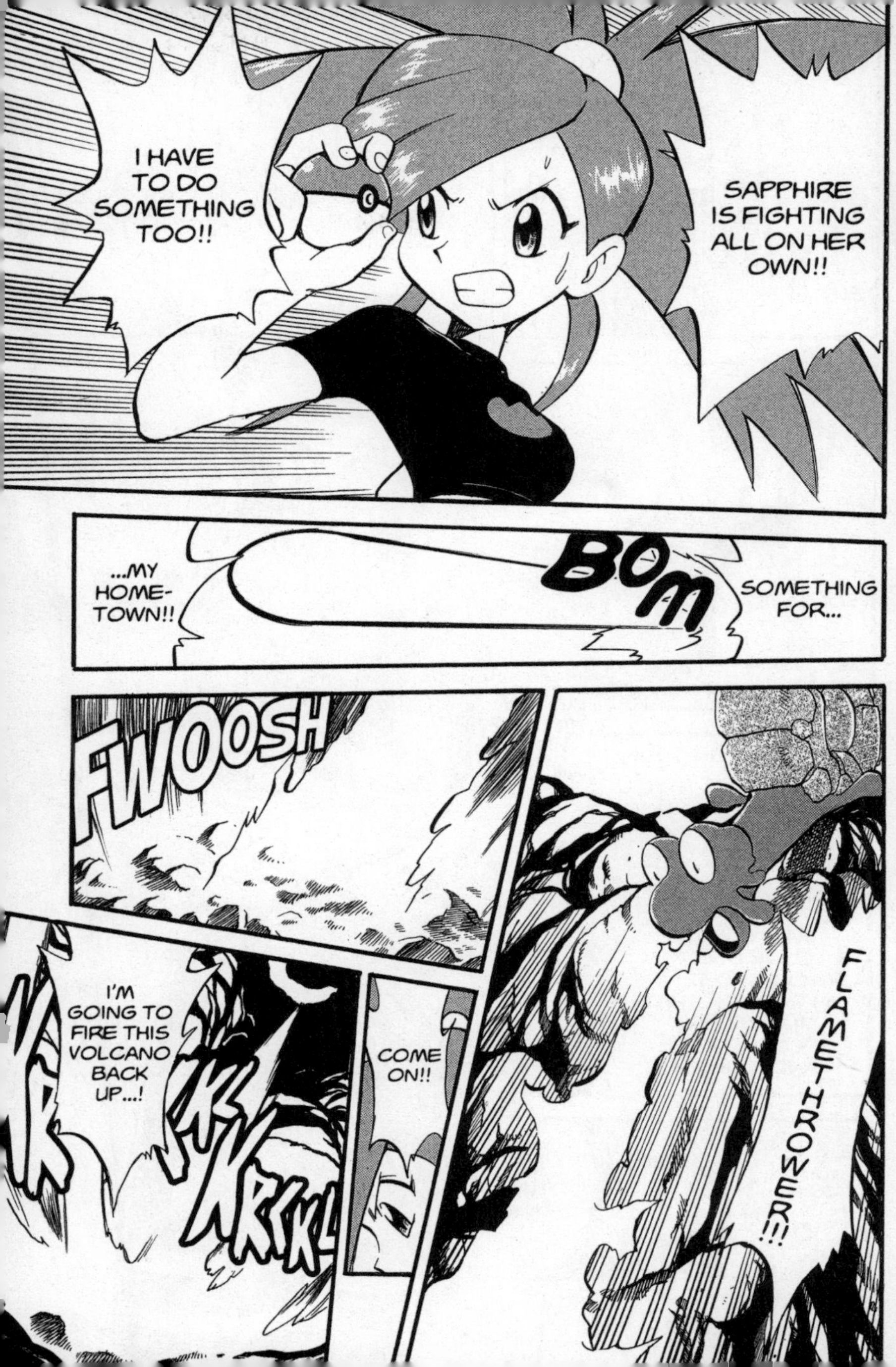
SAPPHIRE IS FIGHTING ALL ON HER OWN!!
I HAVE TO DO SOMETHING TOO!!
SOMETHING FOR...
BOM
...MY HOME-TOWN!!
FLAMETHROWER!!
FWOOSH
COME ON!!
I'M GOING TO FIRE THIS VOLCANO BACK UP...!
KRKL
KRKL

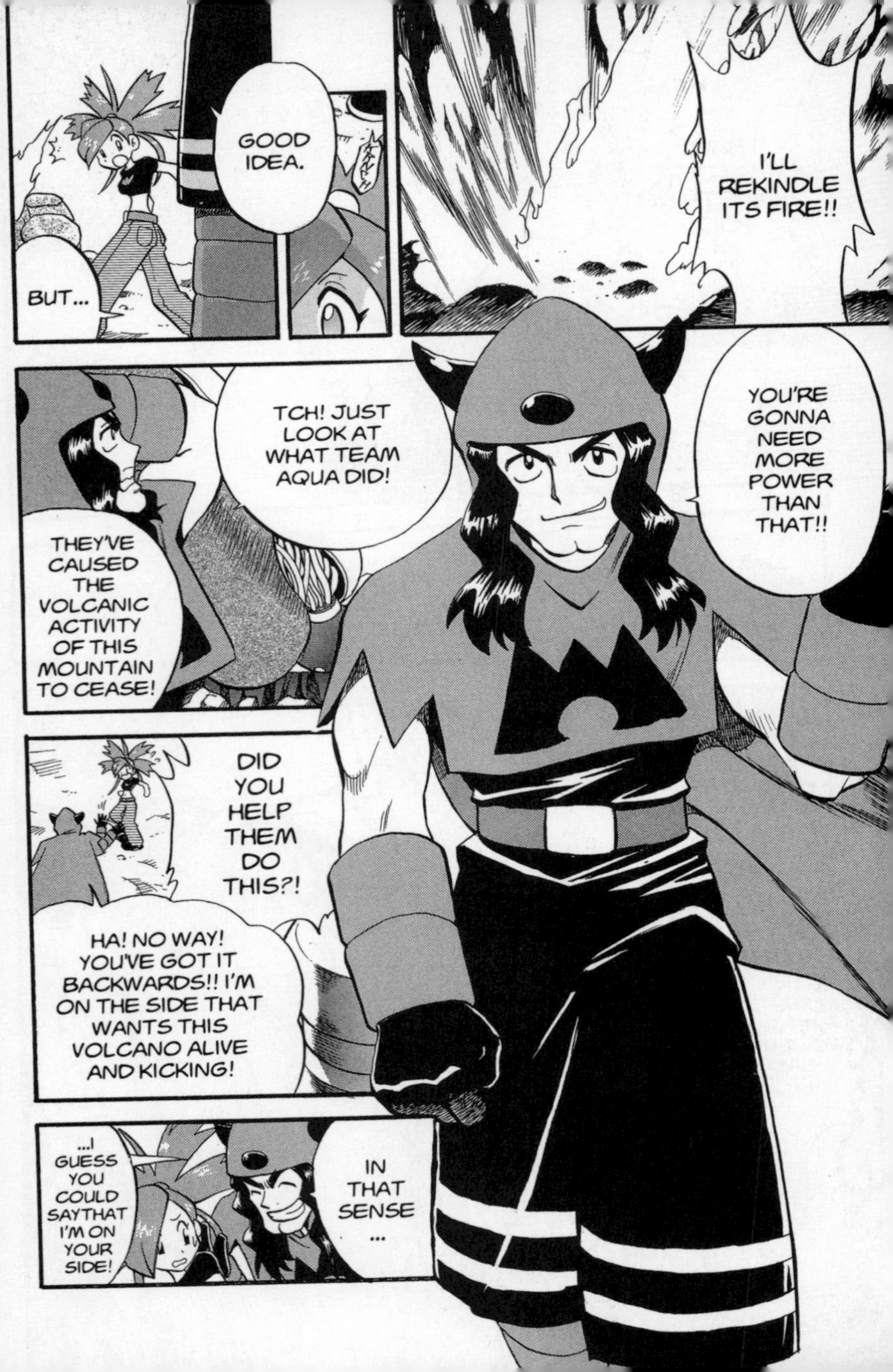
I'LL REKINDLE ITS FIRE!!
GOOD IDEA.
BUT...
YOU'RE GONNA NEED MORE POWER THAN THAT!!
TCH! JUST LOOK AT WHAT TEAM AQUA DID!
THEY'VE CAUSED THE VOLCANIC ACTIVITY OF THIS MOUNTAIN TO CEASE!
DID YOU HELP THEM DO THIS?!
HA! NO WAY! YOU'VE GOT IT BACKWARDS!! I'M ON THE SIDE THAT WANTS THIS VOLCANO ALIVE AND KICKING!
IN THAT SENSE ...
...I GUESS YOU COULD SAY THAT I'M ON YOUR SIDE!

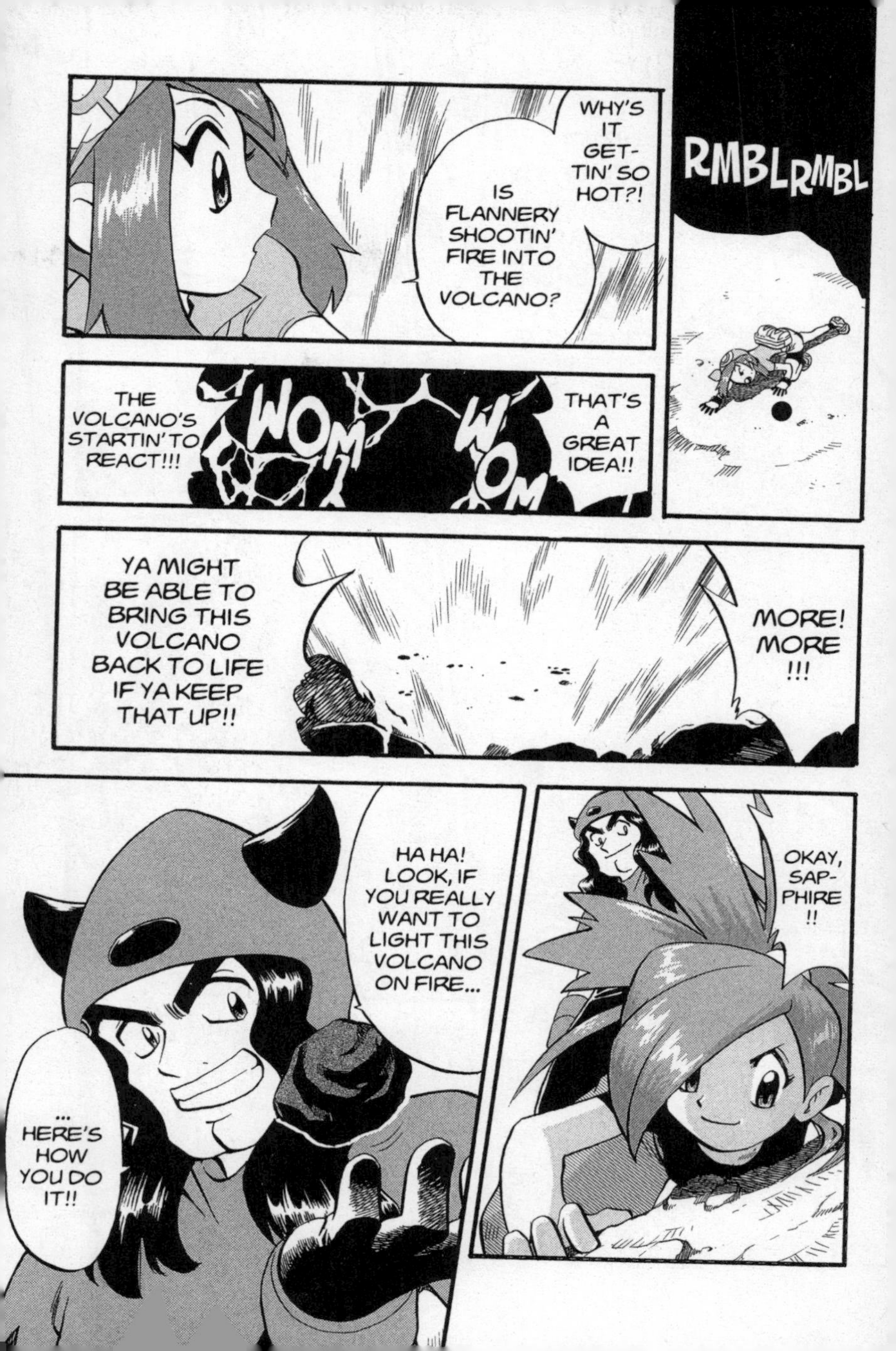
RMBLRMBL
WHY'S IT GET-TIN' SO HOT?!
IS FLANNERY SHOOTIN' FIRE INTO THE VOLCANO?
THAT'S A GREAT IDEA!!
WOM
WOM
WOM
THE VOLCANO'S STARTIN' TO REACT!!!
MORE! MORE!!!
YA MIGHT BE ABLE TO BRING THIS VOLCANO BACK TO LIFE IF YA KEEP THAT UP!!
OKAY, SAP-PHIRE!!
HA HA! LOOK, IF YOU REALLY WANT TO LIGHT THIS VOLCANO ON FIRE...
...HERE'S HOW YOU DO IT!!

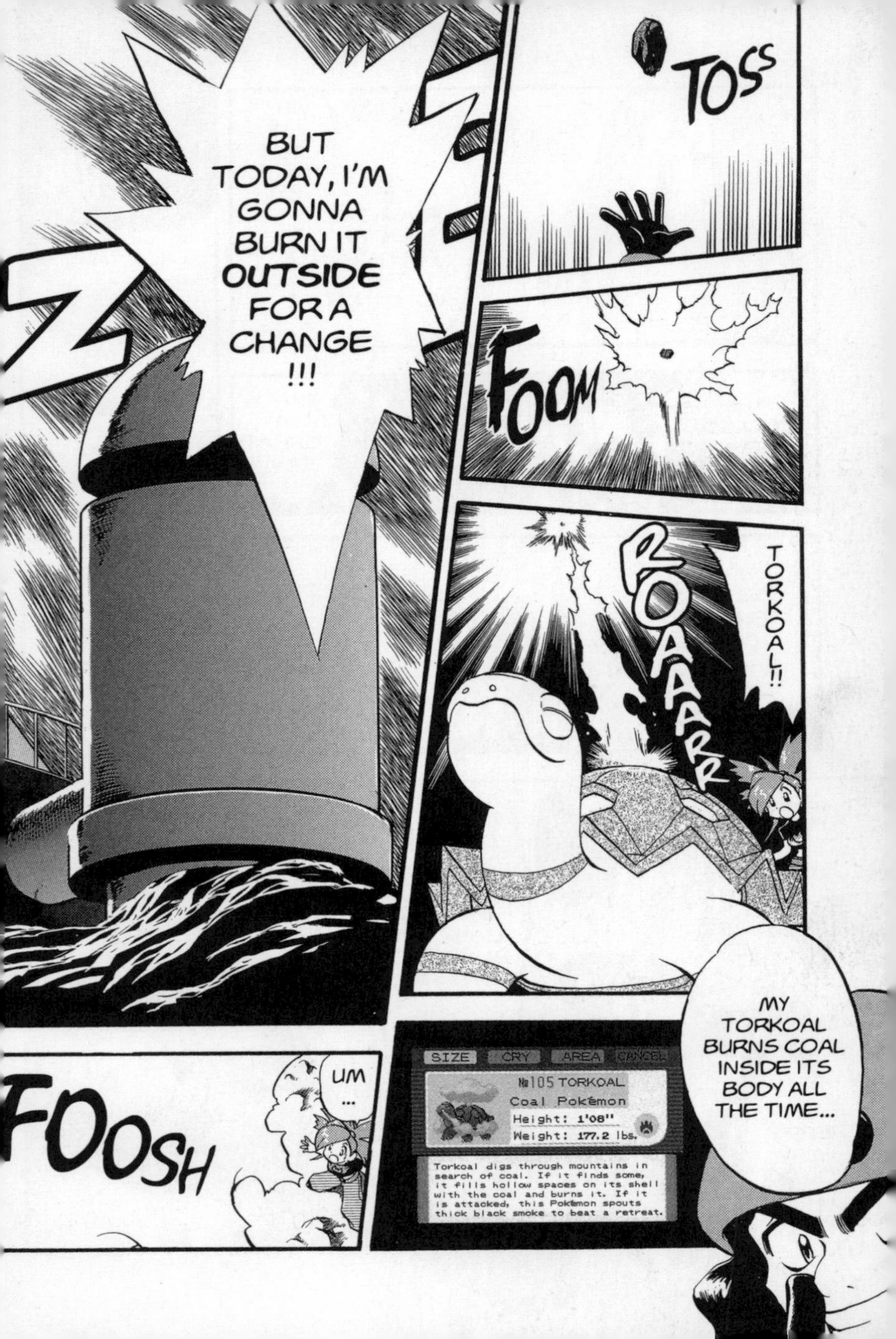
TOSS
FOOM
ROAAARR
TORKOAL!!
BUT TODAY, I'M GONNA BURN IT **OUTSIDE** FOR A CHANGE!!!
MY TORKOAL BURNS COAL INSIDE ITS BODY ALL THE TIME...
SIZE CRY AREA CANCEL
№105 TORKOAL
Coal Pokémon
Height: 1'08"
Weight: 177.2 lbs.
Torkoal digs through mountains in search of coal. If it finds some, it fills hollow spaces on its shell with the coal and burns it. If it is attacked, this Pokémon spouts thick black smoke to beat a retreat.
FOOSH
UM...

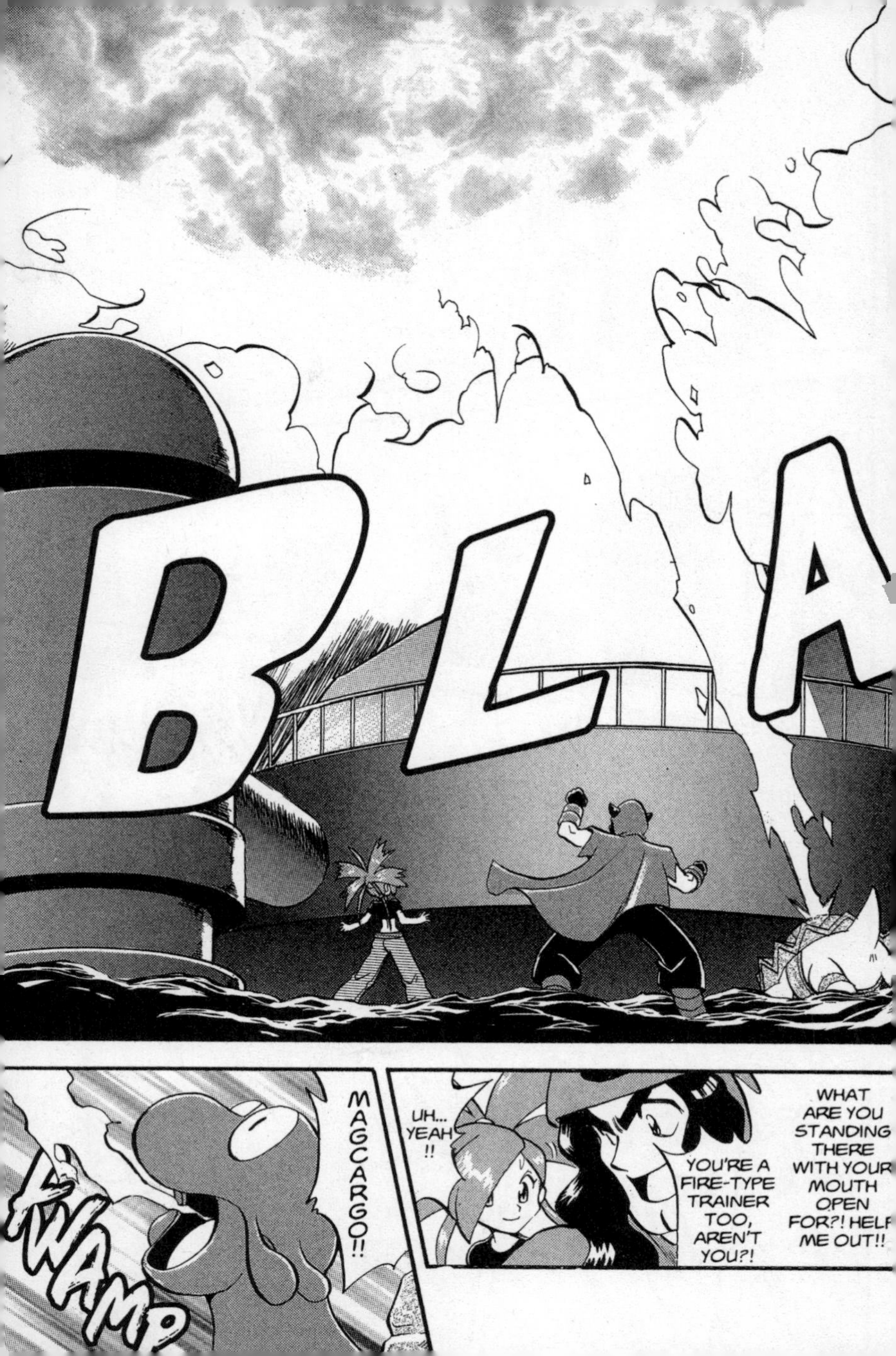
BLA
WHAT ARE YOU STANDING THERE WITH YOUR MOUTH OPEN FOR?! HELP ME OUT!!
YOU'RE A FIRE-TYPE TRAINER TOO, AREN'T YOU?!
UH... YEAH!!
MAGCARGO!!
KWAMP

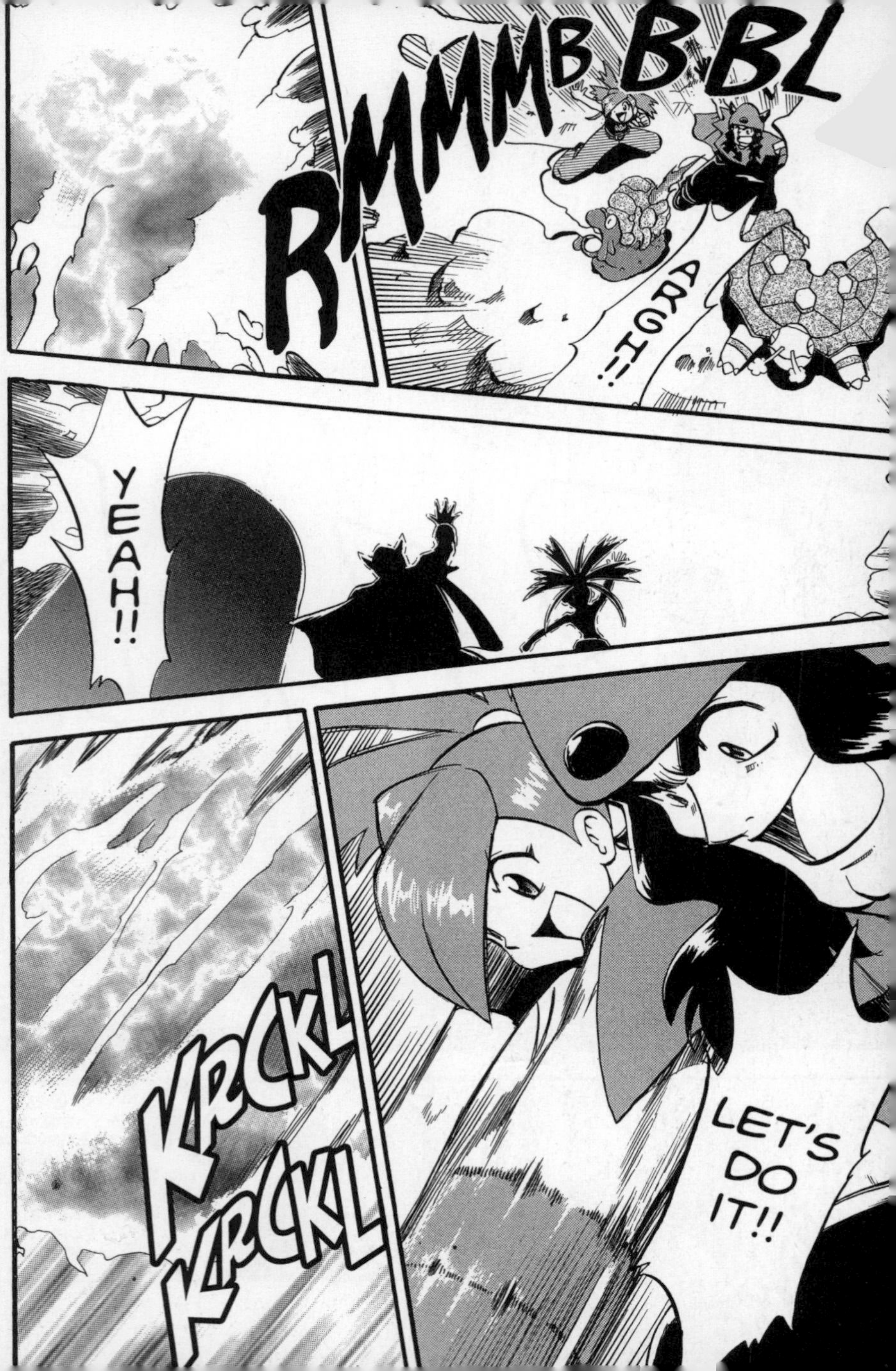
RMMMB BBL
ARGH!!
YEAH!!
LET'S DO IT!!
KRCKL KRCKL

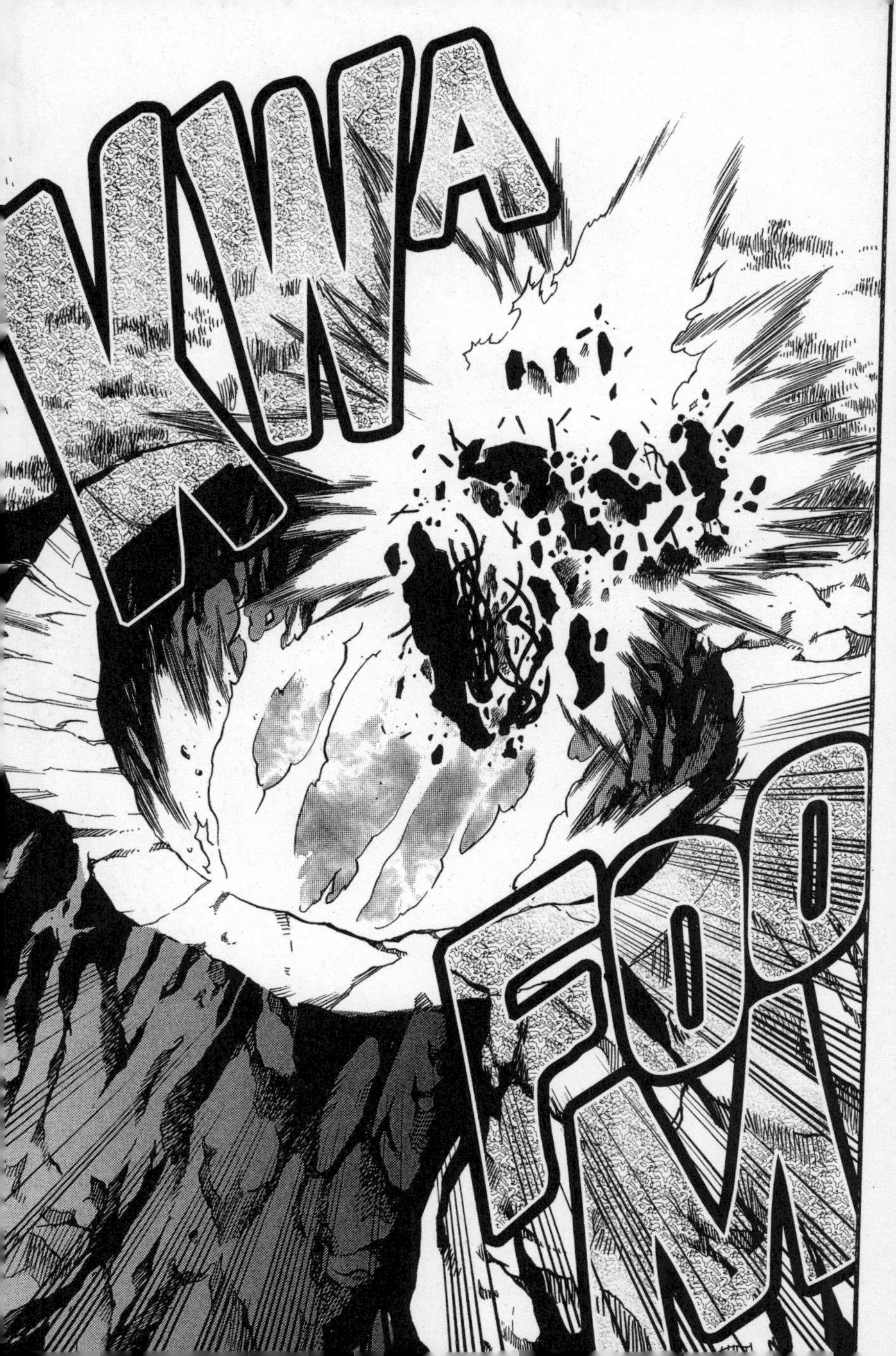
WA
FOOM

● Chapter 216 ●
Mixing It Up with Magcargo

Pokémon Adventures Ruby & Sapphire
The Fourth Chapter

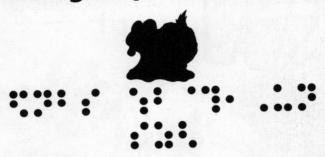

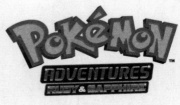

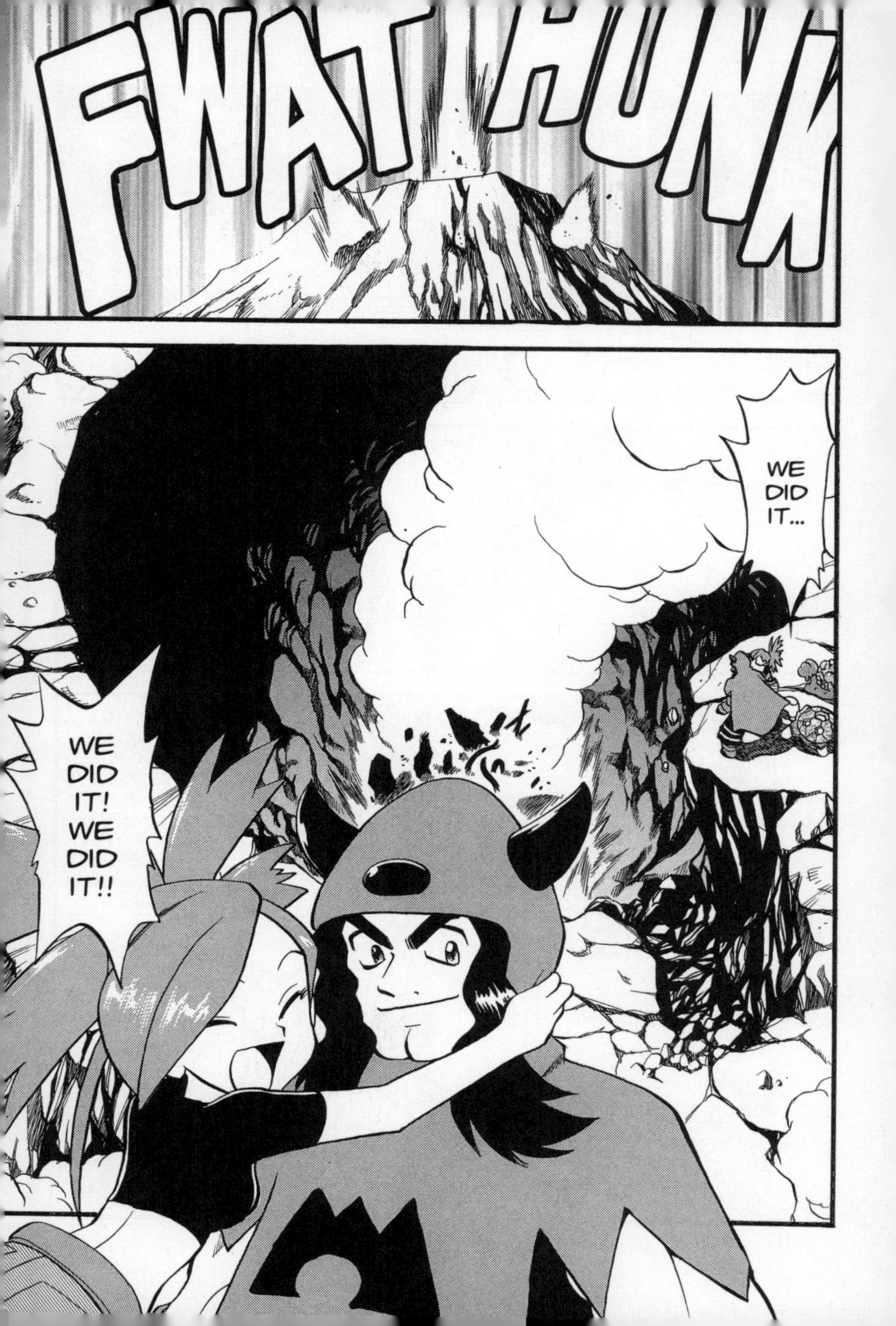
FWAT HUNK
WE DID IT...
WE DID IT! WE DID IT!!

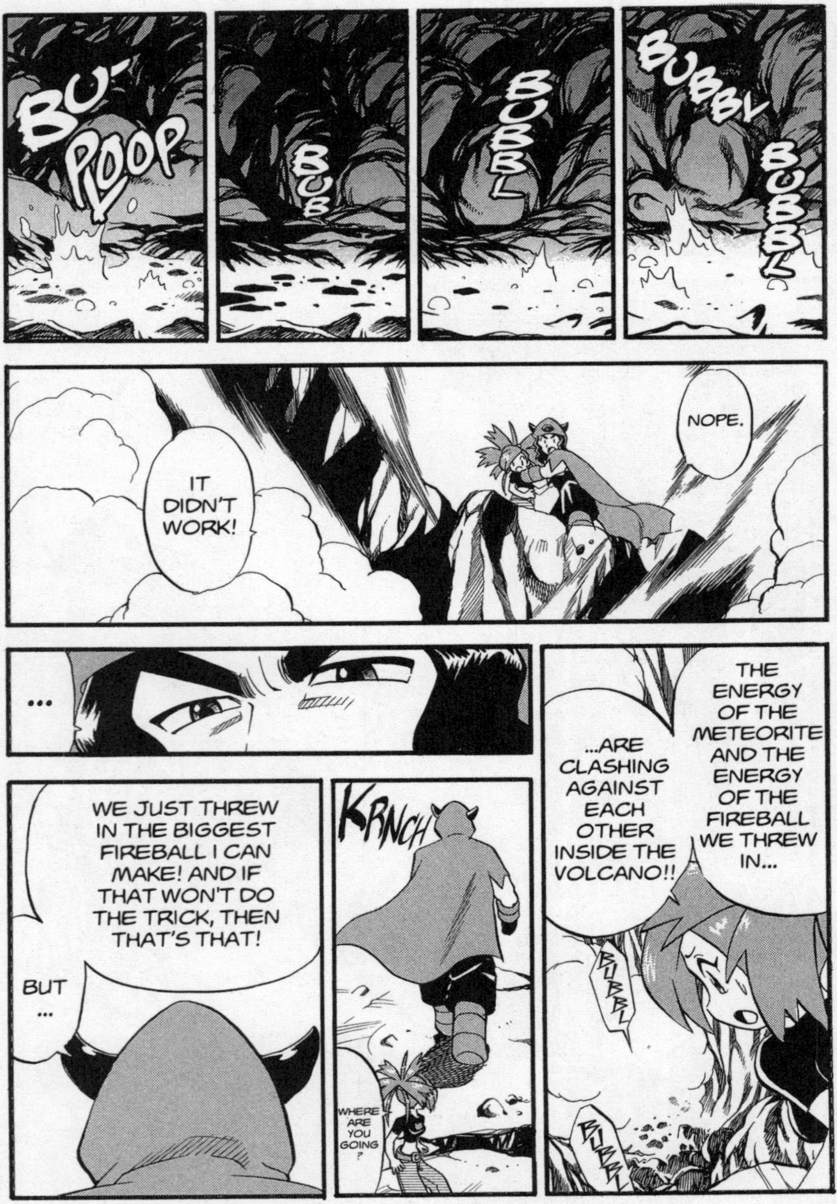
BUBBL
BUBBL
BUBBL
BUB
BU-PLOOP
NOPE.
IT DIDN'T WORK!
THE ENERGY OF THE METEORITE AND THE ENERGY OF THE FIREBALL WE THREW IN...
...ARE CLASHING AGAINST EACH OTHER INSIDE THE VOLCANO!!
BUBBL
BUBBL
...
KRNCH
WHERE ARE YOU GOING?
WE JUST THREW IN THE BIGGEST FIREBALL I CAN MAKE! AND IF THAT WON'T DO THE TRICK, THEN THAT'S THAT!
BUT ...

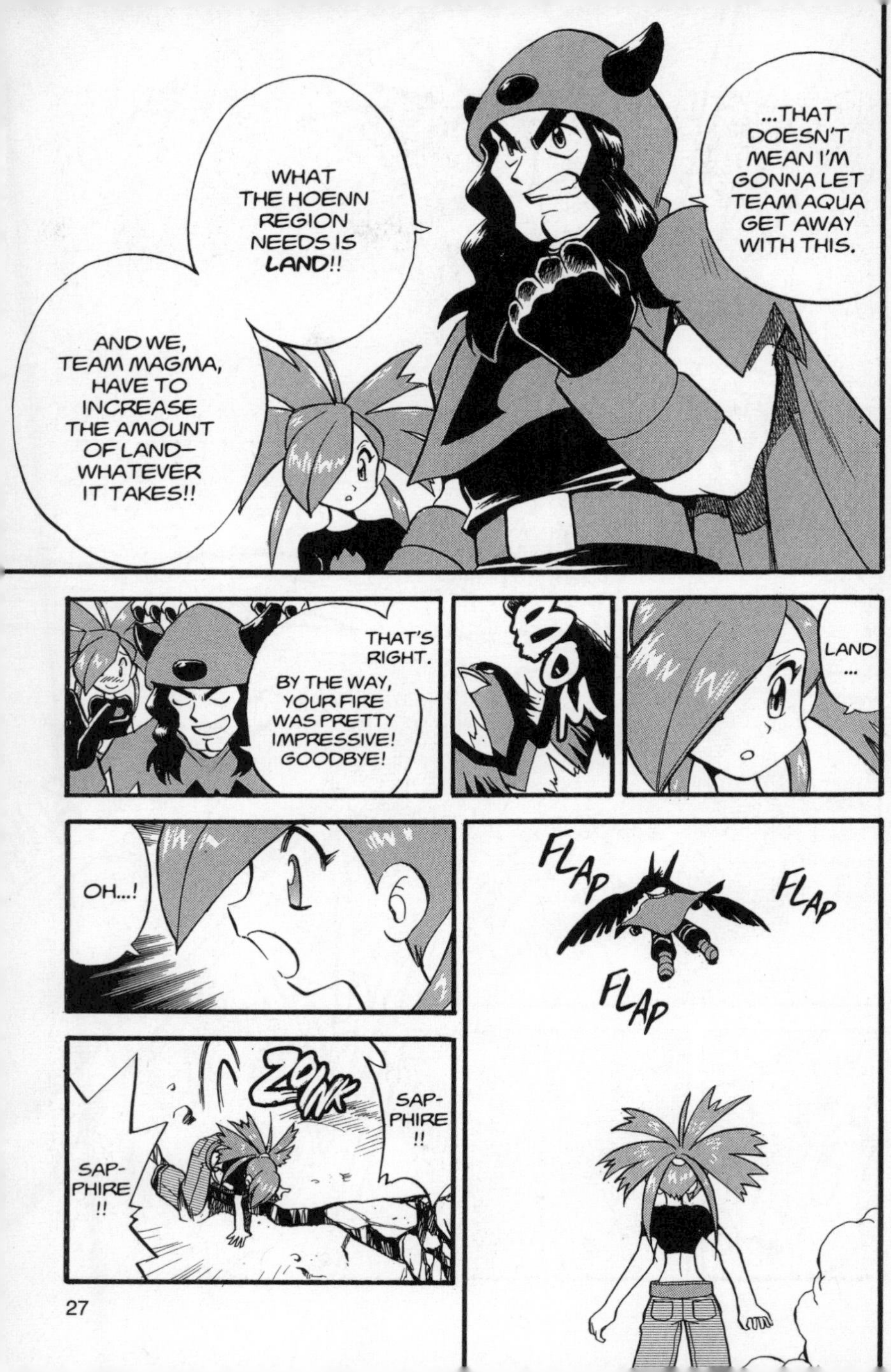
...THAT DOESN'T MEAN I'M GONNA LET TEAM AQUA GET AWAY WITH THIS.
WHAT THE HOENN REGION NEEDS IS **LAND**!!
AND WE, TEAM MAGMA, HAVE TO INCREASE THE AMOUNT OF LAND— WHATEVER IT TAKES!!
LAND ...
BOOM
THAT'S RIGHT.
BY THE WAY, YOUR FIRE WAS PRETTY IMPRESSIVE! GOODBYE!
FLAP
FLAP
FLAP
OH...!
ZOINK
SAP-PHIRE !!
SAP-PHIRE !!

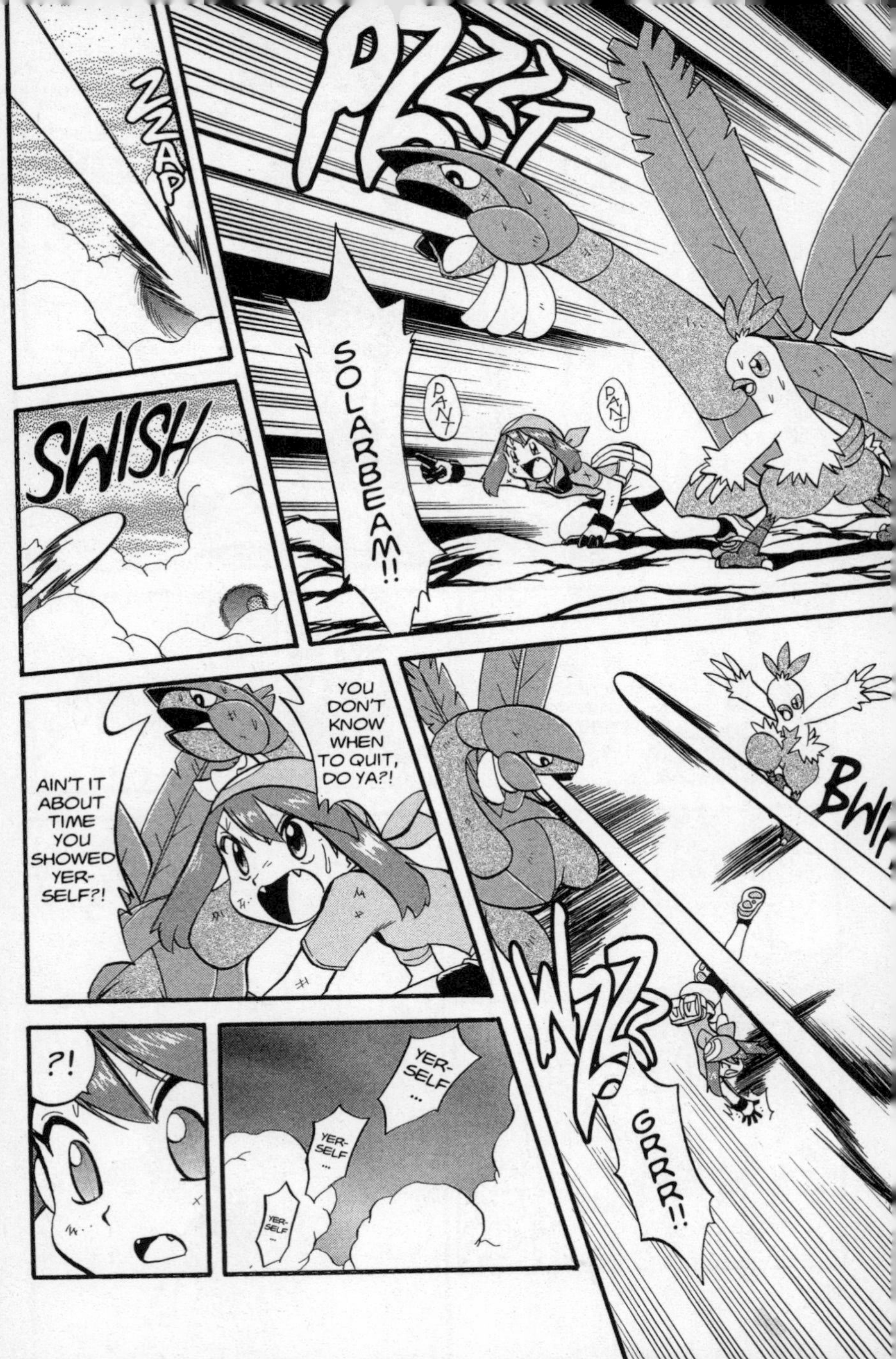
PZZZT
PANT
PANT
SOLARBEAM!!
ZZZAP
SWISH
BWH
WZZZ
GRRRR!!
YOU DON'T KNOW WHEN TO QUIT, DO YA?!
AIN'T IT ABOUT TIME YOU SHOWED YER-SELF?!
YER-SELF...
YER-SELF...
YER-SELF...
?!

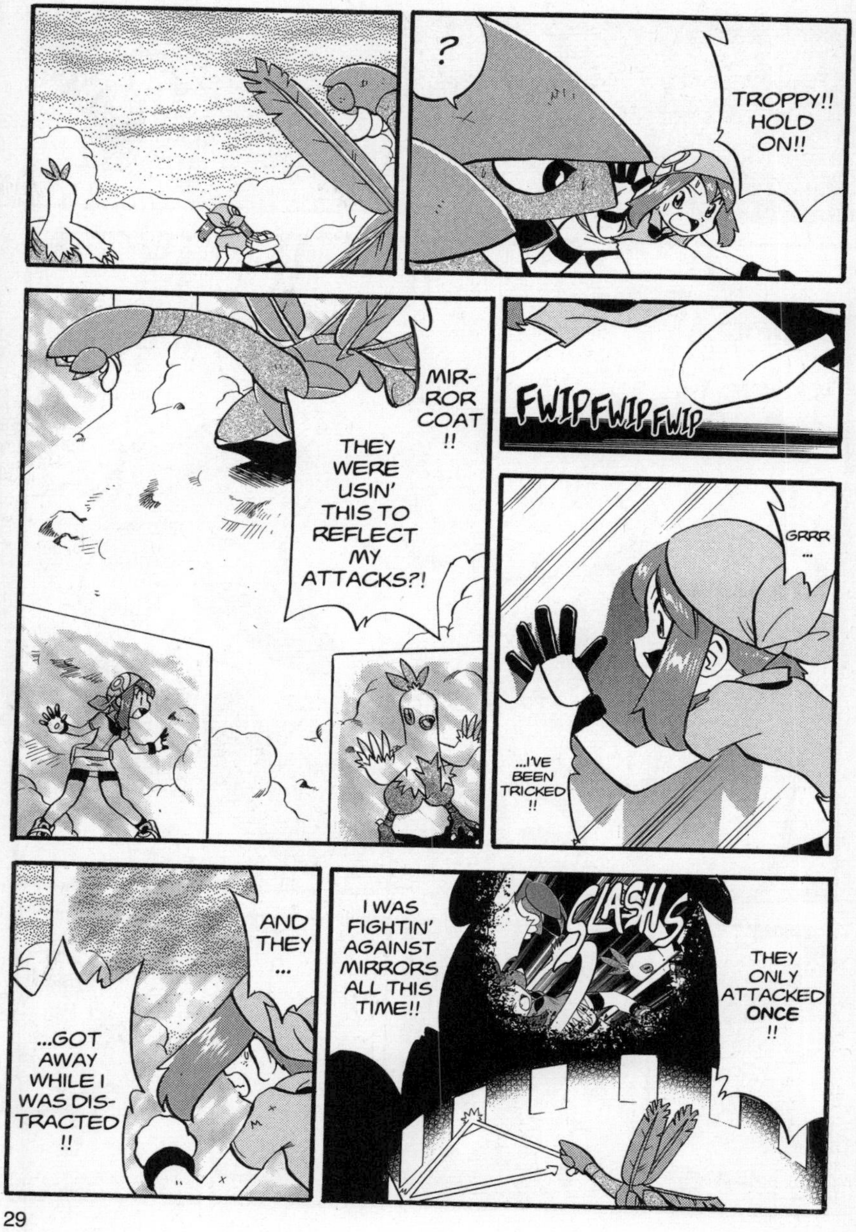
TROPPY!! HOLD ON!!
?
FWIP FWIP FWIP
GRRR...
...I'VE BEEN TRICKED!!
MIR-ROR COAT!!
THEY WERE USIN' THIS TO REFLECT MY ATTACKS?!
THEY ONLY ATTACKED **ONCE**!!
SLASH
I WAS FIGHTIN' AGAINST MIRRORS ALL THIS TIME!!
AND THEY...
...GOT AWAY WHILE I WAS DIS-TRACTED!!

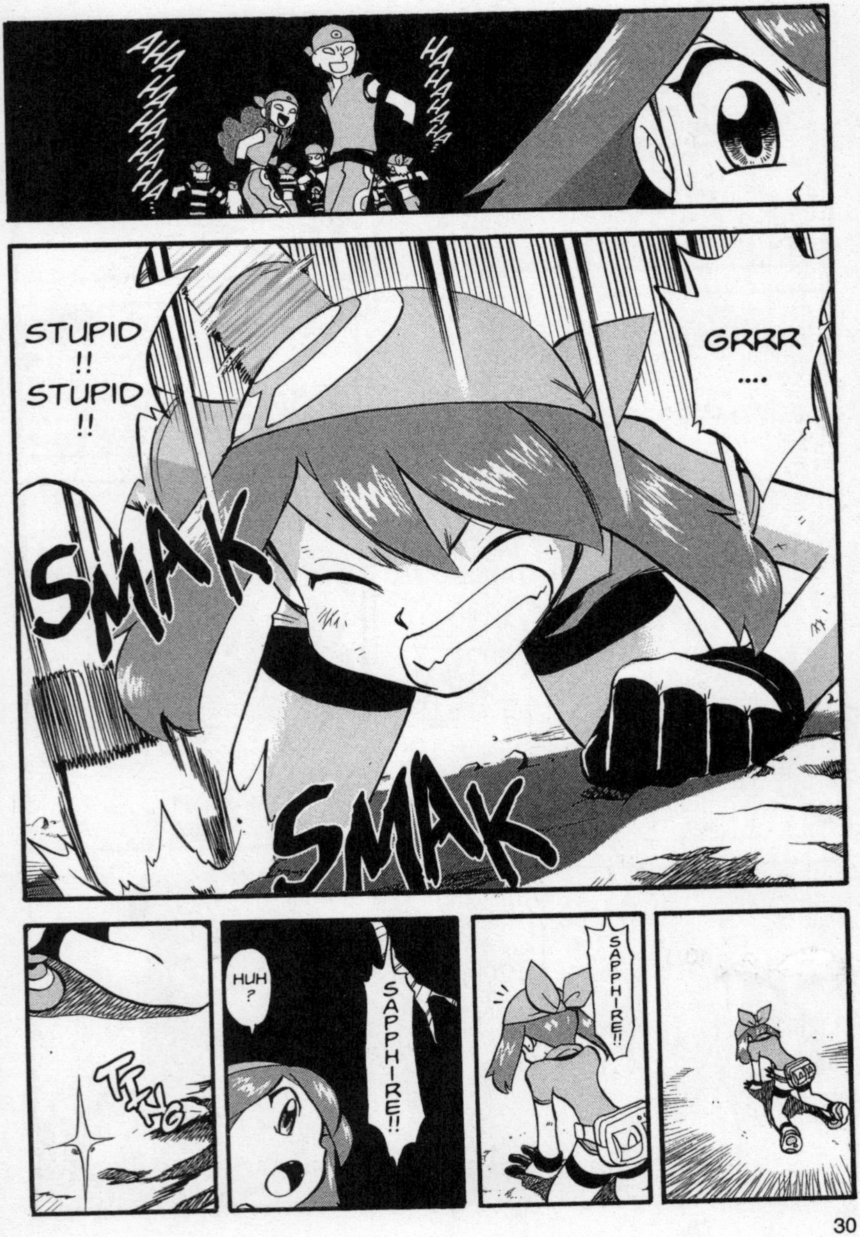
HAHAHAHAHA...
AHAHAHAHAHAHAHA...
GRRR ....
STUPID!! STUPID!!
SMAK
SMAK
...
SAPPHIRE!!
SAPPHIRE!!
HUH?
TING

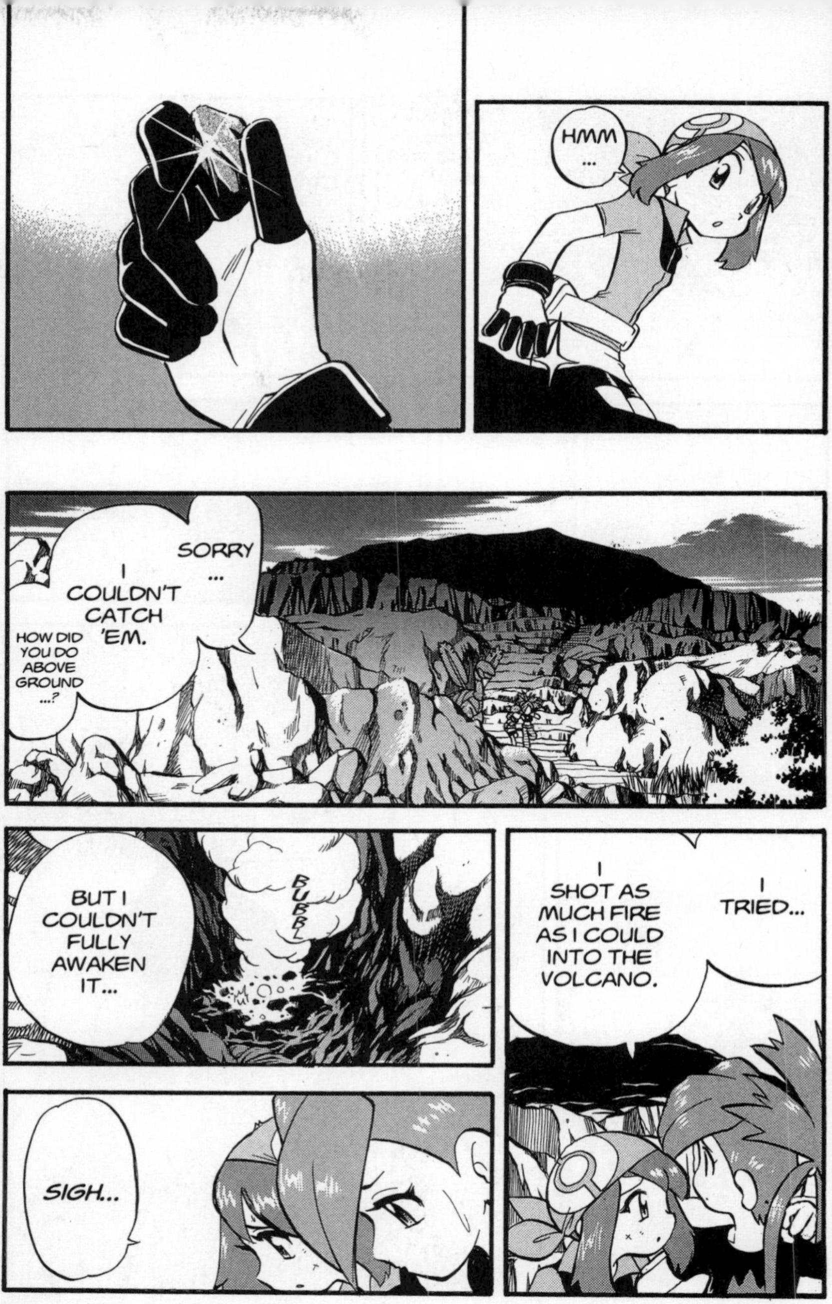
HMM ...
SORRY ... I COULDN'T CATCH 'EM.
HOW DID YOU DO ABOVE GROUND ...?
I TRIED... I SHOT AS MUCH FIRE AS I COULD INTO THE VOLCANO.
BUT I COULDN'T FULLY AWAKEN IT...
BUBBL
SIGH...

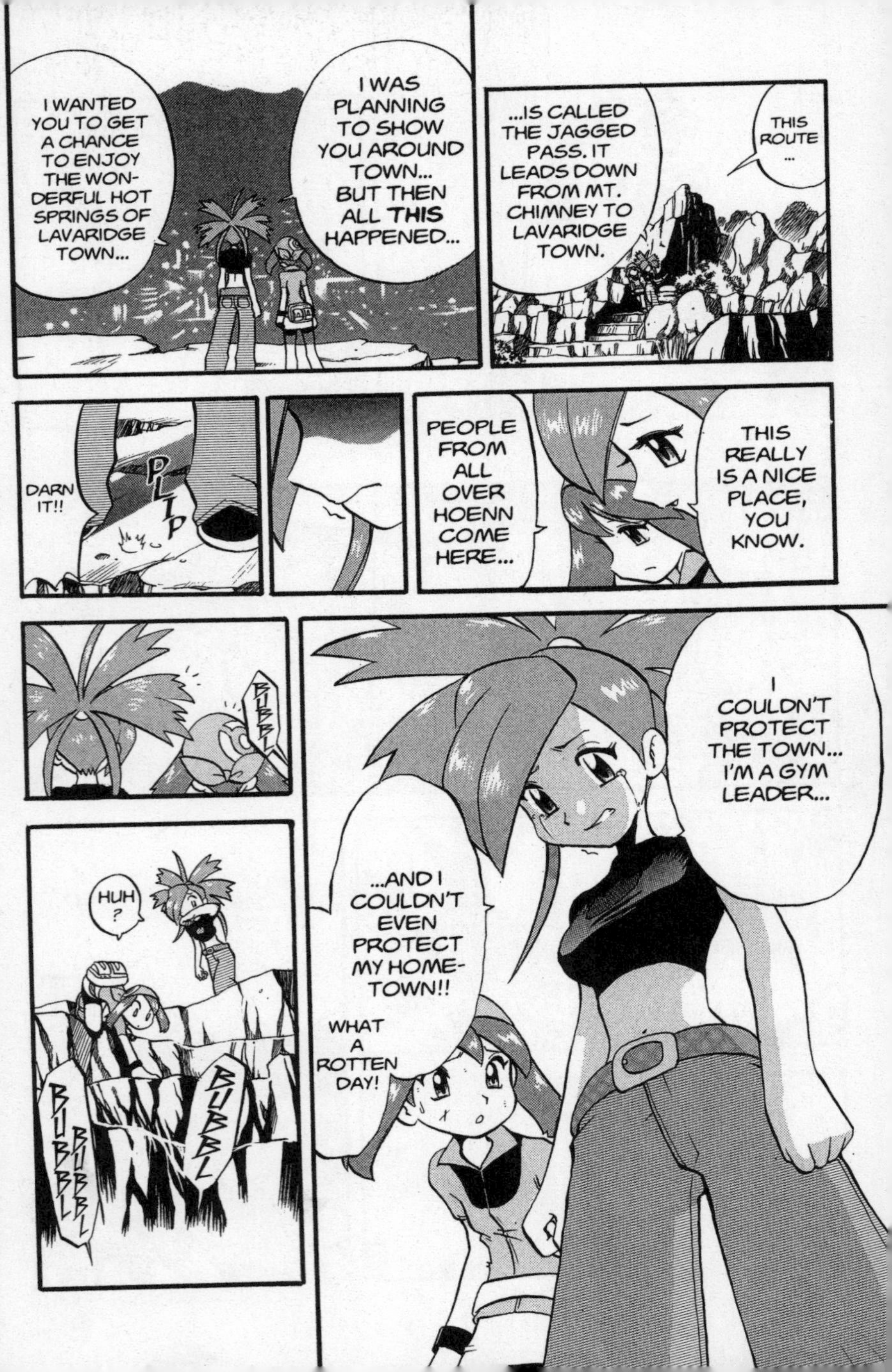
THIS ROUTE ...
...IS CALLED THE JAGGED PASS. IT LEADS DOWN FROM MT. CHIMNEY TO LAVARIDGE TOWN.
I WAS PLANNING TO SHOW YOU AROUND TOWN... BUT THEN ALL **THIS** HAPPENED...
I WANTED YOU TO GET A CHANCE TO ENJOY THE WON-DERFUL HOT SPRINGS OF LAVARIDGE TOWN...
THIS REALLY IS A NICE PLACE, YOU KNOW.
PEOPLE FROM ALL OVER HOENN COME HERE...
PLIP
DARN IT!!
I COULDN'T PROTECT THE TOWN... I'M A GYM LEADER...
...AND I COULDN'T EVEN PROTECT MY HOME-TOWN!!
WHAT A ROTTEN DAY!
BUBBL
HUH?
BUBBL
BUBBL
BUBBL

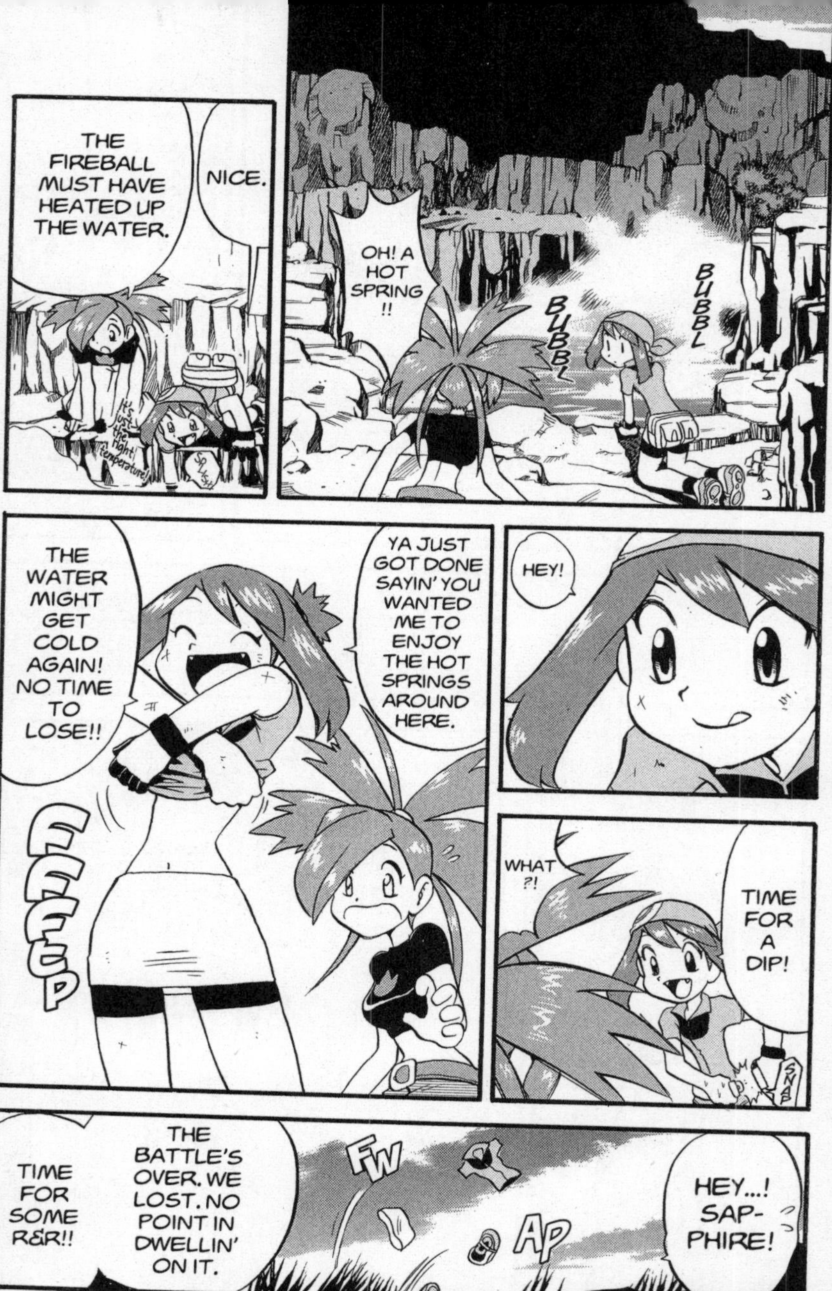
OH! A HOT SPRING!!
BUBBL
BUBBL
NICE.
THE FIREBALL MUST HAVE HEATED UP THE WATER.
It's just the right temperature!
SPLASH
HEY!
TIME FOR A DIP!
WHAT?!
SNAP
YA JUST GOT DONE SAYIN' YOU WANTED ME TO ENJOY THE HOT SPRINGS AROUND HERE.
THE WATER MIGHT GET COLD AGAIN! NO TIME TO LOSE!!
FFFUP
HEY...! SAP-PHIRE!
FW
AP
THE BATTLE'S OVER. WE LOST. NO POINT IN DWELLIN' ON IT.
TIME FOR SOME R&R!!

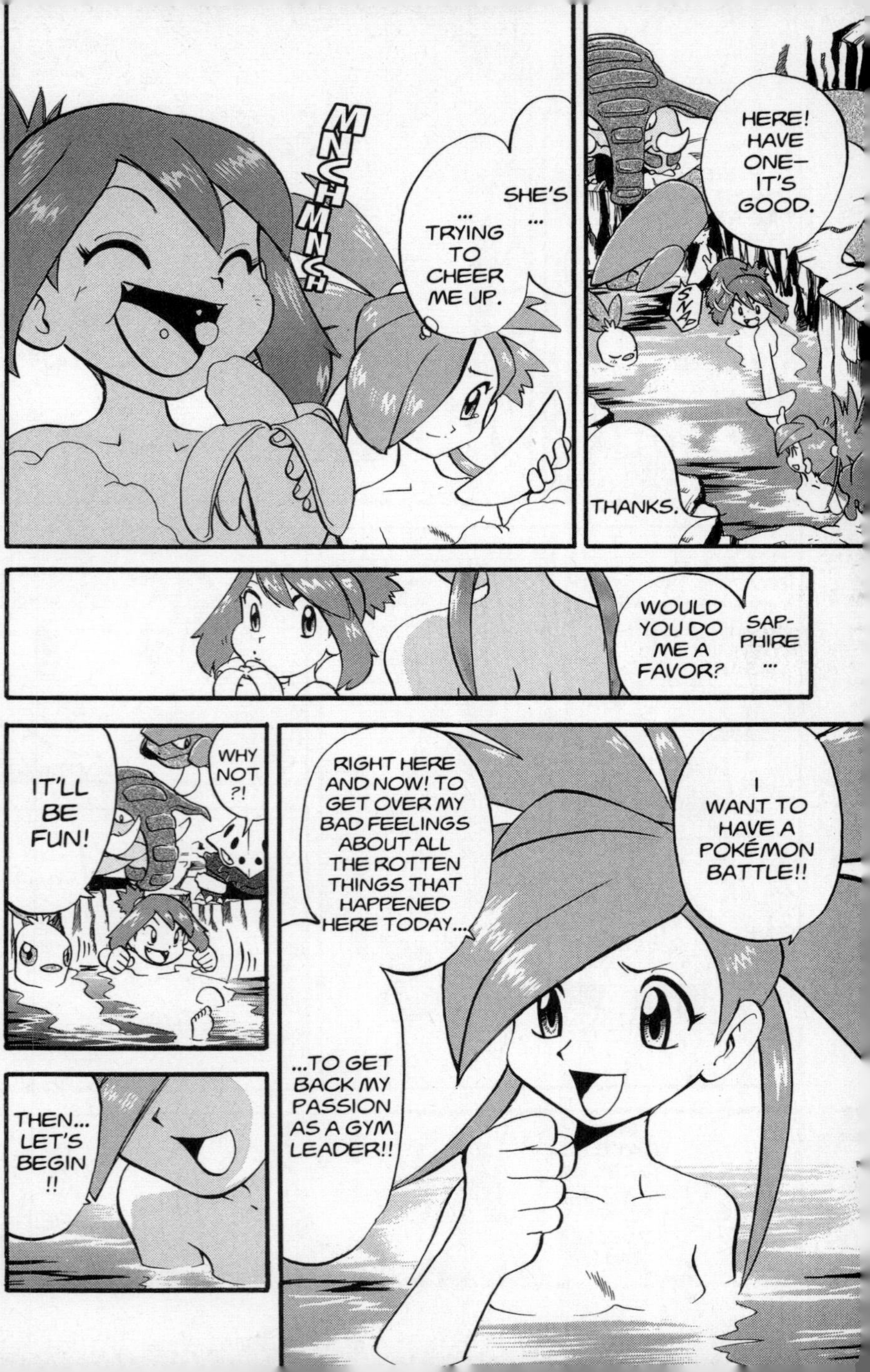
HERE! HAVE ONE— IT'S GOOD.
SNAP
THANKS.
MNCH MNCH
SHE'S ... ... TRYING TO CHEER ME UP.
SAPPHIRE ...
WOULD YOU DO ME A FAVOR?
I WANT TO HAVE A POKÉMON BATTLE!!
RIGHT HERE AND NOW! TO GET OVER MY BAD FEELINGS ABOUT ALL THE ROTTEN THINGS THAT HAPPENED HERE TODAY...
...TO GET BACK MY PASSION AS A GYM LEADER!!
WHY NOT?!
IT'LL BE FUN!
THEN... LET'S BEGIN!!

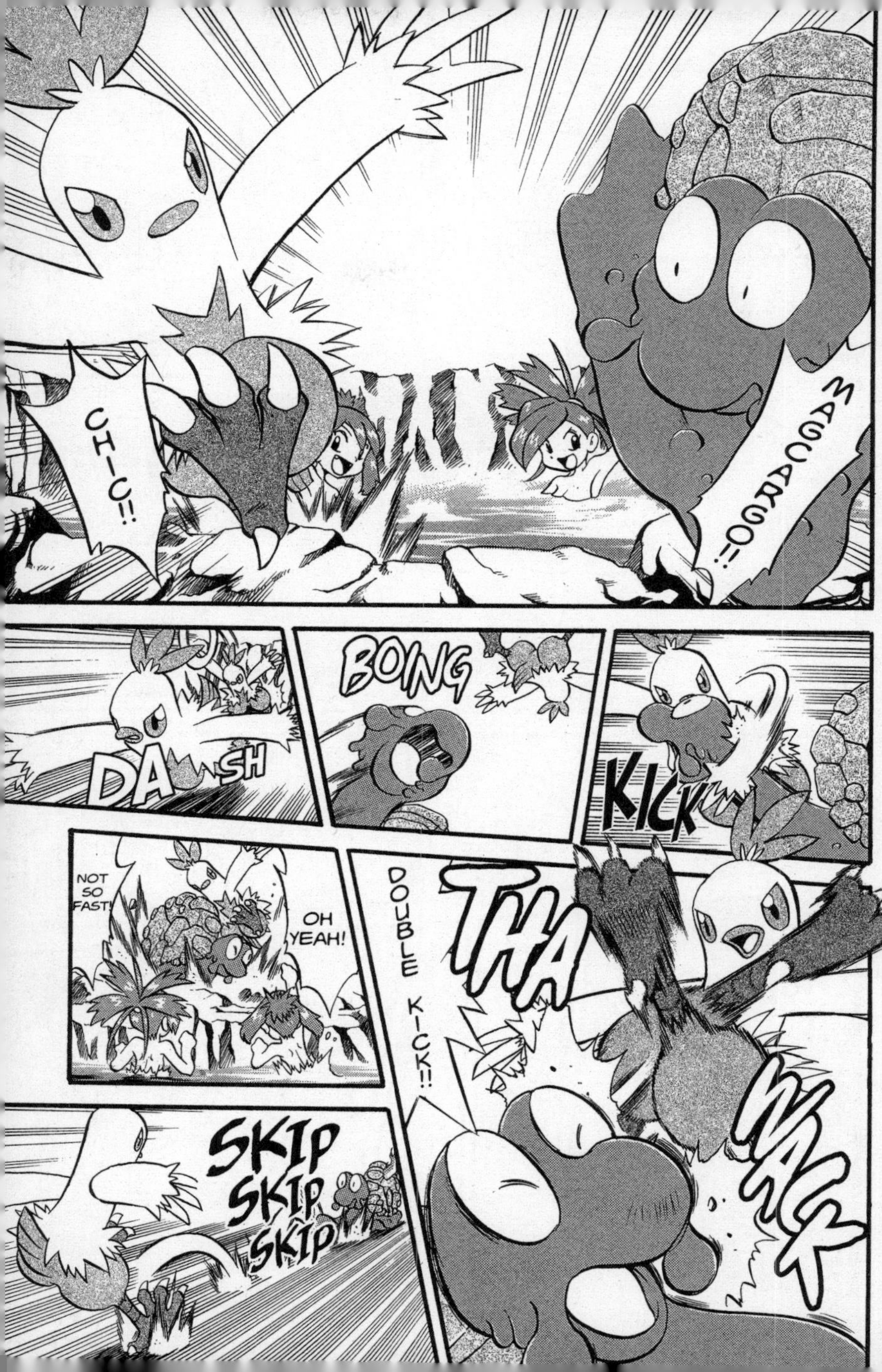
MAGCARGO!!
CHIC!!
KICK
BOING
DASH
THA
DOUBLE KICK!!
WACK
OH YEAH!
NOT SO FAST!
SKIP SKIP SKIP

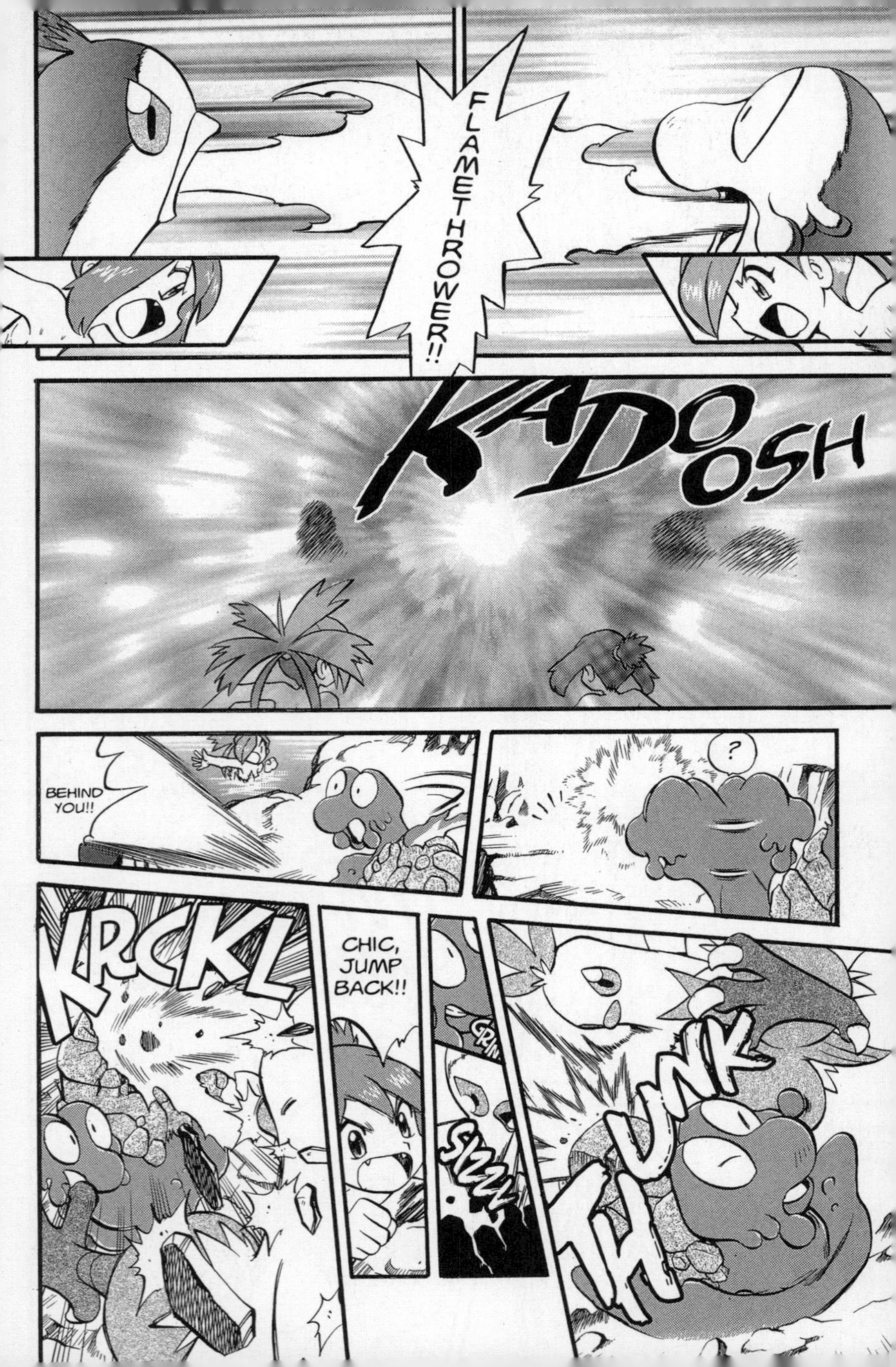
FLAMETHROWER!!
KADOOSH
?
BEHIND YOU!!
THUNK
GRIN
SIZZZ
CHIC, JUMP BACK!!
KRCKL

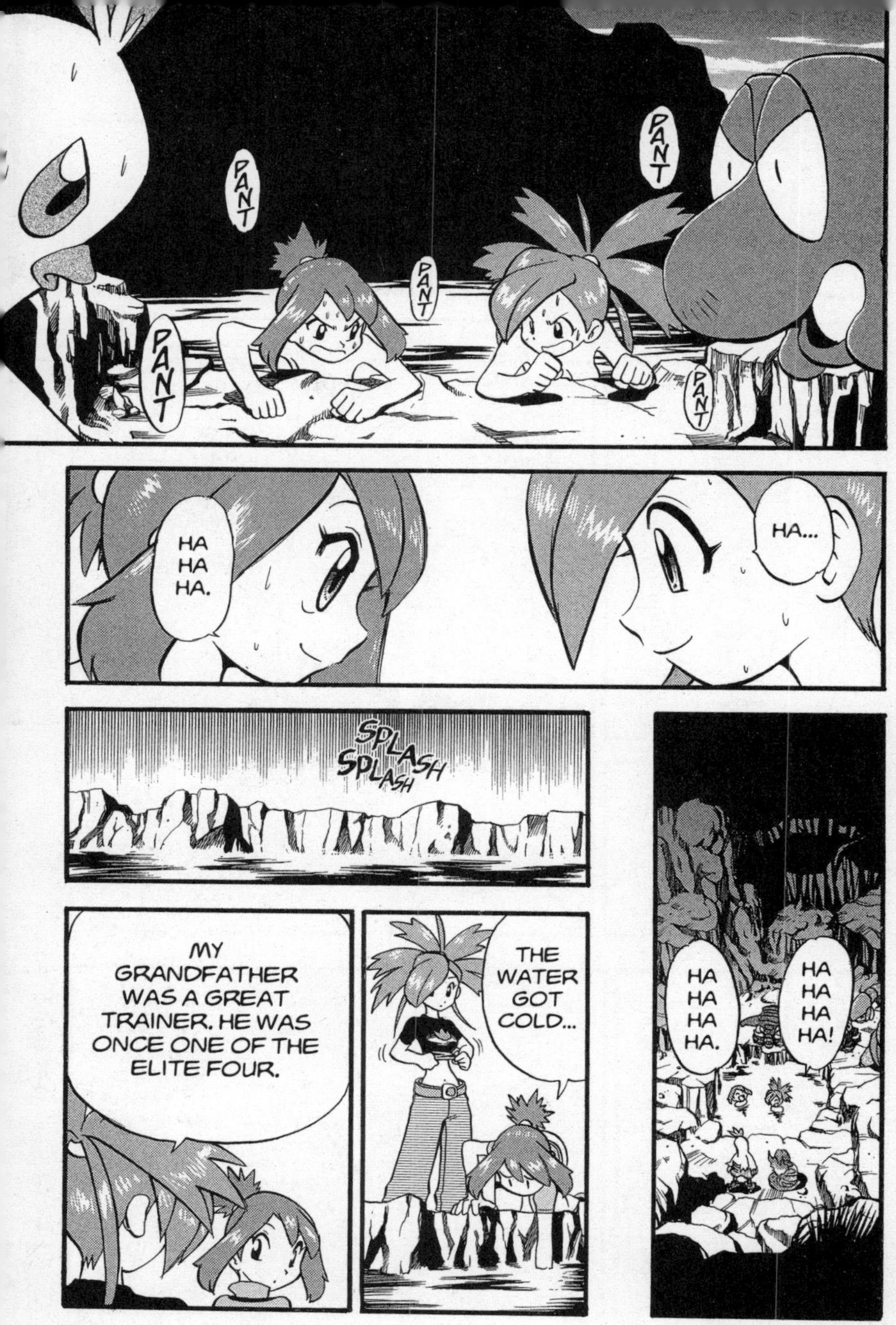
PANT
PANT
PANT
PANT
PANT
HA...
HA HA HA.
HA HA HA HA!
HA HA HA HA.
SPLASH SPLASH
THE WATER GOT COLD...
MY GRANDFATHER WAS A GREAT TRAINER. HE WAS ONCE ONE OF THE ELITE FOUR.

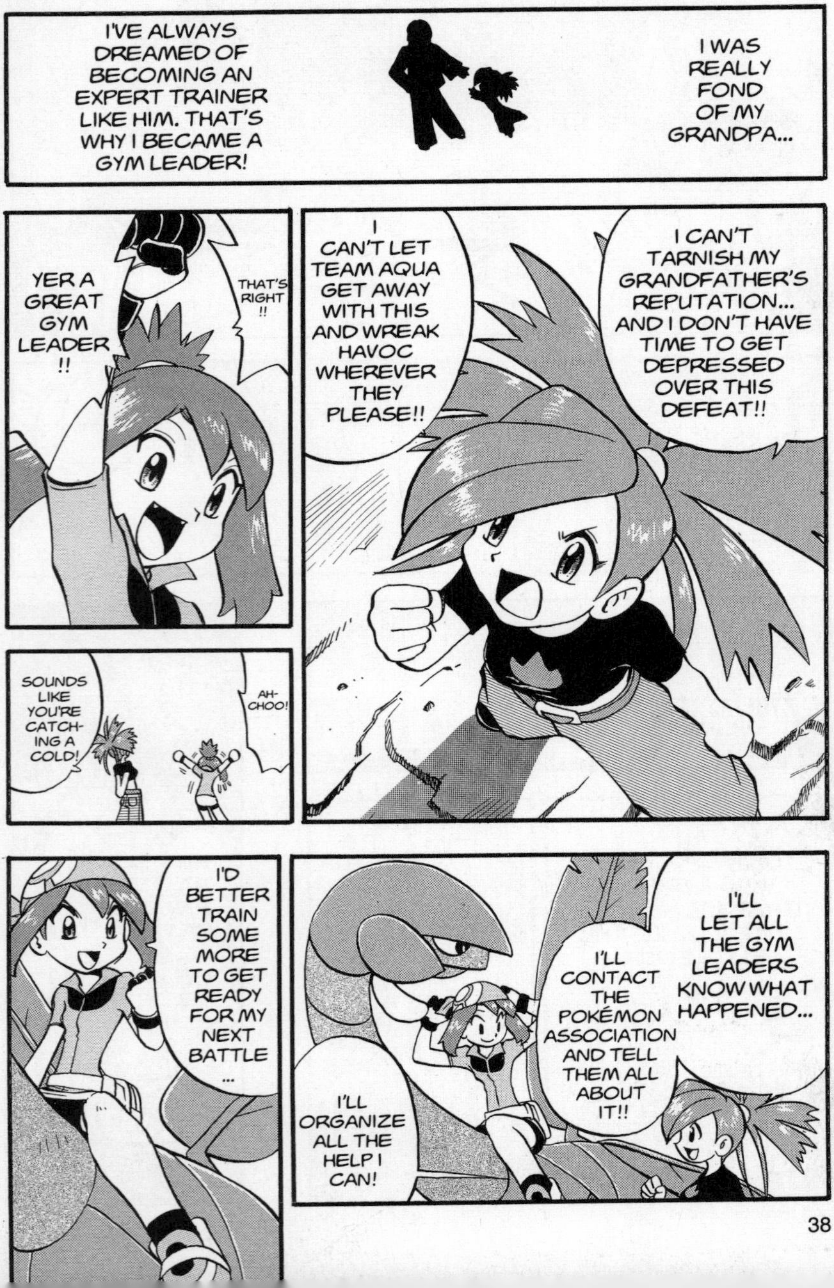
I WAS REALLY FOND OF MY GRANDPA...
I'VE ALWAYS DREAMED OF BECOMING AN EXPERT TRAINER LIKE HIM. THAT'S WHY I BECAME A GYM LEADER!
I CAN'T TARNISH MY GRANDFATHER'S REPUTATION... AND I DON'T HAVE TIME TO GET DEPRESSED OVER THIS DEFEAT!!
I CAN'T LET TEAM AQUA GET AWAY WITH THIS AND WREAK HAVOC WHEREVER THEY PLEASE!!
THAT'S RIGHT!!
YER A GREAT GYM LEADER!!
AH-CHOO!
SOUNDS LIKE YOU'RE CATCHING A COLD!
I'LL LET ALL THE GYM LEADERS KNOW WHAT HAPPENED...
I'LL CONTACT THE POKÉMON ASSOCIATION AND TELL THEM ALL ABOUT IT!!
I'LL ORGANIZE ALL THE HELP I CAN!
I'D BETTER TRAIN SOME MORE TO GET READY FOR MY NEXT BATTLE...

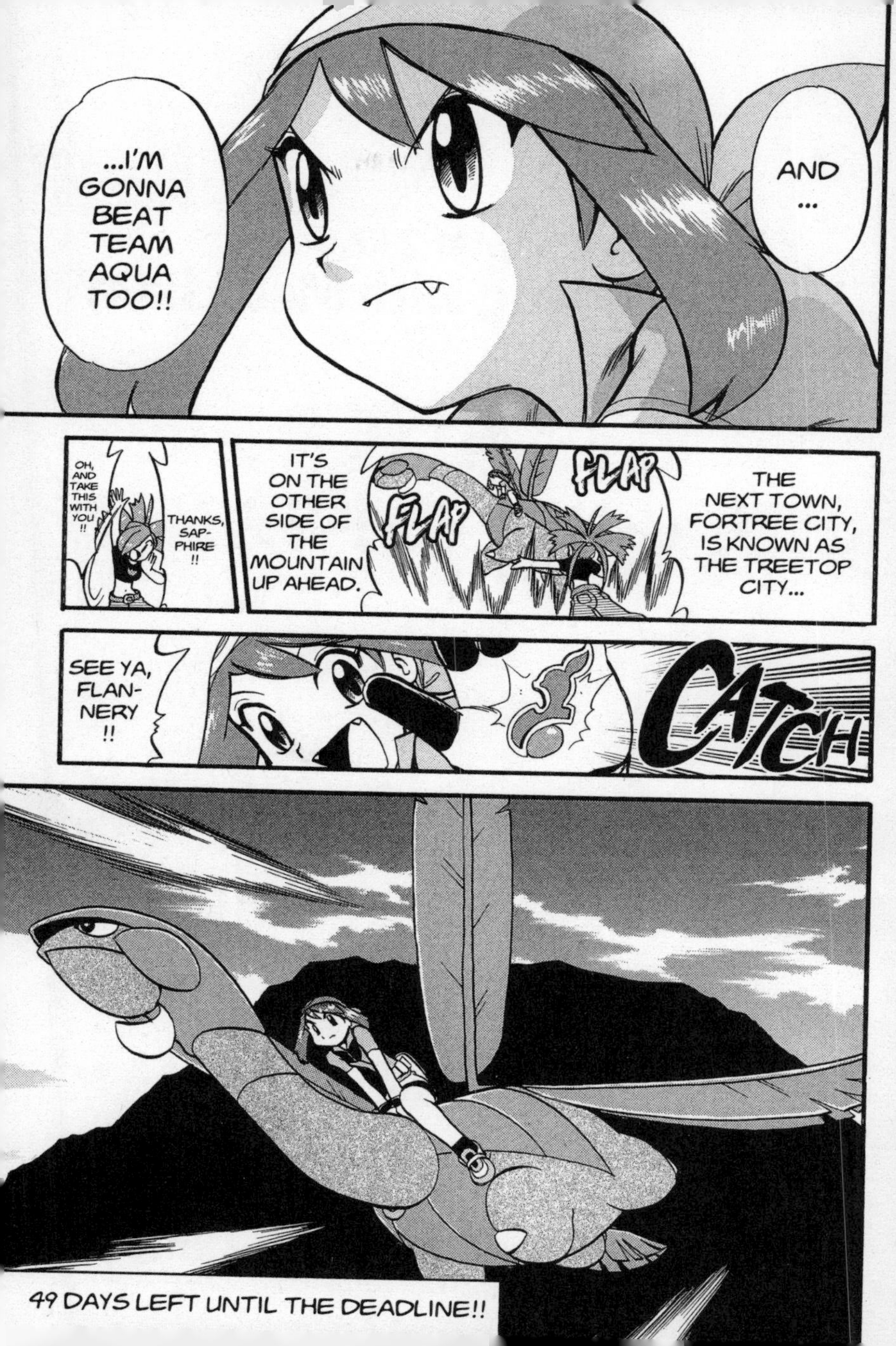
...I'M GONNA BEAT TEAM AQUA TOO!!
AND ...
THE NEXT TOWN, FORTREE CITY, IS KNOWN AS THE TREETOP CITY...
FLAP
FLAP
IT'S ON THE OTHER SIDE OF THE MOUNTAIN UP AHEAD.
OH, AND TAKE THIS WITH YOU!!
THANKS, SAP-PHIRE!!
CATCH
SEE YA, FLAN-NERY!!
49 DAYS LEFT UNTIL THE DEADLINE!!

● Chapter 217 ●
Mind-Boggling with Medicham

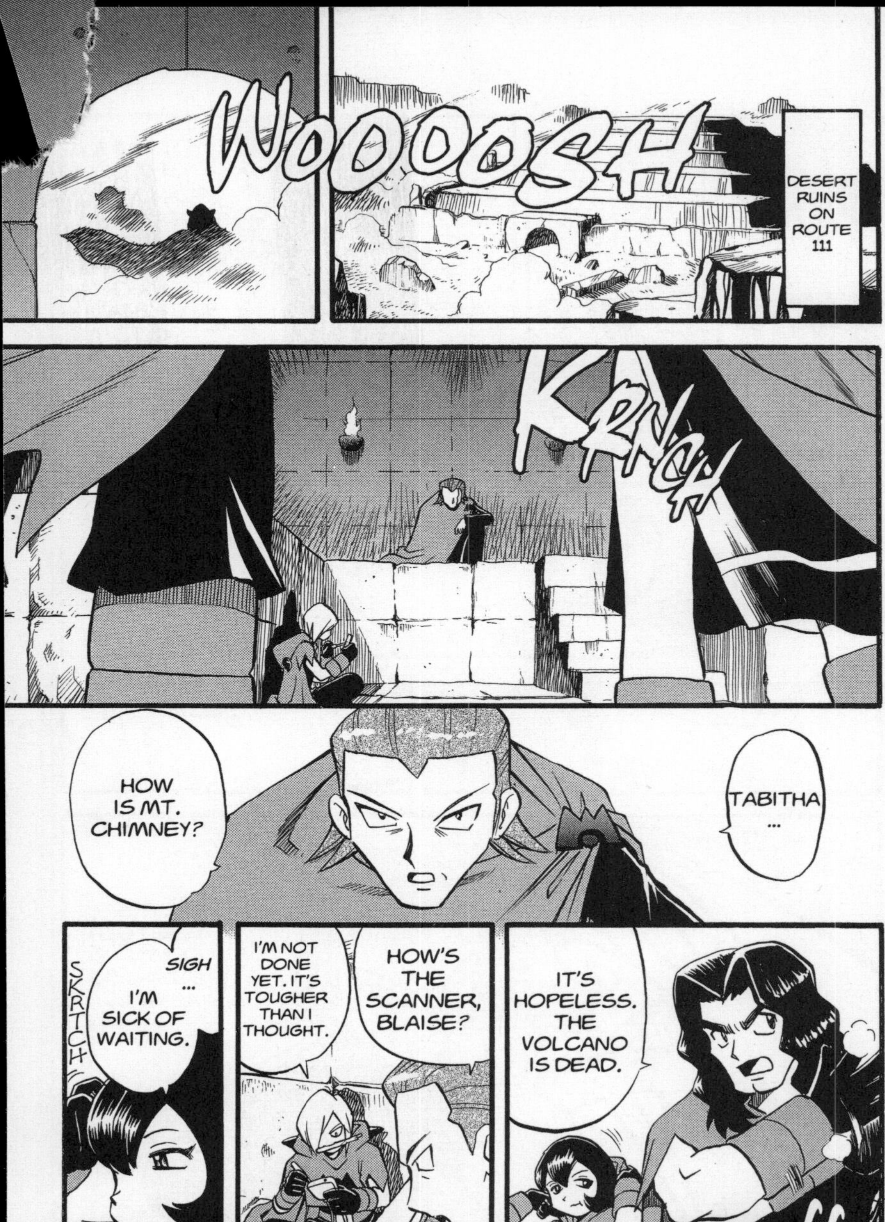
DESERT RUINS ON ROUTE 111
WOOOSH
KRNCH
TABITHA ...
HOW IS MT. CHIMNEY?
IT'S HOPELESS. THE VOLCANO IS DEAD.
FFT FFT
HOW'S THE SCANNER, BLAISE?
I'M NOT DONE YET. IT'S TOUGHER THAN I THOUGHT.
SIGH ...
I'M SICK OF WAITING.
SKRTCH

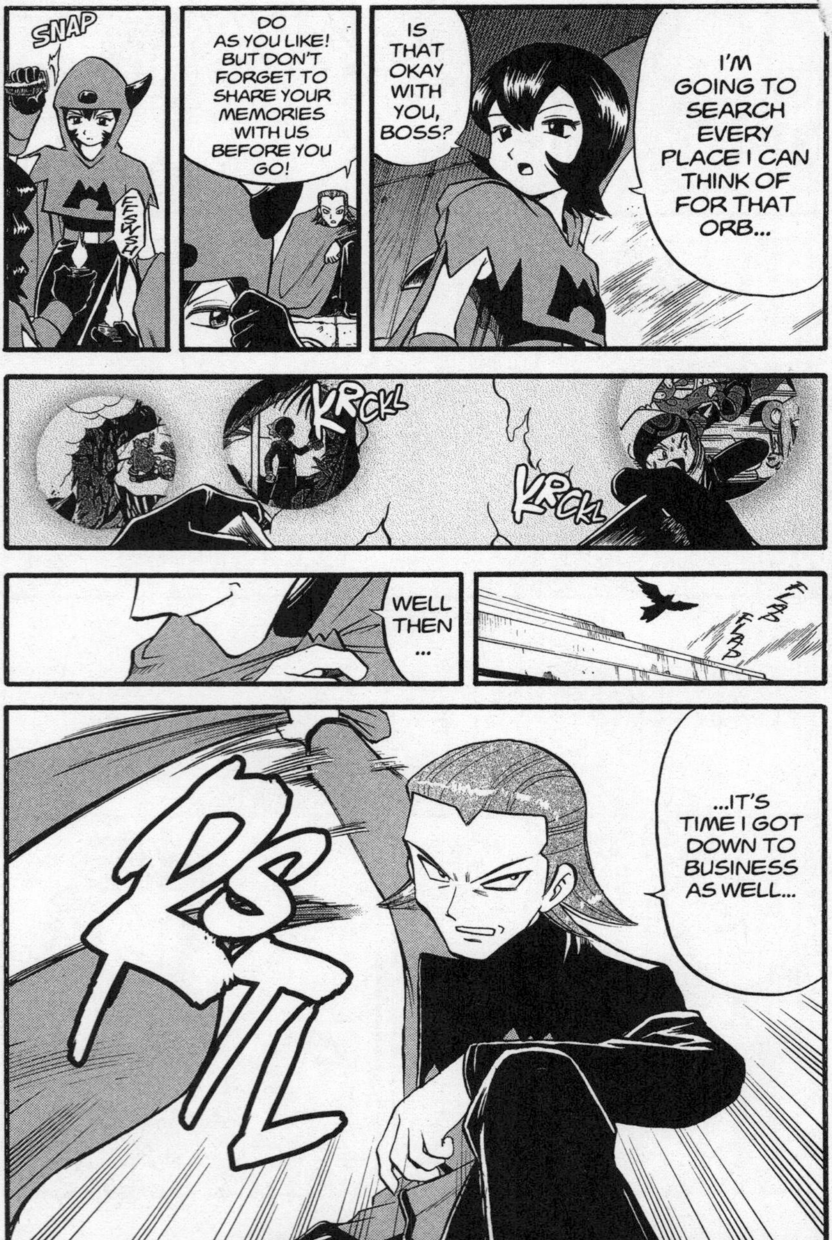
I'M GOING TO SEARCH EVERY PLACE I CAN THINK OF FOR THAT ORB...
IS THAT OKAY WITH YOU, BOSS?
DO AS YOU LIKE! BUT DON'T FORGET TO SHARE YOUR MEMORIES WITH US BEFORE YOU GO!
SNAP
FFSWSH
KRCKL
KRCKL
FLAP FLAP
WELL THEN...
...IT'S TIME I GOT DOWN TO BUSINESS AS WELL...
RSTL

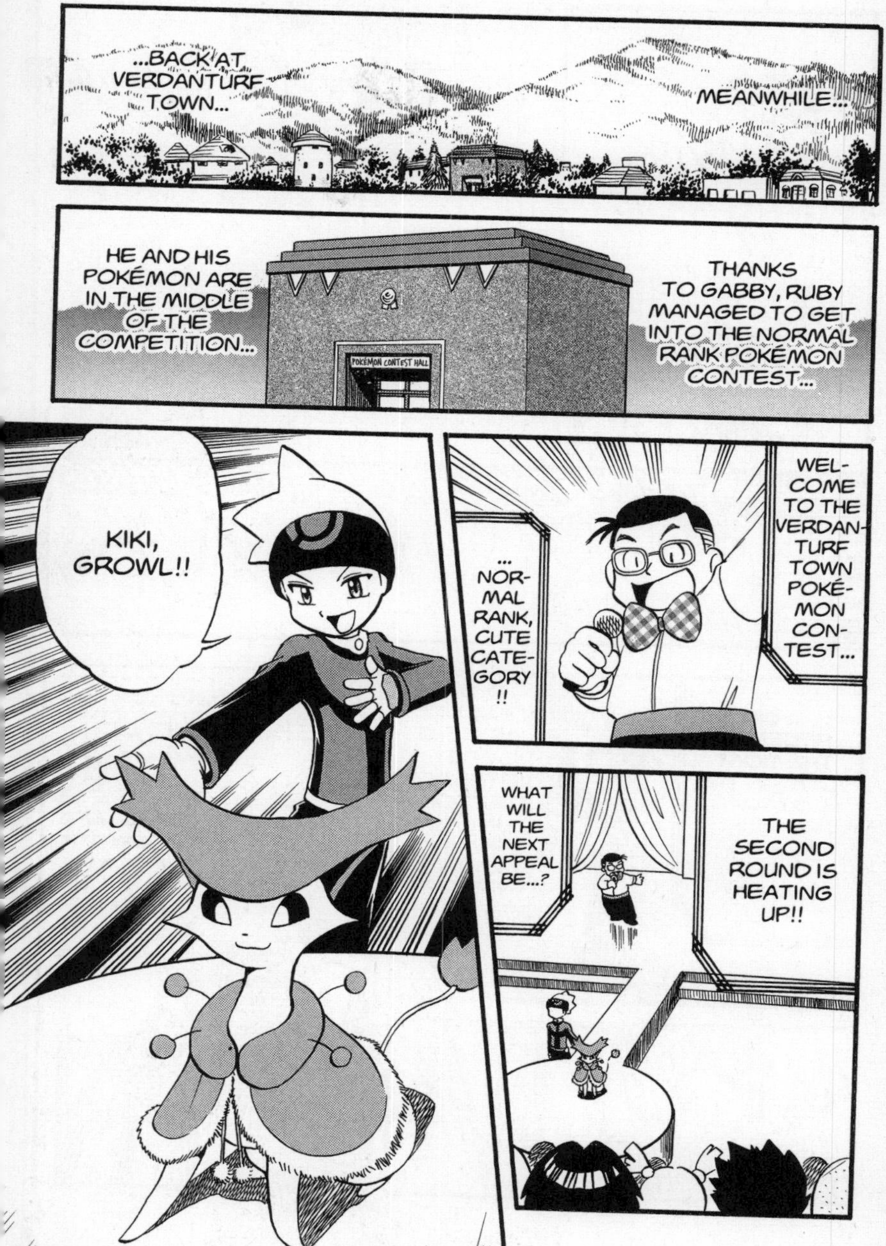
MEANWHILE...
...BACK AT VERDANTURF TOWN...
THANKS TO GABBY, RUBY MANAGED TO GET INTO THE NORMAL RANK POKÉMON CONTEST...
HE AND HIS POKÉMON ARE IN THE MIDDLE OF THE COMPETITION...
POKÉMON CONTEST HALL
WEL-COME TO THE VERDAN-TURF TOWN POKÉ-MON CON-TEST...
...NOR-MAL RANK, CUTE CATE-GORY!!
THE SECOND ROUND IS HEATING UP!!
WHAT WILL THE NEXT APPEAL BE...?
KIKI, GROWL!!

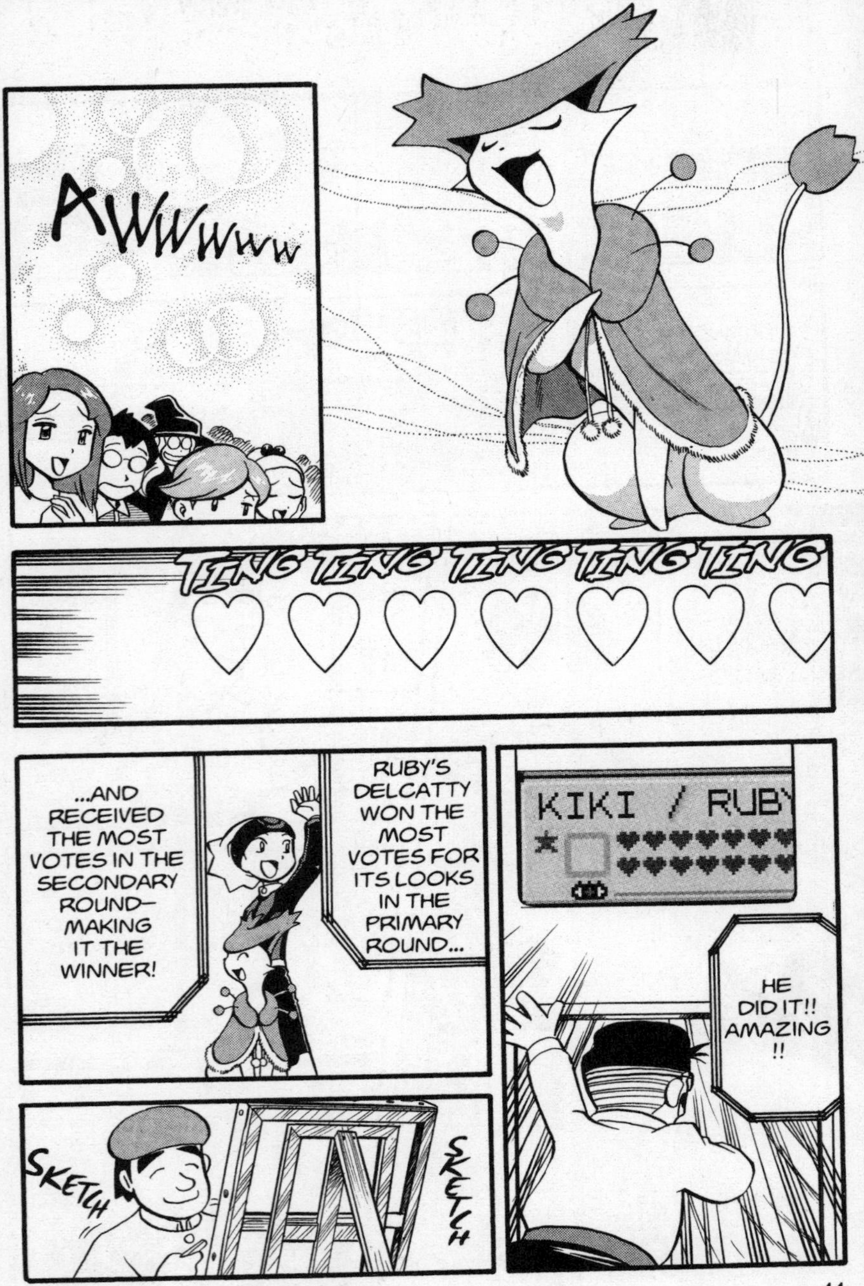
AWWWWWW
TING TING TING TING TING
KIKI / RUBY
HE DID IT!! AMAZING!!
RUBY'S DELCATTY WON THE MOST VOTES FOR ITS LOOKS IN THE PRIMARY ROUND...
...AND RECEIVED THE MOST VOTES IN THE SECONDARY ROUND—MAKING IT THE WINNER!
SKETCH
SKETCH

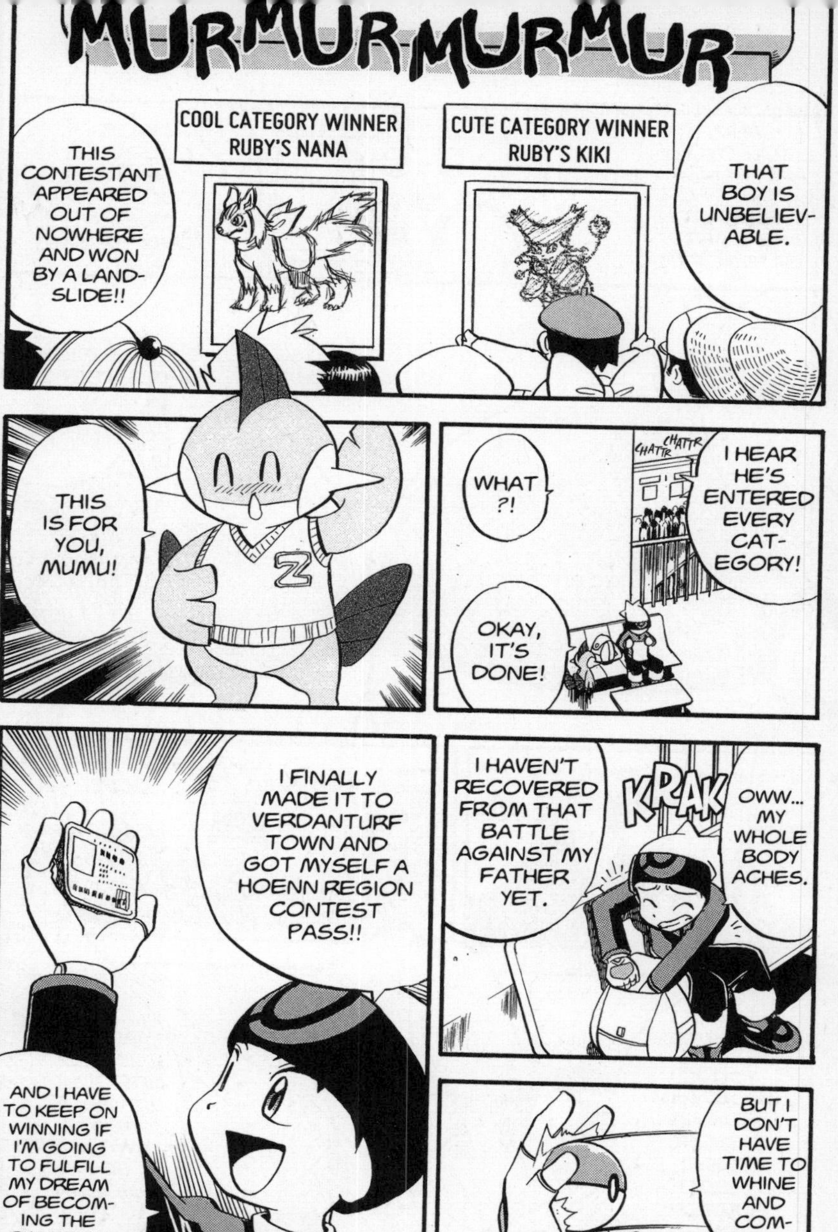
MURMURMURMUR
THAT BOY IS UNBELIEVABLE.
CUTE CATEGORY WINNER RUBY'S KIKI
COOL CATEGORY WINNER RUBY'S NANA
THIS CONTESTANT APPEARED OUT OF NOWHERE AND WON BY A LANDSLIDE!!
CHATTR CHATTR
I HEAR HE'S ENTERED EVERY CATEGORY!
WHAT?!
OKAY, IT'S DONE!
THIS IS FOR YOU, MUMU!
KRAK
OWW... MY WHOLE BODY ACHES.
I HAVEN'T RECOVERED FROM THAT BATTLE AGAINST MY FATHER YET.
BUT I DON'T HAVE TIME TO WHINE AND COMPLAIN.
CATCH
I FINALLY MADE IT TO VERDANTURF TOWN AND GOT MYSELF A HOENN REGION CONTEST PASS!!
AND I HAVE TO KEEP ON WINNING IF I'M GOING TO FULFILL MY DREAM OF BECOMING THE CHAMPION OF EVERY CONTEST!!

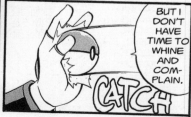

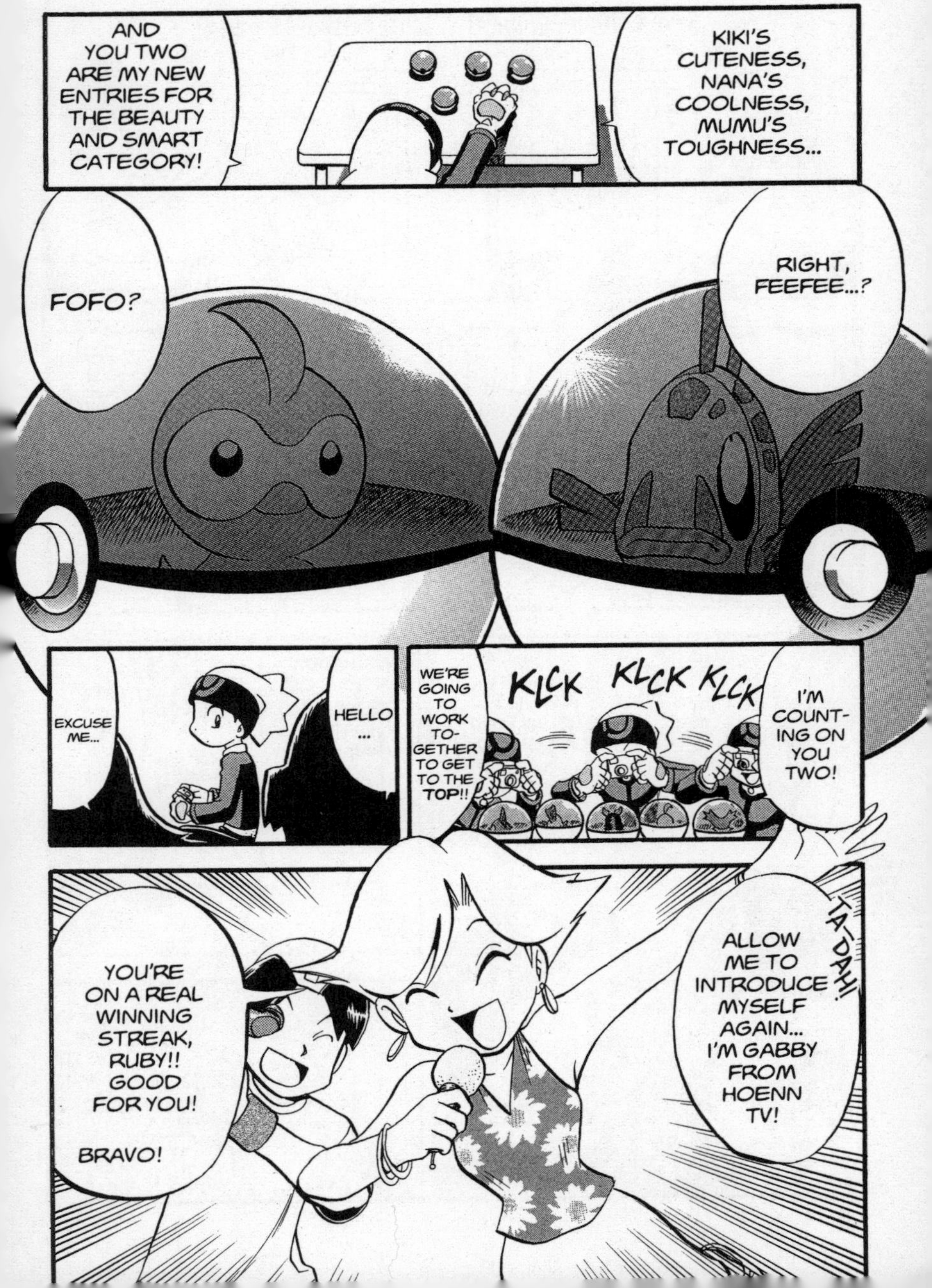
KIKI'S CUTENESS, NANA'S COOLNESS, MUMU'S TOUGHNESS...
AND YOU TWO ARE MY NEW ENTRIES FOR THE BEAUTY AND SMART CATEGORY!
RIGHT, FEEFEE...?
FOFO?
I'M COUNT-ING ON YOU TWO!
KLCK KLCK KLCK
WE'RE GOING TO WORK TO-GETHER TO GET TO THE **TOP**!!
HELLO ...
EXCUSE ME...
TA-DAH!
ALLOW ME TO INTRODUCE MYSELF AGAIN... I'M GABBY FROM HOENN TV!
YOU'RE ON A REAL WINNING STREAK, RUBY!! GOOD FOR YOU!
BRAVO!

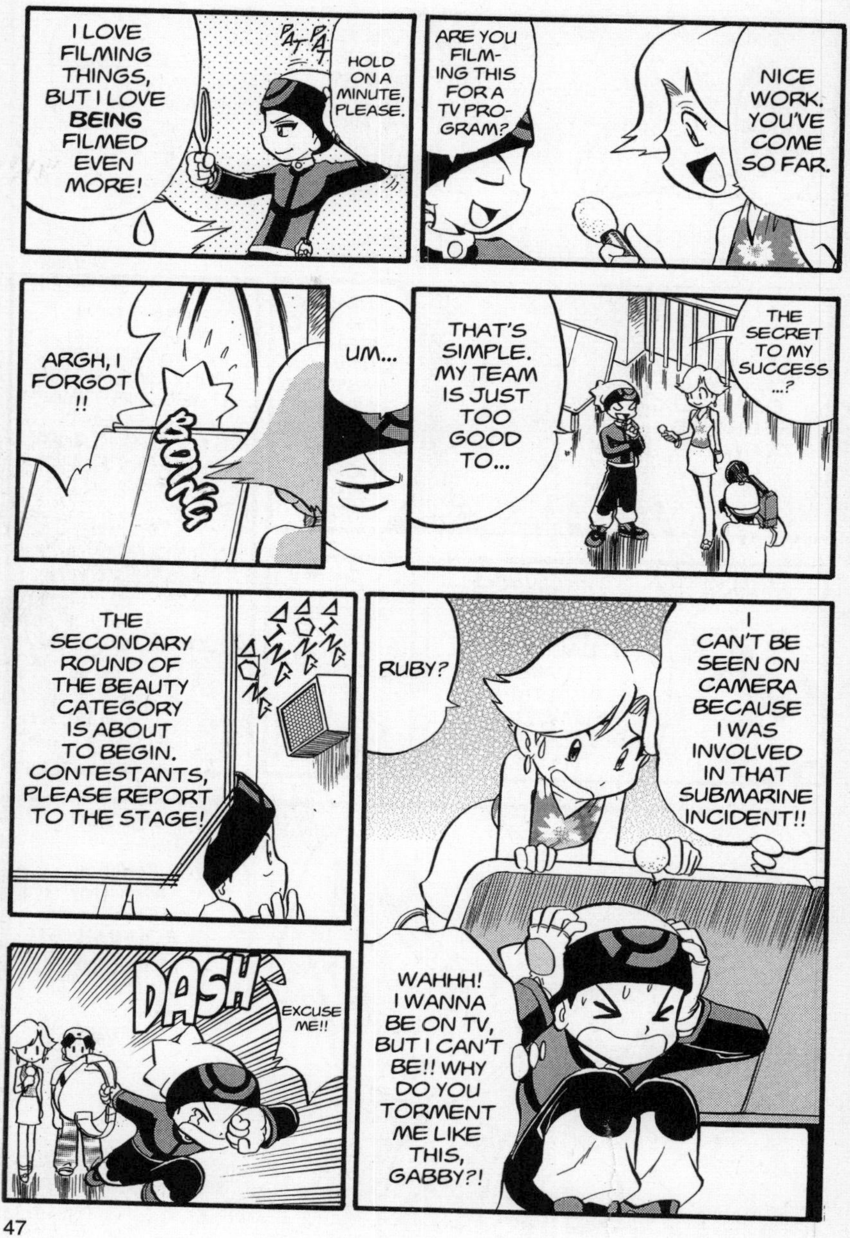
NICE WORK. YOU'VE COME SO FAR.
ARE YOU FILMING THIS FOR A TV PROGRAM?
HOLD ON A MINUTE, PLEASE.
PAT PAT
I LOVE FILMING THINGS, BUT I LOVE **BEING** FILMED EVEN MORE!
THE SECRET TO MY SUCCESS ...?
THAT'S SIMPLE. MY TEAM IS JUST TOO GOOD TO...
UM...
ARGH, I FORGOT !!
BOING
I CAN'T BE SEEN ON CAMERA BECAUSE I WAS INVOLVED IN THAT SUBMARINE INCIDENT!!
RUBY?
WAHHH! I WANNA BE ON TV, BUT I CAN'T BE!! WHY DO YOU TORMENT ME LIKE THIS, GABBY?!
THE SECONDARY ROUND OF THE BEAUTY CATEGORY IS ABOUT TO BEGIN. CONTESTANTS, PLEASE REPORT TO THE STAGE!
DING DING DING DONG DONG DONG
EXCUSE ME!!
DASH

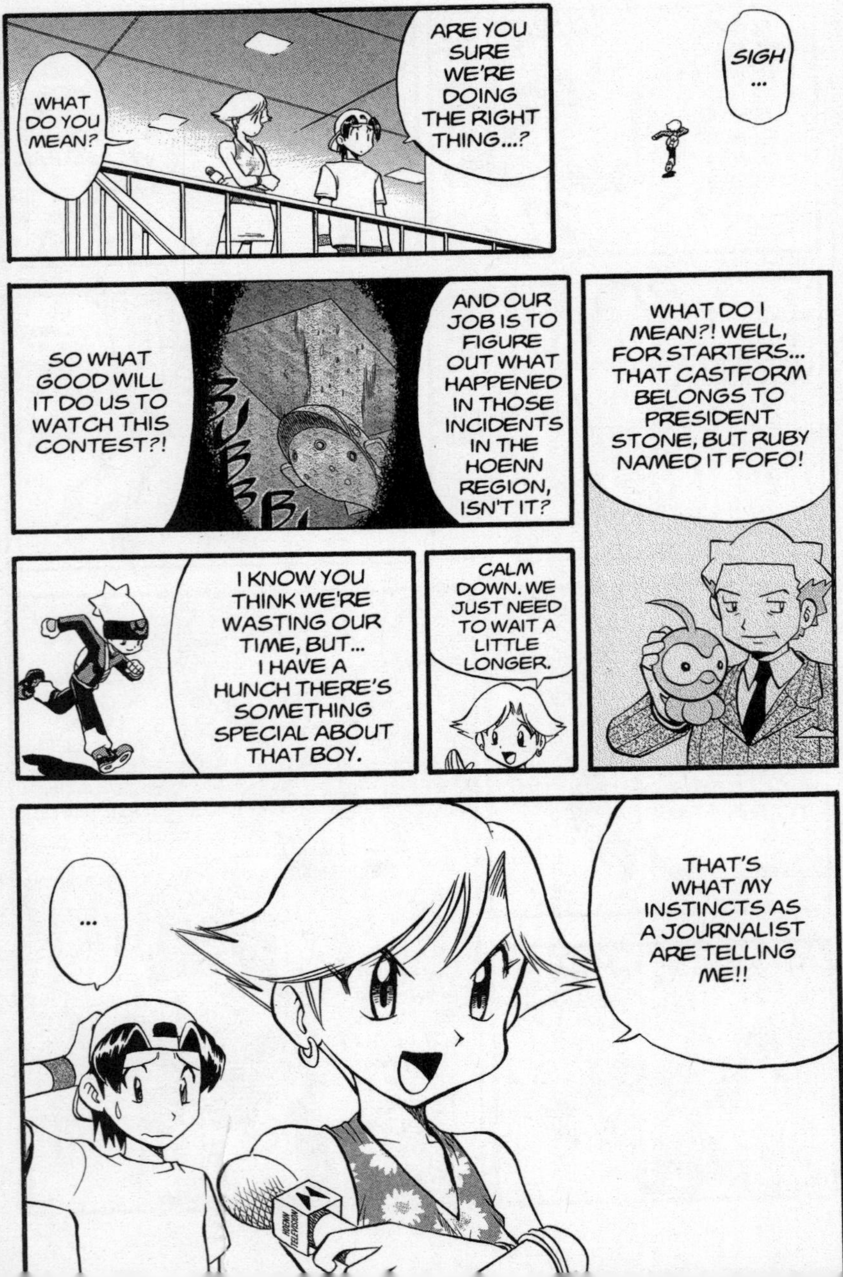
SIGH ...
ARE YOU SURE WE'RE DOING THE RIGHT THING...?
WHAT DO YOU MEAN?
WHAT DO I MEAN?! WELL, FOR STARTERS... THAT CASTFORM BELONGS TO PRESIDENT STONE, BUT RUBY NAMED IT FOFO!
AND OUR JOB IS TO FIGURE OUT WHAT HAPPENED IN THOSE INCIDENTS IN THE HOENN REGION, ISN'T IT?
ZUBBB
SO WHAT GOOD WILL IT DO US TO WATCH THIS CONTEST?!
CALM DOWN. WE JUST NEED TO WAIT A LITTLE LONGER.
I KNOW YOU THINK WE'RE WASTING OUR TIME, BUT... I HAVE A HUNCH THERE'S SOMETHING SPECIAL ABOUT THAT BOY.
THAT'S WHAT MY INSTINCTS AS A JOURNALIST ARE TELLING ME!!
...
HOENN TELEVISION

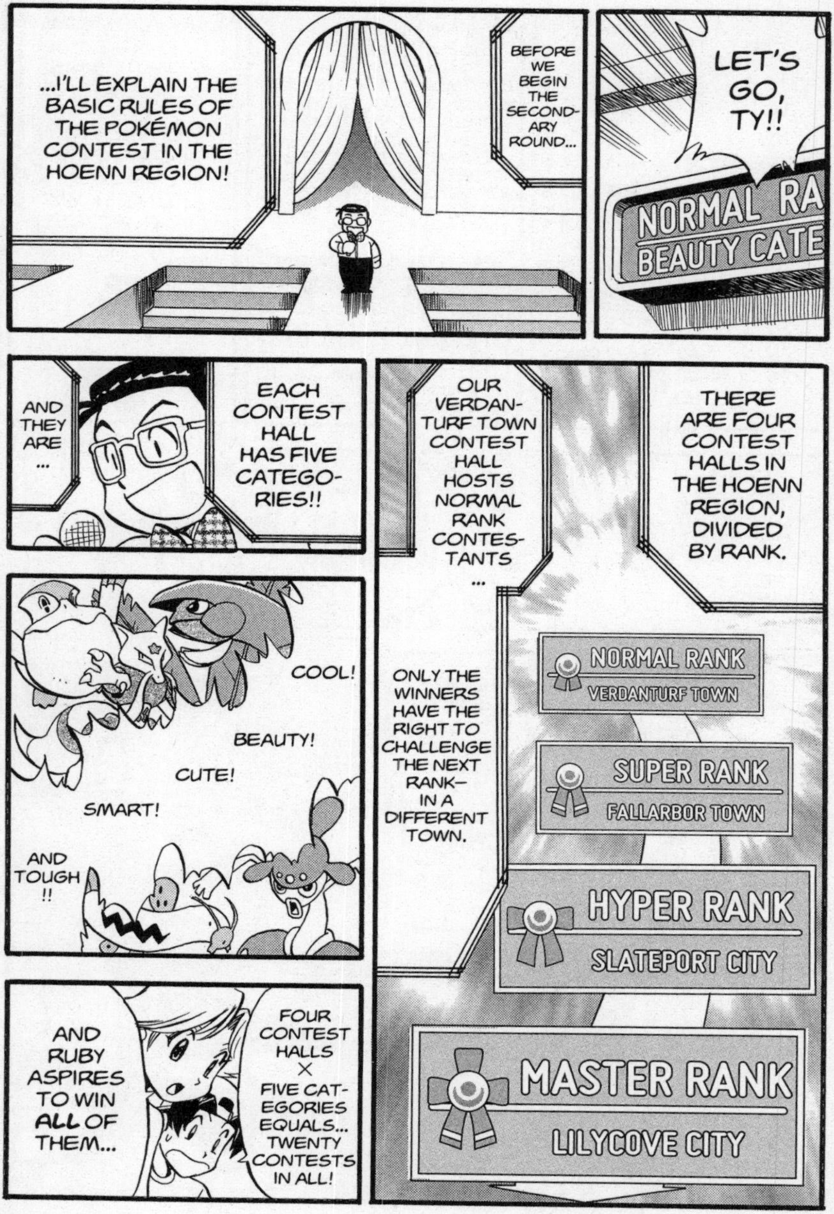
LET'S GO, TY!!
NORMAL RA
BEAUTY CATE
BEFORE WE BEGIN THE SECONDARY ROUND...
...I'LL EXPLAIN THE BASIC RULES OF THE POKÉMON CONTEST IN THE HOENN REGION!
THERE ARE FOUR CONTEST HALLS IN THE HOENN REGION, DIVIDED BY RANK.
OUR VERDANTURF TOWN CONTEST HALL HOSTS NORMAL RANK CONTESTANTS ...
NORMAL RANK
VERDANTURF TOWN
SUPER RANK
FALLARBOR TOWN
HYPER RANK
SLATEPORT CITY
MASTER RANK
LILYCOVE CITY
ONLY THE WINNERS HAVE THE RIGHT TO CHALLENGE THE NEXT RANK—IN A DIFFERENT TOWN.
EACH CONTEST HALL HAS FIVE CATEGORIES!!
AND THEY ARE ...
COOL!
BEAUTY!
CUTE!
SMART!
AND TOUGH !!
FOUR CONTEST HALLS × FIVE CATEGORIES EQUALS... TWENTY CONTESTS IN ALL!
AND RUBY ASPIRES TO WIN **ALL** OF THEM...

WELL THEN, LET'S MOVE ON TO THE SECOND ROUND...

...THE BEAUTY CATE-GORY!!

IN THE FIRST ROUND, THE JUDGES EVALUATE THE LOOKS OF THE POKÉMON. IN THE SECOND ROUND, THE CONTESTANTS APPEAL TO THE JUDGES BY SHOWING OFF THEIR POKÉMON'S MOVES. THE CONTESTANT'S RANK IS DETERMINED BY THE TOTAL POINTS RECEIVED IN THESE TWO ROUNDS.

ERWIN/HILLARY		
MEDDY/CODY		
ALTA/AOI		
FEEFEE/RUBY		

AS YOU KNOW, THE POKÉMON CONTEST IS NOT A BATTLE BUT A COMPETITION COMPARING POKÉMON CONDITIONS AND MOVES!

IS HE SERIOUSLY PLANNING TO USE **THAT** POKÉMON FOR THE BEAUTY CATEGORY?

MURMUR

WHAT? LOOK AT HIS POKÉMON!

MURMUR

MUR MUR

HE WAS LAST PLACE IN THE FIRST ROUND TOO!

ITS MOVES CAN'T BE NICE WITH LOOKS LIKE **THAT**...

MUR MUR

IT'S POINTLESS TO COMPETE JUST TO WIN THE POKÉMON CONTESTS!!

I REAL-IZED SOME-THING AFTER FIGHTING DAD...

50

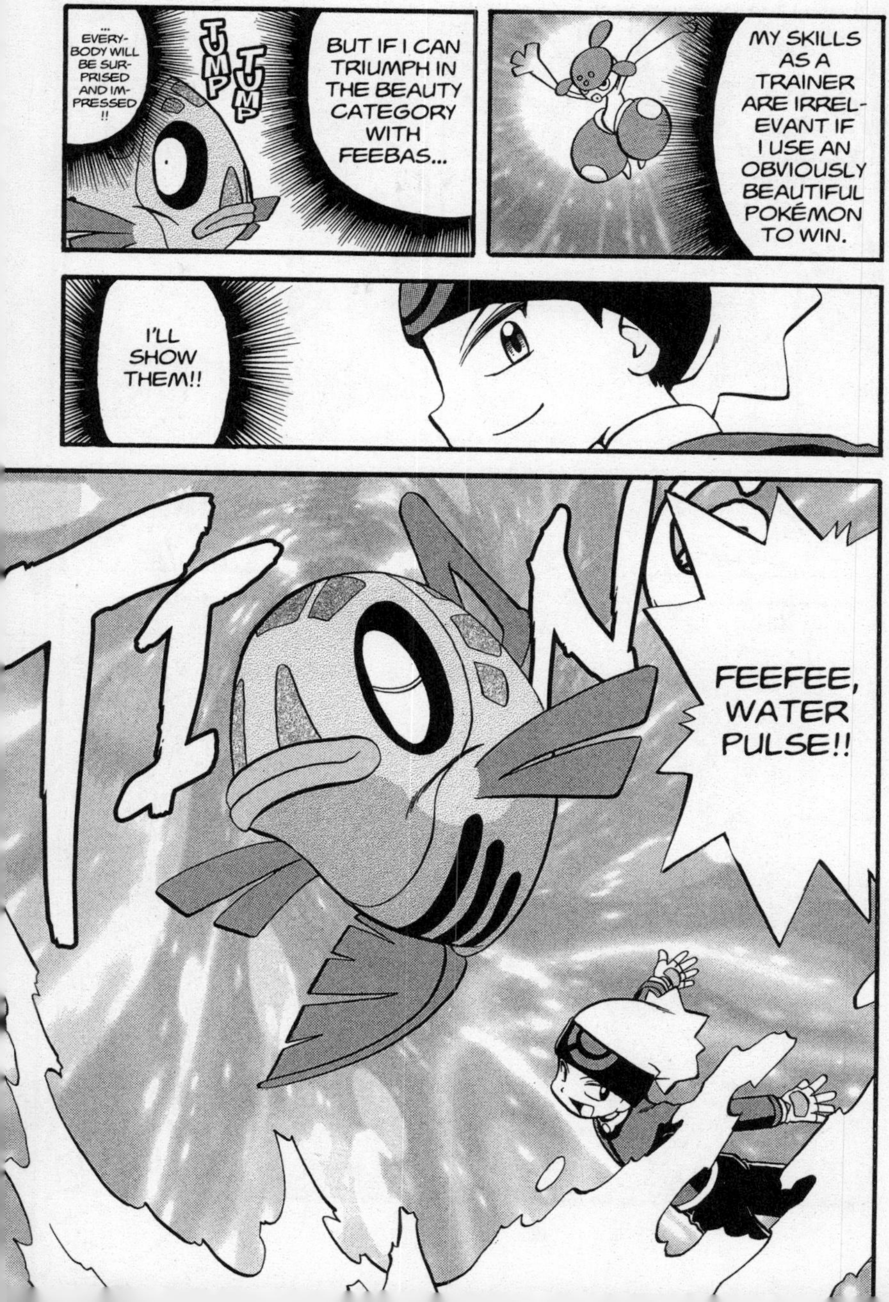
MY SKILLS AS A TRAINER ARE IRREL-EVANT IF I USE AN OBVIOUSLY BEAUTIFUL POKÉMON TO WIN.
BUT IF I CAN TRIUMPH IN THE BEAUTY CATEGORY WITH FEEBAS...
TUMP TUMP
... EVERY-BODY WILL BE SUR-PRISED AND IM-PRESSED !!
I'LL SHOW THEM!!
TION
FEEFEE, WATER PULSE!!

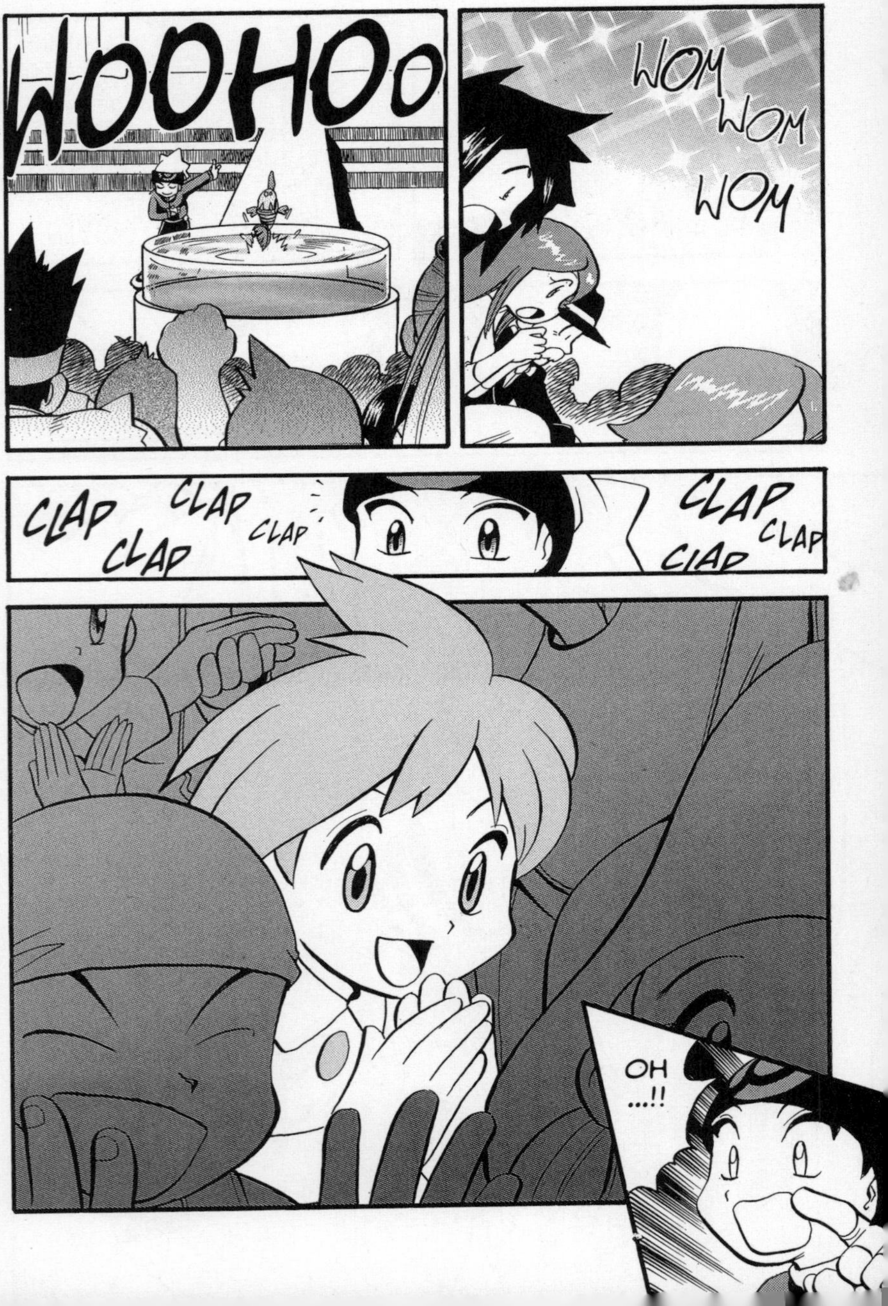
WOM WOM WOM
WOOHOO
CLAP CLAP CLAP
CLAP CLAP CLAP CLAP
OH ...!!

● Chapter 218 ●
It's Absol-lutely a Bad Omen

Pokémon™ Adventures Ruby & Sapphire

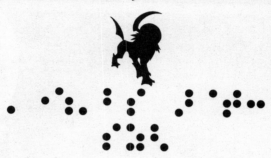

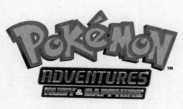

The Fourth Chapter

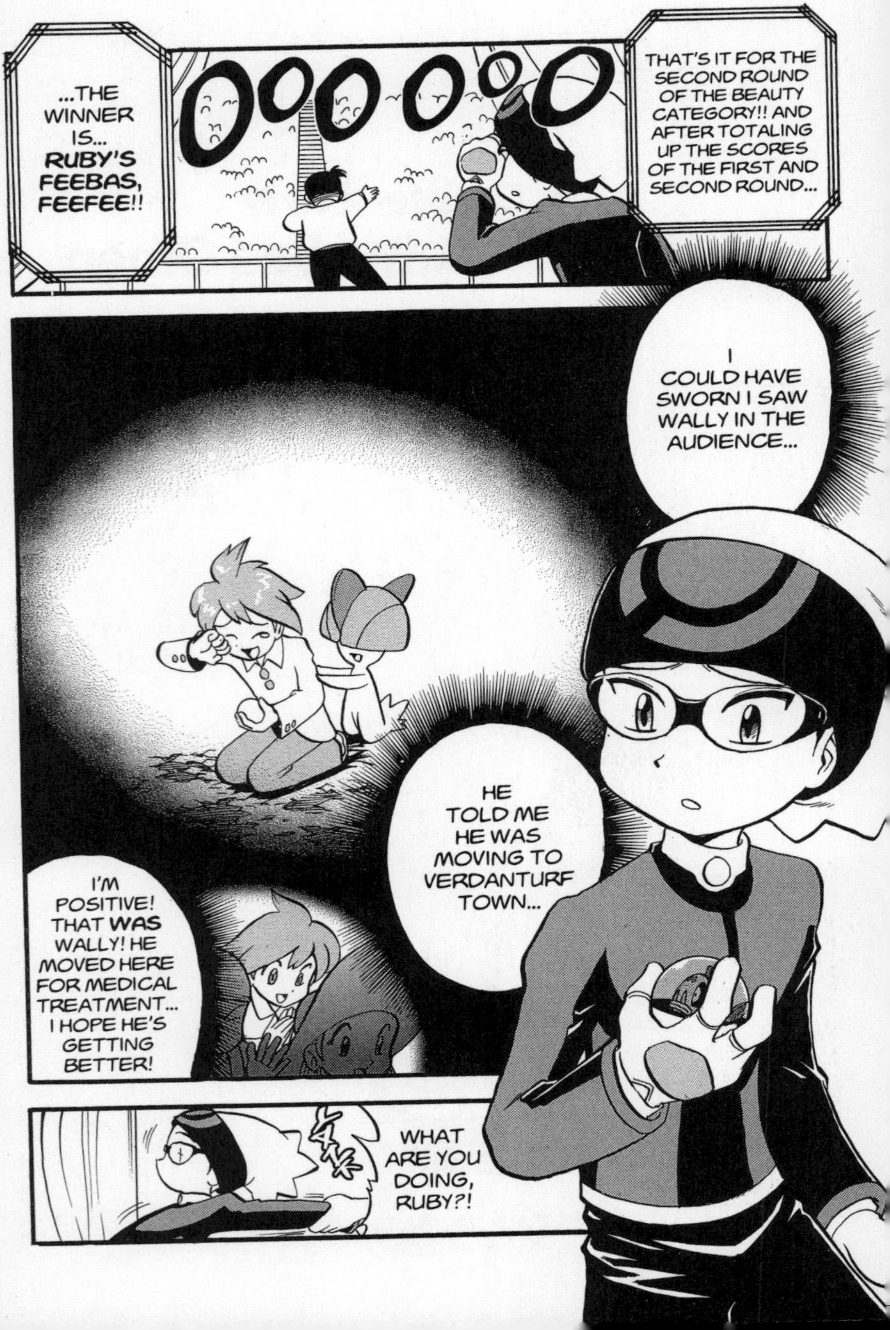
THAT'S IT FOR THE SECOND ROUND OF THE BEAUTY CATEGORY!! AND AFTER TOTALING UP THE SCORES OF THE FIRST AND SECOND ROUND...
OOOOOO
...THE WINNER IS... RUBY'S FEEBAS, FEEFEE!!
I COULD HAVE SWORN I SAW WALLY IN THE AUDIENCE...
HE TOLD ME HE WAS MOVING TO VERDANTURF TOWN...
I'M POSITIVE! THAT WAS WALLY! HE MOVED HERE FOR MEDICAL TREATMENT... I HOPE HE'S GETTING BETTER!
WHAT ARE YOU DOING, RUBY?!

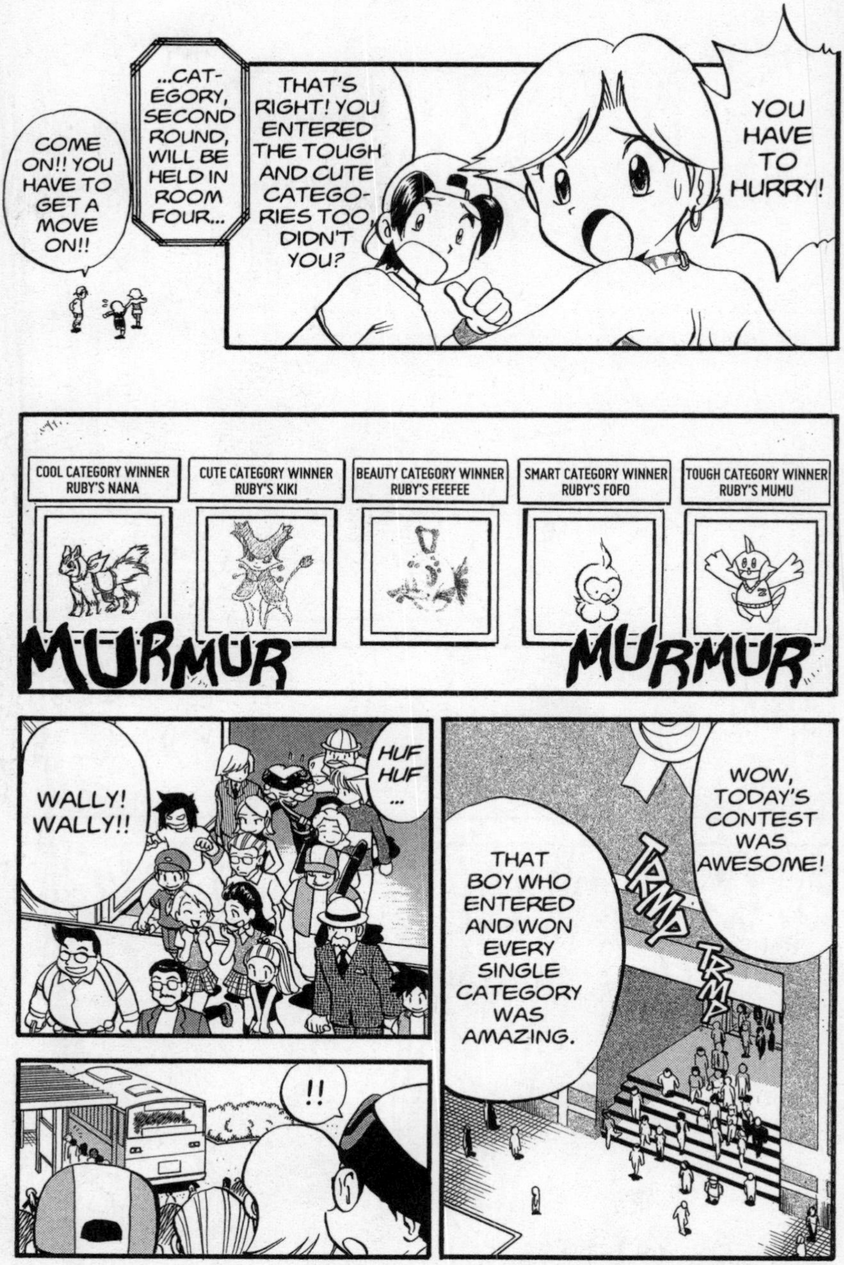

YOU HAVE TO HURRY!
THAT'S RIGHT! YOU ENTERED THE TOUGH AND CUTE CATEGORIES TOO, DIDN'T YOU?
...CATEGORY, SECOND ROUND, WILL BE HELD IN ROOM FOUR...
COME ON!! YOU HAVE TO GET A MOVE ON!!
COOL CATEGORY WINNER RUBY'S NANA
CUTE CATEGORY WINNER RUBY'S KIKI
BEAUTY CATEGORY WINNER RUBY'S FEEFEE
SMART CATEGORY WINNER RUBY'S FOFO
TOUGH CATEGORY WINNER RUBY'S MUMU
MURMUR
MURMUR
WOW, TODAY'S CONTEST WAS AWESOME!
THAT BOY WHO ENTERED AND WON EVERY SINGLE CATEGORY WAS AMAZING.
TRMP
TRMP
HUF HUF ...
WALLY! WALLY!!
!!

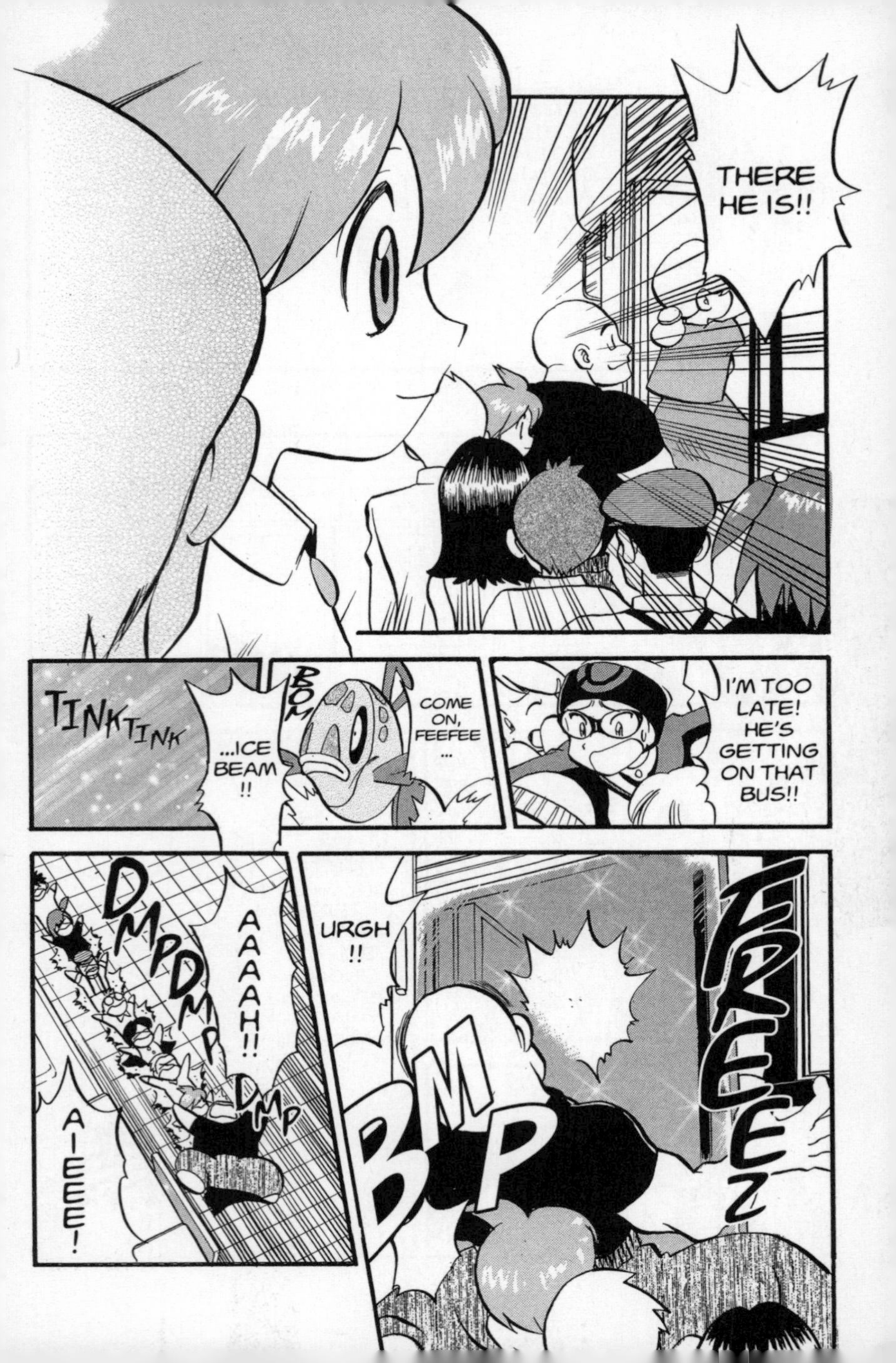
THERE HE IS!!
I'M TOO LATE! HE'S GETTING ON THAT BUS!!
BOM
COME ON, FEEFEE ...
...ICE BEAM !!
TINKTINK
FREEEZ
URGH !!
BMP
AAAAAH!!
DMPDMP
DMP
AIEEE!

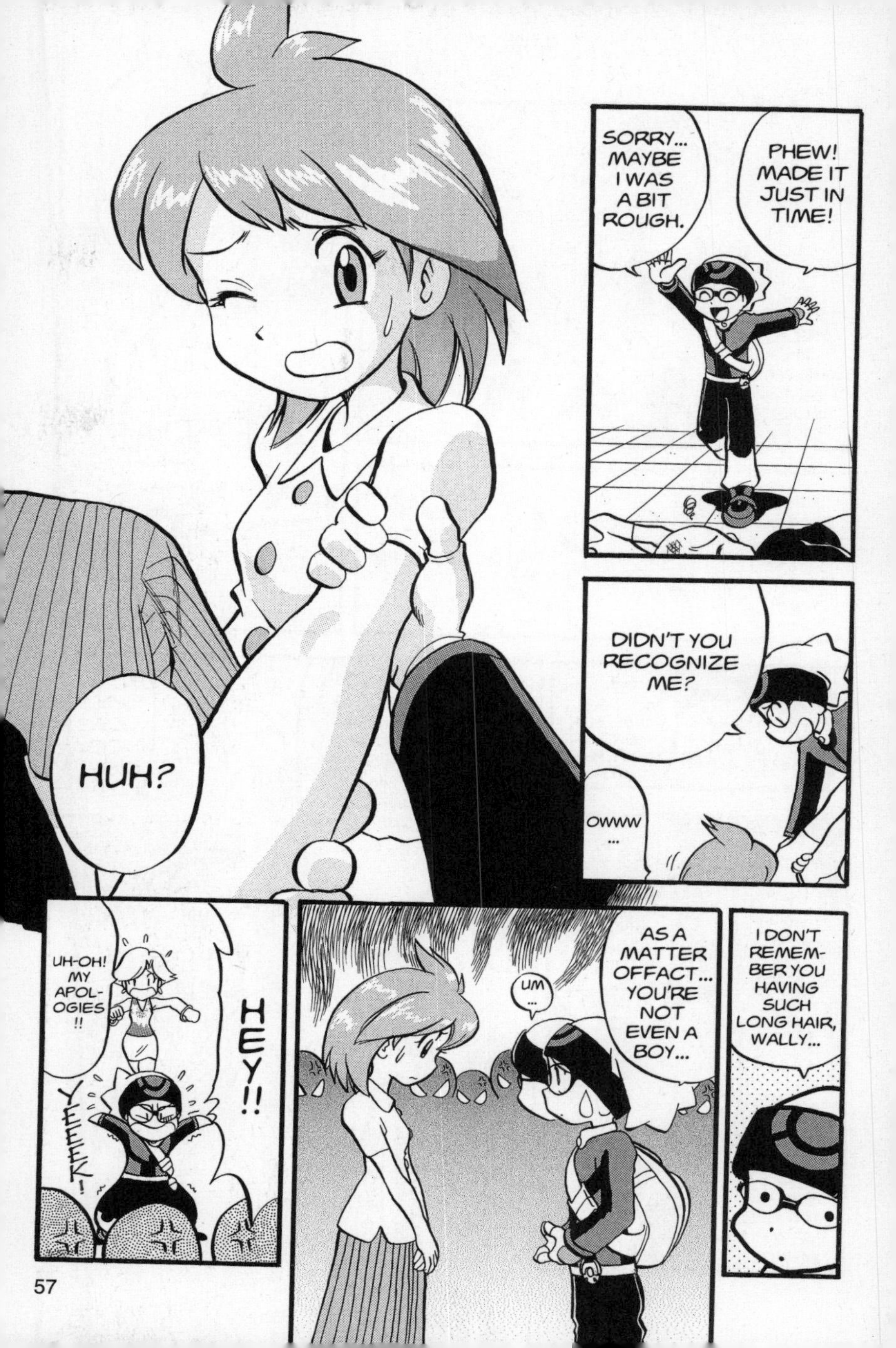
PHEW! MADE IT JUST IN TIME!
SORRY... MAYBE I WAS A BIT ROUGH.
DIDN'T YOU RECOGNIZE ME?
OWWW ...
HUH?
I DON'T REMEM-BER YOU HAVING SUCH LONG HAIR, WALLY...
AS A MATTER OFFACT... YOU'RE NOT EVEN A BOY...
UM ...
HEY!!
UH-OH! MY APOL-OGIES !!
YEEEK!

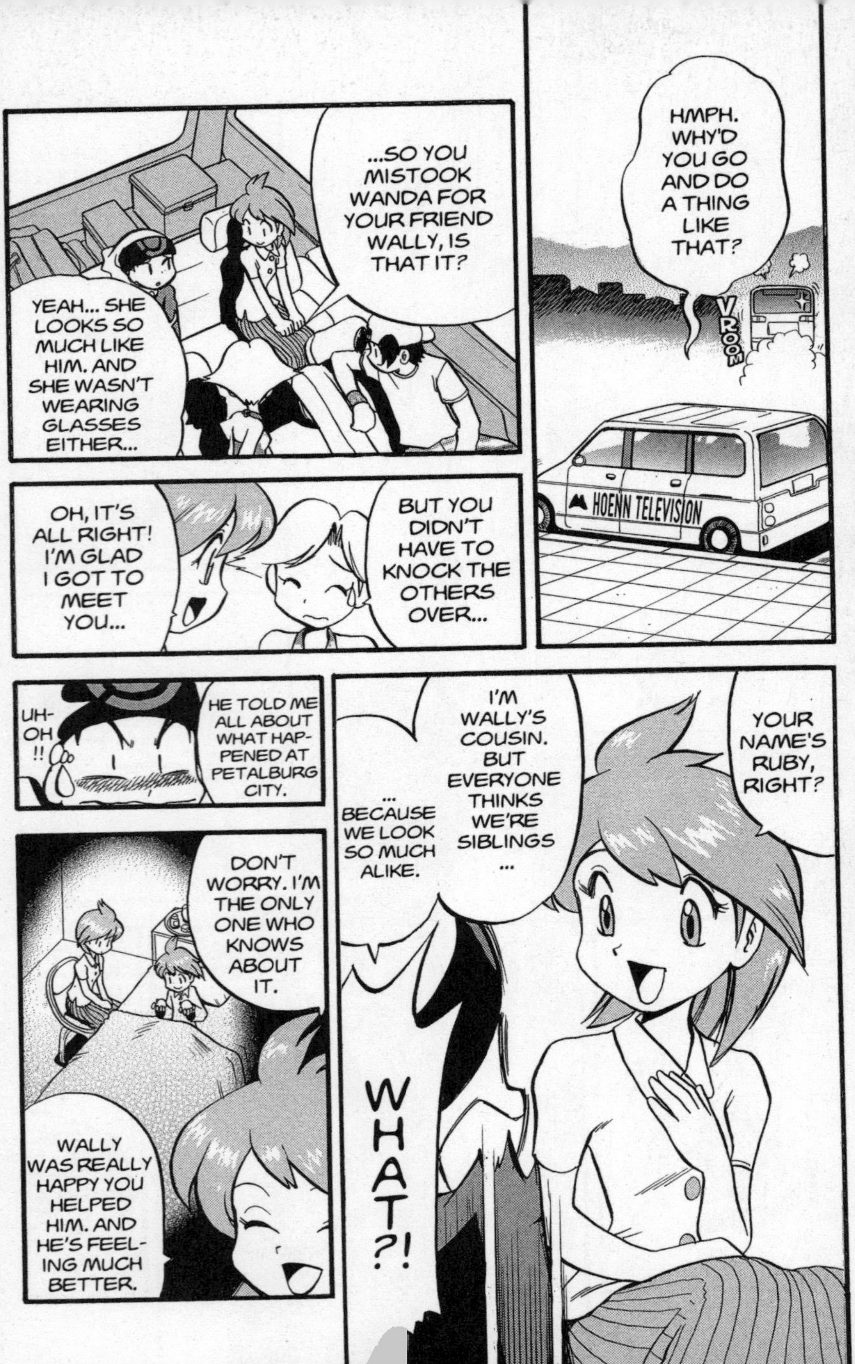
HMPH. WHY'D YOU GO AND DO A THING LIKE THAT?
VROOM
HOENN TELEVISION
...SO YOU MISTOOK WANDA FOR YOUR FRIEND WALLY, IS THAT IT?
YEAH... SHE LOOKS SO MUCH LIKE HIM. AND SHE WASN'T WEARING GLASSES EITHER...
BUT YOU DIDN'T HAVE TO KNOCK THE OTHERS OVER...
OH, IT'S ALL RIGHT! I'M GLAD I GOT TO MEET YOU...
YOUR NAME'S RUBY, RIGHT?
I'M WALLY'S COUSIN. BUT EVERYONE THINKS WE'RE SIBLINGS ...
... BECAUSE WE LOOK SO MUCH ALIKE.
WHAT?!
HE TOLD ME ALL ABOUT WHAT HAPPENED AT PETALBURG CITY.
UH-OH !!
DON'T WORRY. I'M THE ONLY ONE WHO KNOWS ABOUT IT.
WALLY WAS REALLY HAPPY YOU HELPED HIM. AND HE'S FEELING MUCH BETTER.

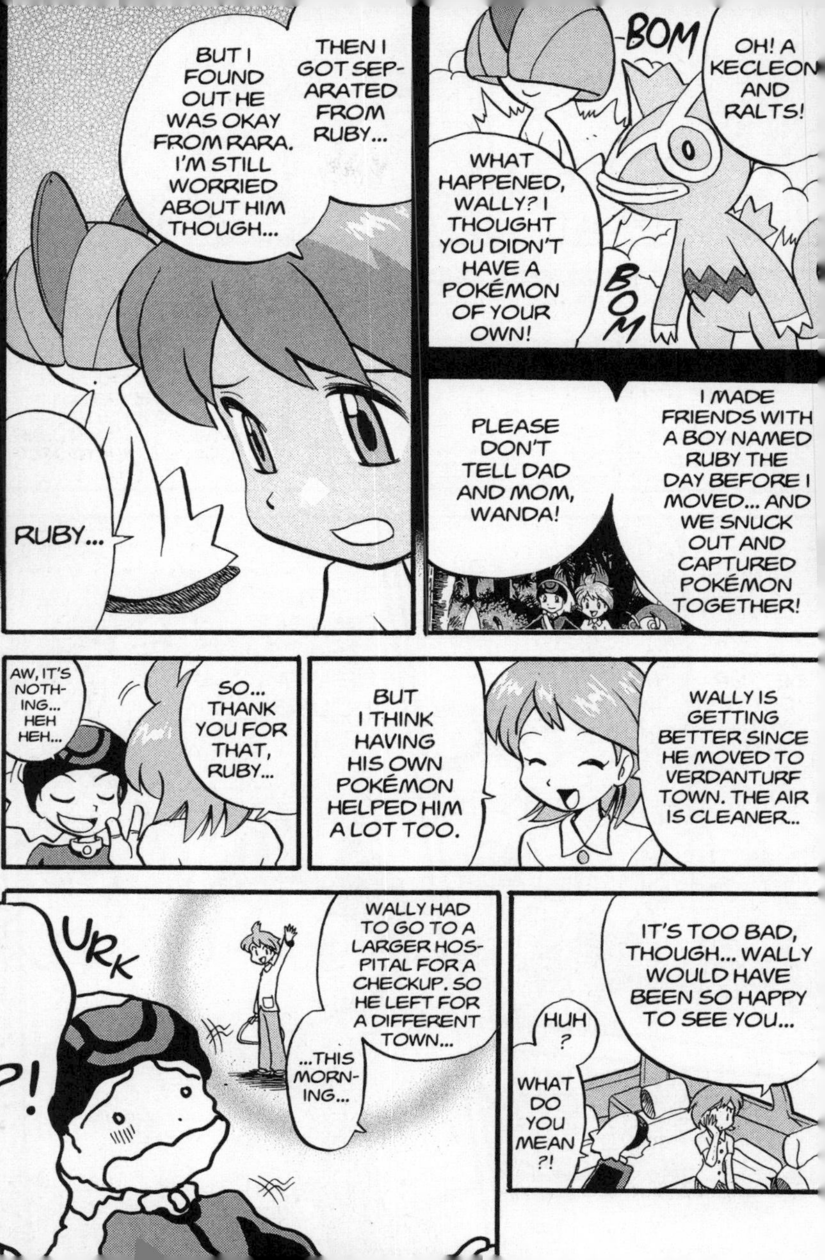
OH! A KECLEON AND RALTS!
-BOM
WHAT HAPPENED, WALLY?! I THOUGHT YOU DIDN'T HAVE A POKÉMON OF YOUR OWN!
BOM
I MADE FRIENDS WITH A BOY NAMED RUBY THE DAY BEFORE I MOVED... AND WE SNUCK OUT AND CAPTURED POKÉMON TOGETHER!
PLEASE DON'T TELL DAD AND MOM, WANDA!
THEN I GOT SEPARATED FROM RUBY...
BUT I FOUND OUT HE WAS OKAY FROM RARA. I'M STILL WORRIED ABOUT HIM THOUGH...
RUBY...
WALLY IS GETTING BETTER SINCE HE MOVED TO VERDANTURF TOWN. THE AIR IS CLEANER...
BUT I THINK HAVING HIS OWN POKÉMON HELPED HIM A LOT TOO.
SO... THANK YOU FOR THAT, RUBY...
AW, IT'S NOTHING... HEH HEH...
IT'S TOO BAD, THOUGH... WALLY WOULD HAVE BEEN SO HAPPY TO SEE YOU...
HUH?
WHAT DO YOU MEAN?!
WALLY HAD TO GO TO A LARGER HOSPITAL FOR A CHECKUP. SO HE LEFT FOR A DIFFERENT TOWN...
...THIS MORNING...
URK
?!

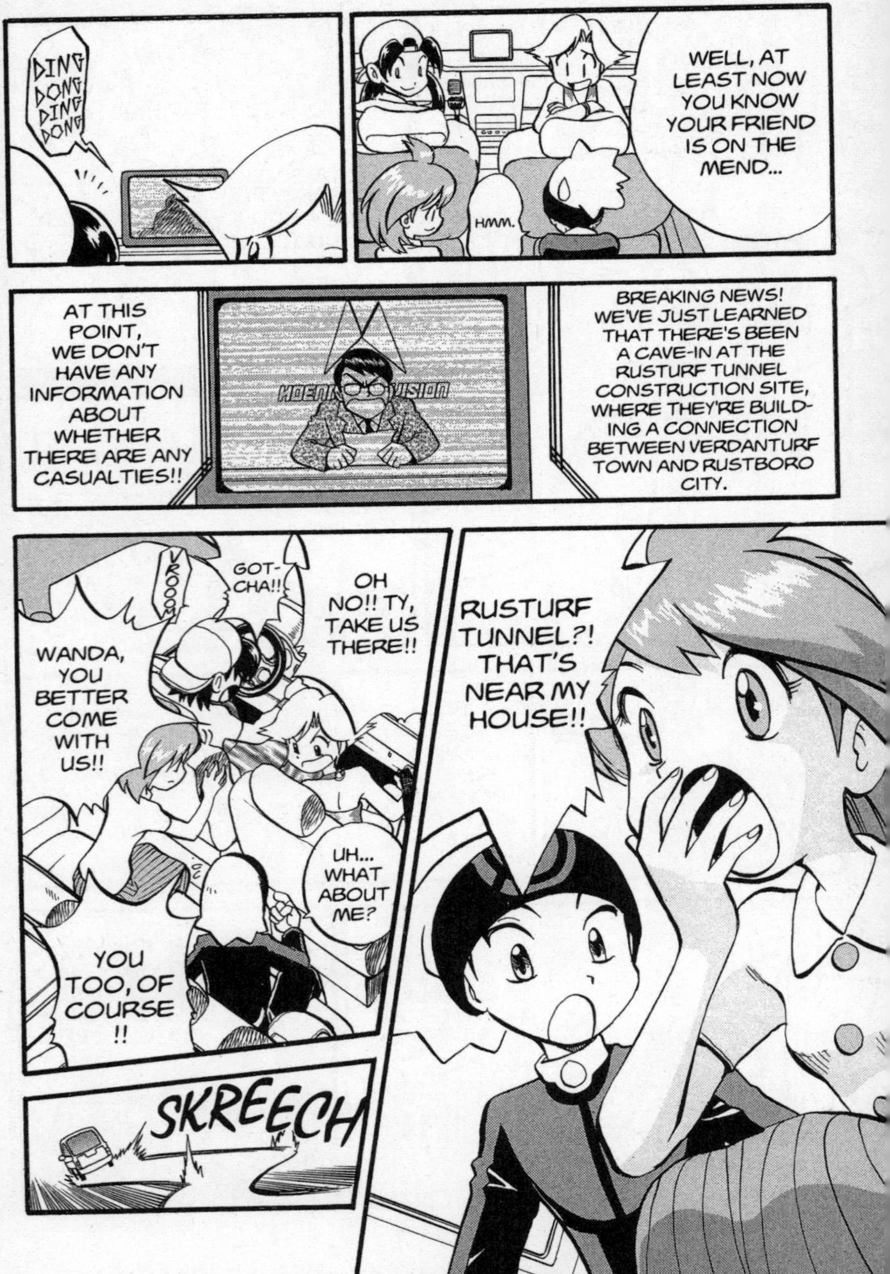
WELL, AT LEAST NOW YOU KNOW YOUR FRIEND IS ON THE MEND...
HMM.
DING DONG DING DONG
BREAKING NEWS! WE'VE JUST LEARNED THAT THERE'S BEEN A CAVE-IN AT THE RUSTURF TUNNEL CONSTRUCTION SITE, WHERE THEY'RE BUILD-ING A CONNECTION BETWEEN VERDANTURF TOWN AND RUSTBORO CITY.
AT THIS POINT, WE DON'T HAVE ANY INFORMATION ABOUT WHETHER THERE ARE ANY CASUALTIES!!
RUSTURF TUNNEL?! THAT'S NEAR MY HOUSE!!
OH NO!! TY, TAKE US THERE!!
GOT-CHA!!
VROOOM
WANDA, YOU BETTER COME WITH US!!
UH... WHAT ABOUT ME?
YOU TOO, OF COURSE!!
SKREECH

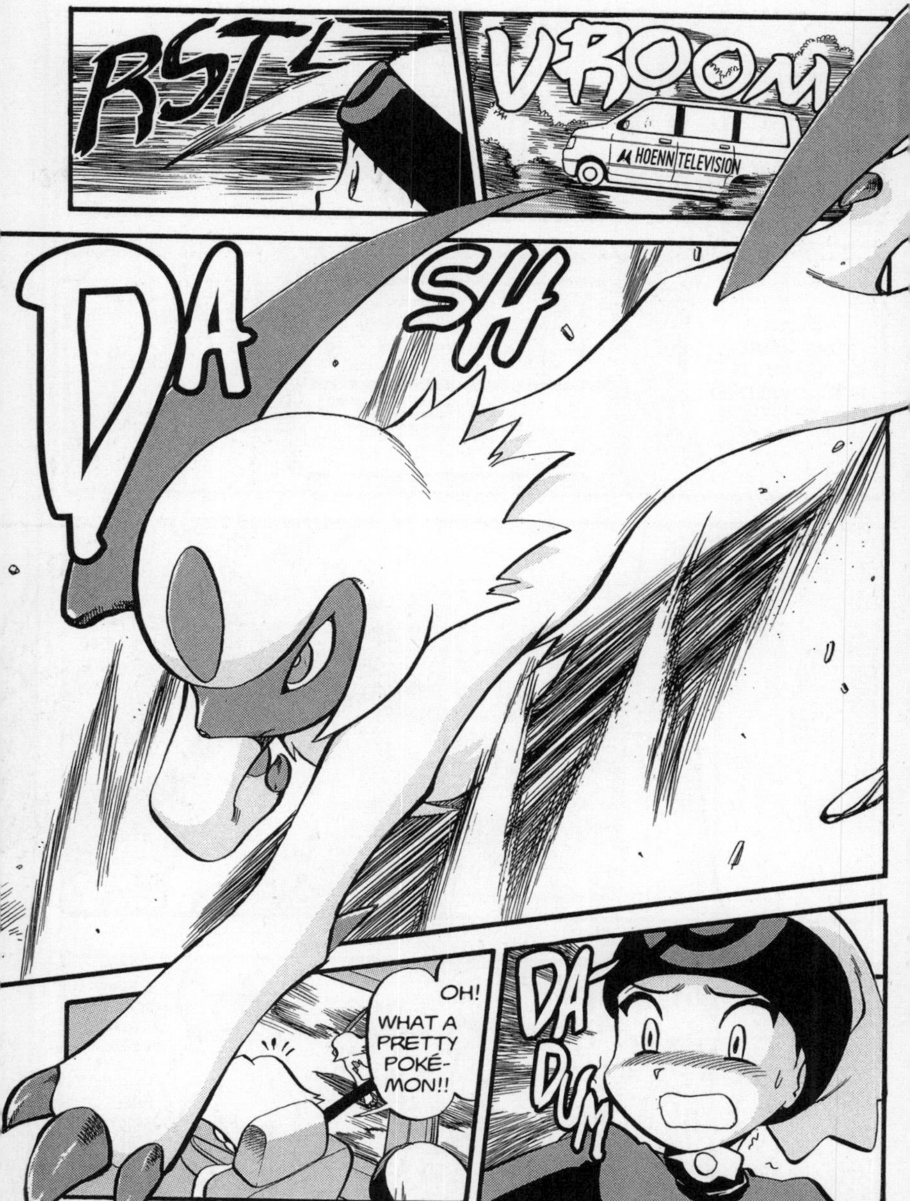
VROOM
HOENN TELEVISION
RSTL
DASH
DA DUM
OH!
WHAT A PRETTY POKÉMON!!

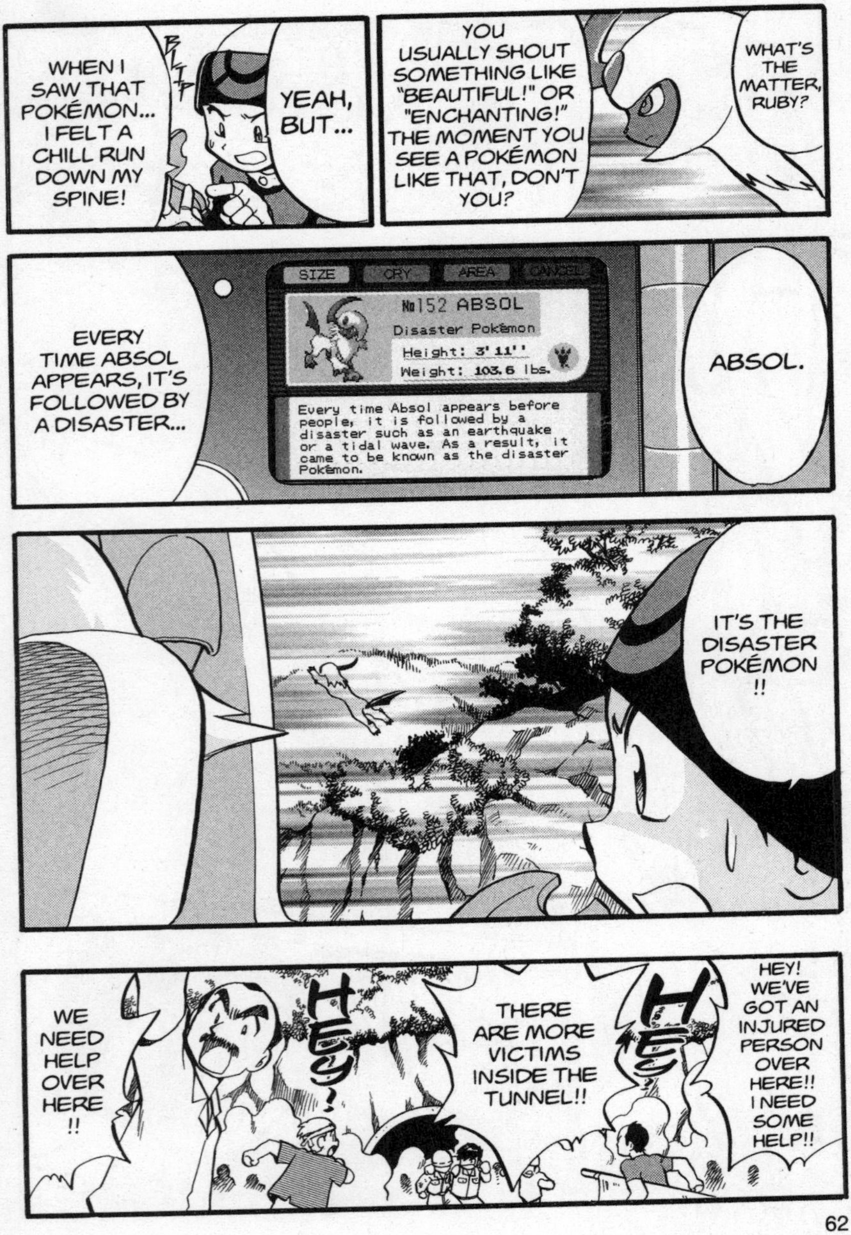
WHAT'S THE MATTER, RUBY?
YOU USUALLY SHOUT SOMETHING LIKE "BEAUTIFUL!" OR "ENCHANTING!" THE MOMENT YOU SEE A POKÉMON LIKE THAT, DON'T YOU?
YEAH, BUT...
BLIP
WHEN I SAW THAT POKÉMON... I FELT A CHILL RUN DOWN MY SPINE!
ABSOL.
SIZE
CRY
AREA
CANCEL
No152 ABSOL
Disaster Pokémon
Height: 3'11''
Weight: 103.6 lbs.
Every time Absol appears before people, it is followed by a disaster such as an earthquake or a tidal wave. As a result, it came to be known as the disaster Pokémon.
EVERY TIME ABSOL APPEARS, IT'S FOLLOWED BY A DISASTER...
IT'S THE DISASTER POKÉMON!!
HEY! WE'VE GOT AN INJURED PERSON OVER HERE!! I NEED SOME HELP!!
HEY
THERE ARE MORE VICTIMS INSIDE THE TUNNEL!!
HEY!
WE NEED HELP OVER HERE!!

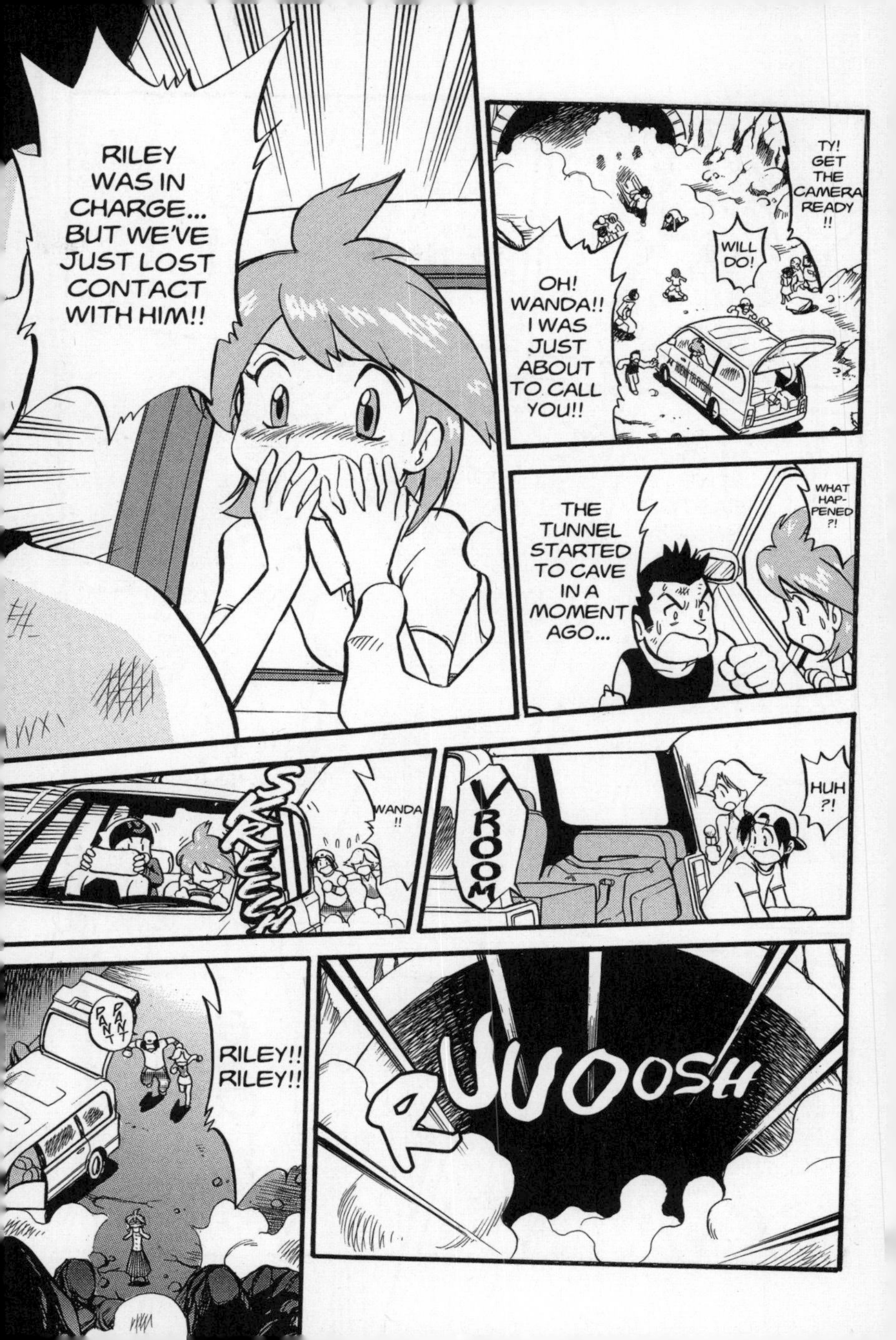
TY! GET THE CAMERA READY!!
WILL DO!
OH! WANDA!! I WAS JUST ABOUT TO CALL YOU!!
WHAT HAP-PENED?!
THE TUNNEL STARTED TO CAVE IN A MOMENT AGO...
RILEY WAS IN CHARGE... BUT WE'VE JUST LOST CONTACT WITH HIM!!
HUH?!
VROOM
WANDA!!
SKREEECH
RUUUOOSH
RILEY!! RILEY!!
PANT PANT

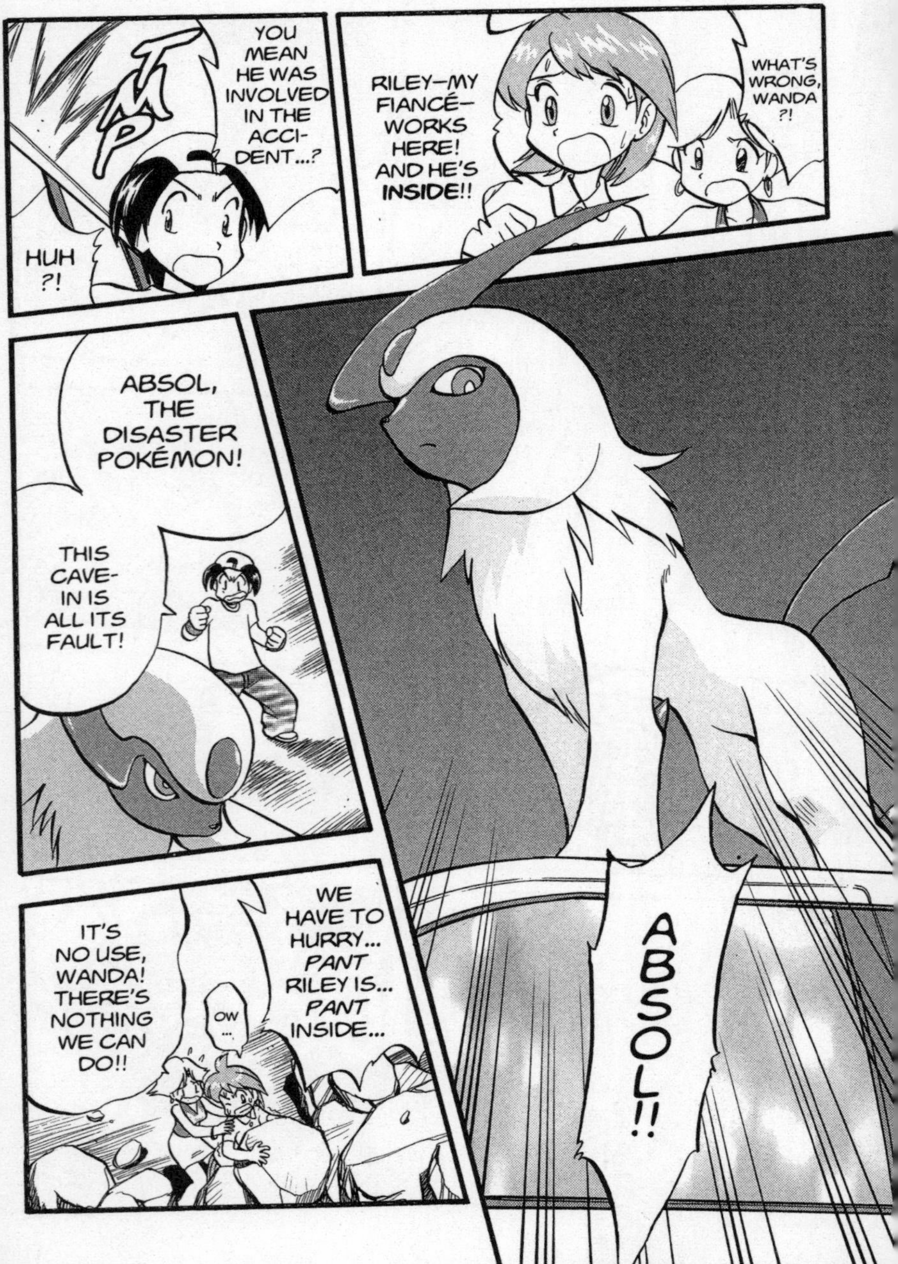
WHAT'S WRONG, WANDA?!
RILEY—MY FIANCÉ—WORKS HERE! AND HE'S INSIDE!!
YOU MEAN HE WAS INVOLVED IN THE ACCIDENT...?
TMP
HUH?!
ABSOL!!
ABSOL, THE DISASTER POKÉMON!
THIS CAVE-IN IS ALL ITS FAULT!
WE HAVE TO HURRY... PANT RILEY IS... PANT INSIDE...
IT'S NO USE, WANDA! THERE'S NOTHING WE CAN DO!!
OW...

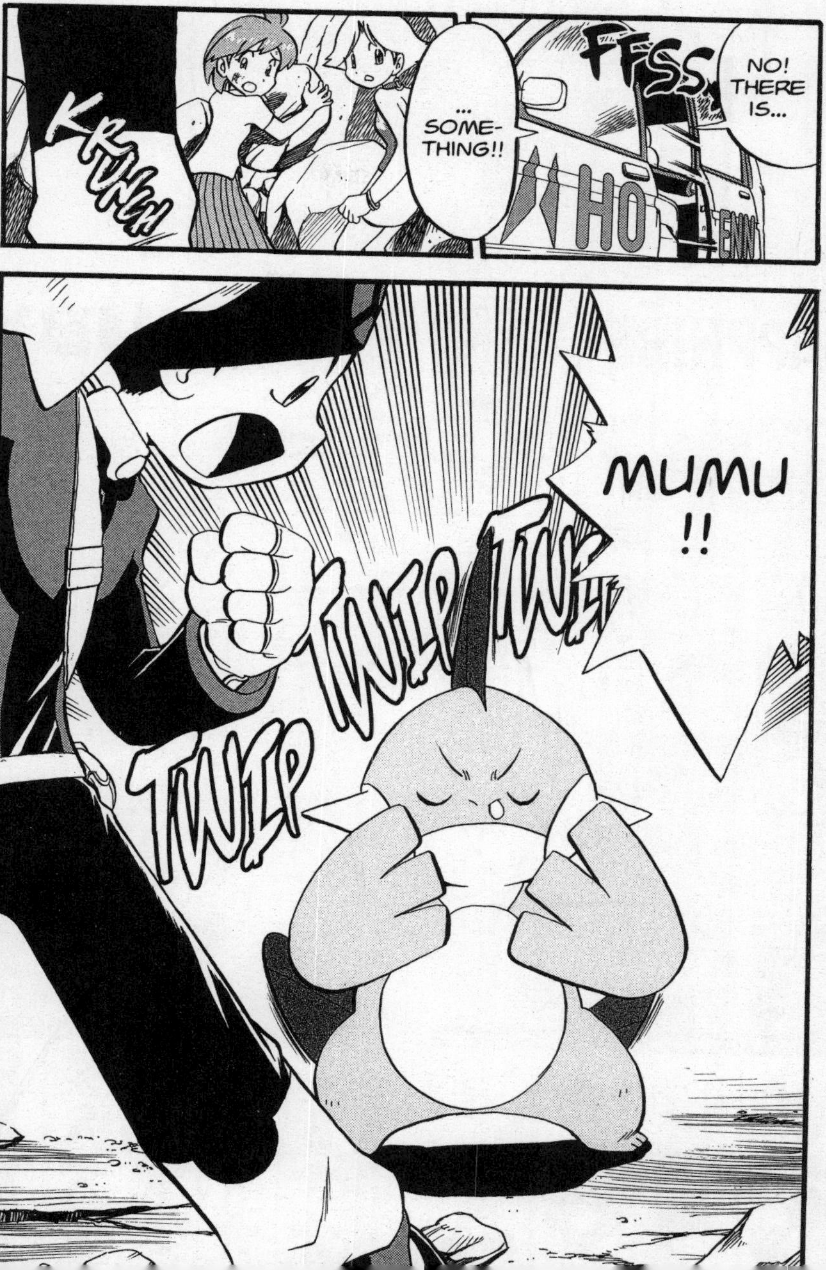
NO! THERE IS...
FFSS
... SOMETHING!!
HO
KRUNCH
MUMU !!
TWIP TWIP TWIP

ADVENTURE MAP

SAPPHIRE

CHIC
Combusken ♀
Lv30

RONO
Lairon ♂
Lv39

LORRY
Wailord ♂
Lv44

PHADO
Donphan ♂
Lv42

TROPPY
Tropius ♂
Lv41

RUBY

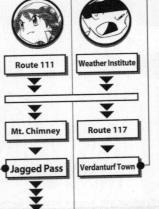

Route 111	Weather Institute
▼	▼
▼	▼
Mt. Chimney	Route 117
▼	▼
Jagged Pass	Verdanturf Town

▼▼▼▼

MUMU
Marshtomp ♂

NANA
Mightyena ♀

KIKI
Delcatty ♀

FEEFEE
Feebas ♀

FOFO
Castform ♀

Stone Badge	Knuckle Badge	Dynamo Badge	Heat Badge
Balance Badge	Feather Badge	Mind Badge	Rain Badge

		Cool	Beauty	Cute	Smart	Tough
Normal	Super					
Super	Hyper					
Hyper	Master					

● Chapter 219 ●

What Would You Do for a Whismur?

Pokémon Adventures Ruby & Sapphire

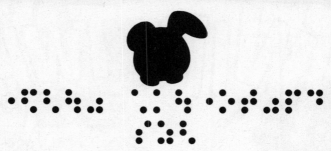

The Fourth Chapter

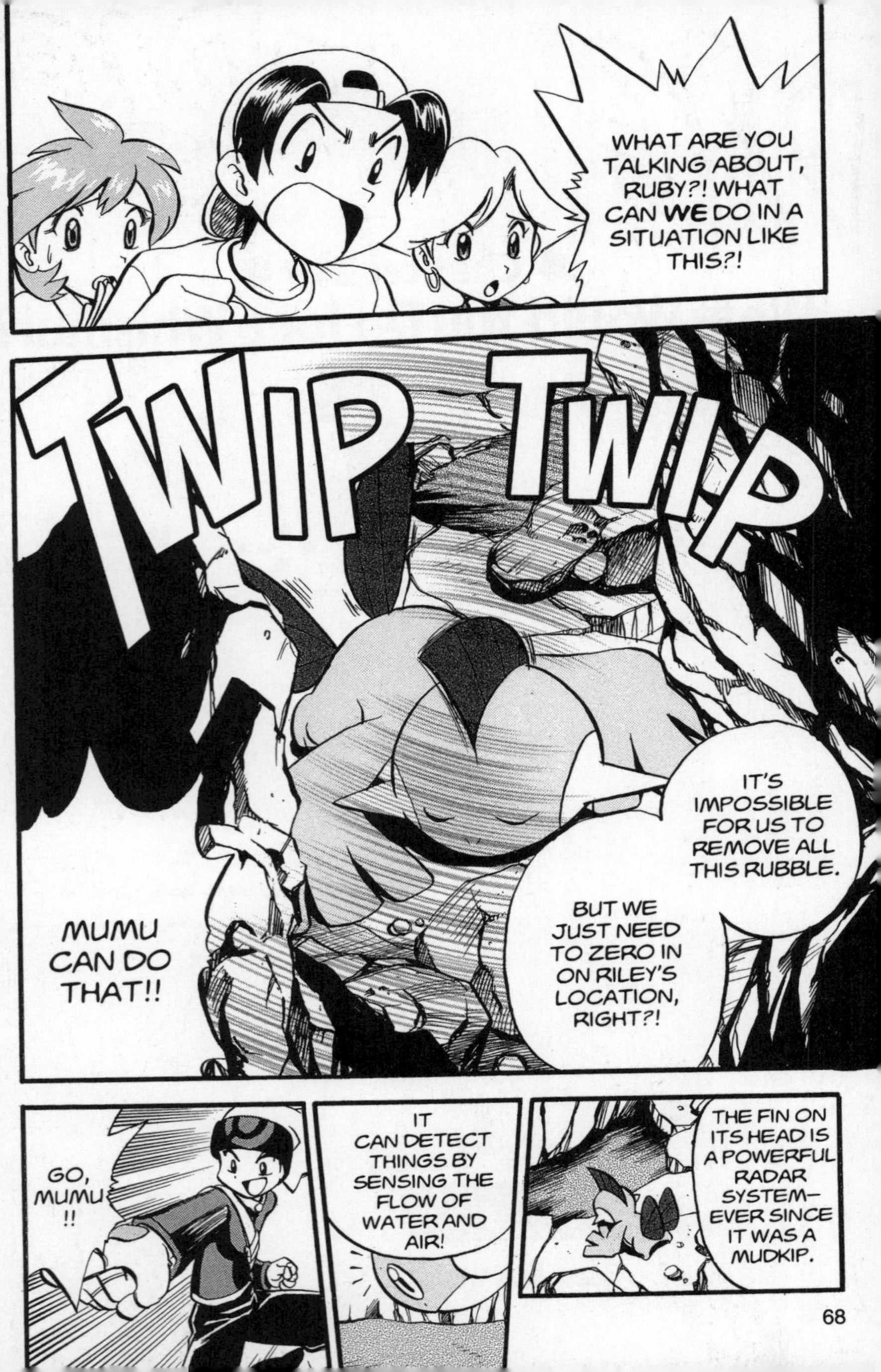
WHAT ARE YOU TALKING ABOUT, RUBY?! WHAT CAN **WE** DO IN A SITUATION LIKE THIS?!
TWIP TWIP
IT'S IMPOSSIBLE FOR US TO REMOVE ALL THIS RUBBLE.
BUT WE JUST NEED TO ZERO IN ON RILEY'S LOCATION, RIGHT?!
MUMU CAN DO THAT!!
THE FIN ON ITS HEAD IS A POWERFUL RADAR SYSTEM— EVER SINCE IT WAS A MUDKIP.
IT CAN DETECT THINGS BY SENSING THE FLOW OF WATER AND AIR!
GO, MUMU!!

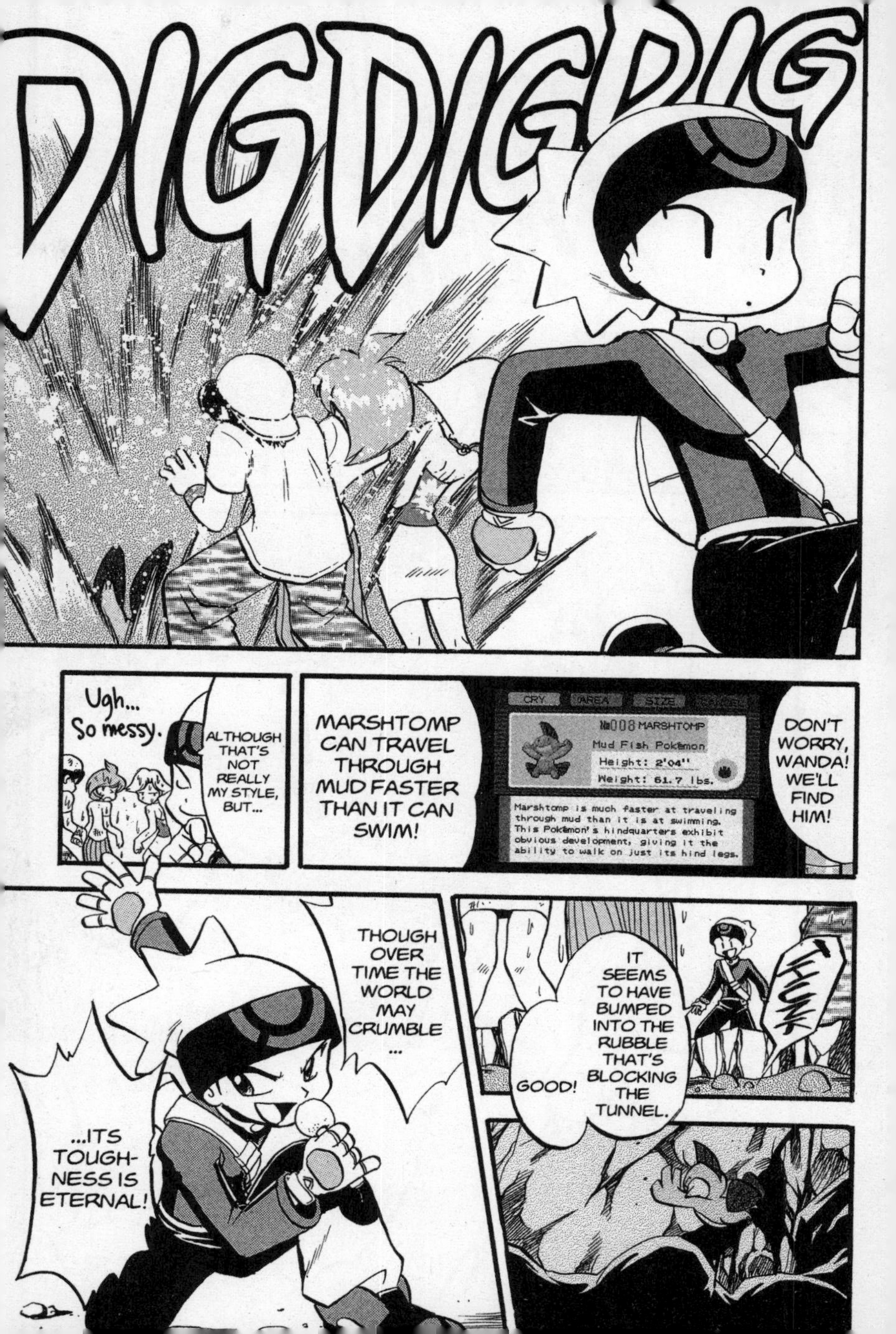
DIGDIGDIG
DON'T WORRY, WANDA! WE'LL FIND HIM!
MARSHTOMP CAN TRAVEL THROUGH MUD FASTER THAN IT CAN SWIM!
CRY AREA SIZE
No008 MARSHTOMP
Mud Fish Pokémon
Height: 2'04''
Weight: 61.7 lbs.
Marshtomp is much faster at traveling through mud than it is at swimming. This Pokémon's hindquarters exhibit obvious development, giving it the ability to walk on just its hind legs.
ALTHOUGH THAT'S NOT REALLY MY STYLE, BUT...
Ugh... So messy.
THUNK
IT SEEMS TO HAVE BUMPED INTO THE RUBBLE THAT'S BLOCKING THE TUNNEL.
GOOD!
THOUGH OVER TIME THE WORLD MAY CRUMBLE ...
...ITS TOUGHNESS IS ETERNAL!

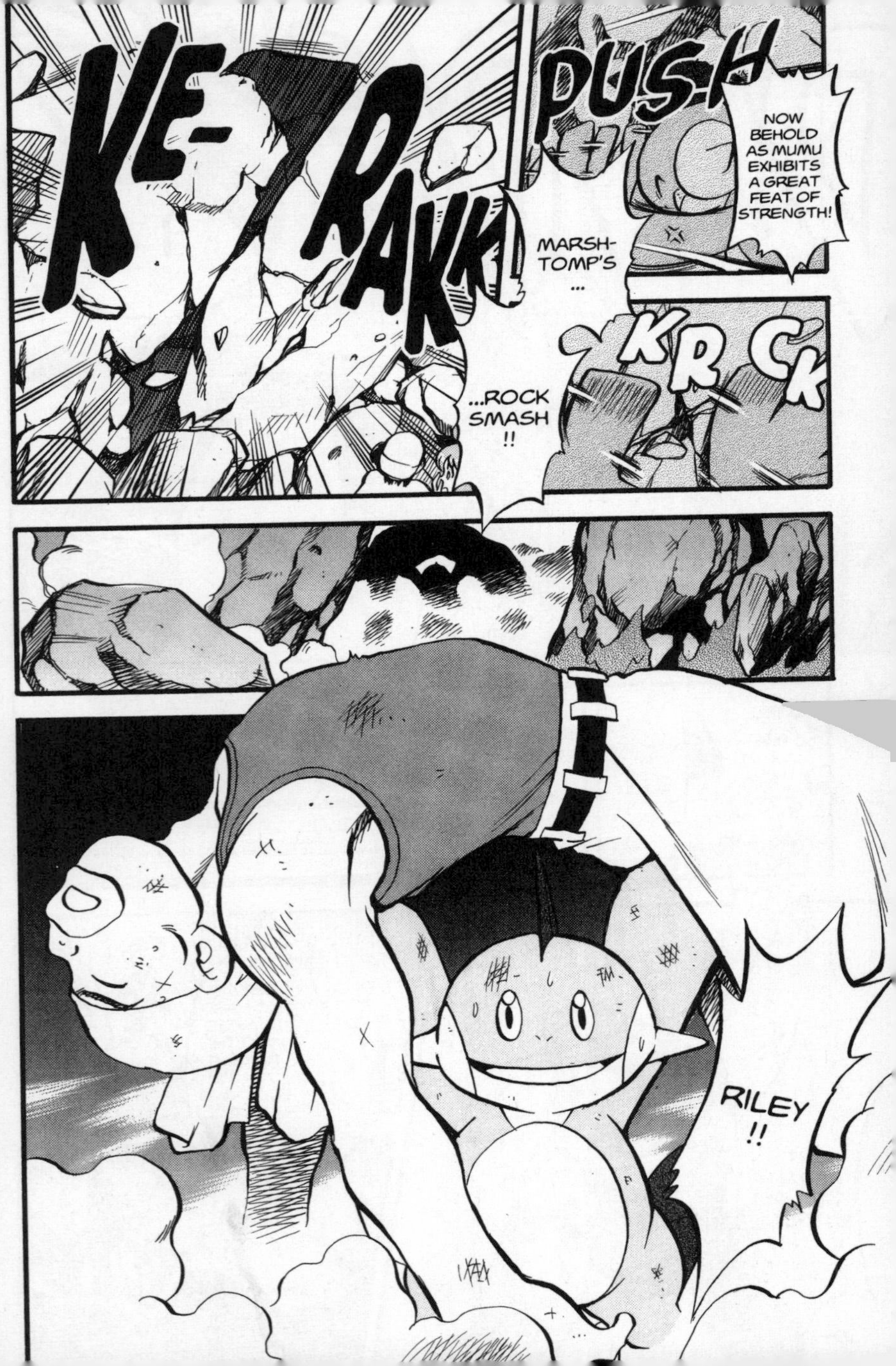
PUSH
NOW BEHOLD AS MUMU EXHIBITS A GREAT FEAT OF STRENGTH!
MARSH-TOMP'S ...
KRCK
...ROCK SMASH !!
KE-RAKK
RILEY !!

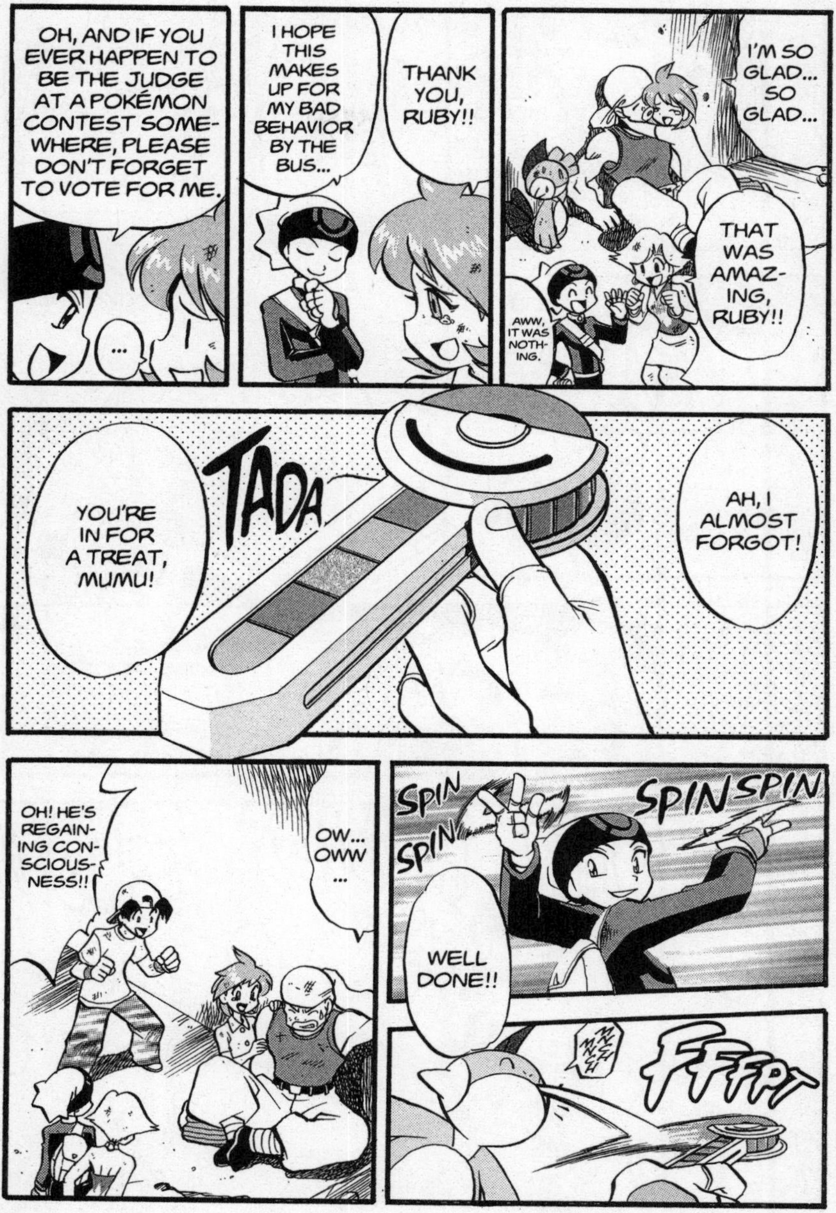
I'M SO GLAD... SO GLAD...
THAT WAS AMAZ-ING, RUBY!!
AWW, IT WAS NOTH-ING.
THANK YOU, RUBY!!
I HOPE THIS MAKES UP FOR MY BAD BEHAVIOR BY THE BUS...
OH, AND IF YOU EVER HAPPEN TO BE THE JUDGE AT A POKÉMON CONTEST SOME-WHERE, PLEASE DON'T FORGET TO VOTE FOR ME.
...
AH, I ALMOST FORGOT!
TADA
YOU'RE IN FOR A TREAT, MUMU!
SPIN SPIN
SPIN SPIN
WELL DONE!!
FFFPT
OW... OWW ...
OH! HE'S REGAIN-ING CON-SCIOUS-NESS!!

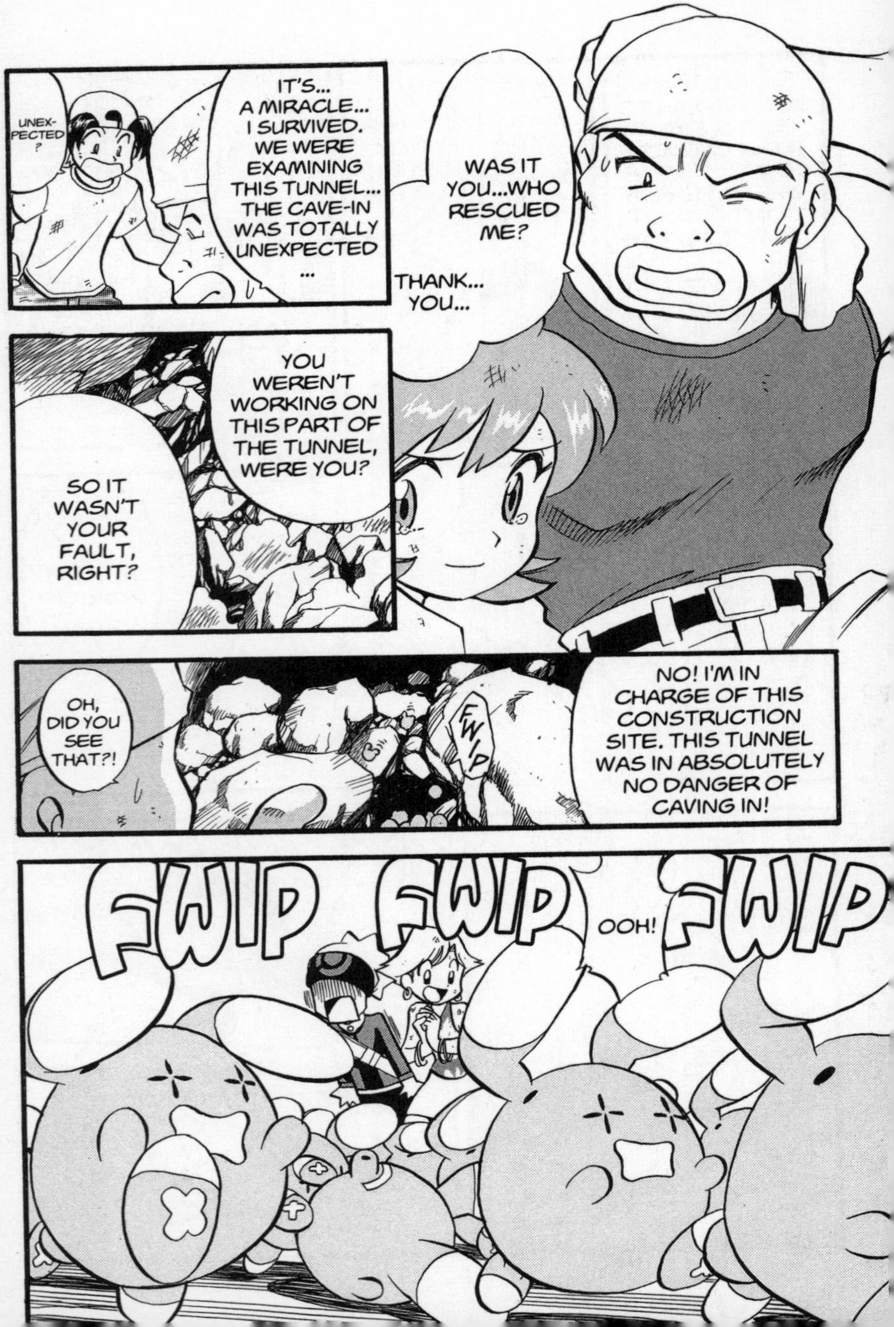
WAS IT YOU...WHO RESCUED ME?
THANK... YOU...
IT'S... A MIRACLE... I SURVIVED. WE WERE EXAMINING THIS TUNNEL... THE CAVE-IN WAS TOTALLY UNEXPECTED ...
UNEX-PECTED ?
YOU WEREN'T WORKING ON THIS PART OF THE TUNNEL, WERE YOU?
SO IT WASN'T YOUR FAULT, RIGHT?
NO! I'M IN CHARGE OF THIS CONSTRUCTION SITE. THIS TUNNEL WAS IN ABSOLUTELY NO DANGER OF CAVING IN!
FWIP
OH, DID YOU SEE THAT?!
FWIP
OOH!
FWIP
FWIP

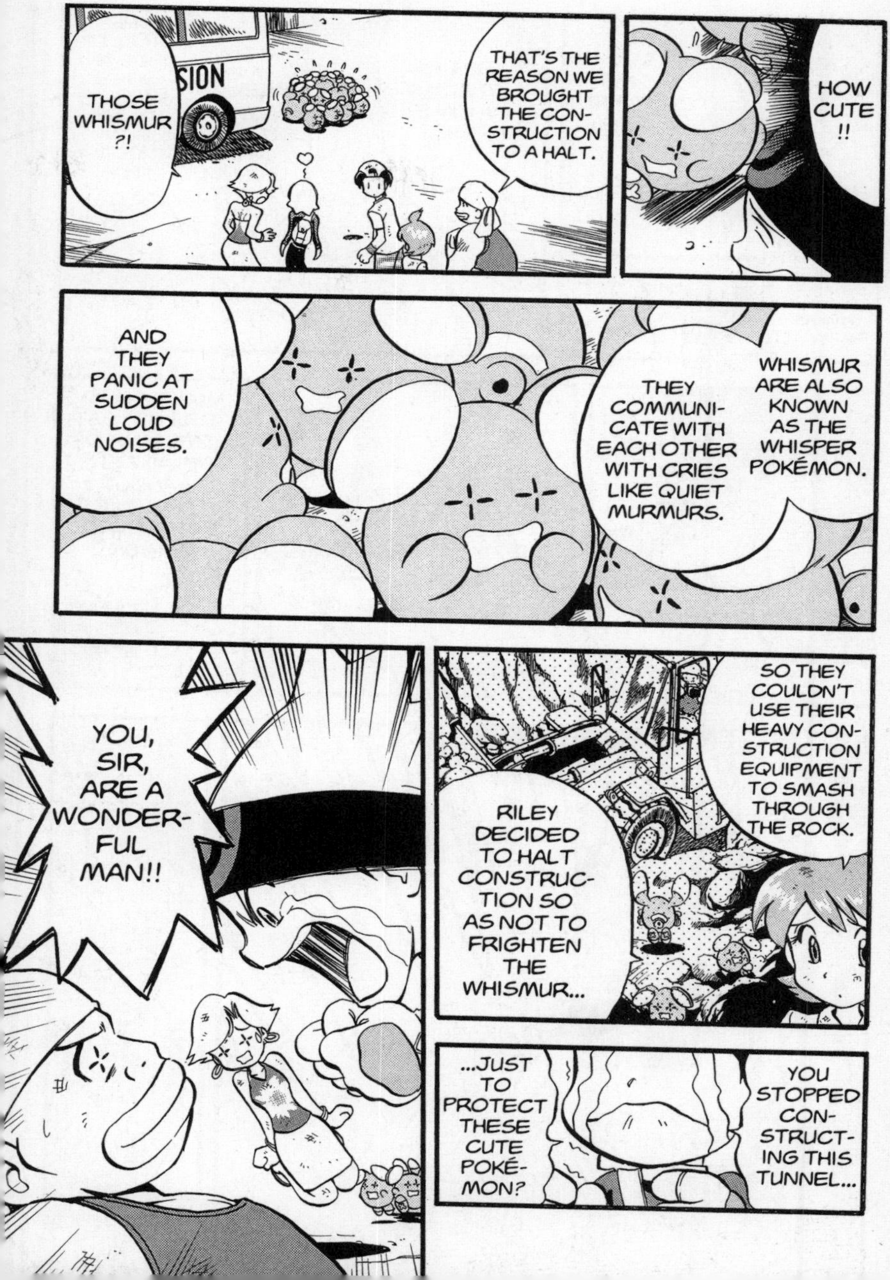
HOW CUTE !!
THAT'S THE REASON WE BROUGHT THE CON-STRUCTION TO A HALT.
THOSE WHISMUR ?!
WHISMUR ARE ALSO KNOWN AS THE WHISPER POKÉMON.
THEY COMMUNI-CATE WITH EACH OTHER WITH CRIES LIKE QUIET MURMURS.
AND THEY PANIC AT SUDDEN LOUD NOISES.
SO THEY COULDN'T USE THEIR HEAVY CON-STRUCTION EQUIPMENT TO SMASH THROUGH THE ROCK.
RILEY DECIDED TO HALT CONSTRUC-TION SO AS NOT TO FRIGHTEN THE WHISMUR...
YOU STOPPED CON-STRUCT-ING THIS TUNNEL...
...JUST TO PROTECT THESE CUTE POKÉ-MON?
YOU, SIR, ARE A WONDER-FUL MAN!!

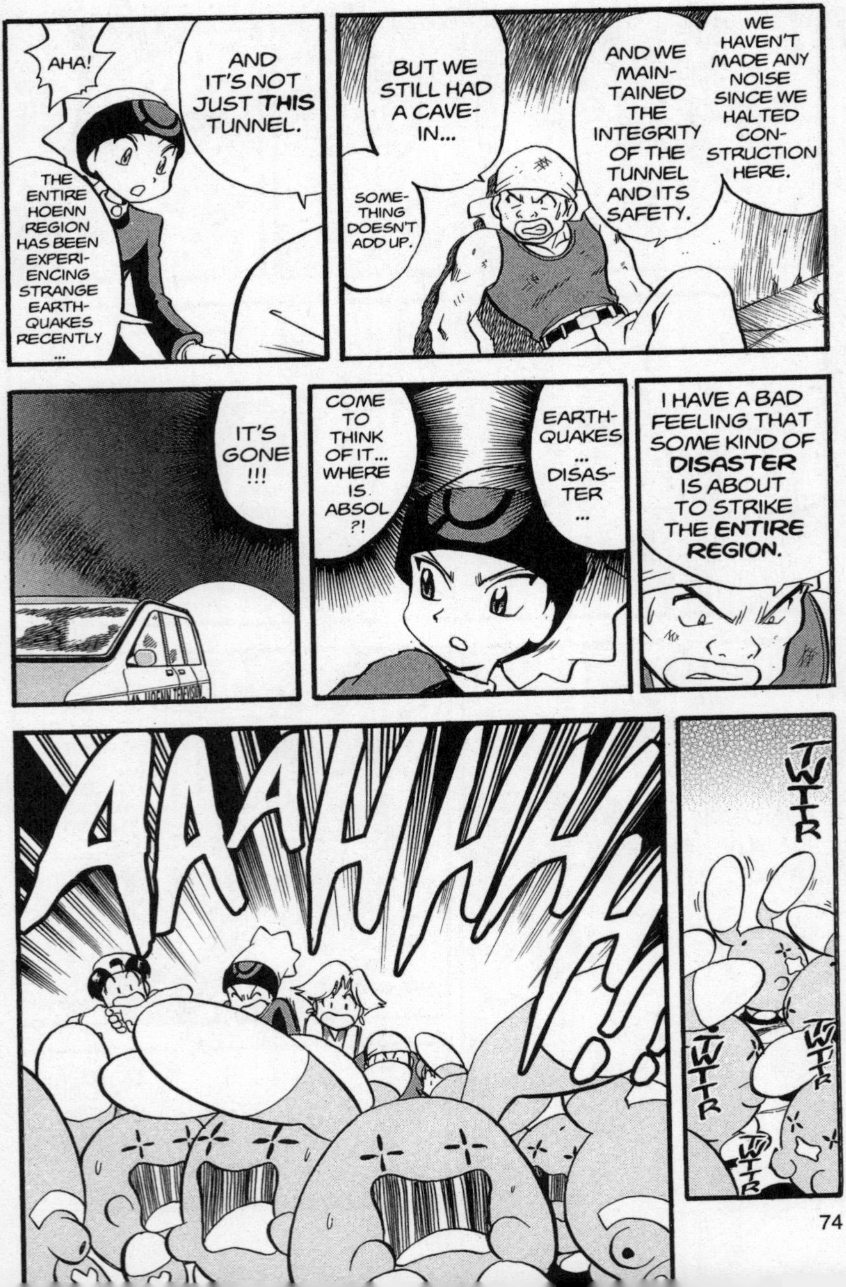
WE HAVEN'T MADE ANY NOISE SINCE WE HALTED CONSTRUCTION HERE.
AND WE MAINTAINED THE INTEGRITY OF THE TUNNEL AND ITS SAFETY.
BUT WE STILL HAD A CAVE-IN...
SOMETHING DOESN'T ADD UP.
AHA!
AND IT'S NOT JUST THIS TUNNEL.
THE ENTIRE HOENN REGION HAS BEEN EXPERIENCING STRANGE EARTHQUAKES RECENTLY...
I HAVE A BAD FEELING THAT SOME KIND OF DISASTER IS ABOUT TO STRIKE THE ENTIRE REGION.
EARTHQUAKES... DISASTER...
COME TO THINK OF IT... WHERE IS ABSOL?!
IT'S GONE!!!
TWTTR
TWTTR
TWTTR
TWTTR
AAHHHH

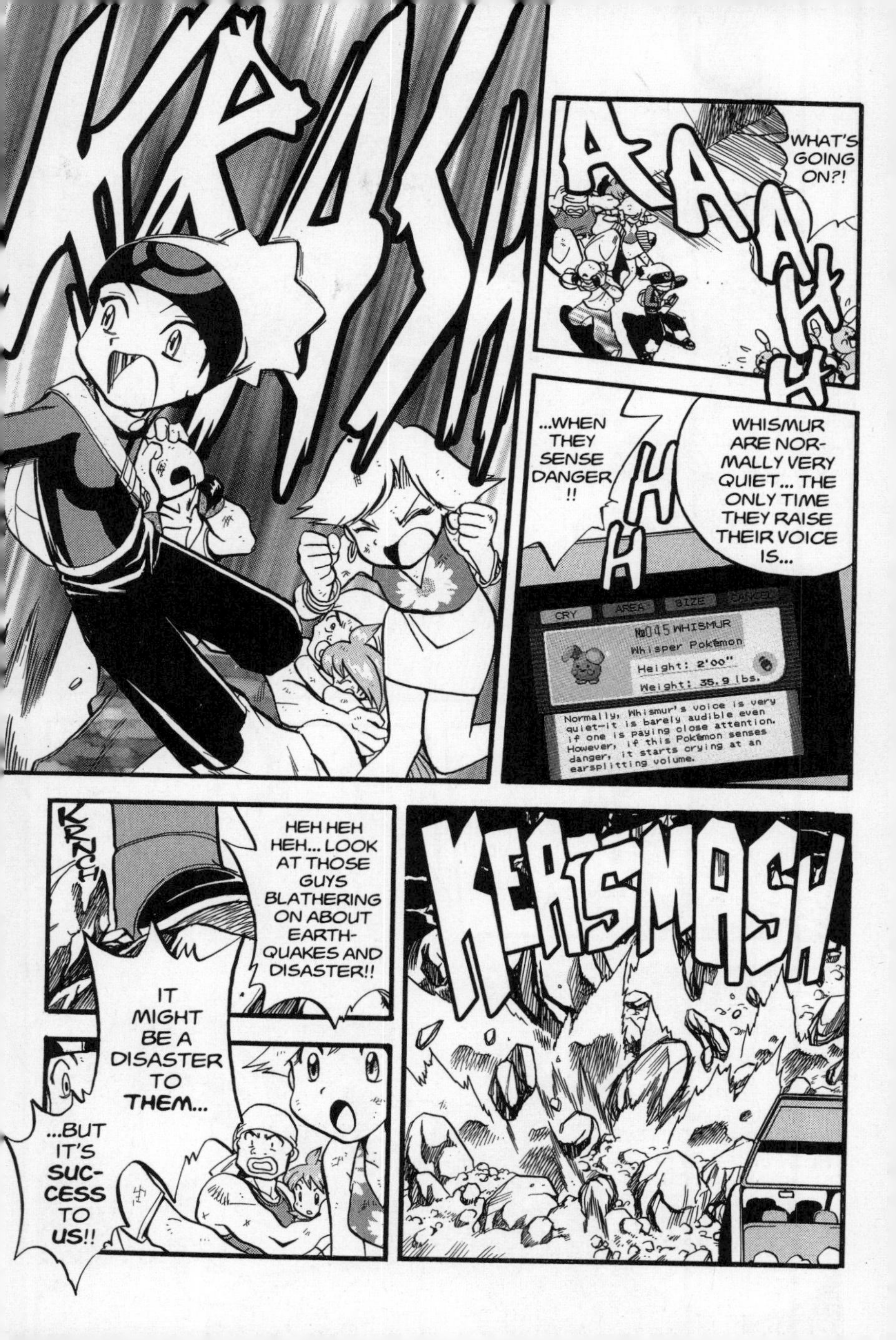
WHAT'S GOING ON?!
WHISMUR ARE NORMALLY VERY QUIET... THE ONLY TIME THEY RAISE THEIR VOICE IS...
...WHEN THEY SENSE DANGER!!
CRY AREA SIZE CANCEL
№045 WHISMUR
Whisper Pokémon
Height: 2'00"
Weight: 35.9 lbs.
Normally, Whismur's voice is very quiet—it is barely audible even if one is paying close attention. However, if this Pokémon senses danger, it starts crying at an earsplitting volume.
KERSMASH
KRNCH
HEH HEH HEH... LOOK AT THOSE GUYS BLATHERING ON ABOUT EARTHQUAKES AND DISASTER!!
IT MIGHT BE A DISASTER TO THEM...
...BUT IT'S SUCCESS TO US!!

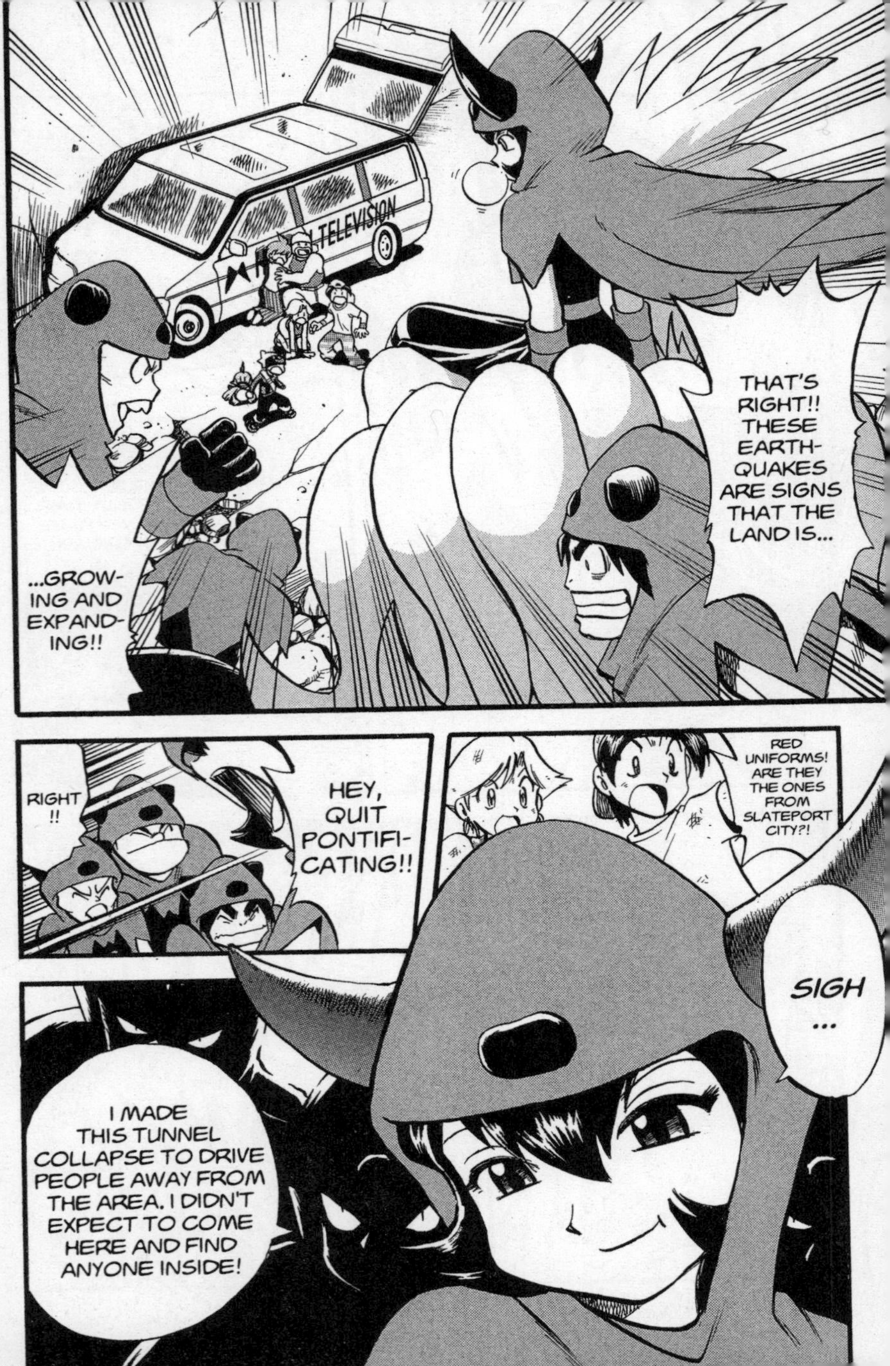
THAT'S RIGHT!! THESE EARTH-QUAKES ARE SIGNS THAT THE LAND IS...
...GROW-ING AND EXPAND-ING!!
RED UNIFORMS! ARE THEY THE ONES FROM SLATEPORT CITY?!
HEY, QUIT PONTIFI-CATING!!
RIGHT !!
SIGH ...
I MADE THIS TUNNEL COLLAPSE TO DRIVE PEOPLE AWAY FROM THE AREA. I DIDN'T EXPECT TO COME HERE AND FIND ANYONE INSIDE!

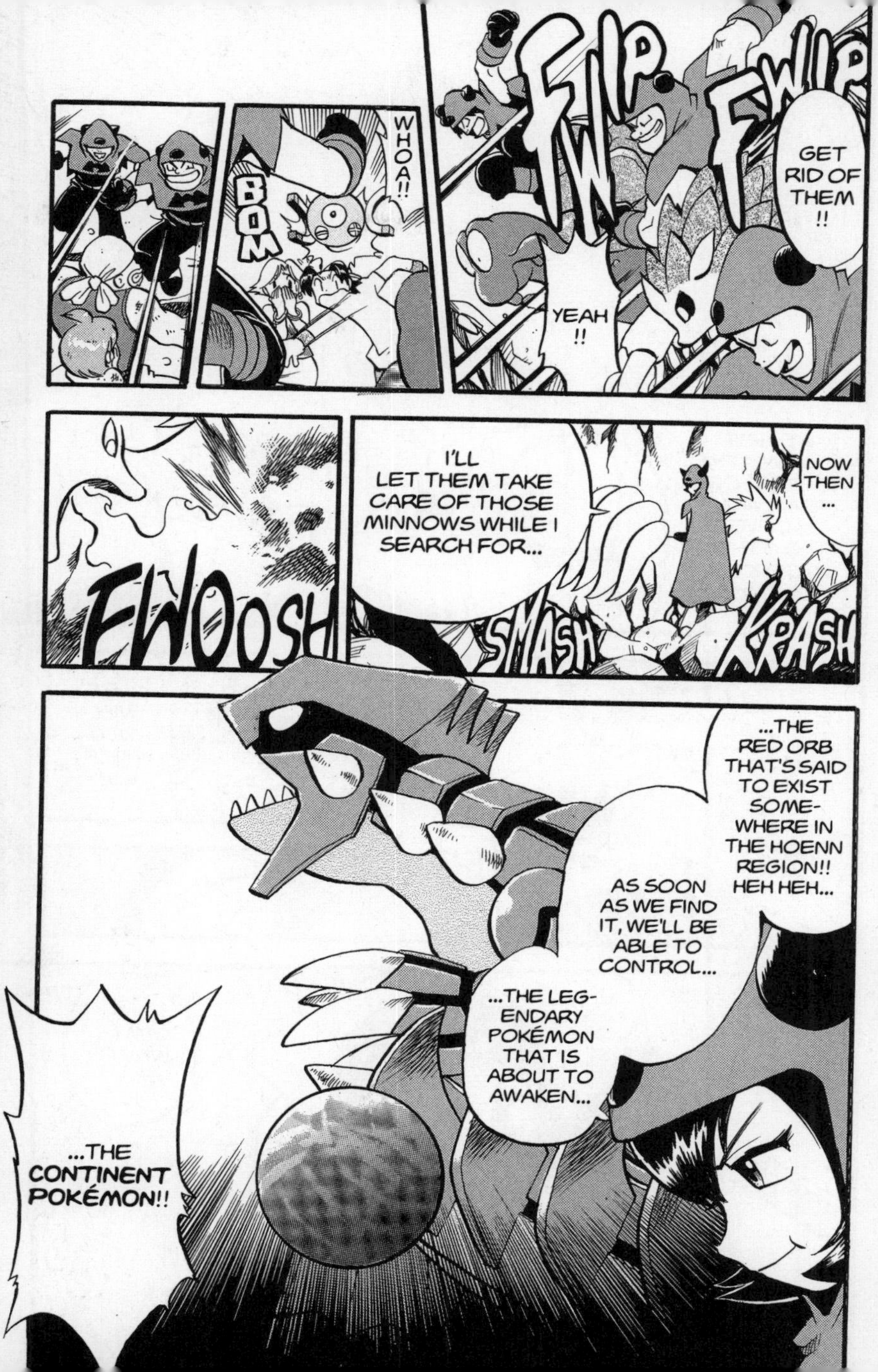
FWIP
FWIP
GET RID OF THEM!!
YEAH!!
WHOA!!
BOM
NOW THEN...
I'LL LET THEM TAKE CARE OF THOSE MINNOWS WHILE I SEARCH FOR...
SMASH
KRASH
FWOOSH
...THE RED ORB THAT'S SAID TO EXIST SOME-WHERE IN THE HOENN REGION!! HEH HEH...
AS SOON AS WE FIND IT, WE'LL BE ABLE TO CONTROL...
...THE LEG-ENDARY POKÉMON THAT IS ABOUT TO AWAKEN...
...THE CONTINENT POKÉMON!!

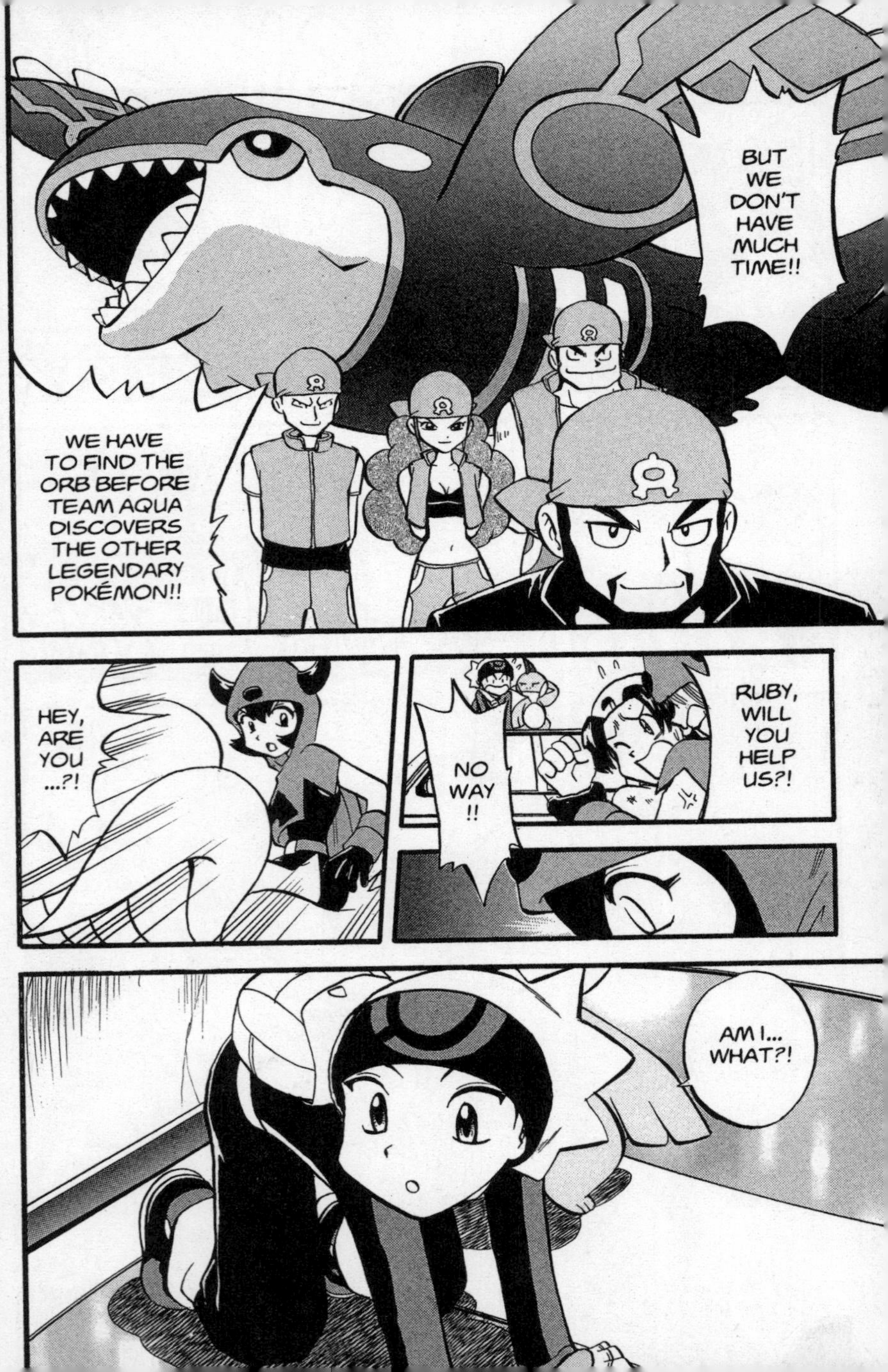
BUT WE DON'T HAVE MUCH TIME!!
WE HAVE TO FIND THE ORB BEFORE TEAM AQUA DISCOVERS THE OTHER LEGENDARY POKÉMON!!
RUBY, WILL YOU HELP US?!
NO WAY !!
HEY, ARE YOU ...?!
AM I... WHAT?!

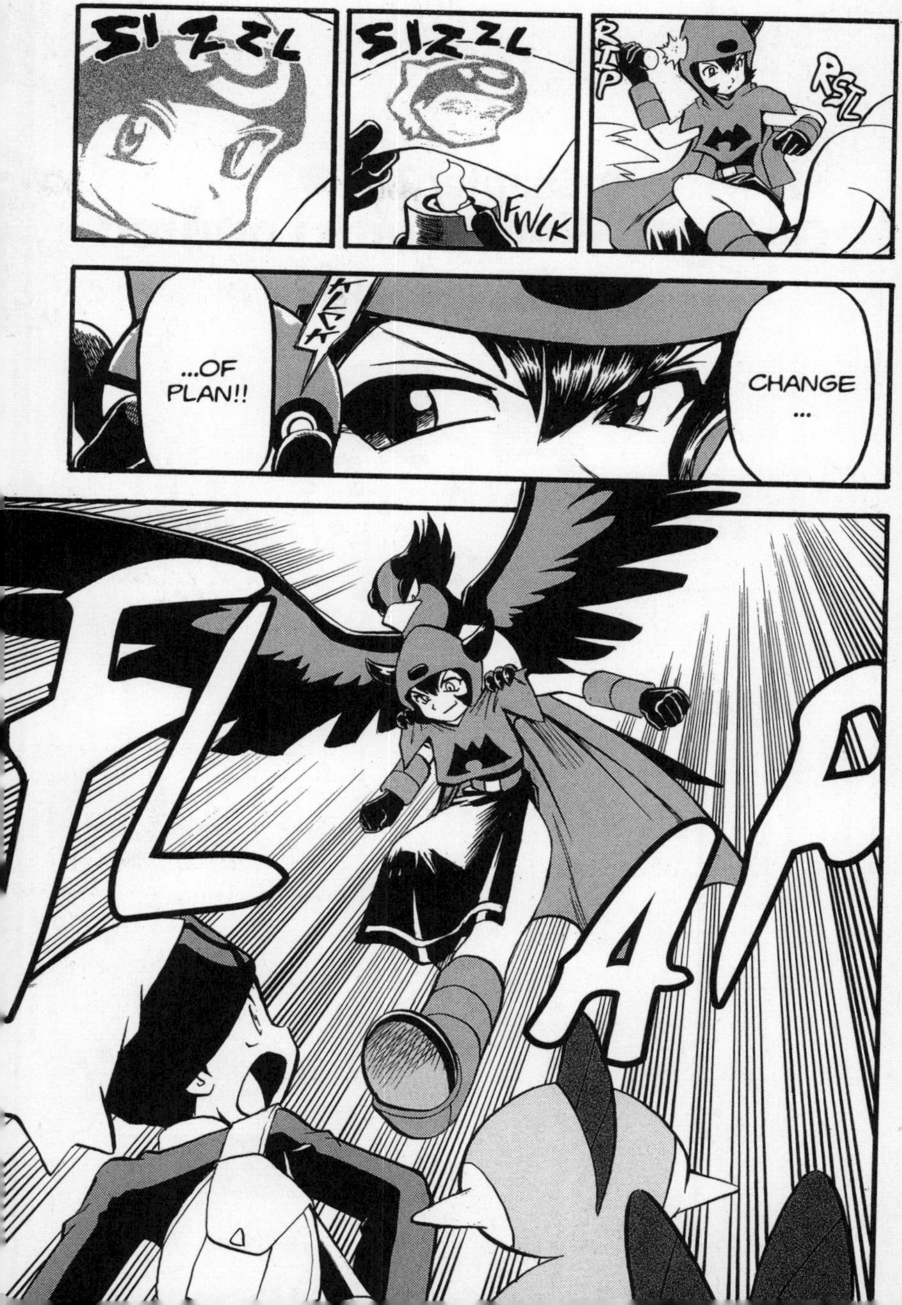
RIP
RSL
SIZZL
FWCK
SIZZL
CHANGE ...
KLICK
...OF PLAN!!
FLAP

● Chapter 220 ●
Going to Eleven with Loudred and Exploud I

The Fourth Chapter

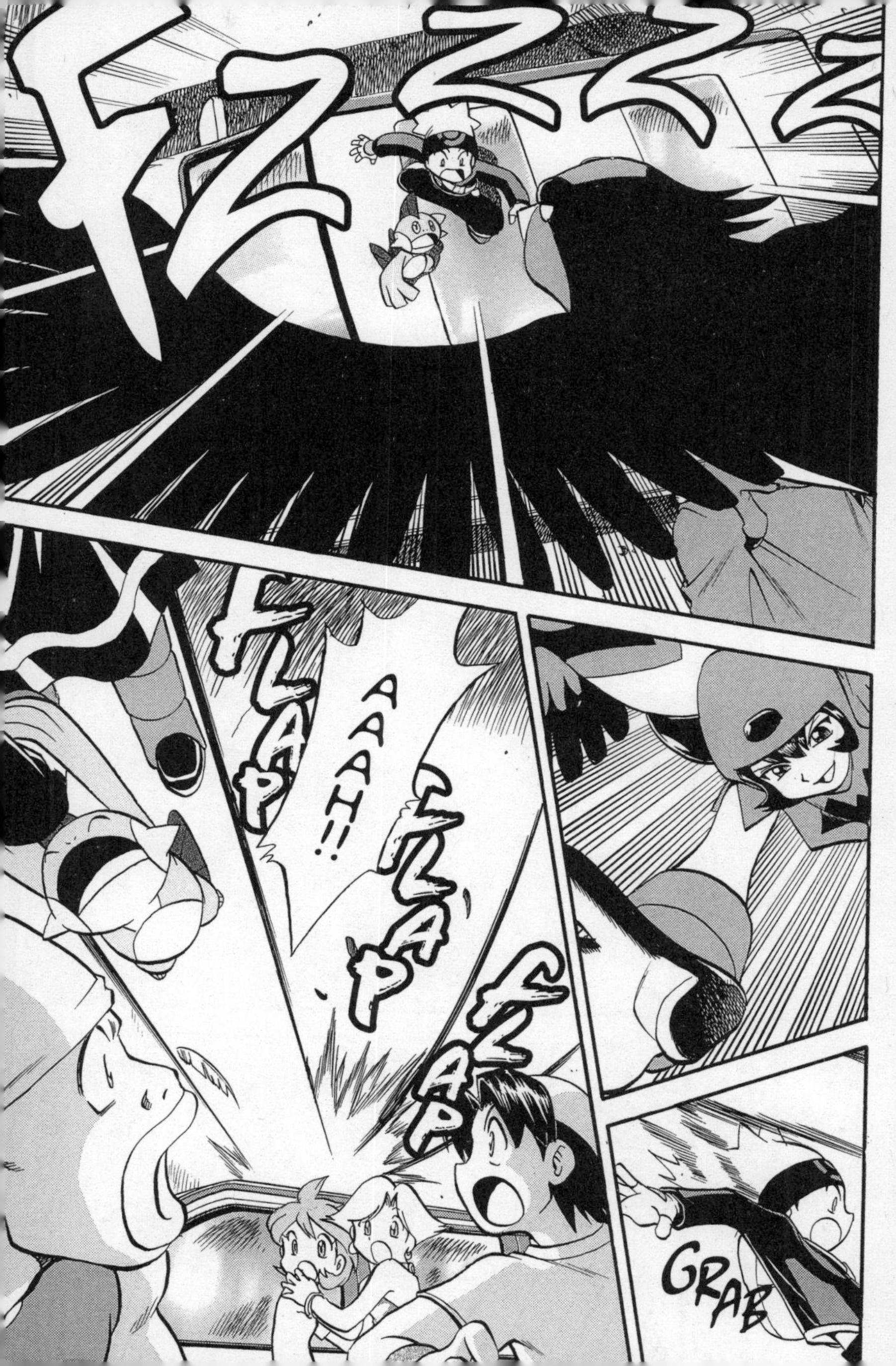
FZZZZ
FLAP
FLAP
AAAAH!!
FLAP
GRAB

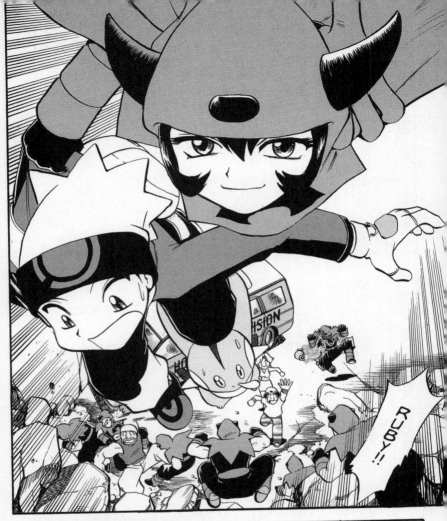

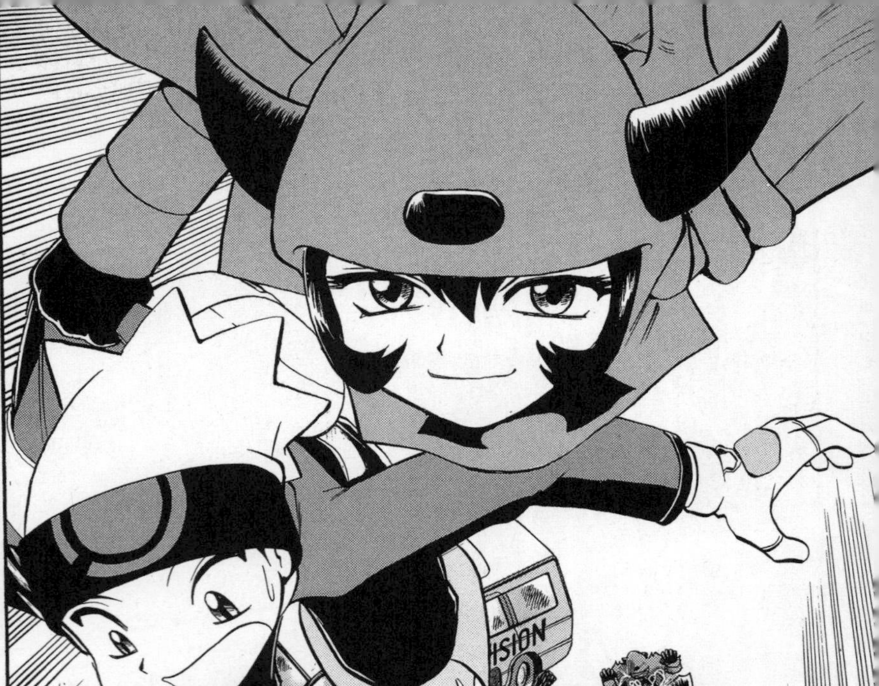
RUBY!!

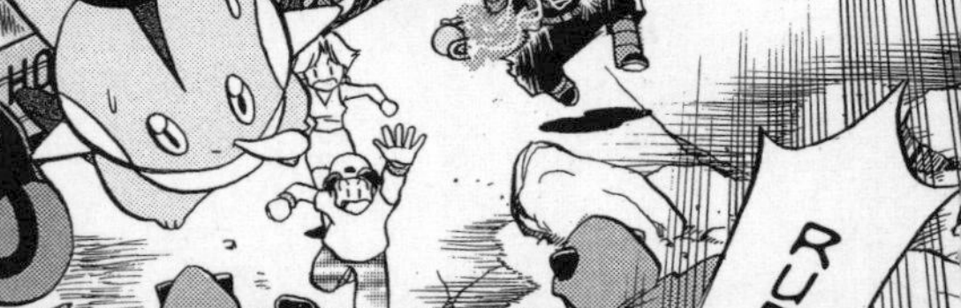
HEY! YOU HAVE TO DEAL WITH US FIRST!!
GRRR ...

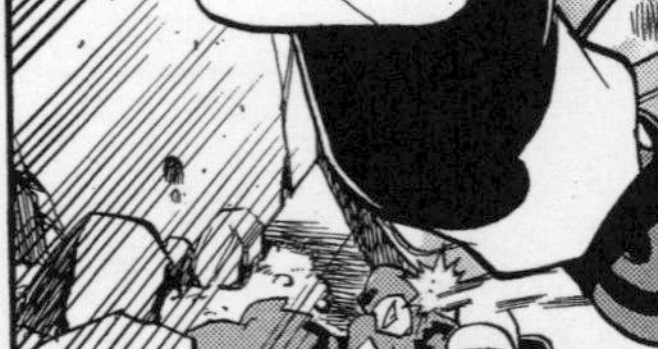
FOOOSH

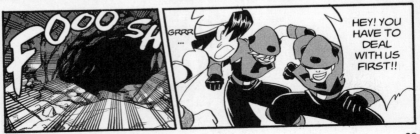

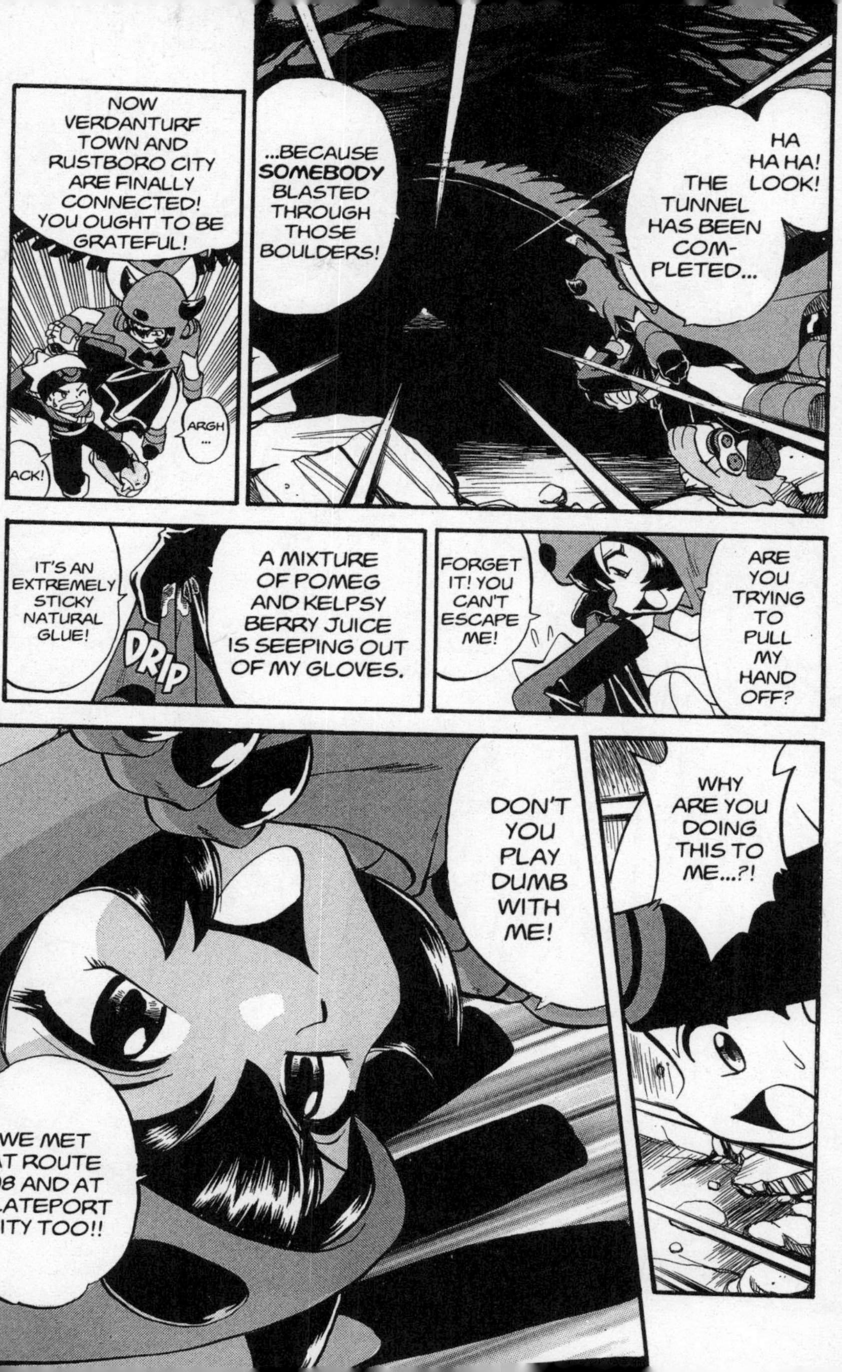
HA HA HA! LOOK! THE TUNNEL HAS BEEN COM-PLETED...
...BECAUSE SOMEBODY BLASTED THROUGH THOSE BOULDERS!
NOW VERDANTURF TOWN AND RUSTBORO CITY ARE FINALLY CONNECTED! YOU OUGHT TO BE GRATEFUL!
ARGH...
ACK!
ARE YOU TRYING TO PULL MY HAND OFF?
FORGET IT! YOU CAN'T ESCAPE ME!
A MIXTURE OF POMEG AND KELPSY BERRY JUICE IS SEEPING OUT OF MY GLOVES.
IT'S AN EXTREMELY STICKY NATURAL GLUE!
DRIP
WHY ARE YOU DOING THIS TO ME...?!
DON'T YOU PLAY DUMB WITH ME!
WE MET AT ROUTE 108 AND AT SLATEPORT CITY TOO!!

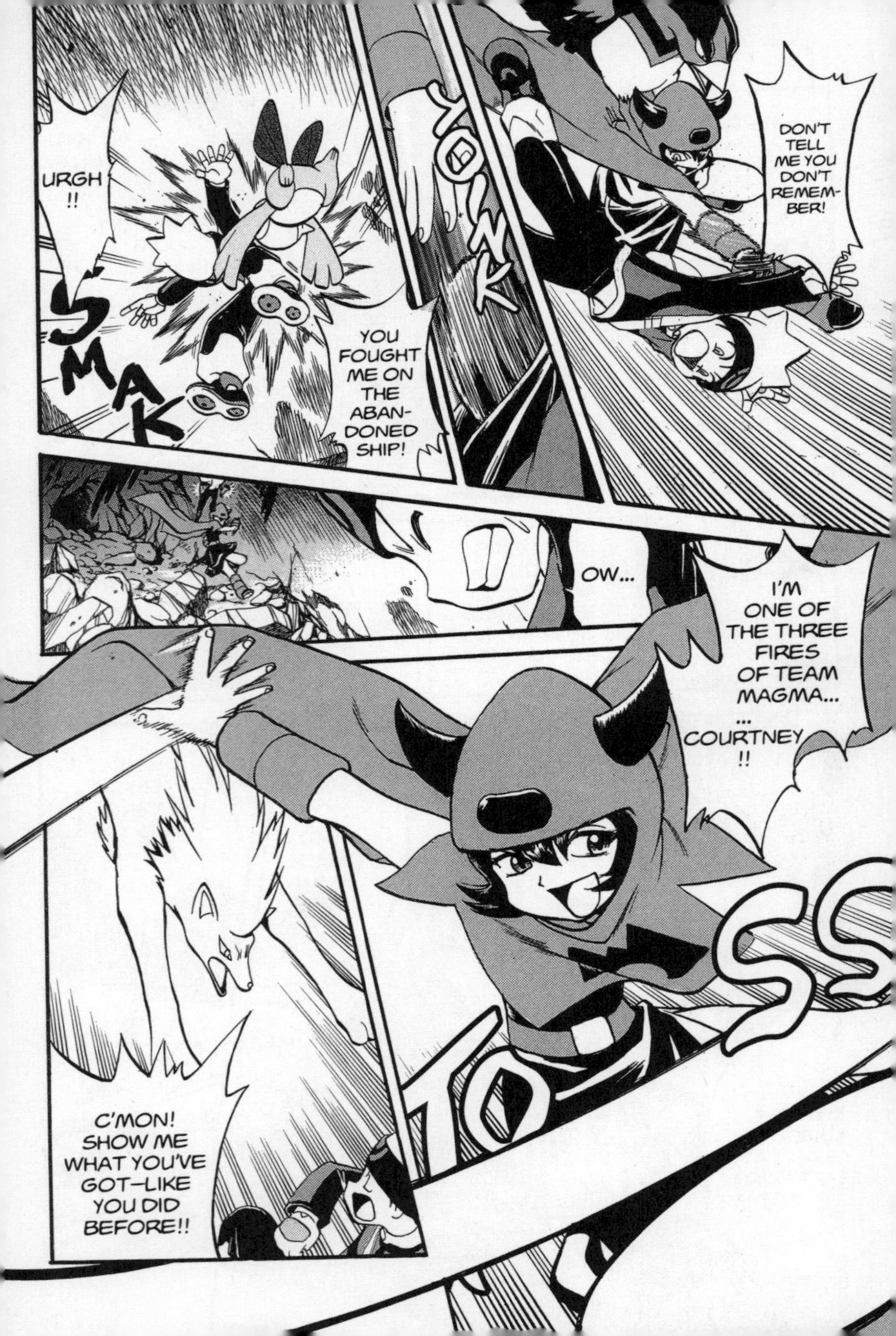
DON'T TELL ME YOU DON'T REMEM-BER!
YOINK
YOU FOUGHT ME ON THE ABAN-DONED SHIP!
URGH!!
SMAK
OW...
I'M ONE OF THE THREE FIRES OF TEAM MAGMA... ...COURTNEY!!
SS
TO
C'MON! SHOW ME WHAT YOU'VE GOT—LIKE YOU DID BEFORE!!

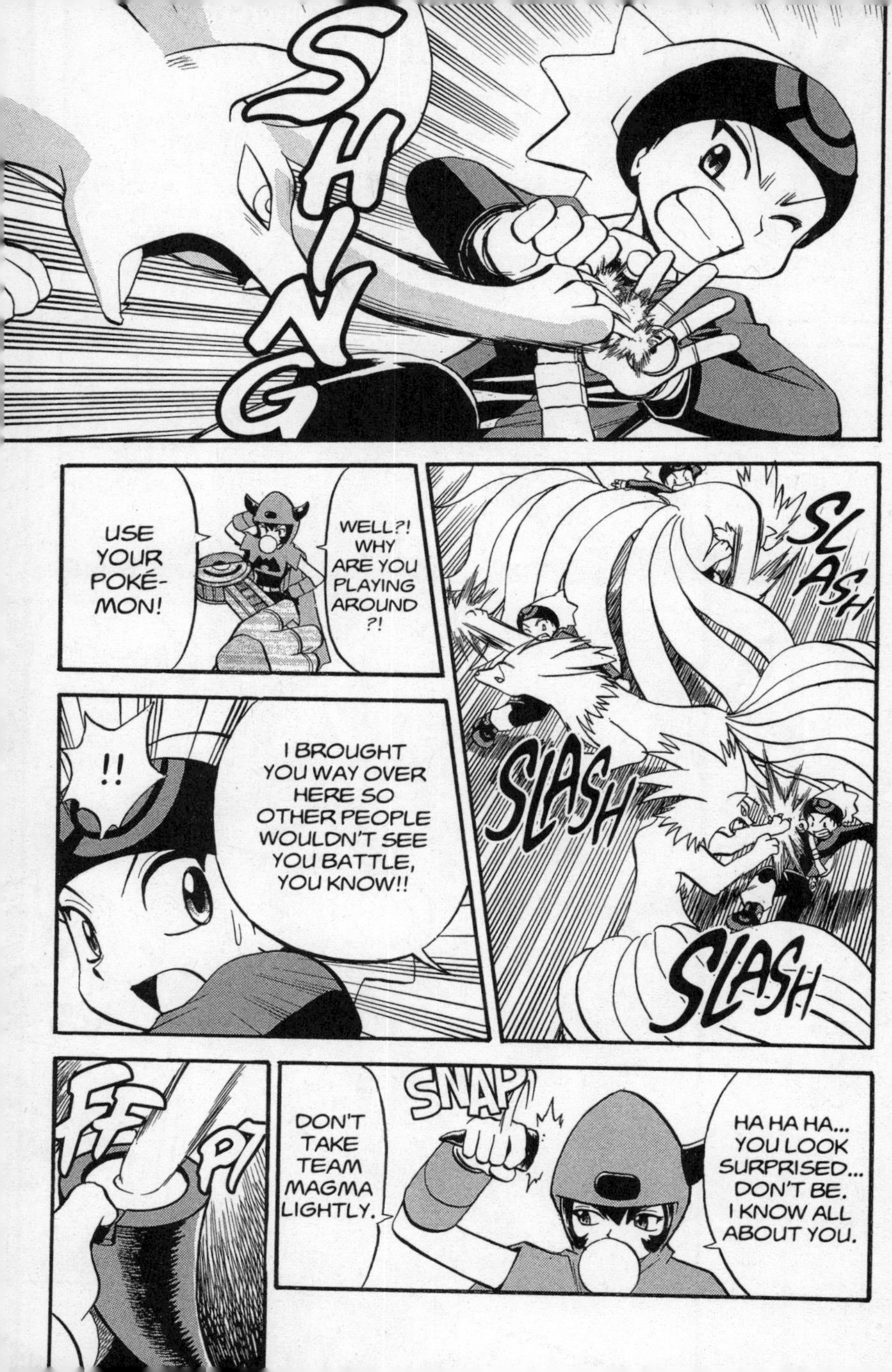
SHING
SLASH
WELL?! WHY ARE YOU PLAYING AROUND ?!
USE YOUR POKÉ-MON!
SLASH
SLASH
I BROUGHT YOU WAY OVER HERE SO OTHER PEOPLE WOULDN'T SEE YOU BATTLE, YOU KNOW!!
!!
HA HA HA... YOU LOOK SURPRISED... DON'T BE. I KNOW ALL ABOUT YOU.
SNAP
DON'T TAKE TEAM MAGMA LIGHTLY.
FFPT

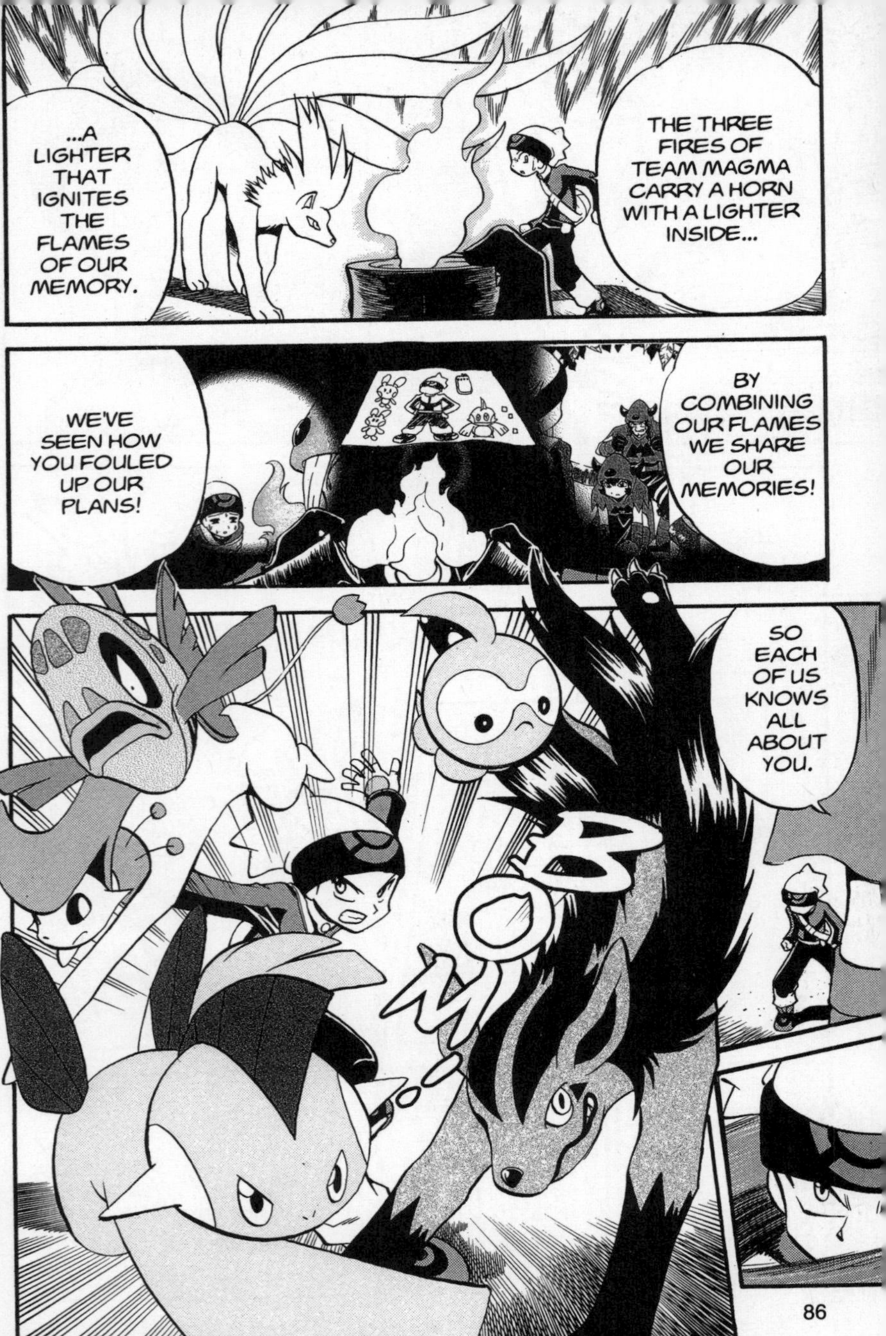
THE THREE FIRES OF TEAM MAGMA CARRY A HORN WITH A LIGHTER INSIDE...
...A LIGHTER THAT IGNITES THE FLAMES OF OUR MEMORY.
BY COMBINING OUR FLAMES WE SHARE OUR MEMORIES!
WE'VE SEEN HOW YOU FOULED UP OUR PLANS!
SO EACH OF US KNOWS ALL ABOUT YOU.
BOM!

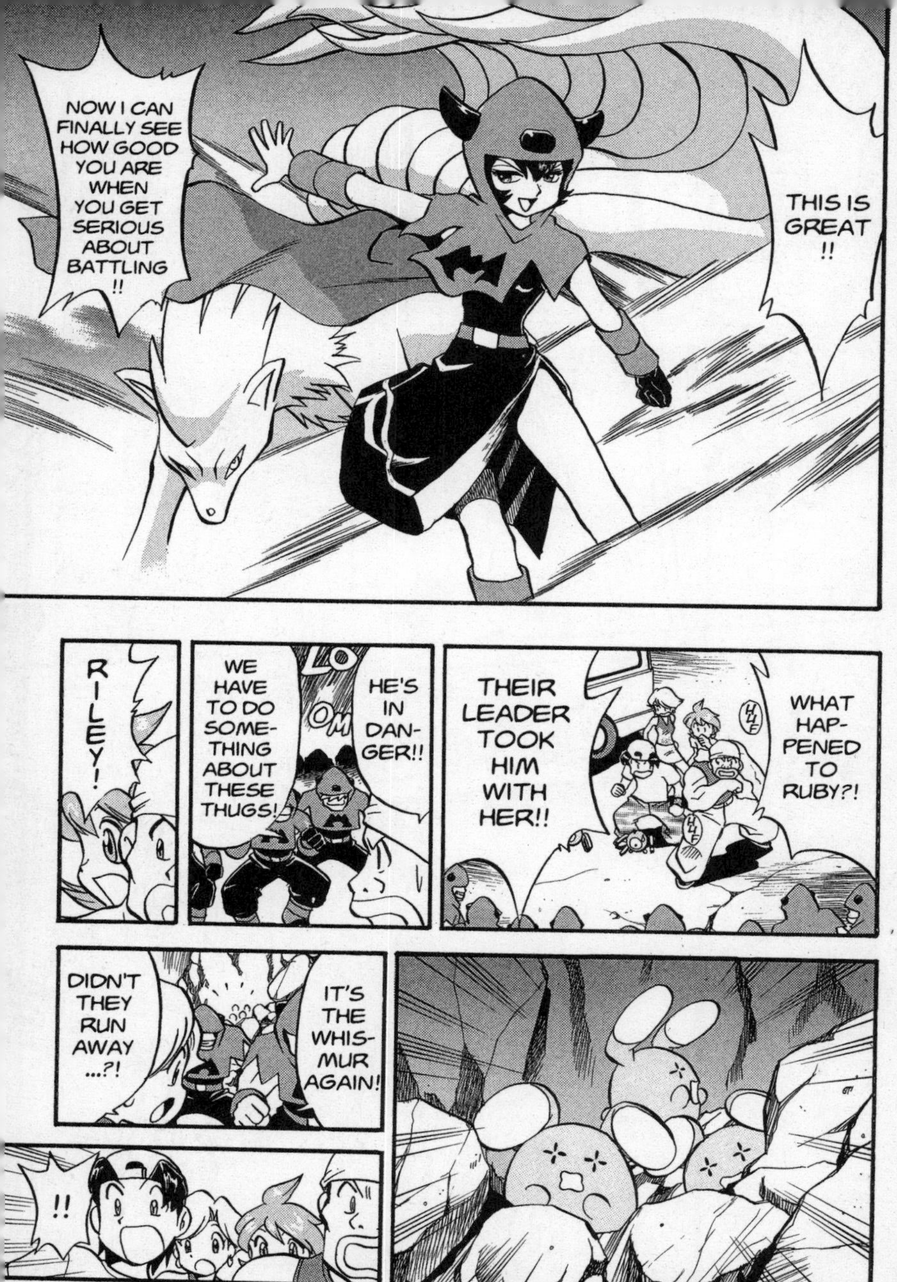
THIS IS GREAT !!
NOW I CAN FINALLY SEE HOW GOOD YOU ARE WHEN YOU GET SERIOUS ABOUT BATTLING !!
WHAT HAPPENED TO RUBY?!
THEIR LEADER TOOK HIM WITH HER!!
HE'S IN DANGER!!
WE HAVE TO DO SOMETHING ABOUT THESE THUGS!
RILEY!
IT'S THE WHISMUR AGAIN!
DIDN'T THEY RUN AWAY ...?!
!!

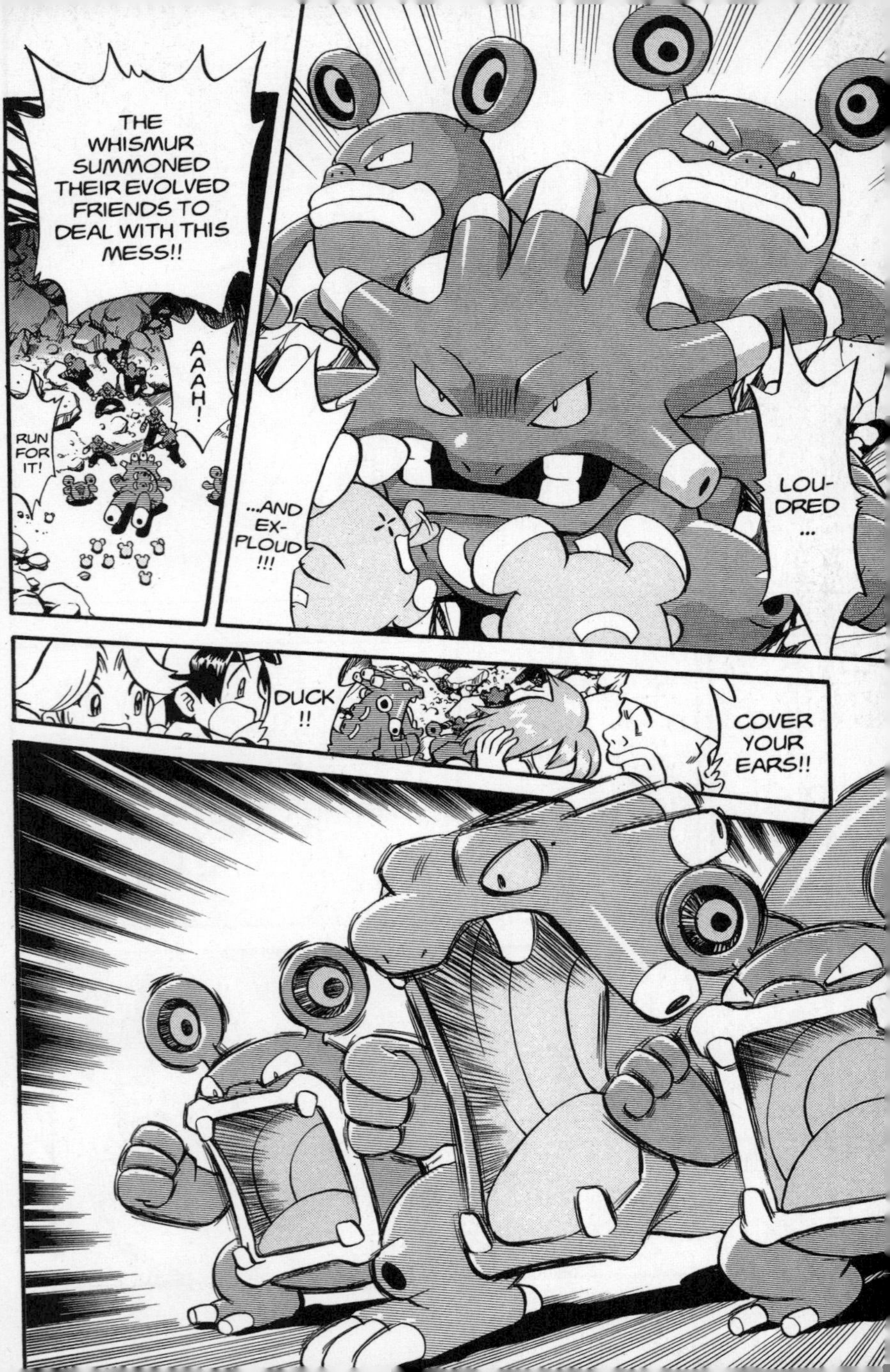
LOU-DRED ...
...AND EX-PLOUD !!!
THE WHISMUR SUMMONED THEIR EVOLVED FRIENDS TO DEAL WITH THIS MESS!!
AAAH!
RUN FOR IT!
COVER YOUR EARS!!
DUCK !!

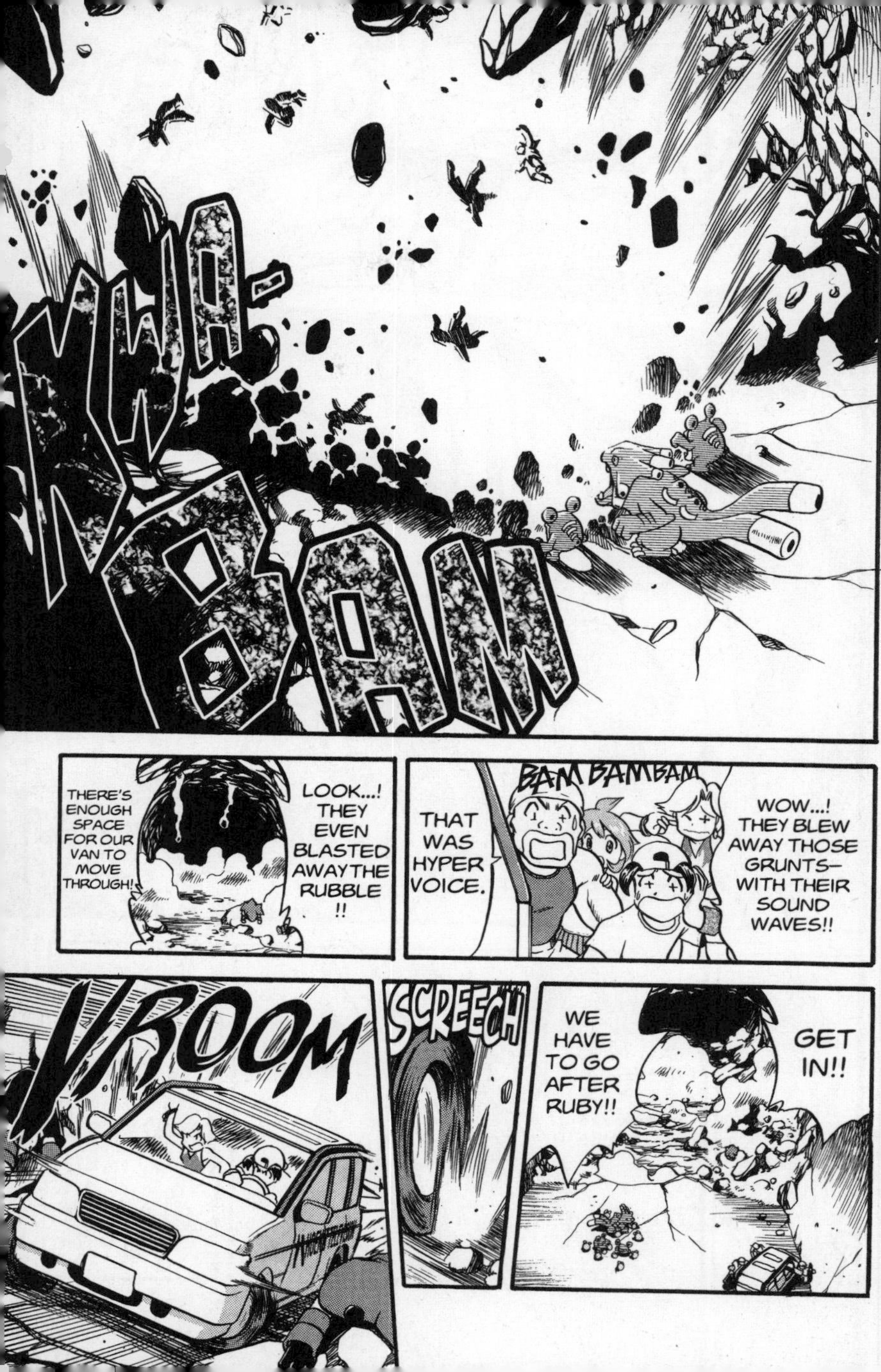
KWA-BOOM
BAM BAMBAM
WOW...! THEY BLEW AWAY THOSE GRUNTS—WITH THEIR SOUND WAVES!!
THAT WAS HYPER VOICE.
LOOK...! THEY EVEN BLASTED AWAY THE RUBBLE!!
THERE'S ENOUGH SPACE FOR OUR VAN TO MOVE THROUGH!
GET IN!!
WE HAVE TO GO AFTER RUBY!!
SCREECH
VROOM

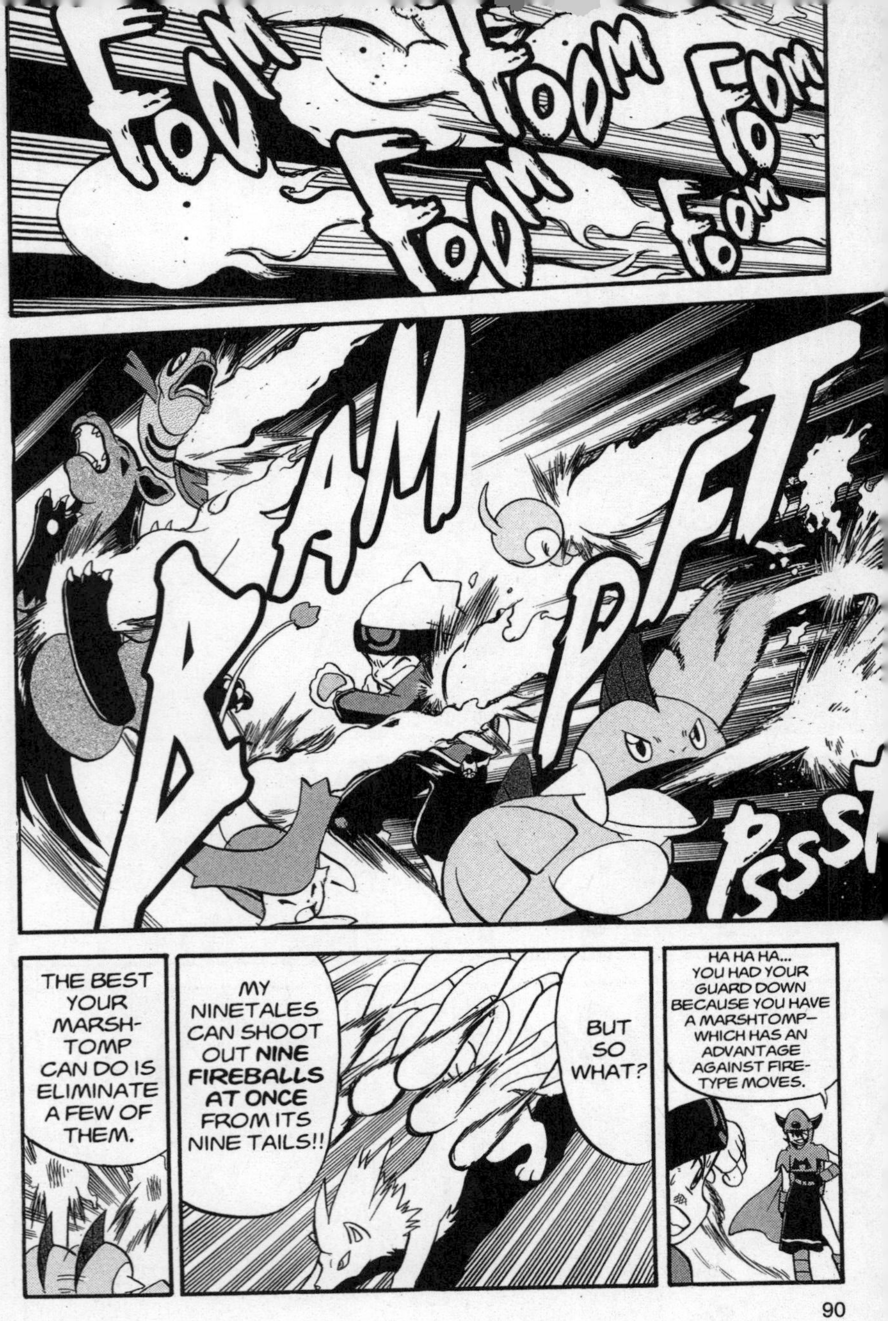
FOOM
FOOM
FOOM
FOOM
FOOM
BAM
HA HA HA... YOU HAD YOUR GUARD DOWN BECAUSE YOU HAVE A MARSHTOMP—WHICH HAS AN ADVANTAGE AGAINST FIRE-TYPE MOVES.
BUT SO WHAT?
MY NINETALES CAN SHOOT OUT **NINE FIREBALLS AT ONCE** FROM ITS NINE TAILS!!
THE BEST YOUR MARSHTOMP CAN DO IS ELIMINATE A FEW OF THEM.

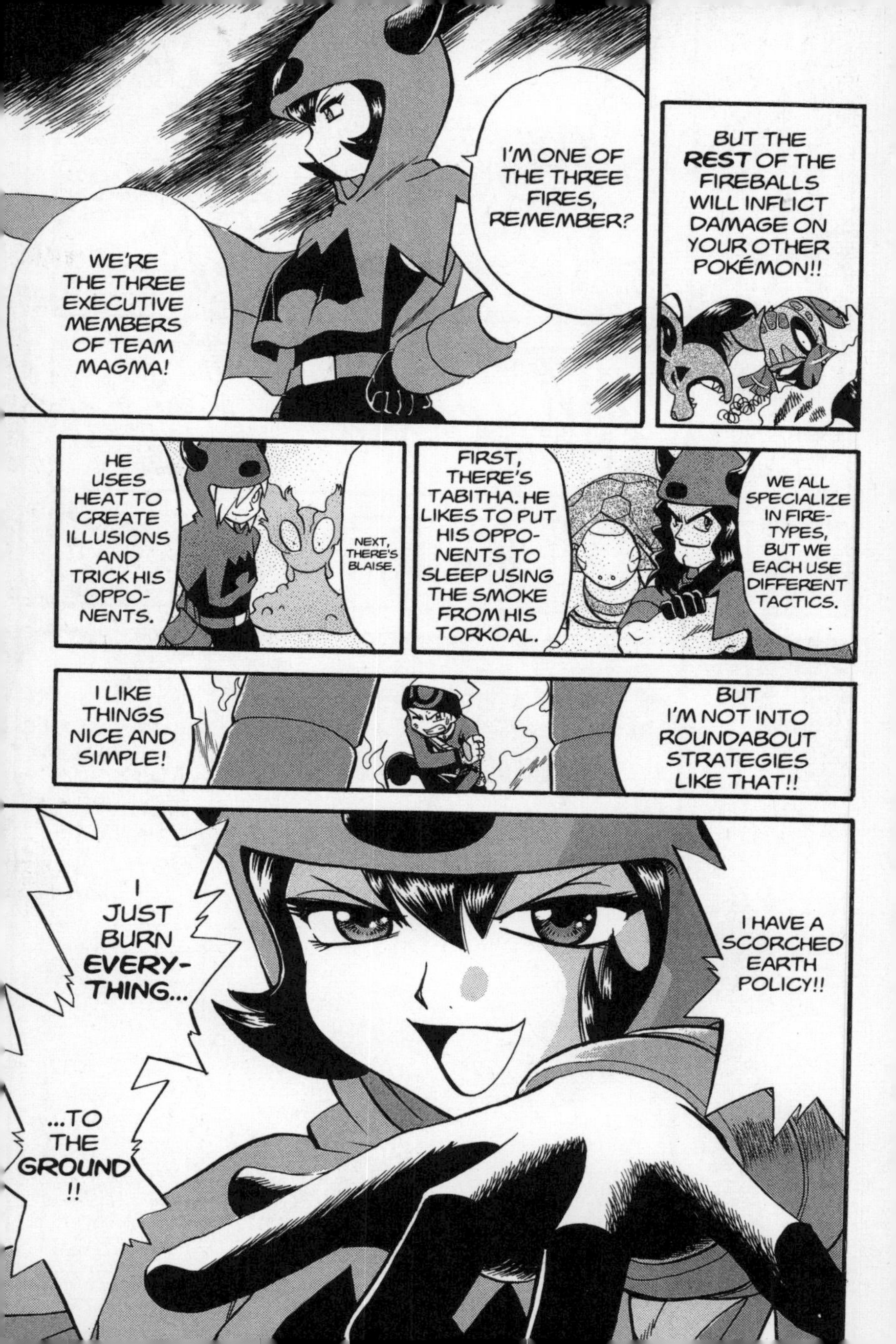
BUT THE **REST** OF THE FIREBALLS WILL INFLICT DAMAGE ON YOUR OTHER POKÉMON!!
I'M ONE OF THE THREE FIRES, REMEMBER?
WE'RE THE THREE EXECUTIVE MEMBERS OF TEAM MAGMA!
WE ALL SPECIALIZE IN FIRE-TYPES, BUT WE EACH USE DIFFERENT TACTICS.
FIRST, THERE'S TABITHA. HE LIKES TO PUT HIS OPPONENTS TO SLEEP USING THE SMOKE FROM HIS TORKOAL.
NEXT, THERE'S BLAISE.
HE USES HEAT TO CREATE ILLUSIONS AND TRICK HIS OPPONENTS.
BUT I'M NOT INTO ROUNDABOUT STRATEGIES LIKE THAT!!
I LIKE THINGS NICE AND SIMPLE!
I HAVE A SCORCHED EARTH POLICY!!
I JUST BURN **EVERYTHING...**
...TO THE **GROUND**!!

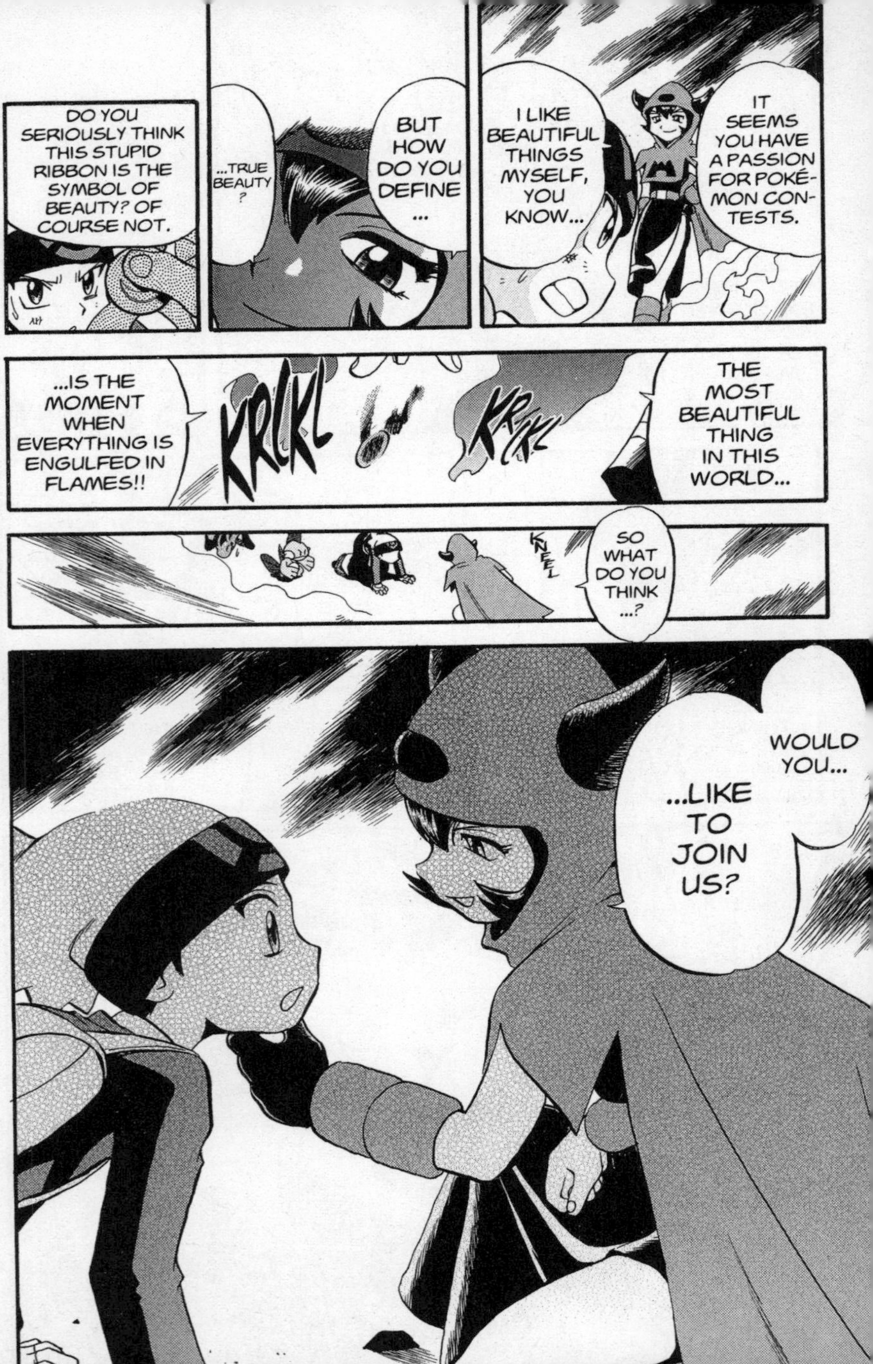

IT SEEMS YOU HAVE A PASSION FOR POKÉMON CONTESTS.
I LIKE BEAUTIFUL THINGS MYSELF, YOU KNOW...
BUT HOW DO YOU DEFINE ...
...TRUE BEAUTY?
DO YOU SERIOUSLY THINK THIS STUPID RIBBON IS THE SYMBOL OF BEAUTY? OF COURSE NOT.
THE MOST BEAUTIFUL THING IN THIS WORLD...
KR-KL
KRLKL
...IS THE MOMENT WHEN EVERYTHING IS ENGULFED IN FLAMES!!
SO WHAT DO YOU THINK ...?
KNEEL
WOULD YOU...
...LIKE TO JOIN US?

ADVENTURE MAP

SAPPHIRE

Name	Pokémon	Level
CHIC	Combusken ♀	Lv31
RONO	Lairon ♂	Lv40
LORRY	Wailord ♂	Lv45
PHADO	Donphan ♂	Lv43
TROPPY	Tropius ♂	Lv42

Sapphire: Route 111 ▼ Mt. Chimney ▼ Jagged Pass ▼

Ruby: Weather Institute ▼ Route 117 ▼ Verdanturf Town ▼ Rusturf Tunnel

RUBY

Name	Pokémon
MUMU	Marshtomp ♂
NANA	Mightyena ♀
KIKI	Delcatty ♀
FEEFEE	Feebas ♀
FOFO	Castform ♀

Stone Badge	Knuckle Badge	Dynamo Badge	Heat Badge
Balance Badge	Feather Badge	Mind Badge	Rain Badge

	Cool	Beauty	Cute	Smart	Tough
Normal					
Super					
Hyper					
Master					

● Chapter 221 ●
Going to Eleven with Loudred and Exploud II

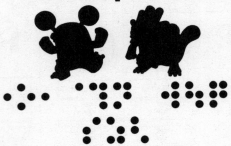

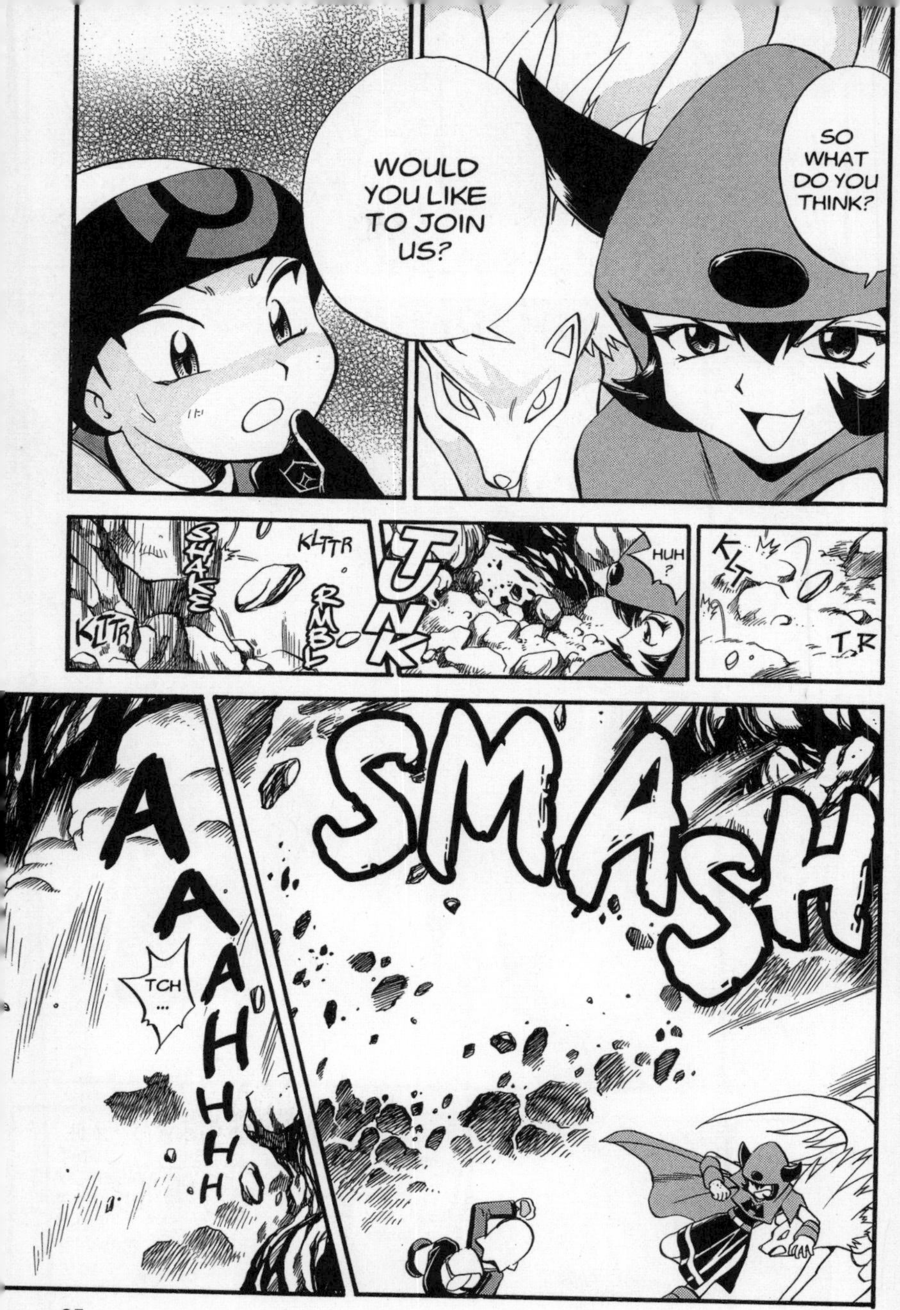
SO WHAT DO YOU THINK?
WOULD YOU LIKE TO JOIN US?
KLT
T.R
HUH?
TUNK
KLTTR
SHAKE
RMBL
KLTTR
SMASH
AAAHHHHH
TCH...

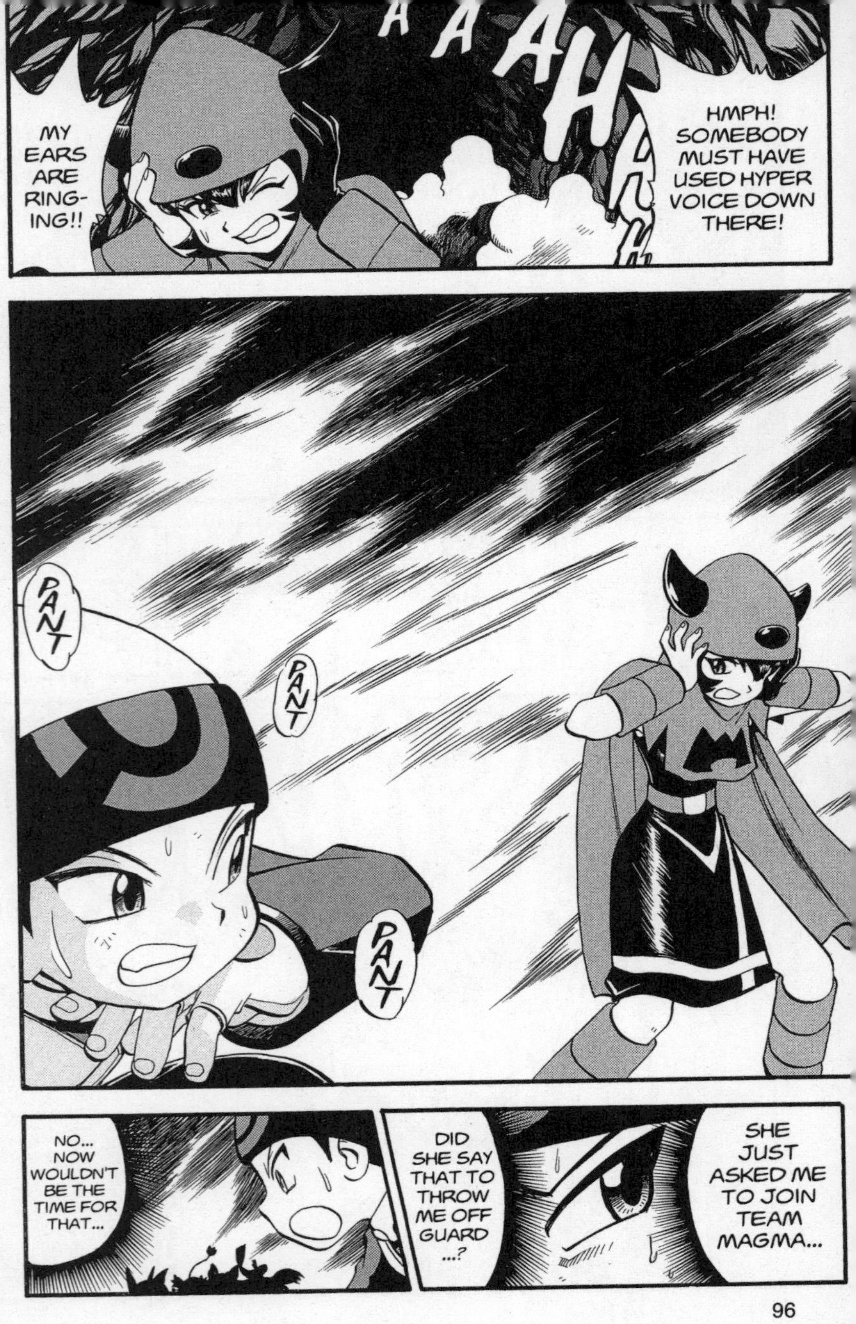
A A AH
HMPH! SOMEBODY MUST HAVE USED HYPER VOICE DOWN THERE!
MY EARS ARE RINGING!!
PANT
PANT
PANT
SHE JUST ASKED ME TO JOIN TEAM MAGMA...
DID SHE SAY THAT TO THROW ME OFF GUARD ...?
NO... NOW WOULDN'T BE THE TIME FOR THAT...

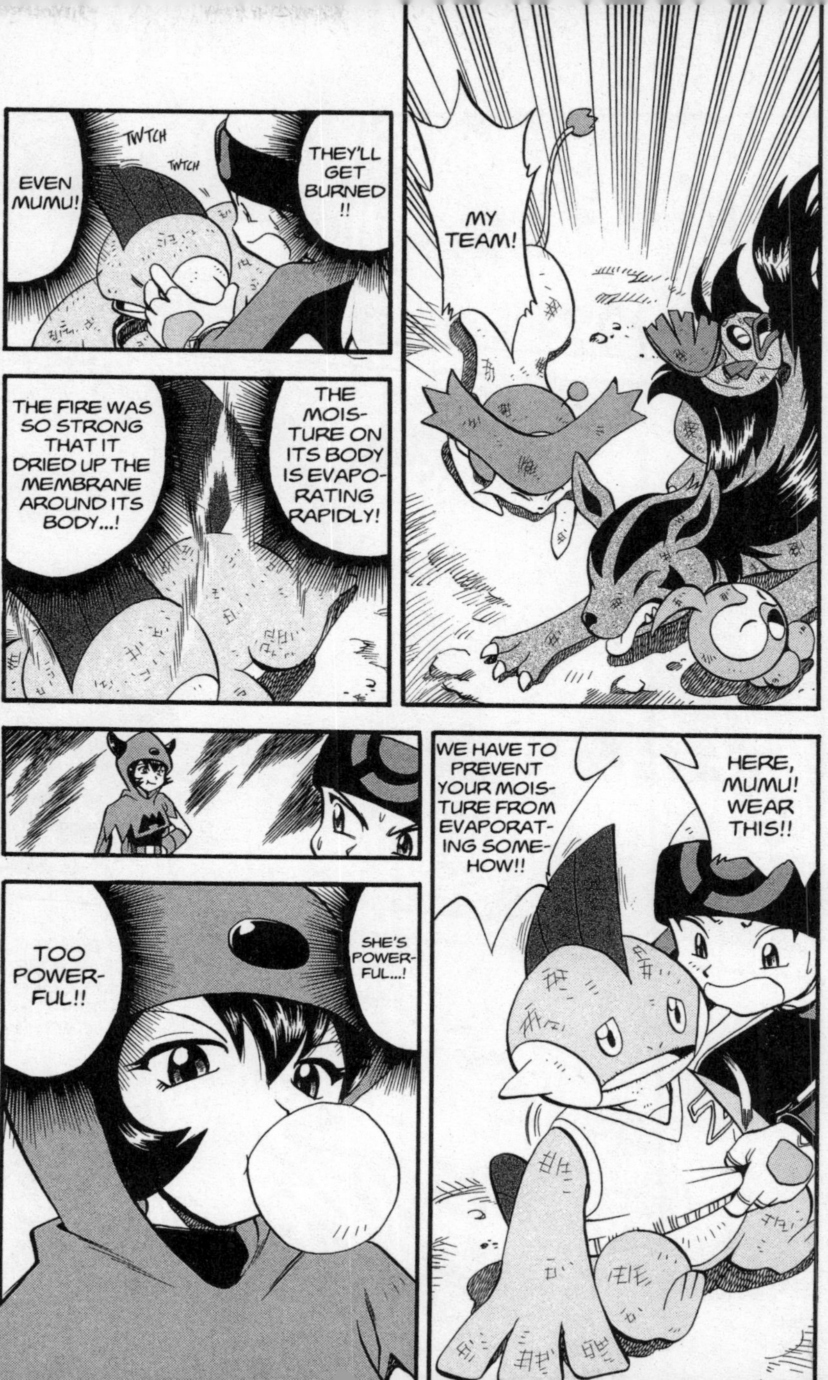
MY TEAM!
TWTCH
TWTCH
THEY'LL GET BURNED !!
EVEN MUMU!
THE MOIS-TURE ON ITS BODY IS EVAPO-RATING RAPIDLY!
THE FIRE WAS SO STRONG THAT IT DRIED UP THE MEMBRANE AROUND ITS BODY...!
HERE, MUMU! WEAR THIS!!
WE HAVE TO PREVENT YOUR MOIS-TURE FROM EVAPORAT-ING SOME-HOW!!
SHE'S POWER-FUL...!
TOO POWER-FUL!!

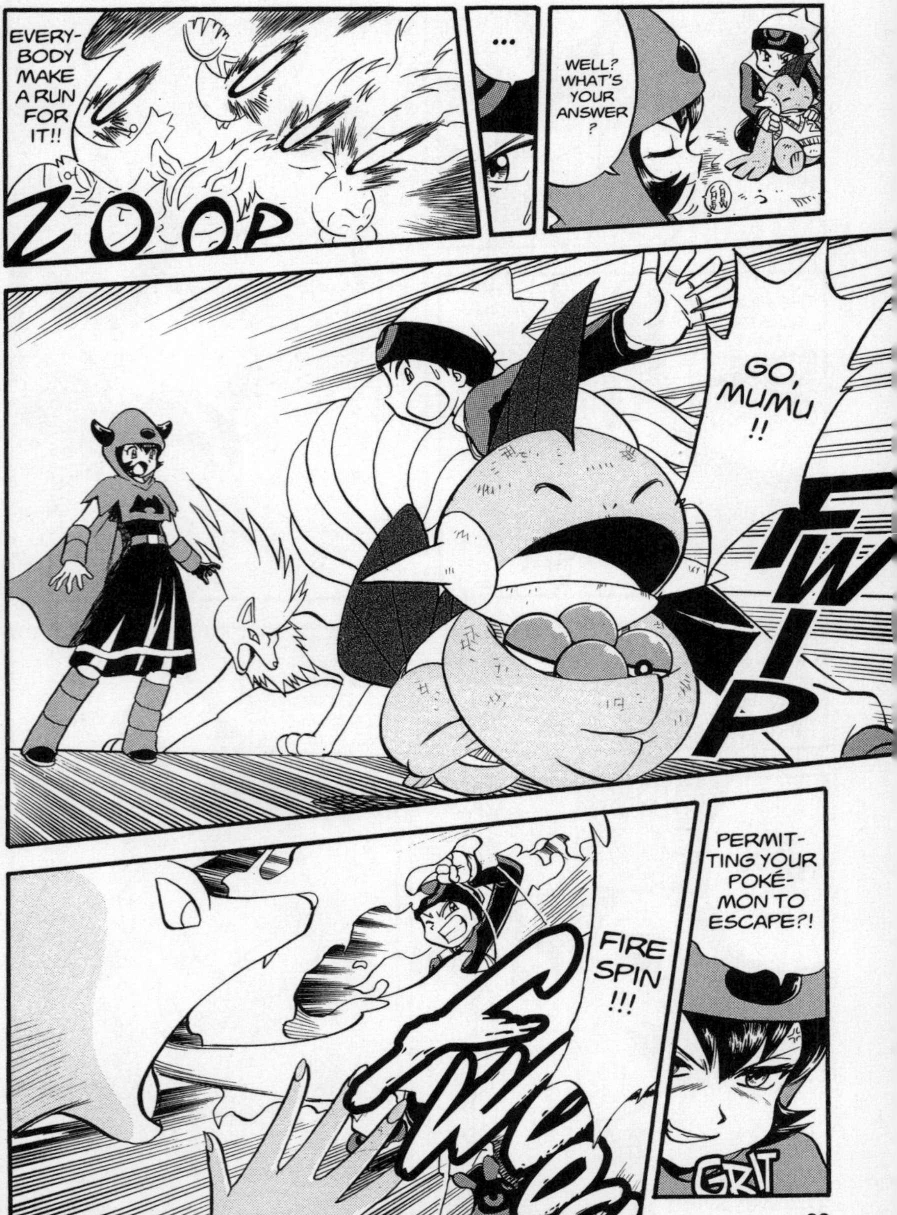
WELL? WHAT'S YOUR ANSWER?
...
EVERYBODY MAKE A RUN FOR IT!!
ZOOP
GO, MUMU!!
FWIP
PERMITTING YOUR POKÉMON TO ESCAPE?!
GRIT
FIRE SPIN!!!

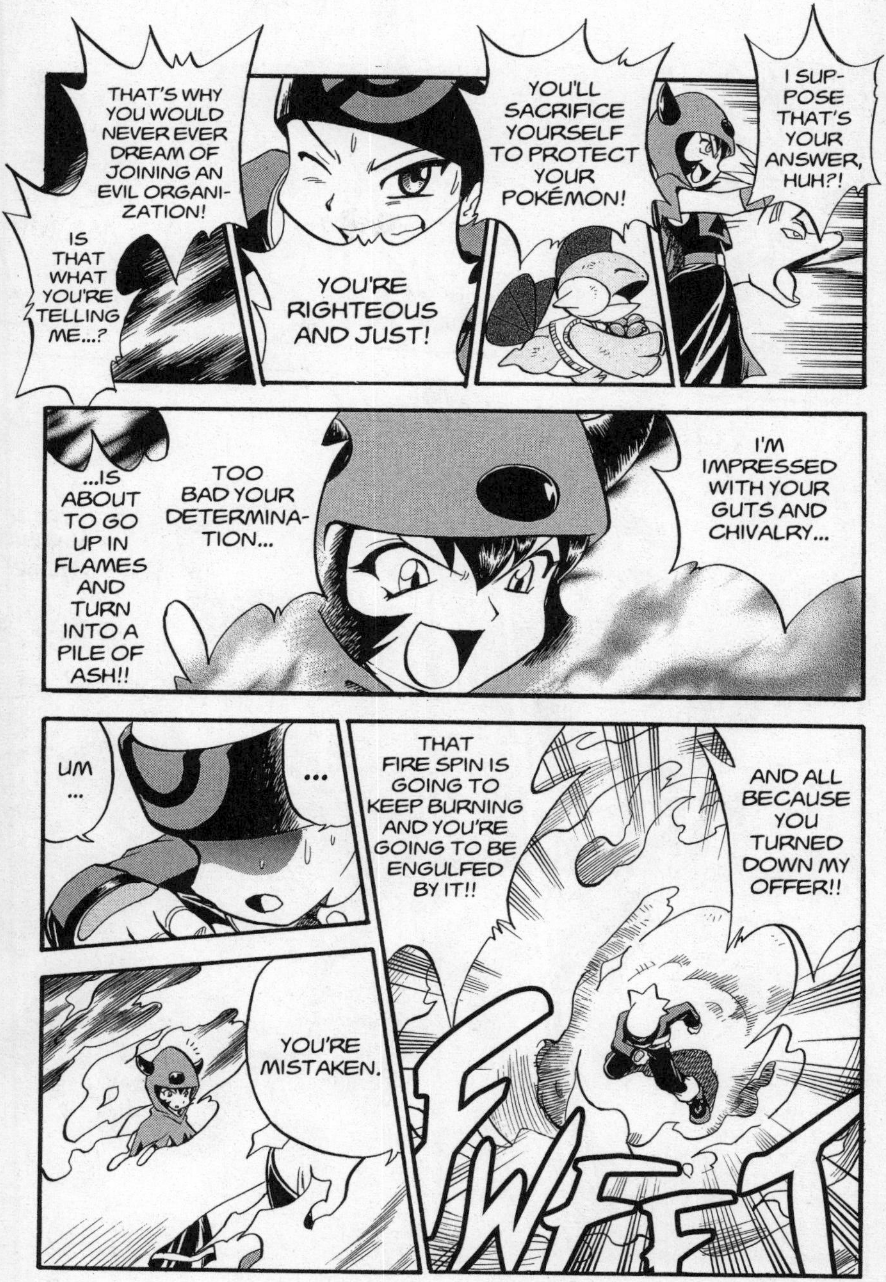
I SUPPOSE THAT'S YOUR ANSWER, HUH?!
YOU'LL SACRIFICE YOURSELF TO PROTECT YOUR POKÉMON!
YOU'RE RIGHTEOUS AND JUST!
THAT'S WHY YOU WOULD NEVER EVER DREAM OF JOINING AN EVIL ORGANIZATION!
IS THAT WHAT YOU'RE TELLING ME...?
I'M IMPRESSED WITH YOUR GUTS AND CHIVALRY...
TOO BAD YOUR DETERMINATION...
...IS ABOUT TO GO UP IN FLAMES AND TURN INTO A PILE OF ASH!!
AND ALL BECAUSE YOU TURNED DOWN MY OFFER!!
THAT FIRE SPIN IS GOING TO KEEP BURNING AND YOU'RE GOING TO BE ENGULFED BY IT!!
SWFT
...
UM ...
YOU'RE MISTAKEN.

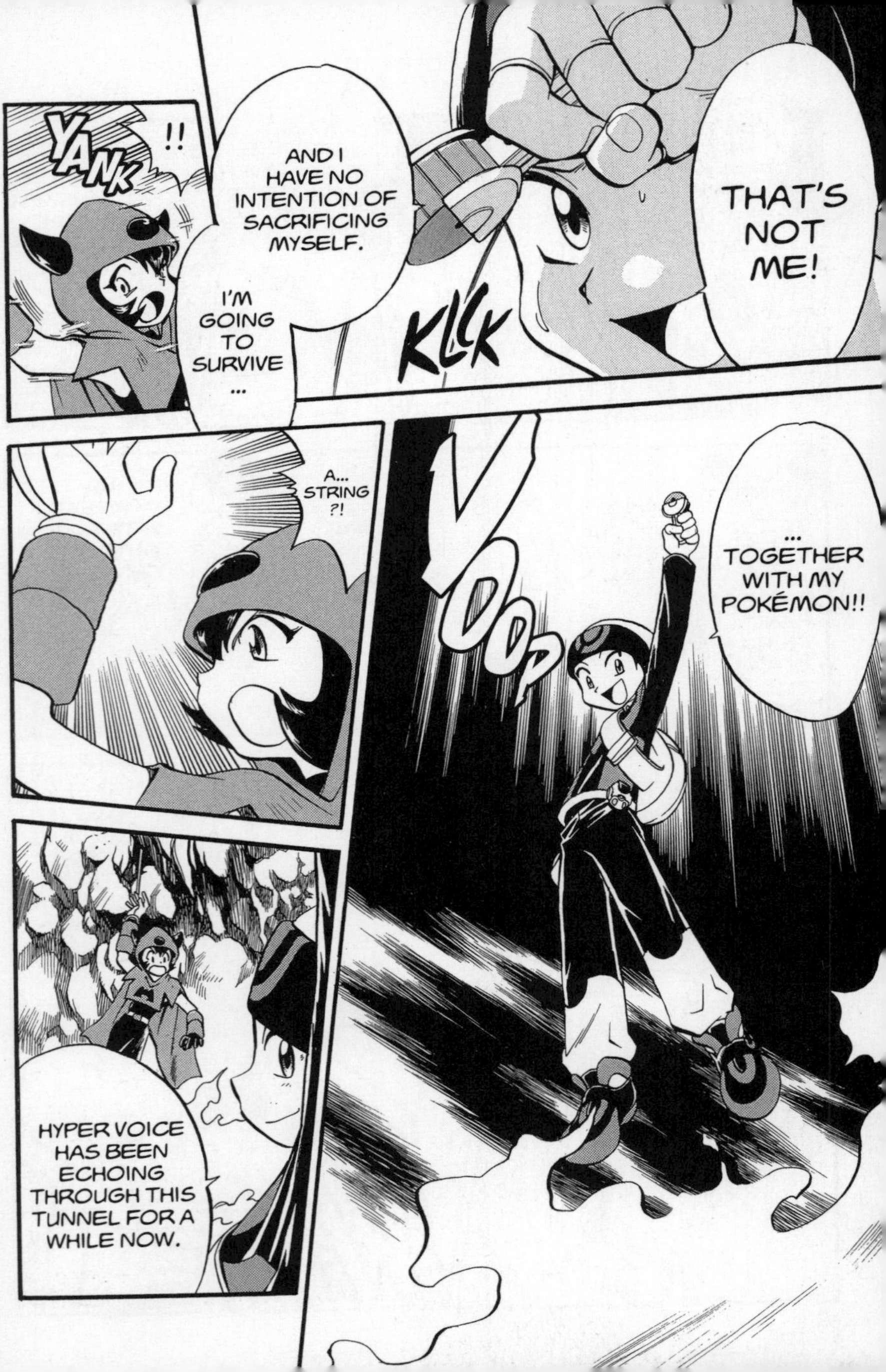
THAT'S NOT ME!
KLICK
AND I HAVE NO INTENTION OF SACRIFICING MYSELF.
I'M GOING TO SURVIVE ...
YANK !!
... TOGETHER WITH MY POKÉMON!!
VOOOP
A... STRING ?!
HYPER VOICE HAS BEEN ECHOING THROUGH THIS TUNNEL FOR A WHILE NOW.

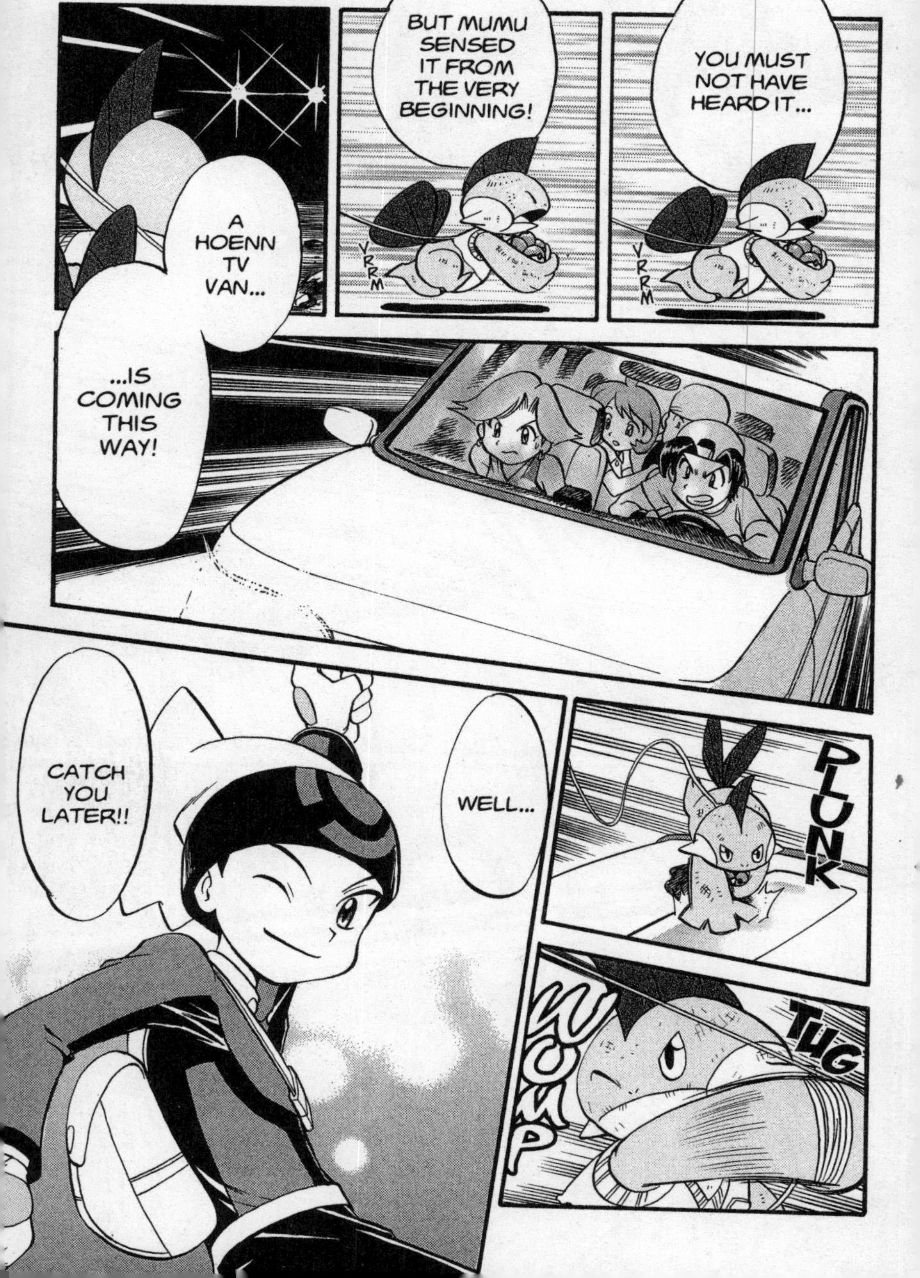

YOU MUST NOT HAVE HEARD IT...
VRRM
BUT MUMU SENSED IT FROM THE VERY BEGINNING!
VRRM
A HOENN TV VAN...
...IS COMING THIS WAY!
PLUNK
TUG
WOMP
WELL...
CATCH YOU LATER!!

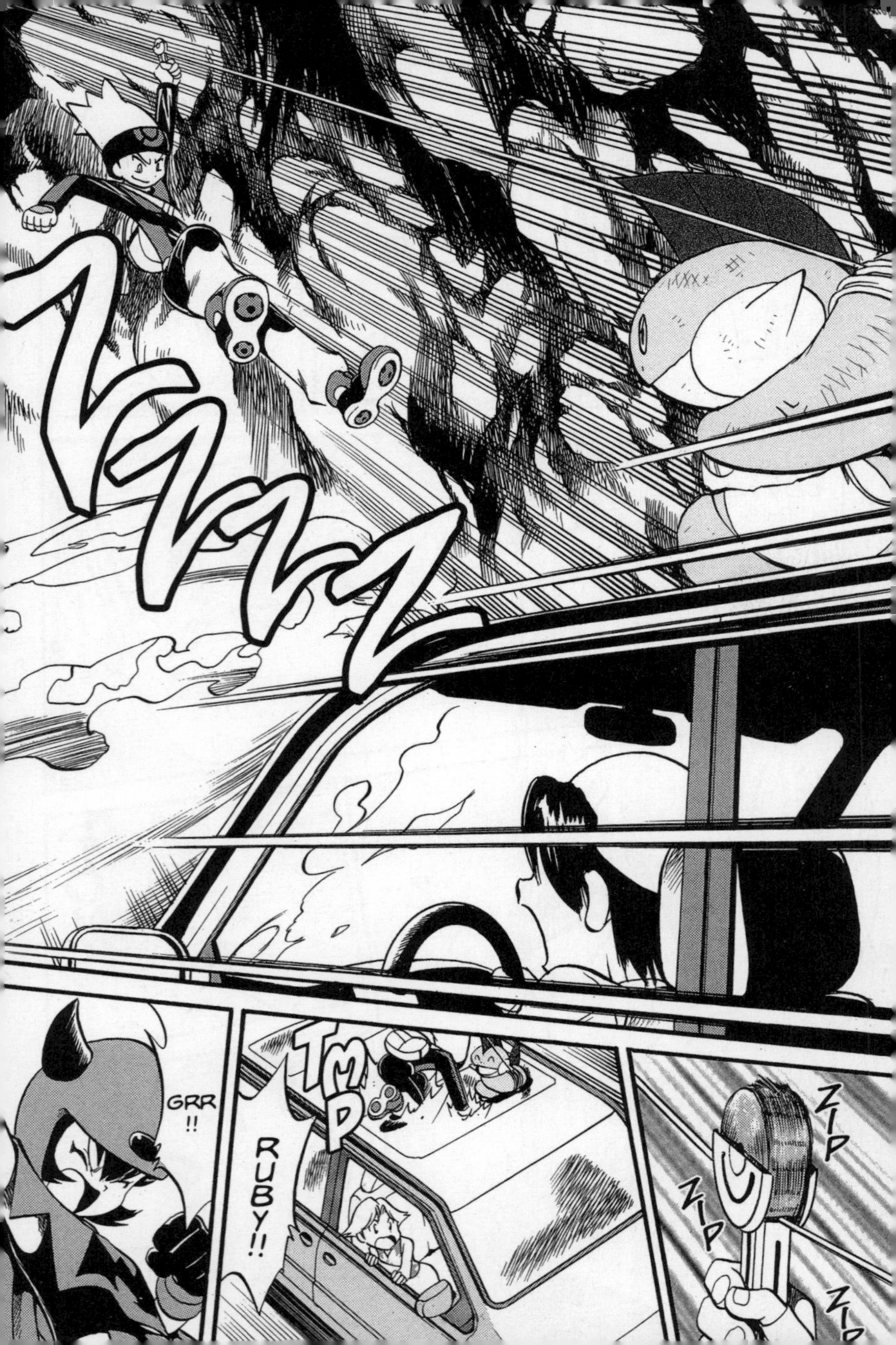
ZIP
ZIP
ZIP
TMP
RUBY!!
GRR !!

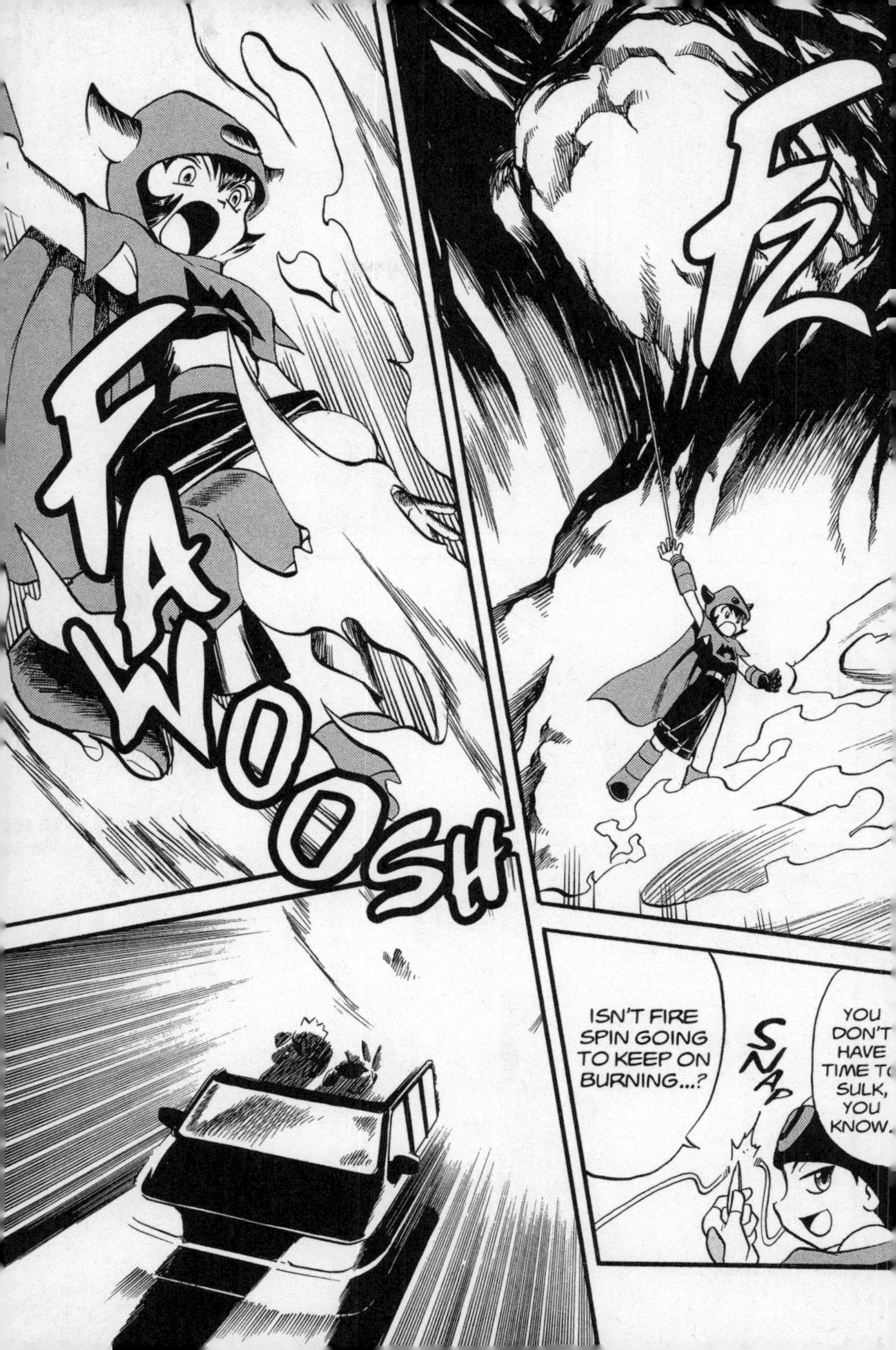
FWOOSH
YOU DON'T HAVE TIME TO SULK, YOU KNOW.
SNAP
ISN'T FIRE SPIN GOING TO KEEP ON BURNING...?

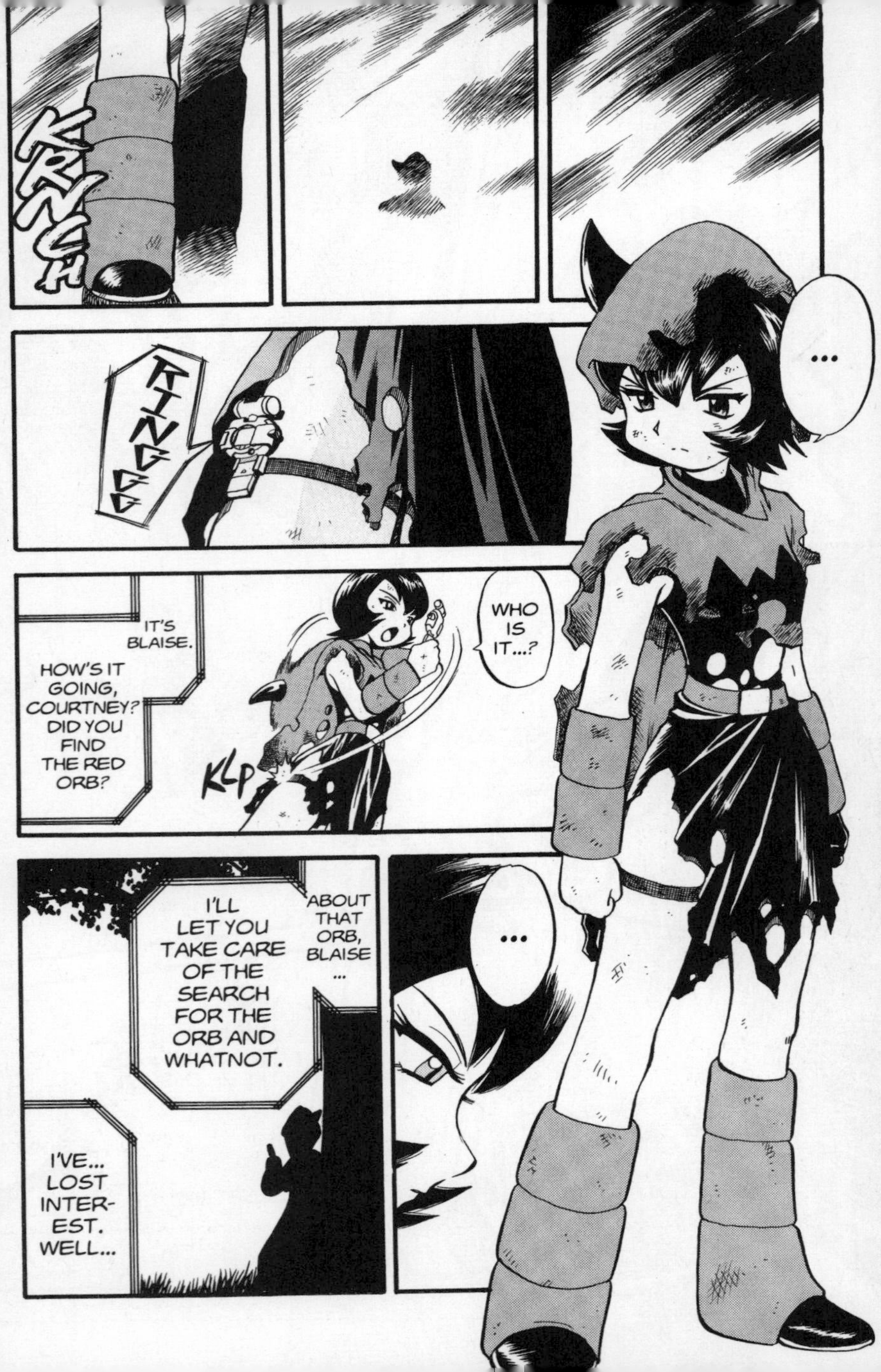
KRNCH
...
RINGGG
WHO IS IT...?
KLP
IT'S BLAISE.
HOW'S IT GOING, COURTNEY? DID YOU FIND THE RED ORB?
...
ABOUT THAT ORB, BLAISE...
I'LL LET YOU TAKE CARE OF THE SEARCH FOR THE ORB AND WHATNOT.
I'VE... LOST INTEREST. WELL...

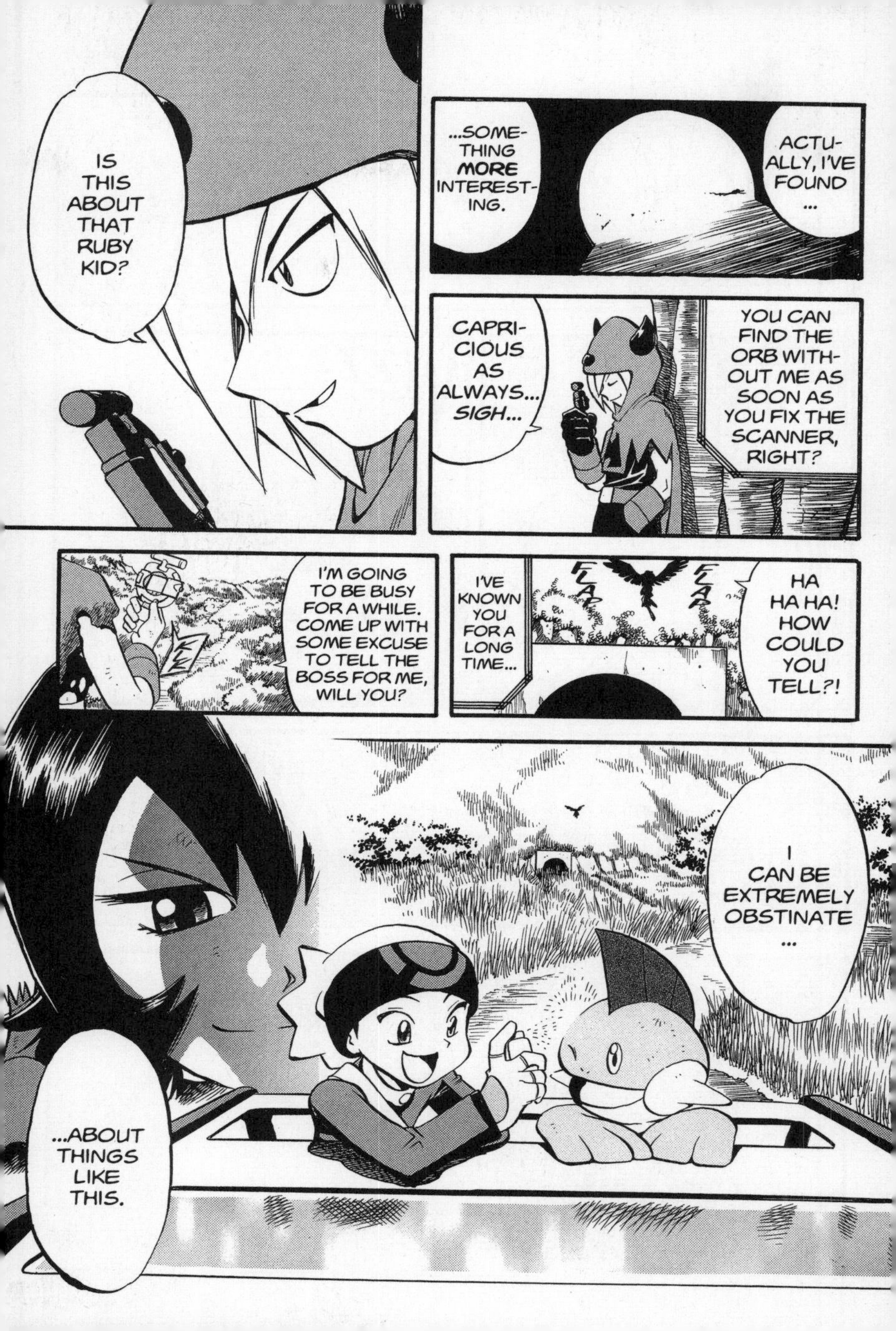
ACTUALLY, I'VE FOUND ...
...SOMETHING **MORE** INTERESTING.
YOU CAN FIND THE ORB WITHOUT ME AS SOON AS YOU FIX THE SCANNER, RIGHT?
CAPRICIOUS AS ALWAYS... *SIGH*...
IS THIS ABOUT THAT RUBY KID?
HA HA HA! HOW COULD YOU TELL?!
FLAP
FLAP
I'VE KNOWN YOU FOR A LONG TIME...
I'M GOING TO BE BUSY FOR A WHILE. COME UP WITH SOME EXCUSE TO TELL THE BOSS FOR ME, WILL YOU?
I CAN BE EXTREMELY OBSTINATE ...
...ABOUT THINGS LIKE THIS.

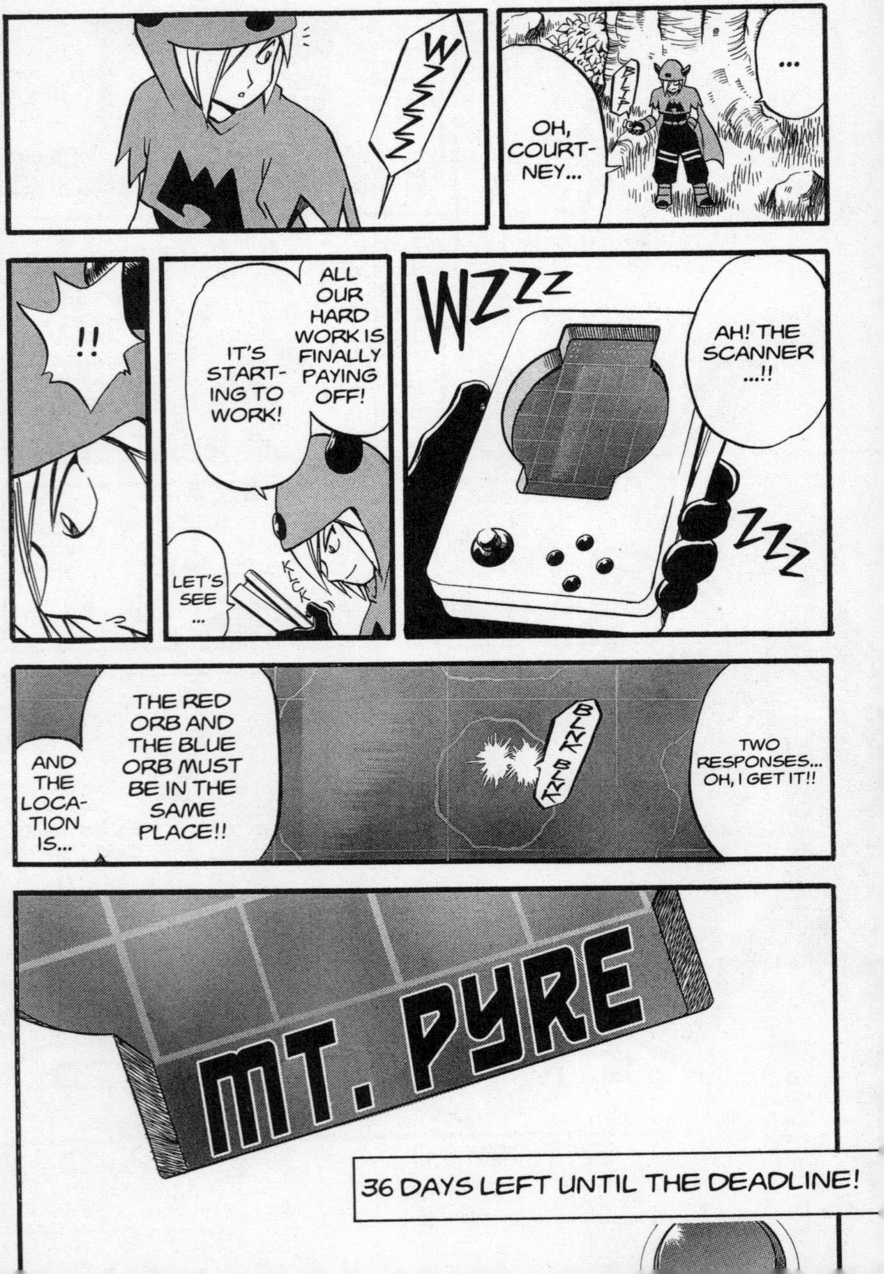
...
BLIP
OH, COURTNEY...
WZZZZ
WZZZ
AH! THE SCANNER ...!!
ZZZ
ALL OUR HARD WORK IS FINALLY PAYING OFF!
IT'S STARTING TO WORK!
KLICK
LET'S SEE ...
!!
TWO RESPONSES... OH, I GET IT!!
BLNK BLNK
THE RED ORB AND THE BLUE ORB MUST BE IN THE SAME PLACE!!
AND THE LOCATION IS...
MT. PYRE
36 DAYS LEFT UNTIL THE DEADLINE!

● Chapter 222 ●
Short Shrift for Shiftry

Pokémon™ Adventures Ruby & Sapphire

The Fourth Chapter

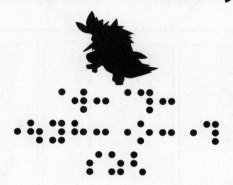

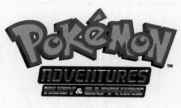

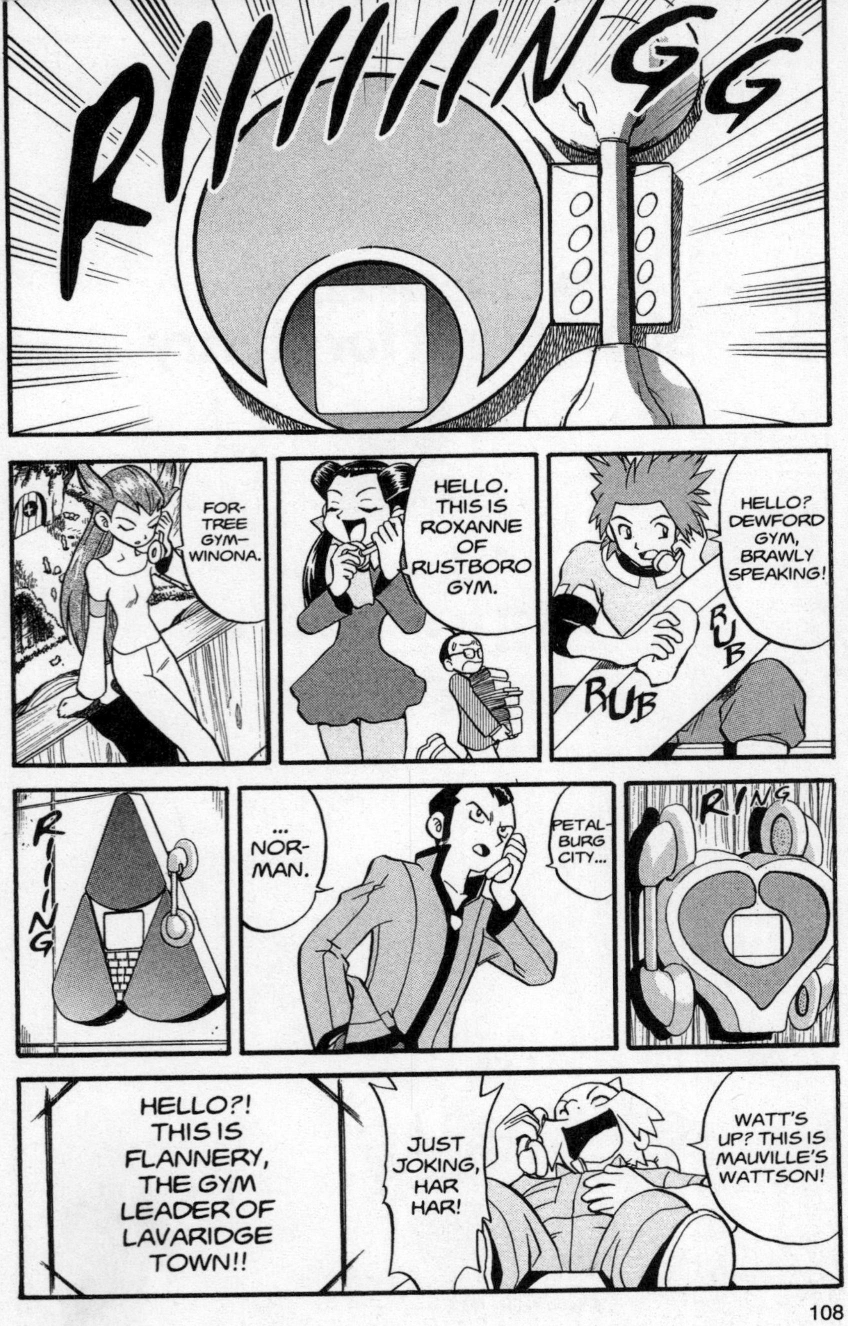
RIIIIINGG
HELLO? DEWFORD GYM, BRAWLY SPEAKING!
RUB
RUB
HELLO. THIS IS ROXANNE OF RUSTBORO GYM.
FOR-TREE GYM– WINONA.
RING
PETAL-BURG CITY...
... NOR-MAN.
RIIIING
WATT'S UP? THIS IS MAUVILLE'S WATTSON!
JUST JOKING, HAR HAR!
HELLO?! THIS IS FLANNERY, THE GYM LEADER OF LAVARIDGE TOWN!!

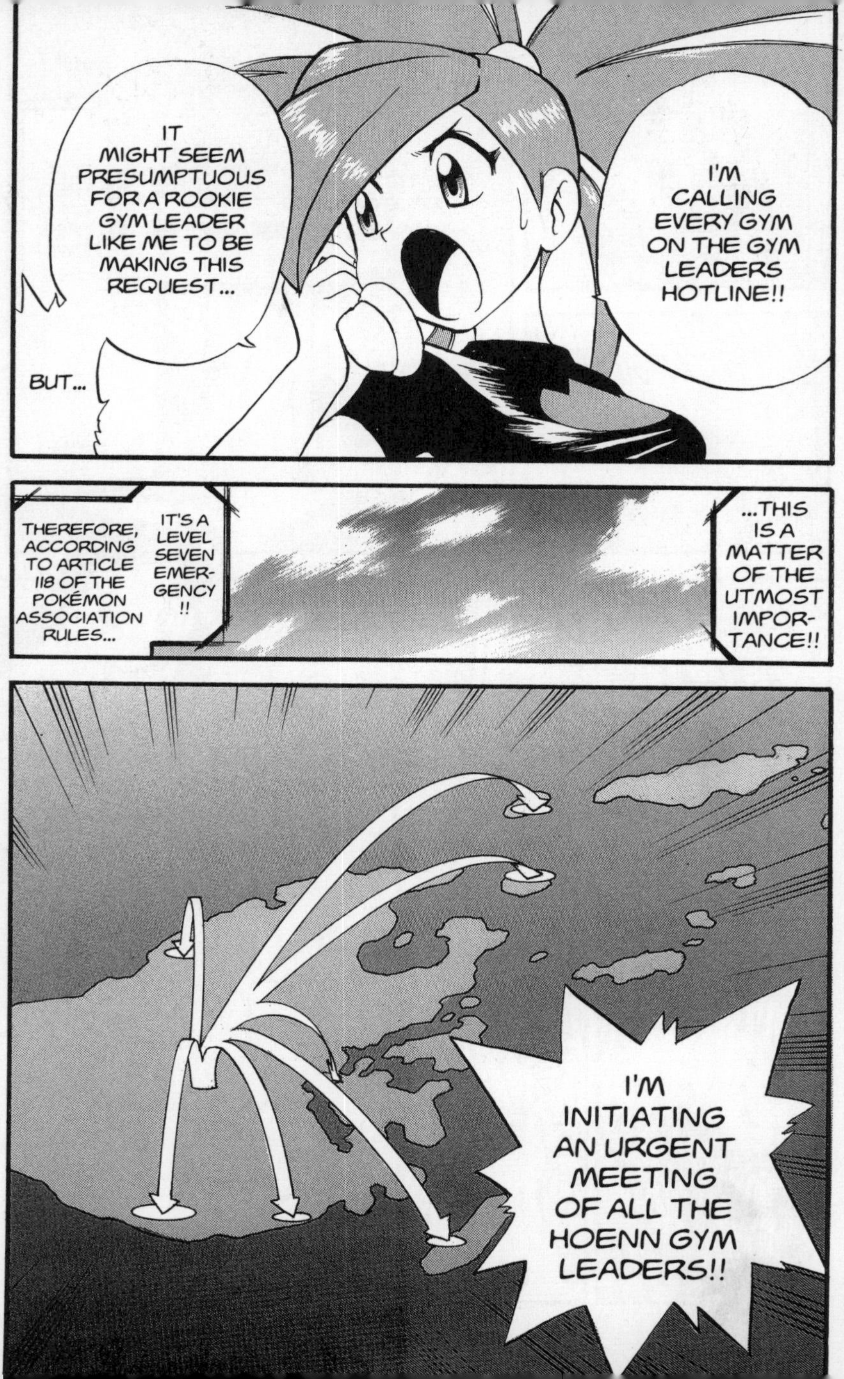
I'M CALLING EVERY GYM ON THE GYM LEADERS HOTLINE!!
IT MIGHT SEEM PRESUMPTUOUS FOR A ROOKIE GYM LEADER LIKE ME TO BE MAKING THIS REQUEST...
BUT...
...THIS IS A MATTER OF THE UTMOST IMPORTANCE!!
IT'S A LEVEL SEVEN EMERGENCY!!
THEREFORE, ACCORDING TO ARTICLE 118 OF THE POKÉMON ASSOCIATION RULES...
I'M INITIATING AN URGENT MEETING OF ALL THE HOENN GYM LEADERS!!

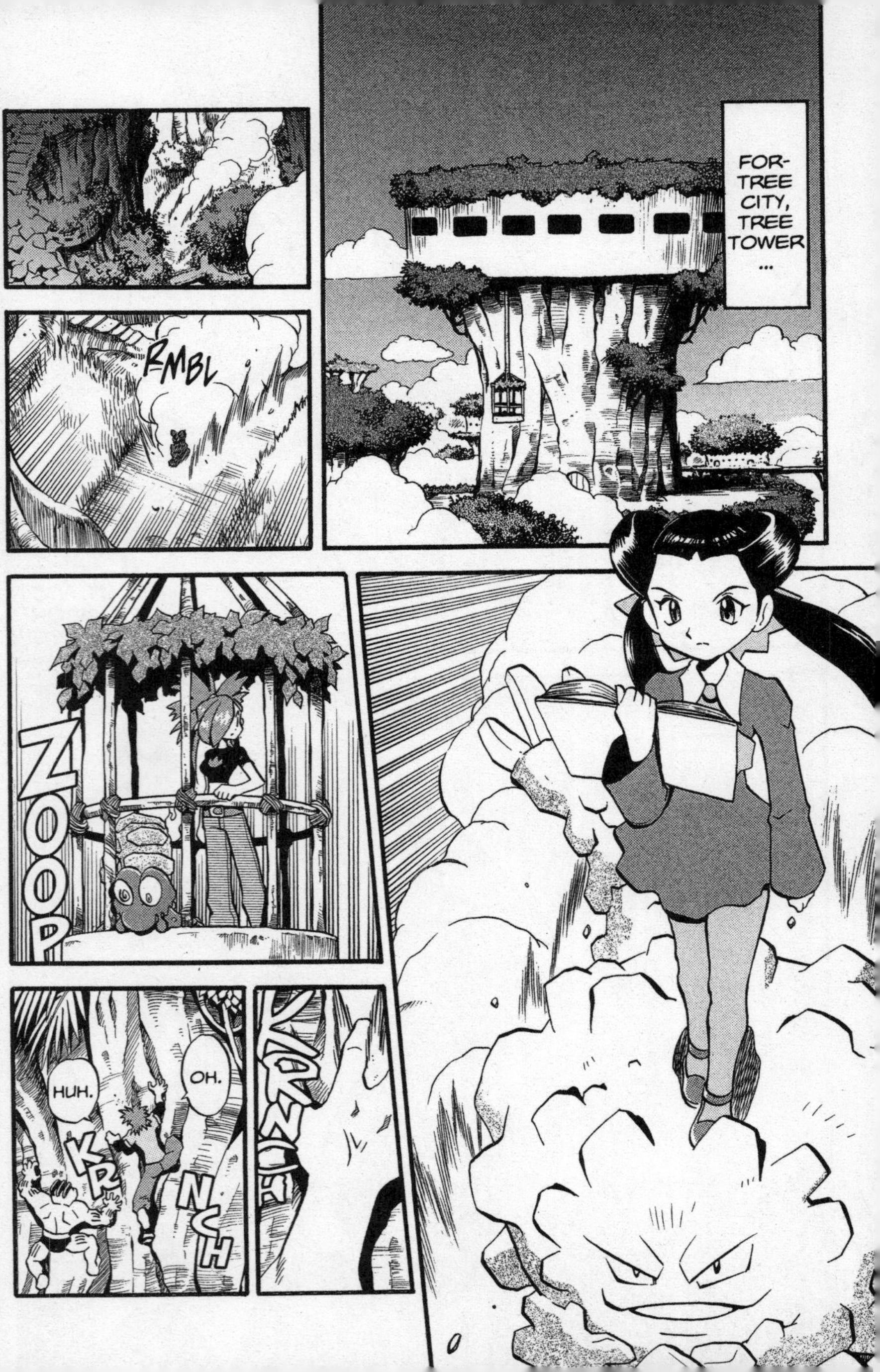
FOR-
TREE
CITY,
TREE
TOWER
...
RMBL
ZOOP
KRNCH
OH.
HUH.
KRNCH

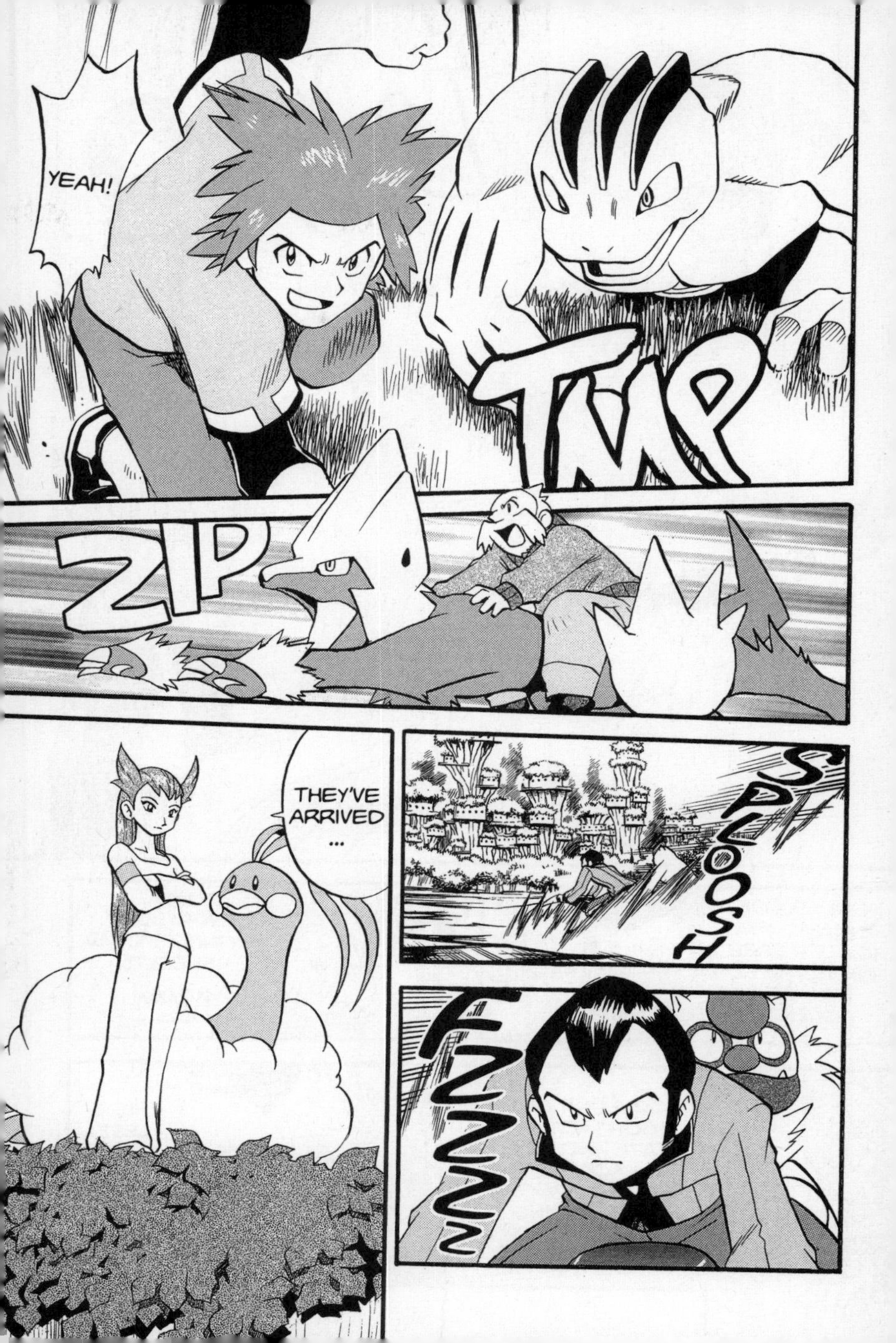
YEAH!
TMP
ZIP
SPLOOSH
FZZZZ
THEY'VE ARRIVED ...

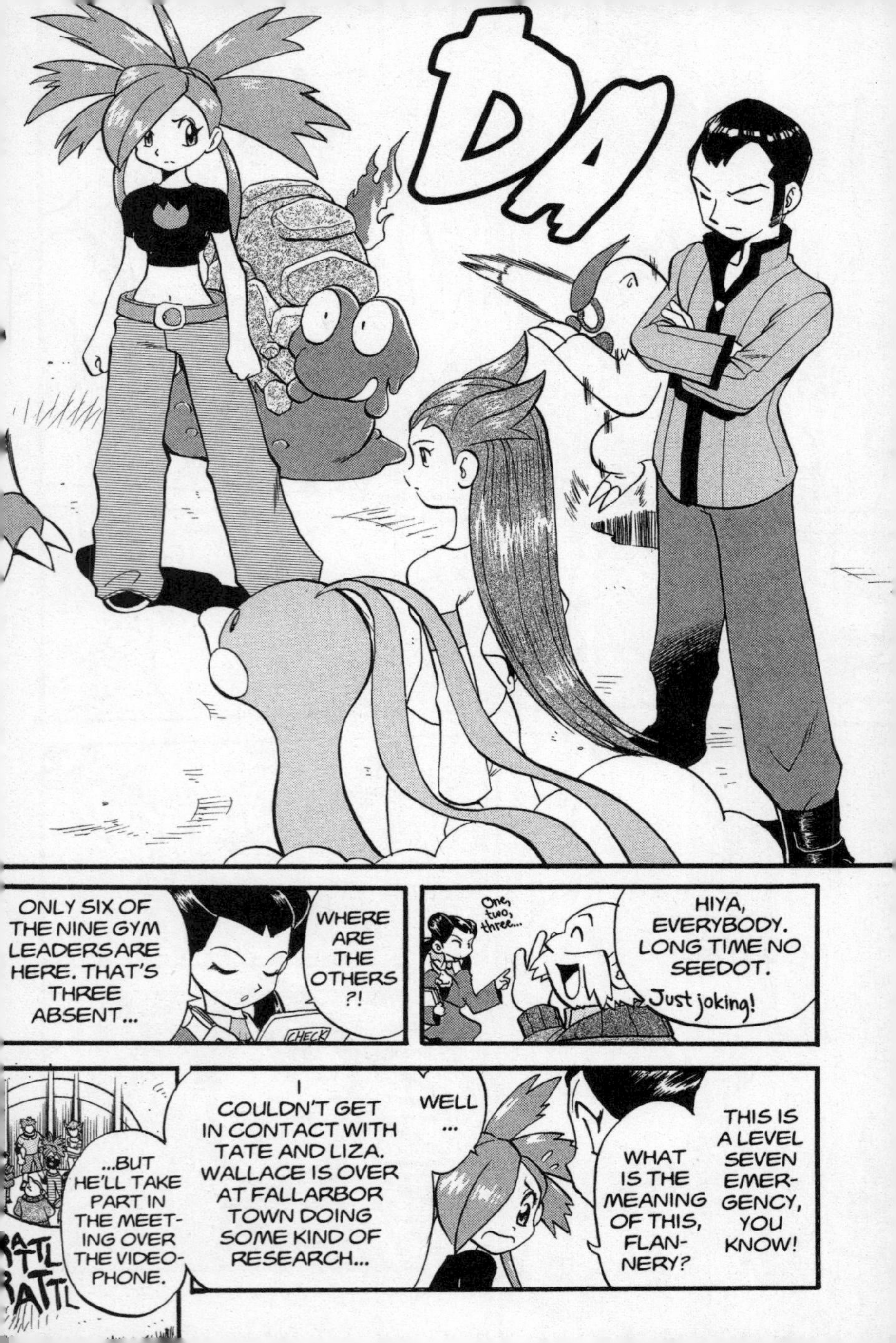
DA
HIYA, EVERYBODY. LONG TIME NO SEEDOT.
Just joking!
One, two, three...
WHERE ARE THE OTHERS?!
ONLY SIX OF THE NINE GYM LEADERS ARE HERE. THAT'S THREE ABSENT...
CHECK
THIS IS A LEVEL SEVEN EMERGENCY, YOU KNOW!
WHAT IS THE MEANING OF THIS, FLANNERY?
WELL...
I COULDN'T GET IN CONTACT WITH TATE AND LIZA. WALLACE IS OVER AT FALLARBOR TOWN DOING SOME KIND OF RESEARCH...
...BUT HE'LL TAKE PART IN THE MEETING OVER THE VIDEOPHONE.
RATTL RATTL

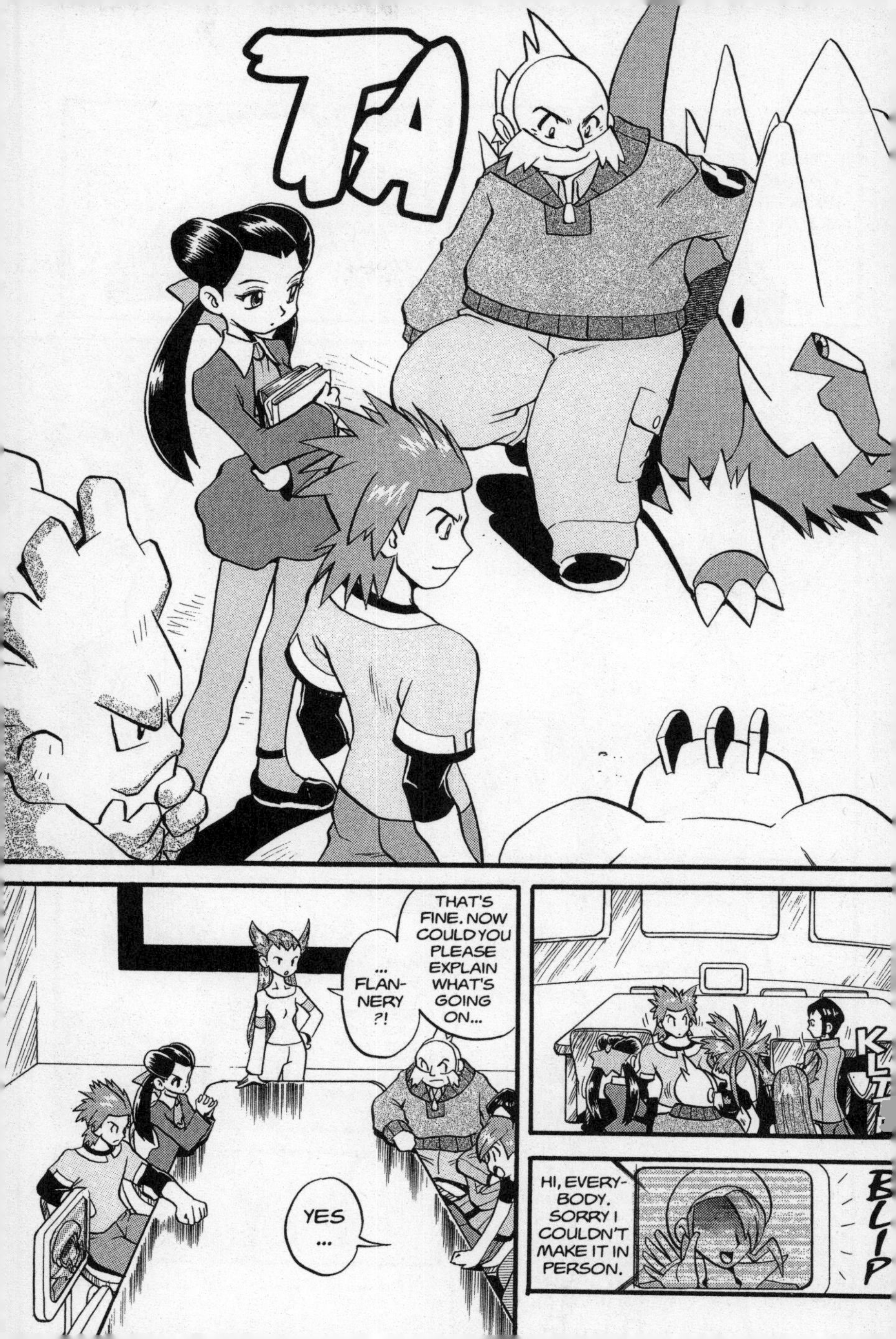
TA
KLI
HI, EVERYBODY. SORRY I COULDN'T MAKE IT IN PERSON.
BLIP
THAT'S FINE. NOW COULD YOU PLEASE EXPLAIN WHAT'S GOING ON...
... FLANNERY?!
YES ...

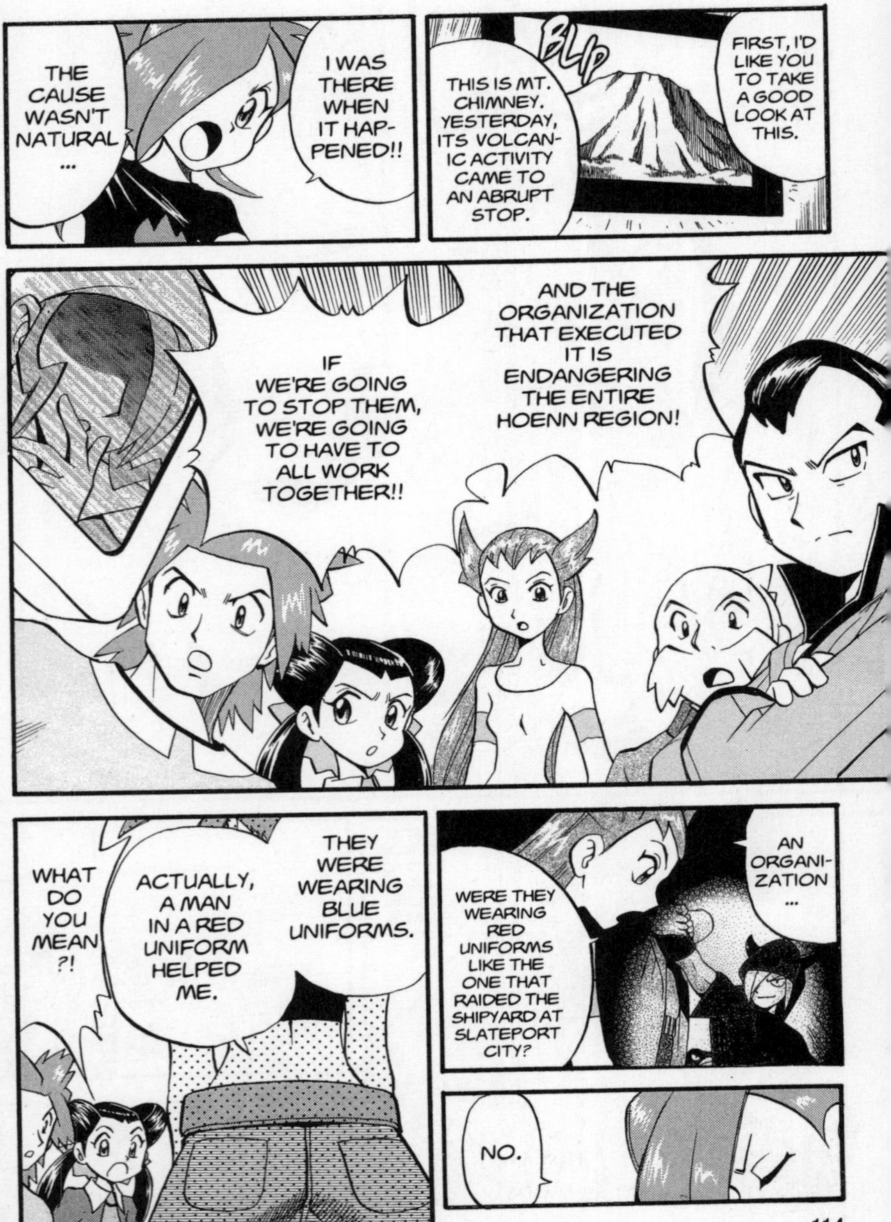
FIRST, I'D LIKE YOU TO TAKE A GOOD LOOK AT THIS.
BLIP
THIS IS MT. CHIMNEY. YESTERDAY, ITS VOLCANIC ACTIVITY CAME TO AN ABRUPT STOP.
I WAS THERE WHEN IT HAPPENED!!
THE CAUSE WASN'T NATURAL...
AND THE ORGANIZATION THAT EXECUTED IT IS ENDANGERING THE ENTIRE HOENN REGION!
IF WE'RE GOING TO STOP THEM, WE'RE GOING TO HAVE TO ALL WORK TOGETHER!!
AN ORGANIZATION...
WERE THEY WEARING RED UNIFORMS LIKE THE ONE THAT RAIDED THE SHIPYARD AT SLATEPORT CITY?
NO.
THEY WERE WEARING BLUE UNIFORMS.
ACTUALLY, A MAN IN A RED UNIFORM HELPED ME.
WHAT DO YOU MEAN?!

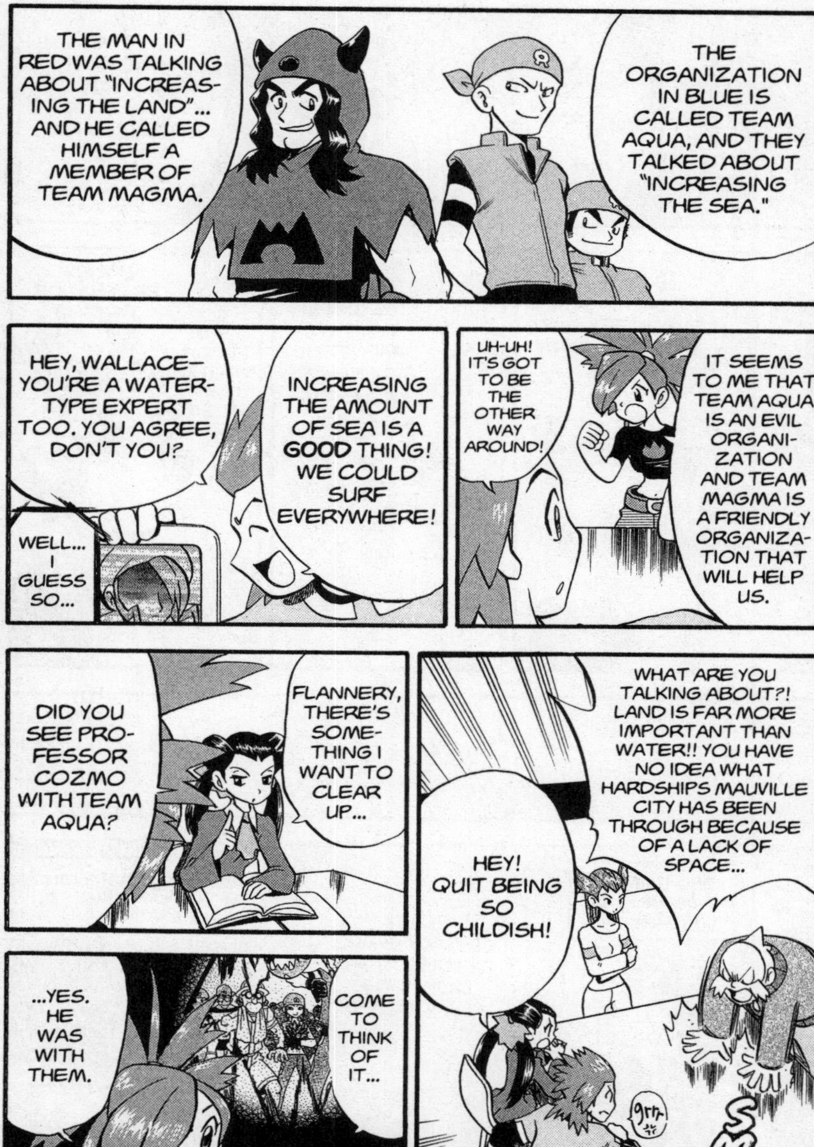
THE ORGANIZATION IN BLUE IS CALLED TEAM AQUA, AND THEY TALKED ABOUT "INCREASING THE SEA."
THE MAN IN RED WAS TALKING ABOUT "INCREASING THE LAND"... AND HE CALLED HIMSELF A MEMBER OF TEAM MAGMA.
IT SEEMS TO ME THAT TEAM AQUA IS AN EVIL ORGANIZATION AND TEAM MAGMA IS A FRIENDLY ORGANIZATION THAT WILL HELP US.
UH-UH! IT'S GOT TO BE THE OTHER WAY AROUND!
INCREASING THE AMOUNT OF SEA IS A **GOOD** THING! WE COULD SURF EVERYWHERE!
HEY, WALLACE— YOU'RE A WATER-TYPE EXPERT TOO. YOU AGREE, DON'T YOU?
WELL... I GUESS SO...
WHAT ARE YOU TALKING ABOUT?! LAND IS FAR MORE IMPORTANT THAN WATER!! YOU HAVE NO IDEA WHAT HARDSHIPS MAUVILLE CITY HAS BEEN THROUGH BECAUSE OF A LACK OF SPACE...
HEY! QUIT BEING SO CHILDISH!
grrr
SMAK
FLANNERY, THERE'S SOMETHING I WANT TO CLEAR UP...
DID YOU SEE PROFESSOR COZMO WITH TEAM AQUA?
COME TO THINK OF IT...
...YES. HE WAS WITH THEM.

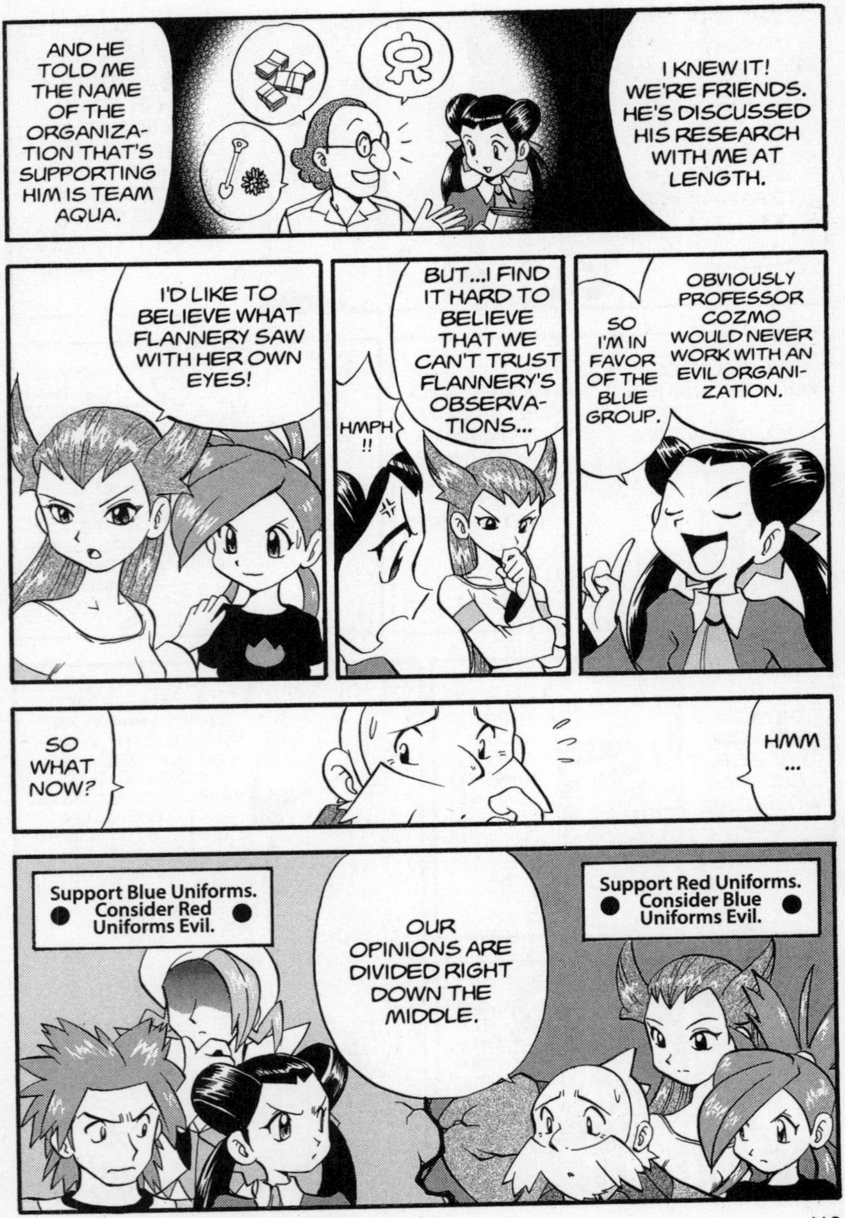
I KNEW IT! WE'RE FRIENDS. HE'S DISCUSSED HIS RESEARCH WITH ME AT LENGTH.
AND HE TOLD ME THE NAME OF THE ORGANIZATION THAT'S SUPPORTING HIM IS TEAM AQUA.
OBVIOUSLY PROFESSOR COZMO WOULD NEVER WORK WITH AN EVIL ORGANIZATION.
SO I'M IN FAVOR OF THE BLUE GROUP.
BUT...I FIND IT HARD TO BELIEVE THAT WE CAN'T TRUST FLANNERY'S OBSERVATIONS...
HMPH !!
I'D LIKE TO BELIEVE WHAT FLANNERY SAW WITH HER OWN EYES!
HMM ...
SO WHAT NOW?
Support Red Uniforms. Consider Blue Uniforms Evil.
Support Blue Uniforms. Consider Red Uniforms Evil.
OUR OPINIONS ARE DIVIDED RIGHT DOWN THE MIDDLE.

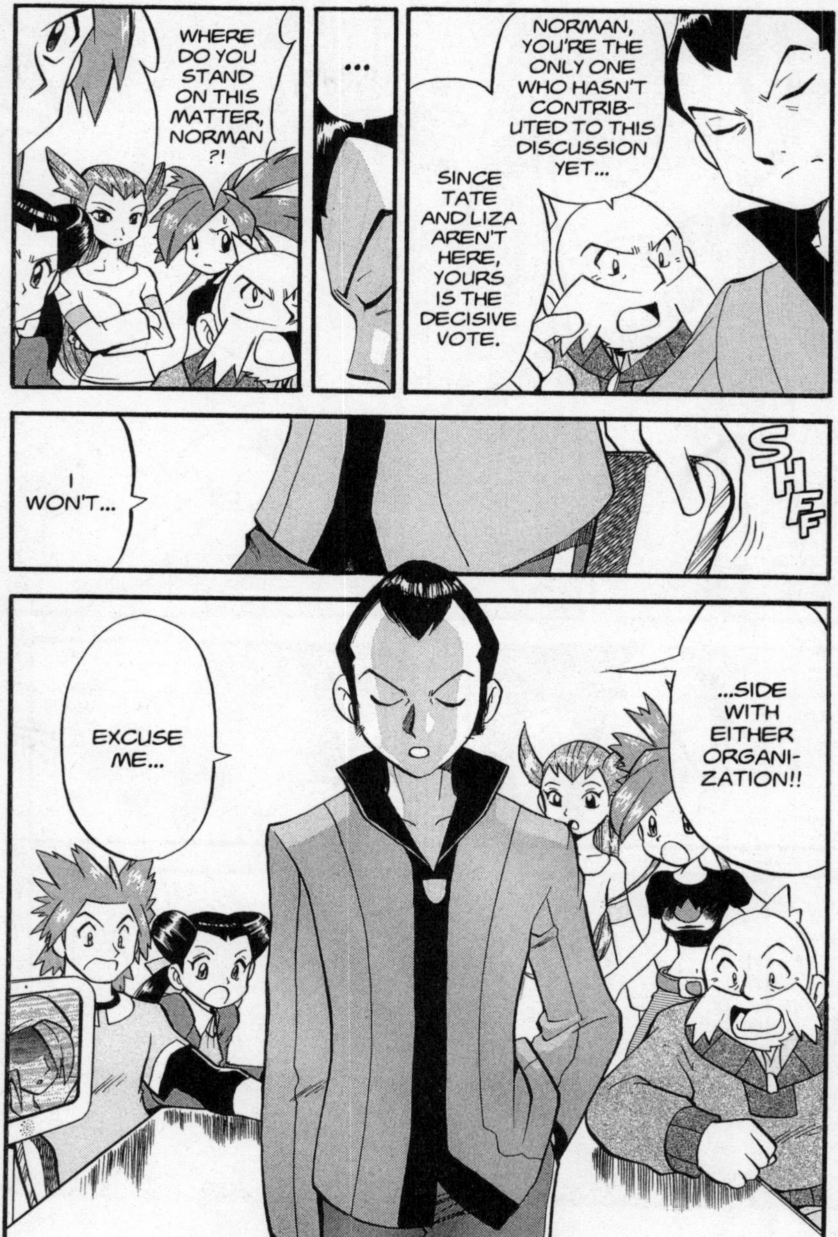
NORMAN, YOU'RE THE ONLY ONE WHO HASN'T CONTRIB-UTED TO THIS DISCUSSION YET...
SINCE TATE AND LIZA AREN'T HERE, YOURS IS THE DECISIVE VOTE.
...
WHERE DO YOU STAND ON THIS MATTER, NORMAN?!
SHFF
I WON'T...
...SIDE WITH EITHER ORGANI-ZATION!!
EXCUSE ME...

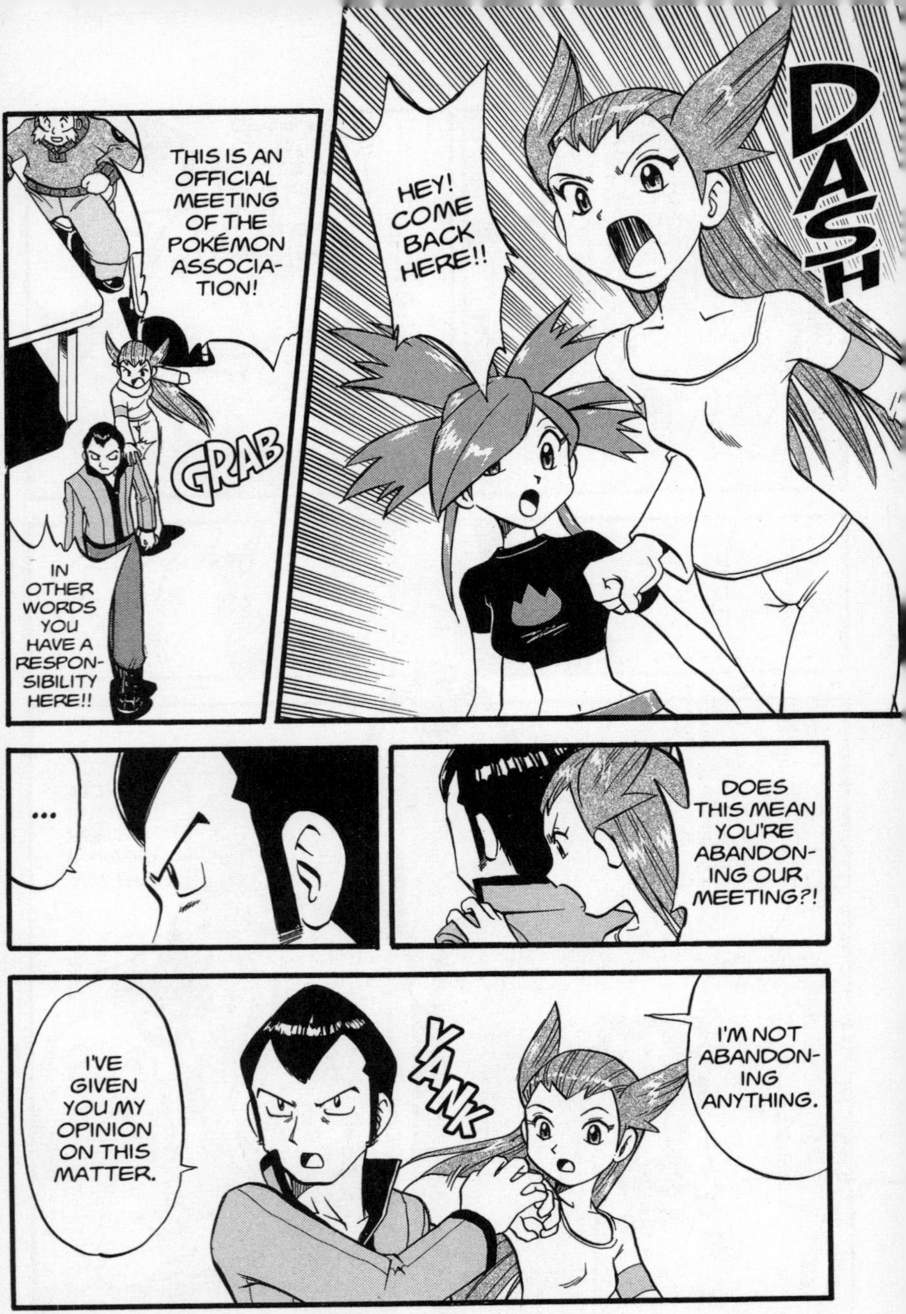
DASH
HEY! COME BACK HERE!!
THIS IS AN OFFICIAL MEETING OF THE POKÉMON ASSOCIA-TION!
GRAB
IN OTHER WORDS YOU HAVE A RESPON-SIBILITY HERE!!
DOES THIS MEAN YOU'RE ABANDON-ING OUR MEETING?!
...
I'M NOT ABANDON-ING ANYTHING.
YANK
I'VE GIVEN YOU MY OPINION ON THIS MATTER.

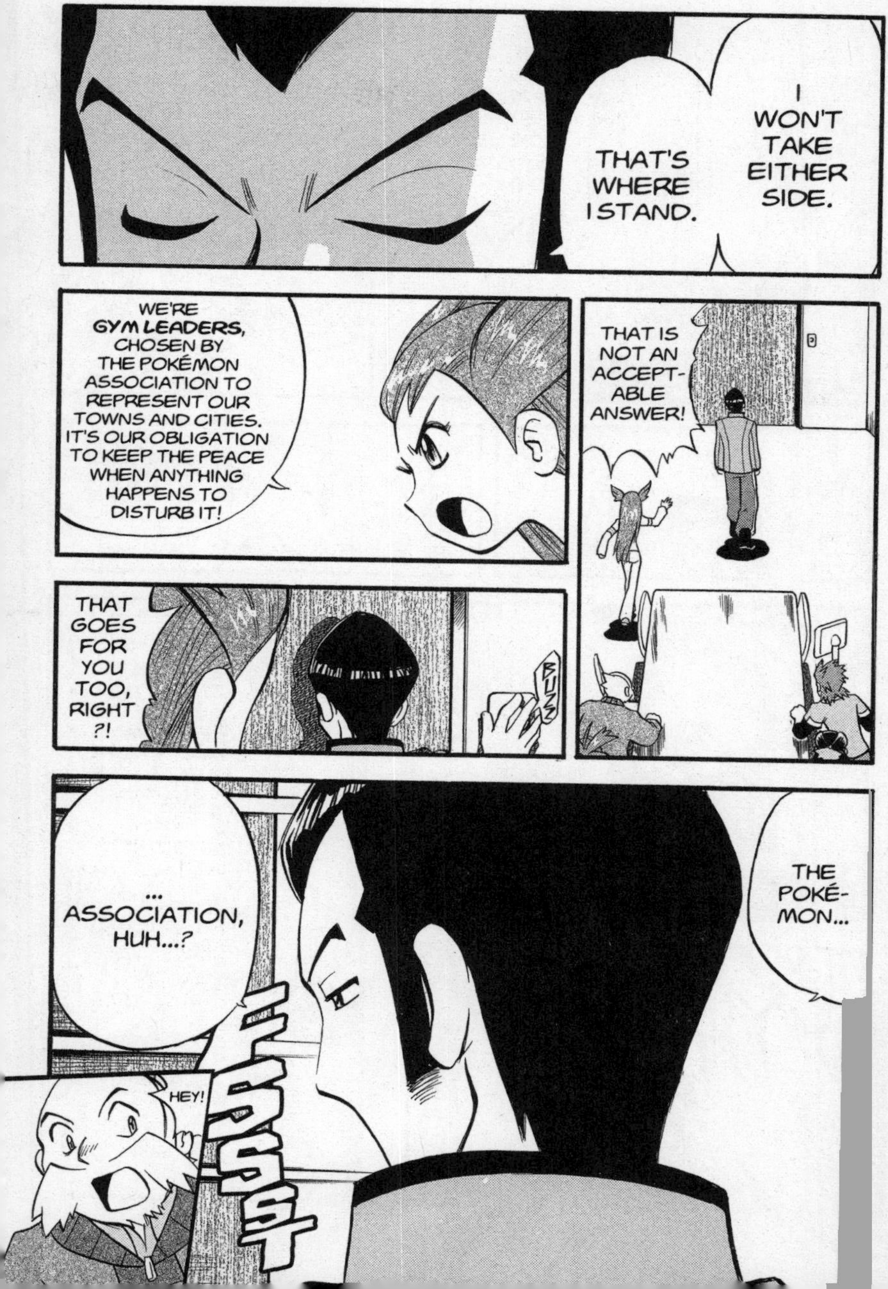

I WON'T TAKE EITHER SIDE.
THAT'S WHERE I STAND.
THAT IS NOT AN ACCEPTABLE ANSWER!
WE'RE **GYM LEADERS**, CHOSEN BY THE POKÉMON ASSOCIATION TO REPRESENT OUR TOWNS AND CITIES. IT'S OUR OBLIGATION TO KEEP THE PEACE WHEN ANYTHING HAPPENS TO DISTURB IT!
BUZZ
THAT GOES FOR YOU TOO, RIGHT?!
THE POKÉMON...
...ASSOCIATION, HUH...?
FSSST
HEY!

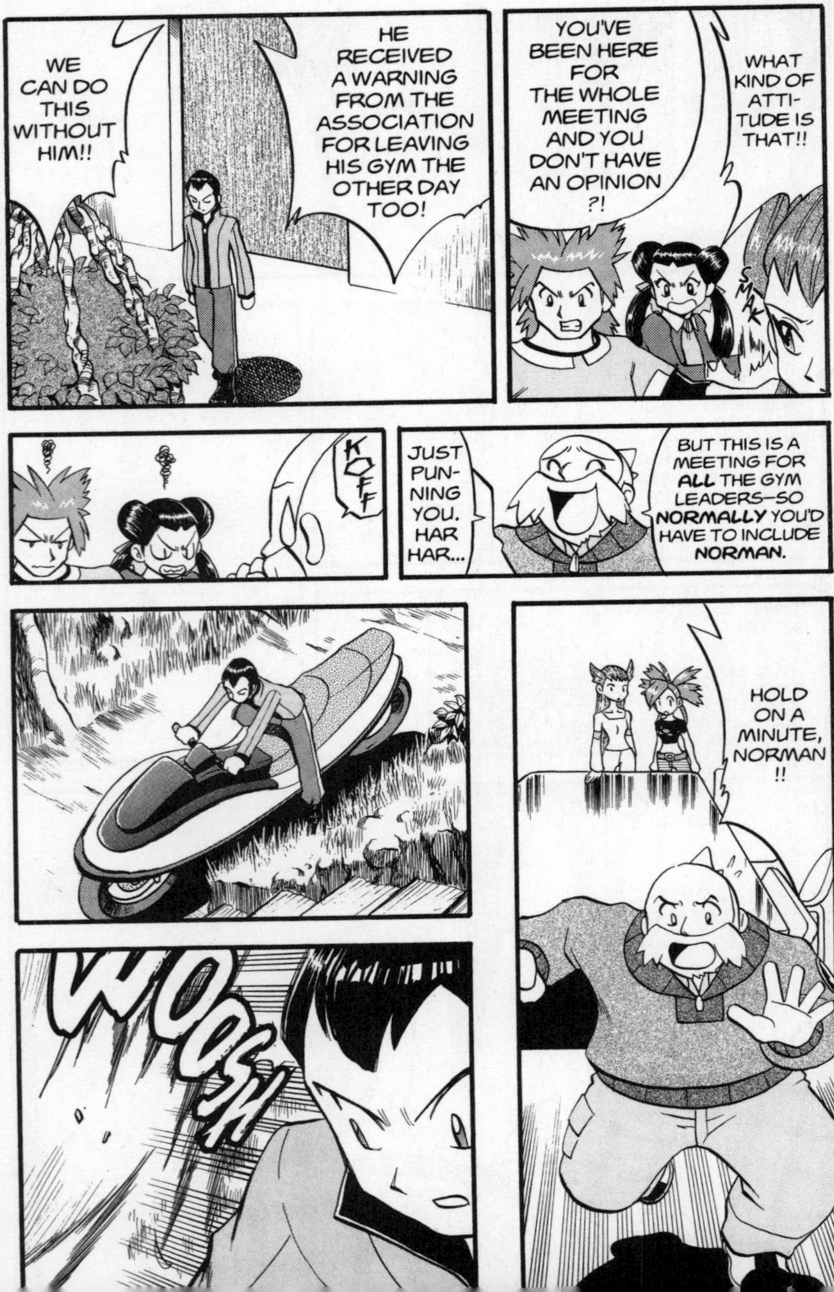
WHAT KIND OF ATTI-TUDE IS THAT!!
YOU'VE BEEN HERE FOR THE WHOLE MEETING AND YOU DON'T HAVE AN OPINION ?!
SMAK
HE RECEIVED A WARNING FROM THE ASSOCIATION FOR LEAVING HIS GYM THE OTHER DAY TOO!
WE CAN DO THIS WITHOUT HIM!!
BUT THIS IS A MEETING FOR **ALL** THE GYM LEADERS—SO **NORMALLY** YOU'D HAVE TO INCLUDE **NORMAN.**
JUST PUN-NING YOU. HAR HAR...
KOFF
HOLD ON A MINUTE, NORMAN !!
WOOSH

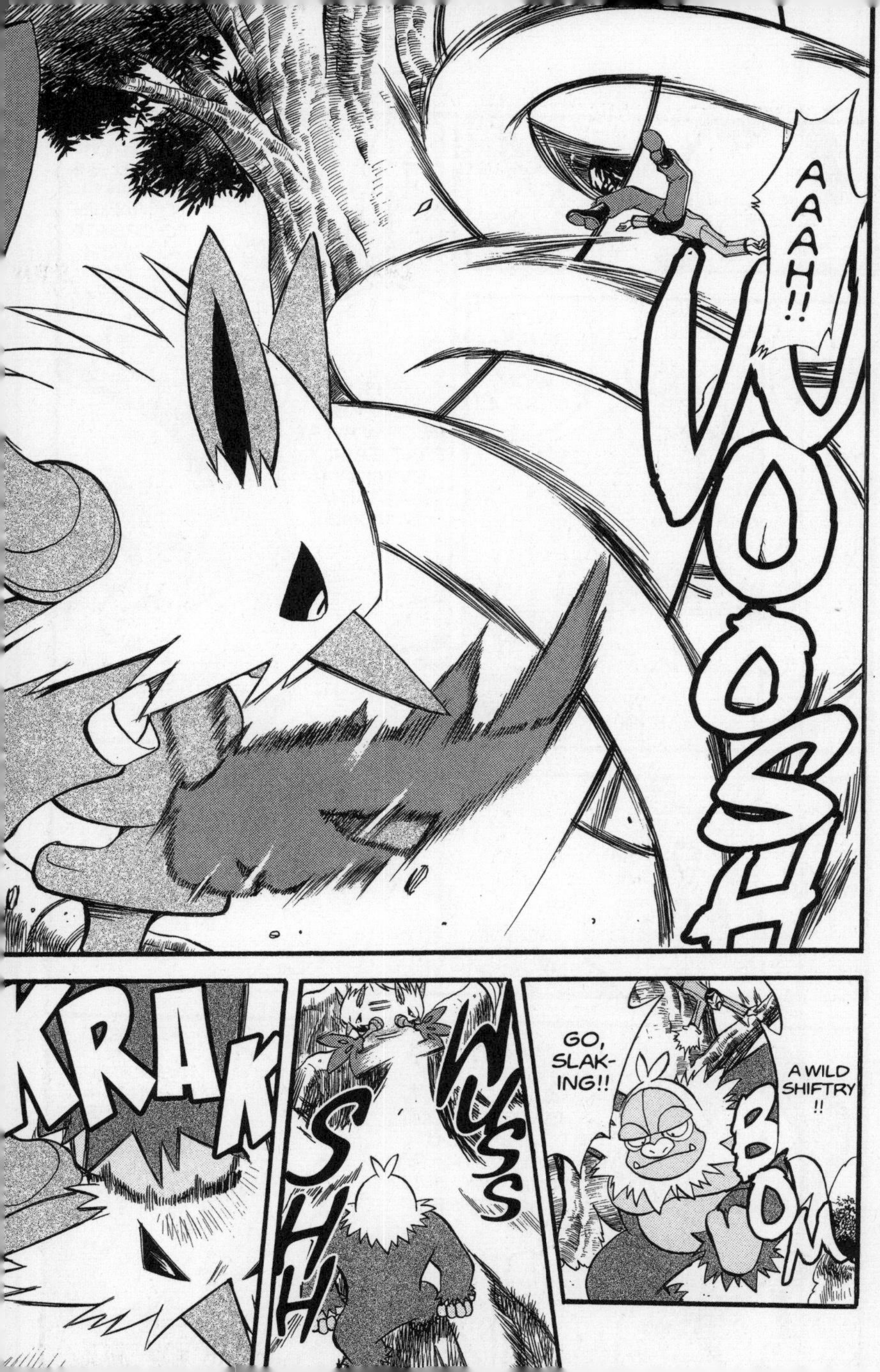
AAAAH!!
WOOOSH
A WILD SHIFTRY!!
GO, SLAK-ING!!
BOM
WHUSS
SHH
KRAK

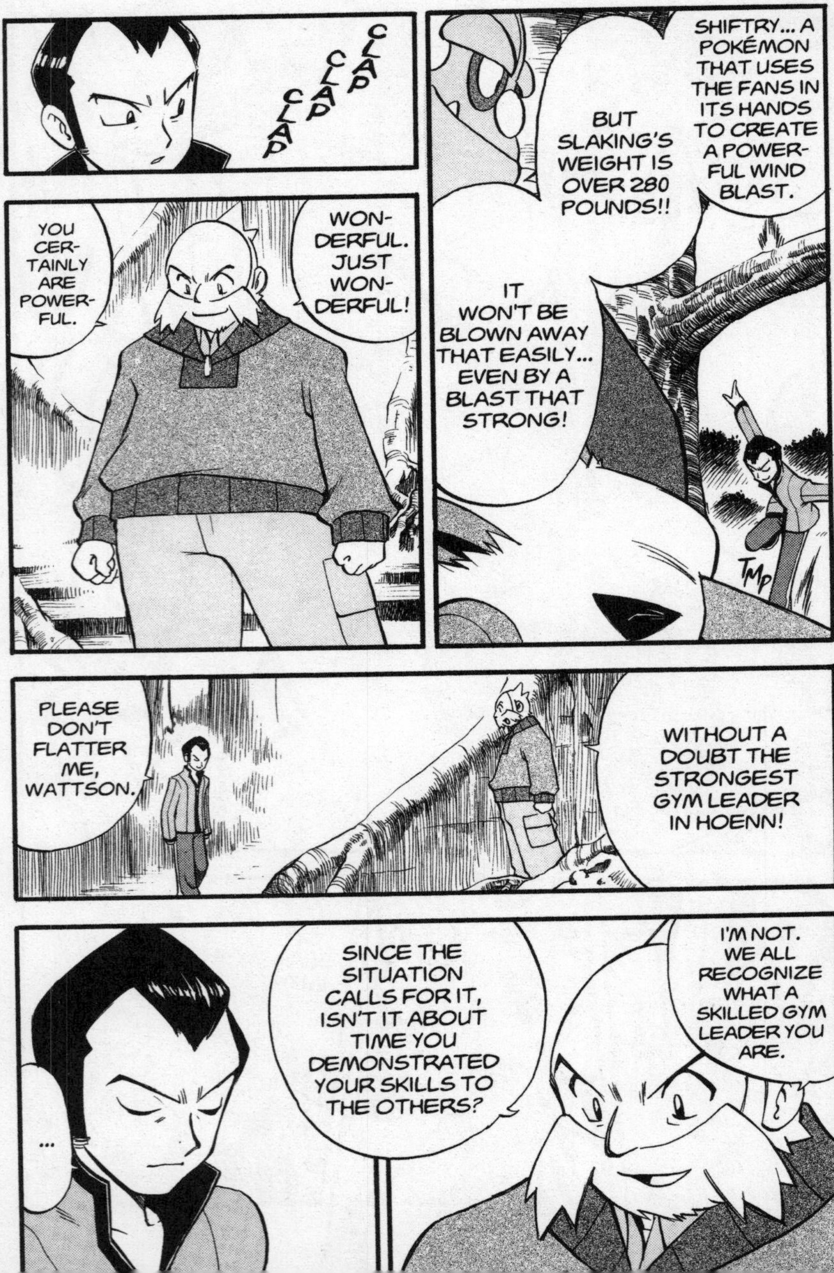
SHIFTRY... A POKÉMON THAT USES THE FANS IN ITS HANDS TO CREATE A POWERFUL WIND BLAST.
BUT SLAKING'S WEIGHT IS OVER 280 POUNDS!!
IT WON'T BE BLOWN AWAY THAT EASILY... EVEN BY A BLAST THAT STRONG!
TMP
CLAP CLAP CLAP
WONDERFUL. JUST WONDERFUL!
YOU CERTAINLY ARE POWERFUL.
WITHOUT A DOUBT THE STRONGEST GYM LEADER IN HOENN!
PLEASE DON'T FLATTER ME, WATTSON.
I'M NOT. WE ALL RECOGNIZE WHAT A SKILLED GYM LEADER YOU ARE.
SINCE THE SITUATION CALLS FOR IT, ISN'T IT ABOUT TIME YOU DEMONSTRATED YOUR SKILLS TO THE OTHERS?
...

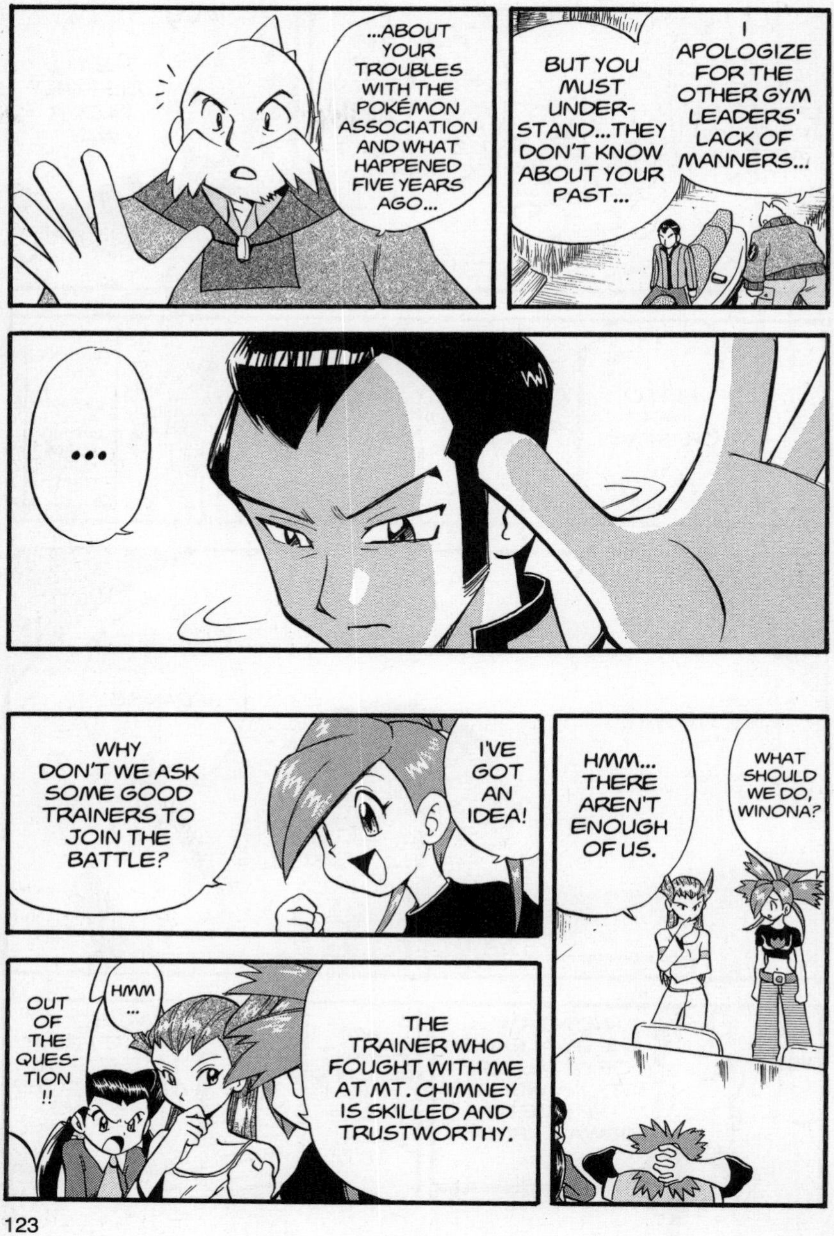
I APOLOGIZE FOR THE OTHER GYM LEADERS' LACK OF MANNERS...
BUT YOU MUST UNDER-STAND...THEY DON'T KNOW ABOUT YOUR PAST...
...ABOUT YOUR TROUBLES WITH THE POKÉMON ASSOCIATION AND WHAT HAPPENED FIVE YEARS AGO...
...
WHAT SHOULD WE DO, WINONA?
HMM... THERE AREN'T ENOUGH OF US.
I'VE GOT AN IDEA!
WHY DON'T WE ASK SOME GOOD TRAINERS TO JOIN THE BATTLE?
THE TRAINER WHO FOUGHT WITH ME AT MT. CHIMNEY IS SKILLED AND TRUSTWORTHY.
HMM ...
OUT OF THE QUES-TION !!

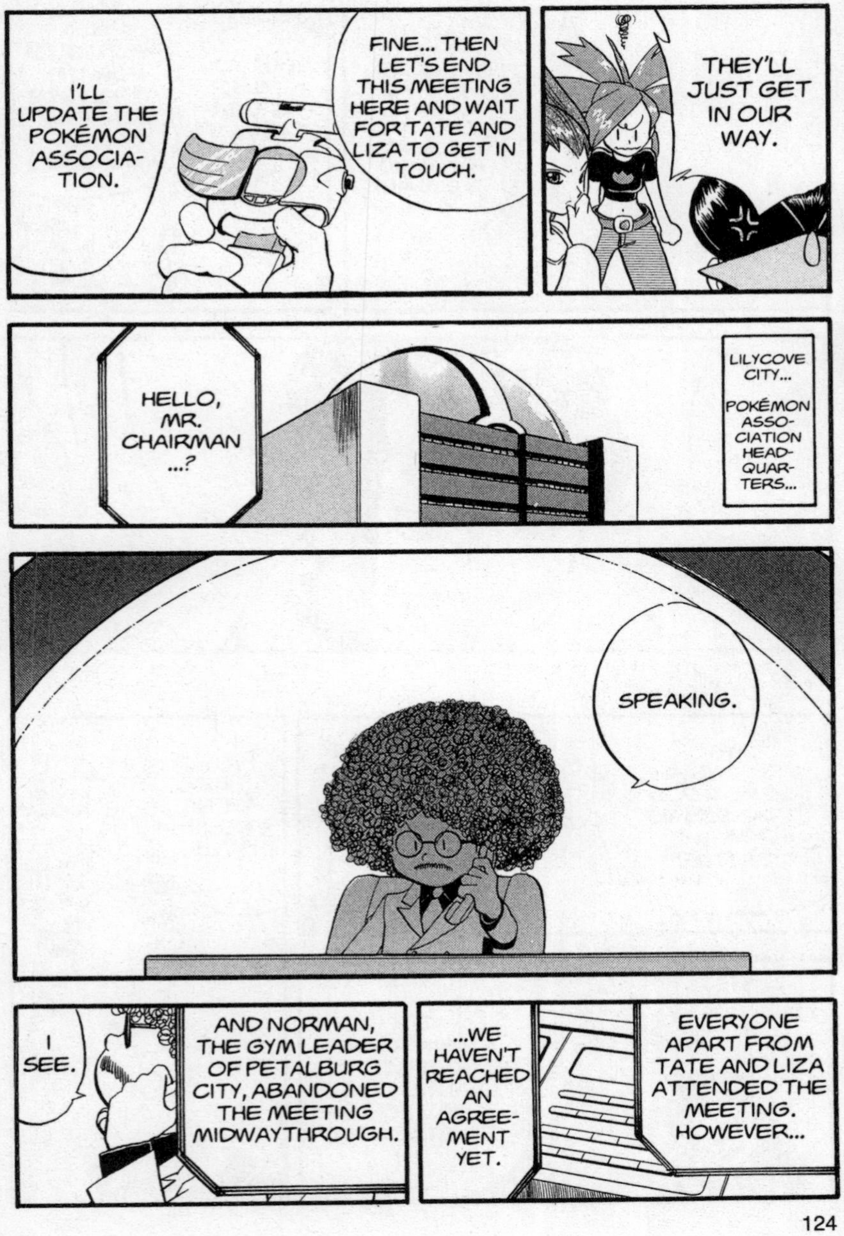
THEY'LL JUST GET IN OUR WAY.
FINE... THEN LET'S END THIS MEETING HERE AND WAIT FOR TATE AND LIZA TO GET IN TOUCH.
I'LL UPDATE THE POKÉMON ASSOCIATION.
LILYCOVE CITY... POKÉMON ASSOCIATION HEADQUARTERS...
HELLO, MR. CHAIRMAN ...?
SPEAKING.
EVERYONE APART FROM TATE AND LIZA ATTENDED THE MEETING. HOWEVER...
...WE HAVEN'T REACHED AN AGREEMENT YET.
AND NORMAN, THE GYM LEADER OF PETALBURG CITY, ABANDONED THE MEETING MIDWAYTHROUGH.
I SEE.

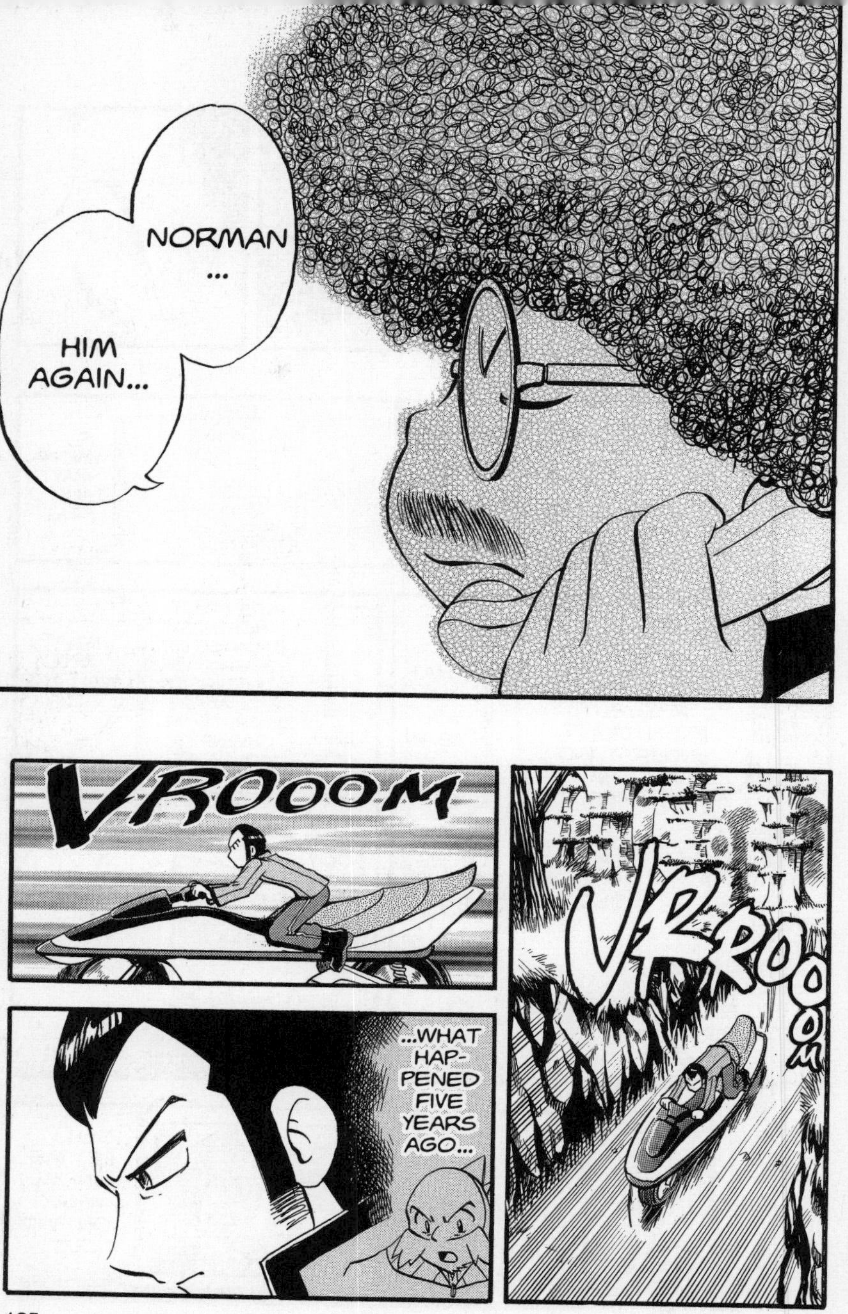
NORMAN ...
HIM AGAIN...
VRROOOOM
VROOOM
...WHAT HAP-PENED FIVE YEARS AGO...

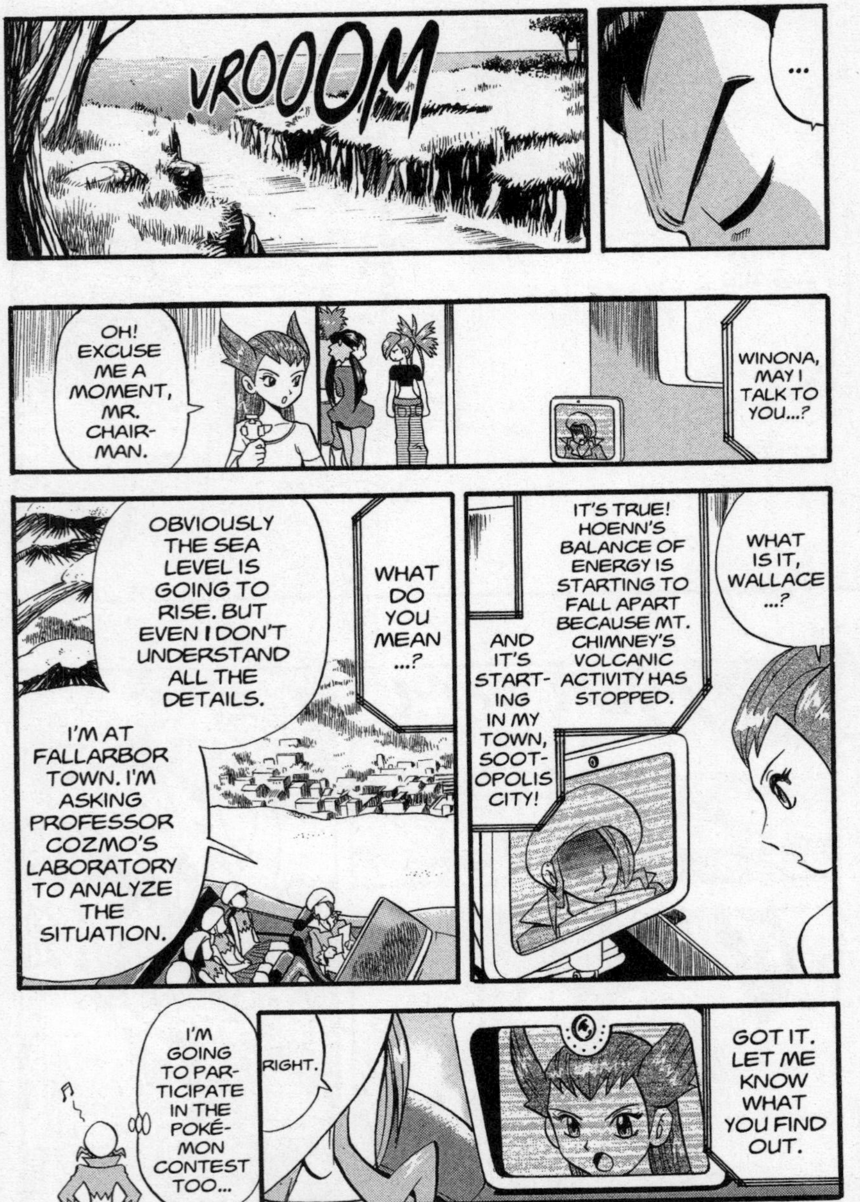
...
VROOOM
WINONA, MAY I TALK TO YOU...?
OH! EXCUSE ME A MOMENT, MR. CHAIRMAN.
WHAT IS IT, WALLACE...?
IT'S TRUE! HOENN'S BALANCE OF ENERGY IS STARTING TO FALL APART BECAUSE MT. CHIMNEY'S VOLCANIC ACTIVITY HAS STOPPED.
AND IT'S STARTING IN MY TOWN, SOOTOPOLIS CITY!
WHAT DO YOU MEAN...?
OBVIOUSLY THE SEA LEVEL IS GOING TO RISE. BUT EVEN I DON'T UNDERSTAND ALL THE DETAILS.
I'M AT FALLARBOR TOWN. I'M ASKING PROFESSOR COZMO'S LABORATORY TO ANALYZE THE SITUATION.
GOT IT. LET ME KNOW WHAT YOU FIND OUT.
RIGHT.
I'M GOING TO PARTICIPATE IN THE POKÉMON CONTEST TOO...

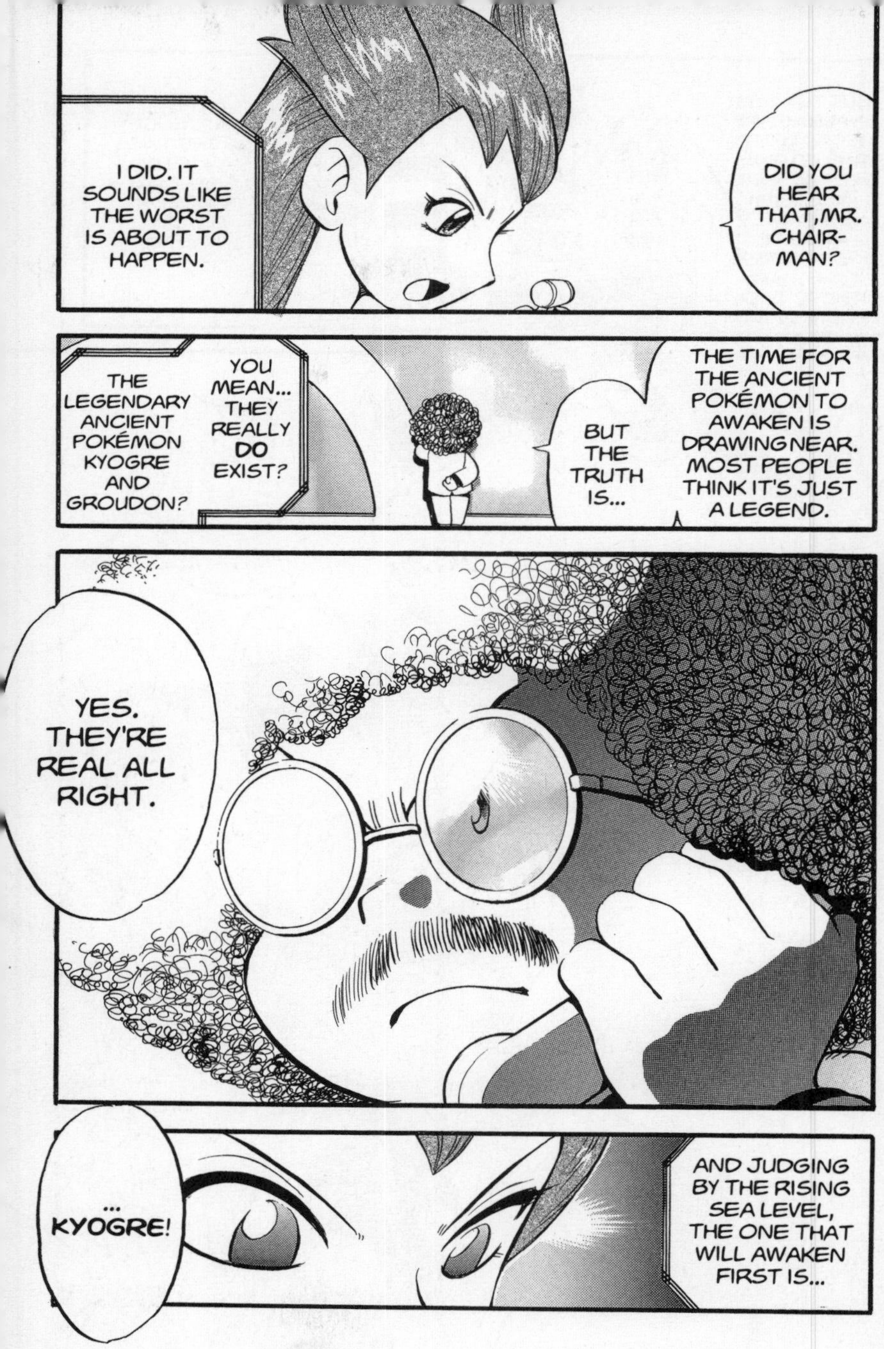
DID YOU HEAR THAT, MR. CHAIRMAN?
I DID. IT SOUNDS LIKE THE WORST IS ABOUT TO HAPPEN.
THE TIME FOR THE ANCIENT POKÉMON TO AWAKEN IS DRAWING NEAR. MOST PEOPLE THINK IT'S JUST A LEGEND.
BUT THE TRUTH IS...
YOU MEAN... THEY REALLY DO EXIST?
THE LEGENDARY ANCIENT POKÉMON KYOGRE AND GROUDON?
YES. THEY'RE REAL ALL RIGHT.
AND JUDGING BY THE RISING SEA LEVEL, THE ONE THAT WILL AWAKEN FIRST IS...
...KYOGRE!

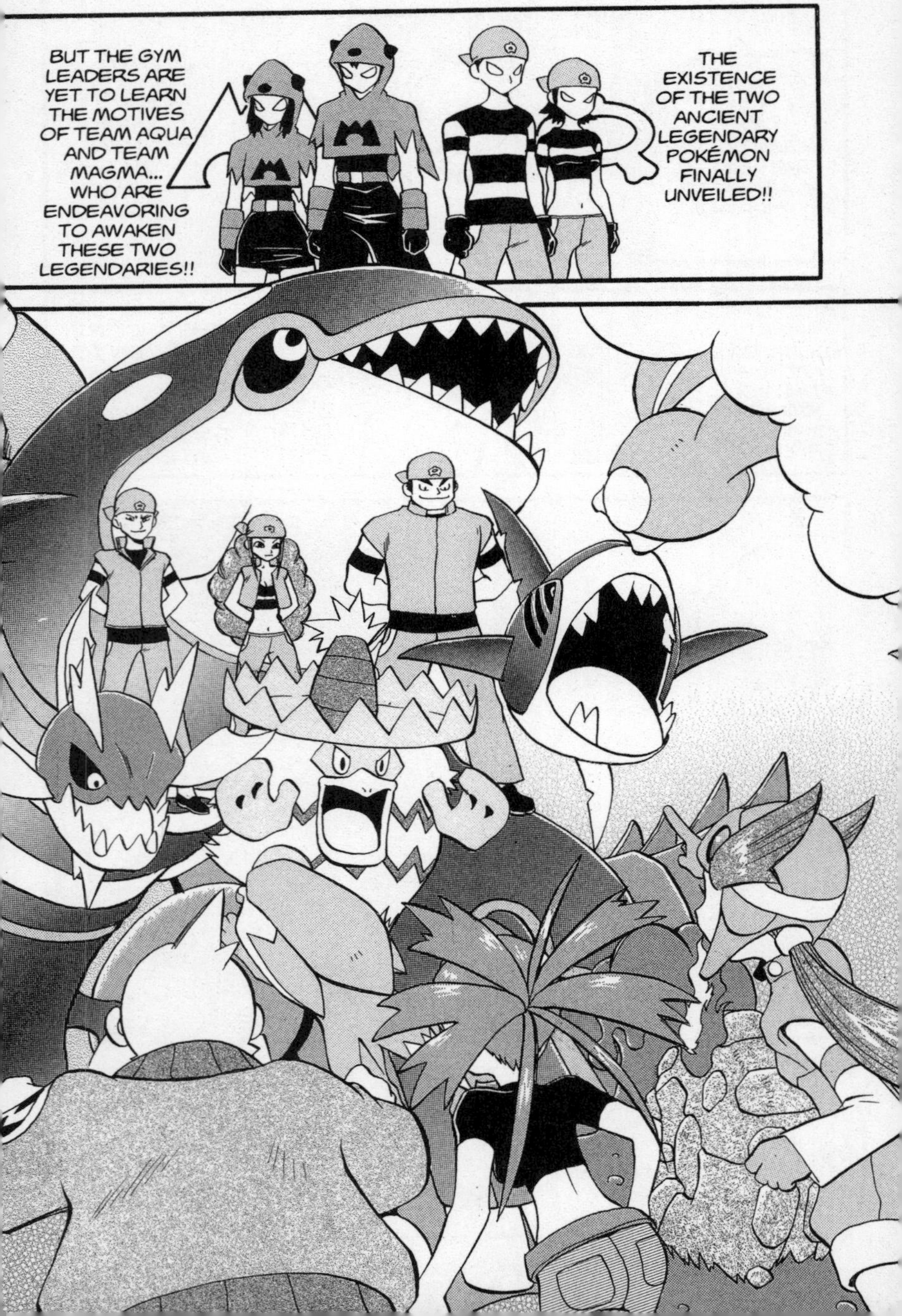
THE EXISTENCE OF THE TWO ANCIENT LEGENDARY POKÉMON FINALLY UNVEILED!!
BUT THE GYM LEADERS ARE YET TO LEARN THE MOTIVES OF TEAM AQUA AND TEAM MAGMA... WHO ARE ENDEAVORING TO AWAKEN THESE TWO LEGENDARIES!!

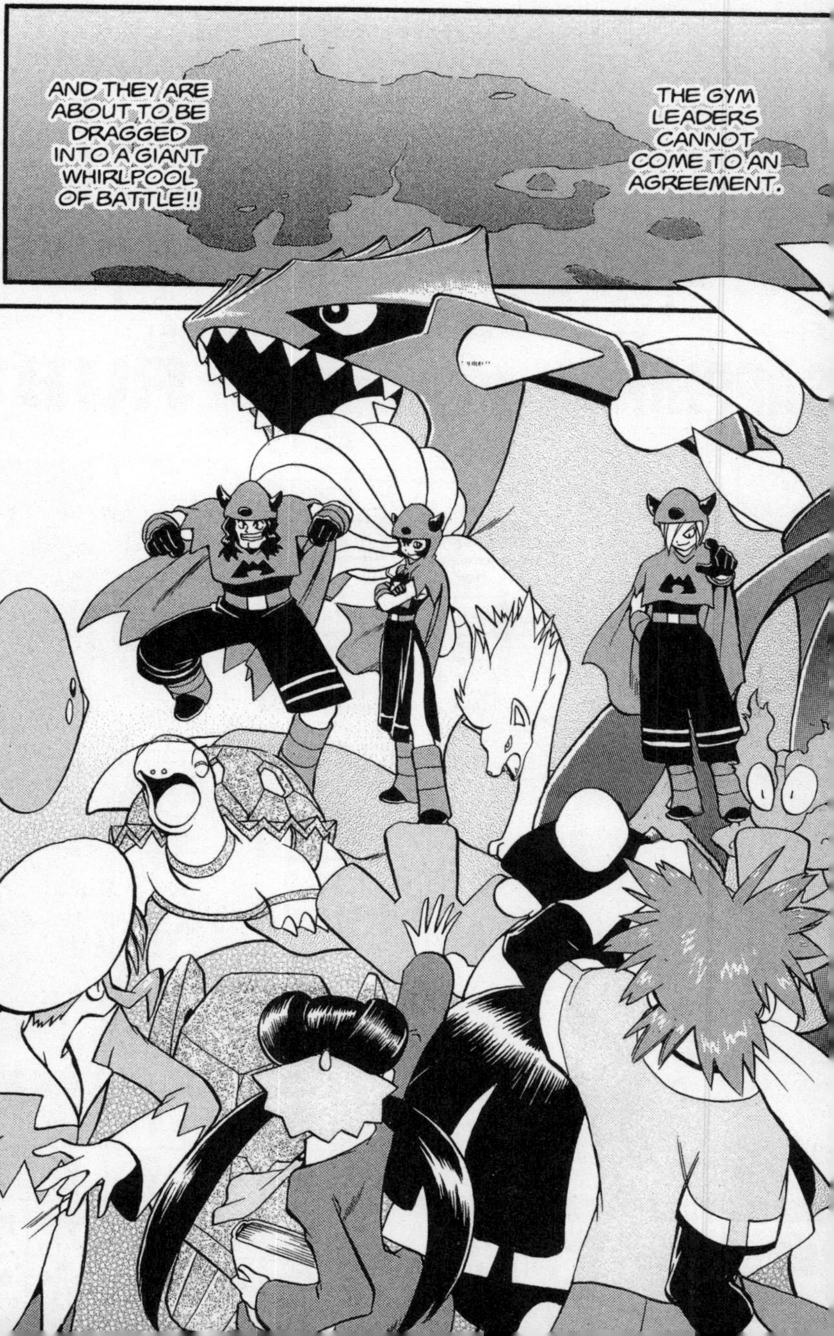
THE GYM LEADERS CANNOT COME TO AN AGREEMENT.
AND THEY ARE ABOUT TO BE DRAGGED INTO A GIANT WHIRLPOOL OF BATTLE!!

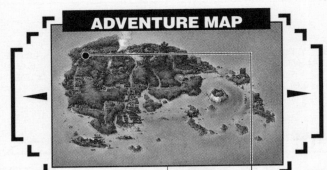

ADVENTURE MAP

SAPPHIRE

Nickname	Pokémon	Level
CHIC	Combusken ♀	Lv33
RONO	Lairon ♂	Lv41
LORRY	Wailord ♂	Lv46
PHADO	Donphan ♂	Lv44
TROPPY	Tropius ♂	Lv43

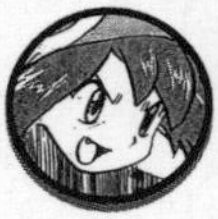

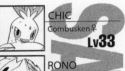

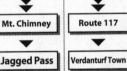

Mt. Chimney
▼
Jagged Pass
▼

RUBY

Route 117
▼
Verdanturf Town
▼
Rusturf Tunnel
▼
Rustboro City
▼
Route 115
▼
Route 114

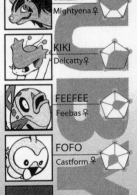

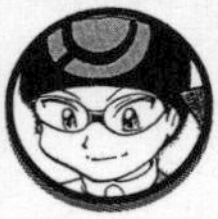

Nickname	Pokémon
MUMU	Marshtomp ♂
NANA	Mightyena ♀
KIKI	Delcatty ♀
FEEFEE	Feebas ♀
FOFO	Castform ♀

Stone Badge	Knuckle Badge	Dynamo Badge	Heat Badge
Balance Badge	Feather Badge	Mind Badge	Rain Badge

	Cool	Beauty	Cute	Smart	Tough
Normal					
Super					
Hyper					
Master					

● Chapter 223 ●

I More Than Like You, Luvdisc I

POKÉMON ADVENTURES RUBY & SAPPHIRE

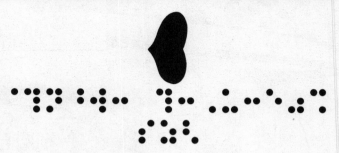

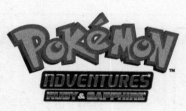

The Fourth Chapter

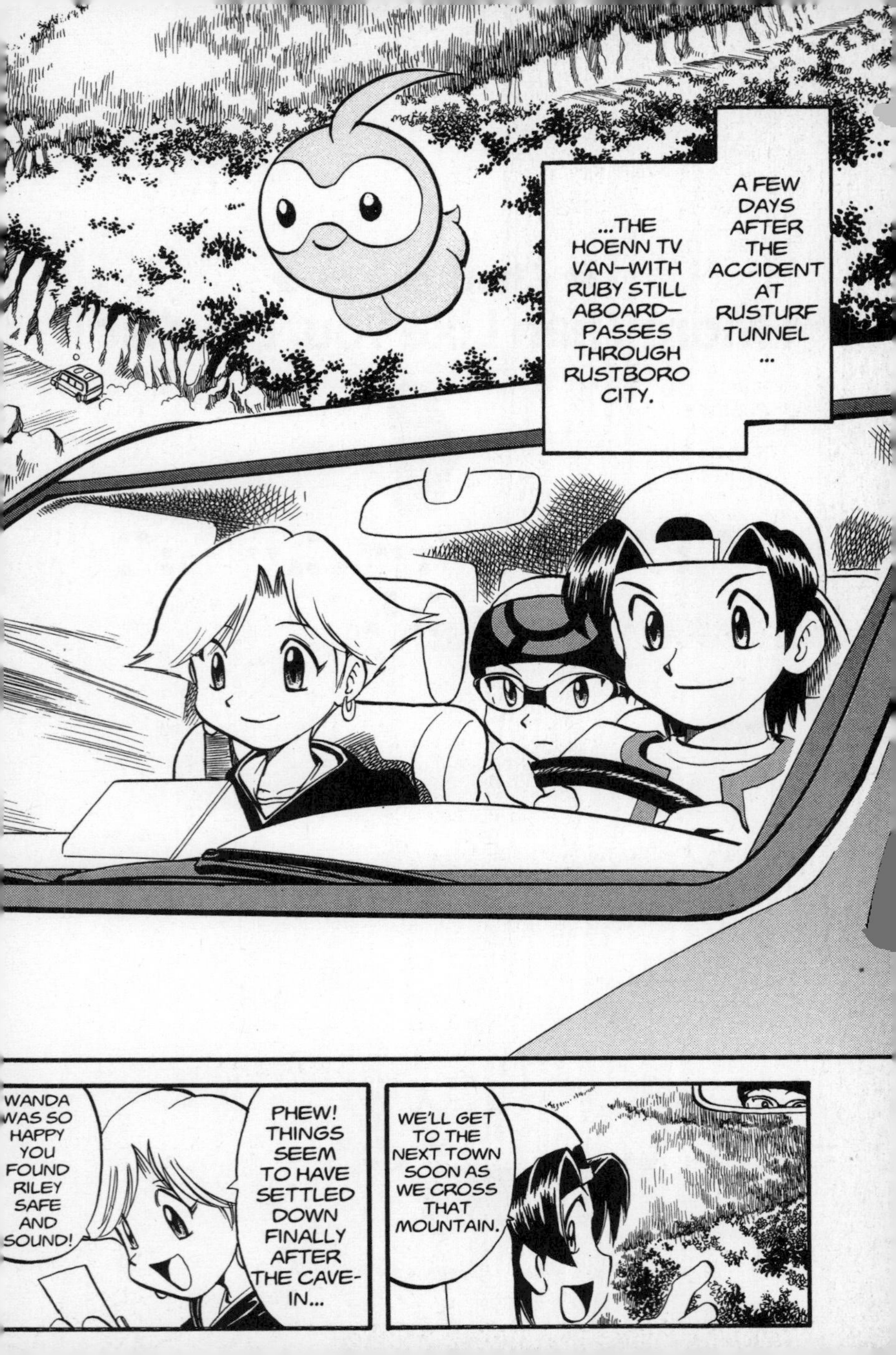
A FEW DAYS AFTER THE ACCIDENT AT RUSTURF TUNNEL ...
...THE HOENN TV VAN—WITH RUBY STILL ABOARD—PASSES THROUGH RUSTBORO CITY.
WE'LL GET TO THE NEXT TOWN SOON AS WE CROSS THAT MOUNTAIN.
PHEW! THINGS SEEM TO HAVE SETTLED DOWN FINALLY AFTER THE CAVE-IN...
WANDA WAS SO HAPPY YOU FOUND RILEY SAFE AND SOUND!

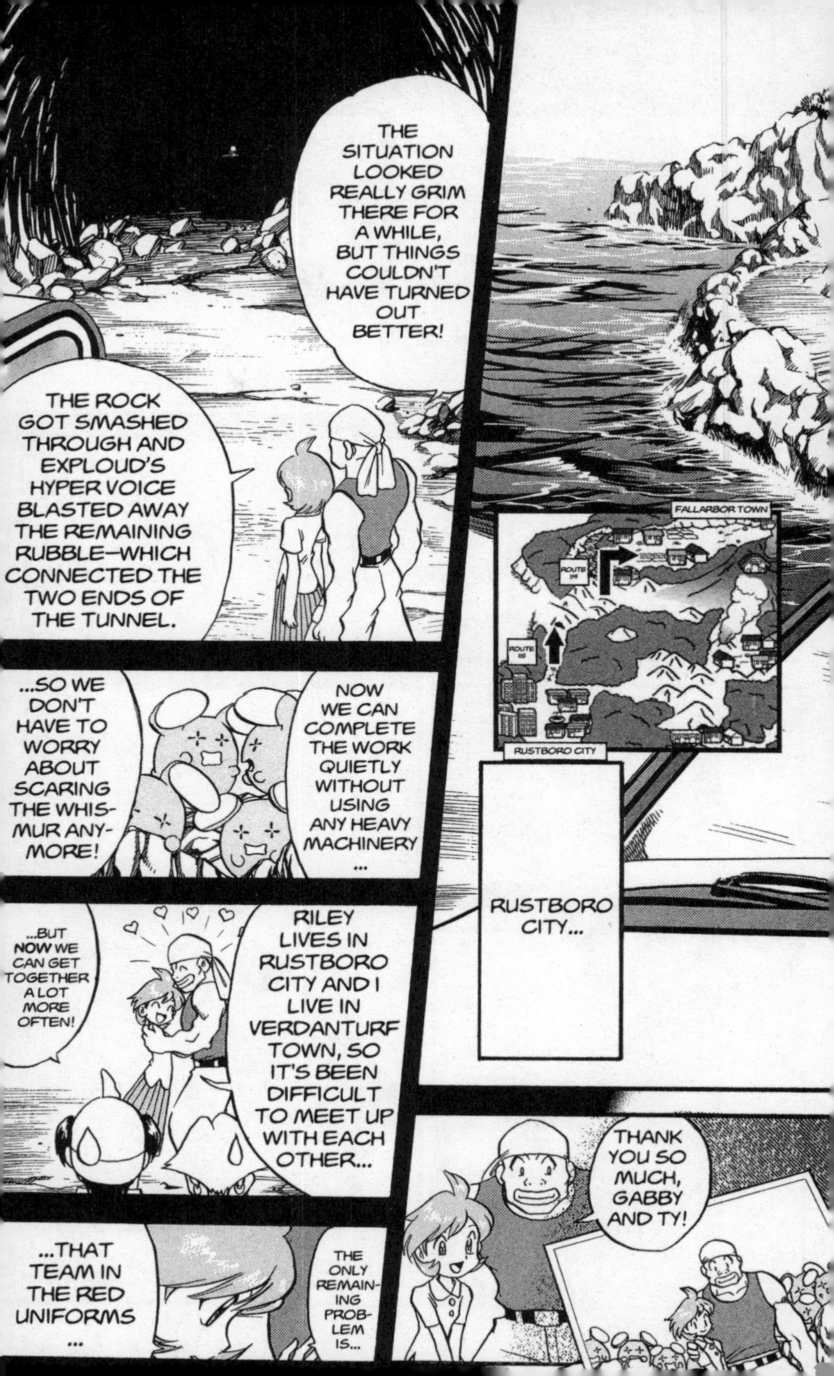
FALLARBOR TOWN
ROUTE 114
ROUTE 116
RUSTBORO CITY
RUSTBORO CITY...
THANK YOU SO MUCH, GABBY AND TY!
THE SITUATION LOOKED REALLY GRIM THERE FOR A WHILE, BUT THINGS COULDN'T HAVE TURNED OUT BETTER!
THE ROCK GOT SMASHED THROUGH AND EXPLOUD'S HYPER VOICE BLASTED AWAY THE REMAINING RUBBLE—WHICH CONNECTED THE TWO ENDS OF THE TUNNEL.
NOW WE CAN COMPLETE THE WORK QUIETLY WITHOUT USING ANY HEAVY MACHINERY ...
...SO WE DON'T HAVE TO WORRY ABOUT SCARING THE WHIS-MUR ANY-MORE!
RILEY LIVES IN RUSTBORO CITY AND I LIVE IN VERDANTURF TOWN, SO IT'S BEEN DIFFICULT TO MEET UP WITH EACH OTHER...
...BUT NOW WE CAN GET TOGETHER A LOT MORE OFTEN!
THE ONLY REMAIN-ING PROB-LEM IS...
...THAT TEAM IN THE RED UNIFORMS ...

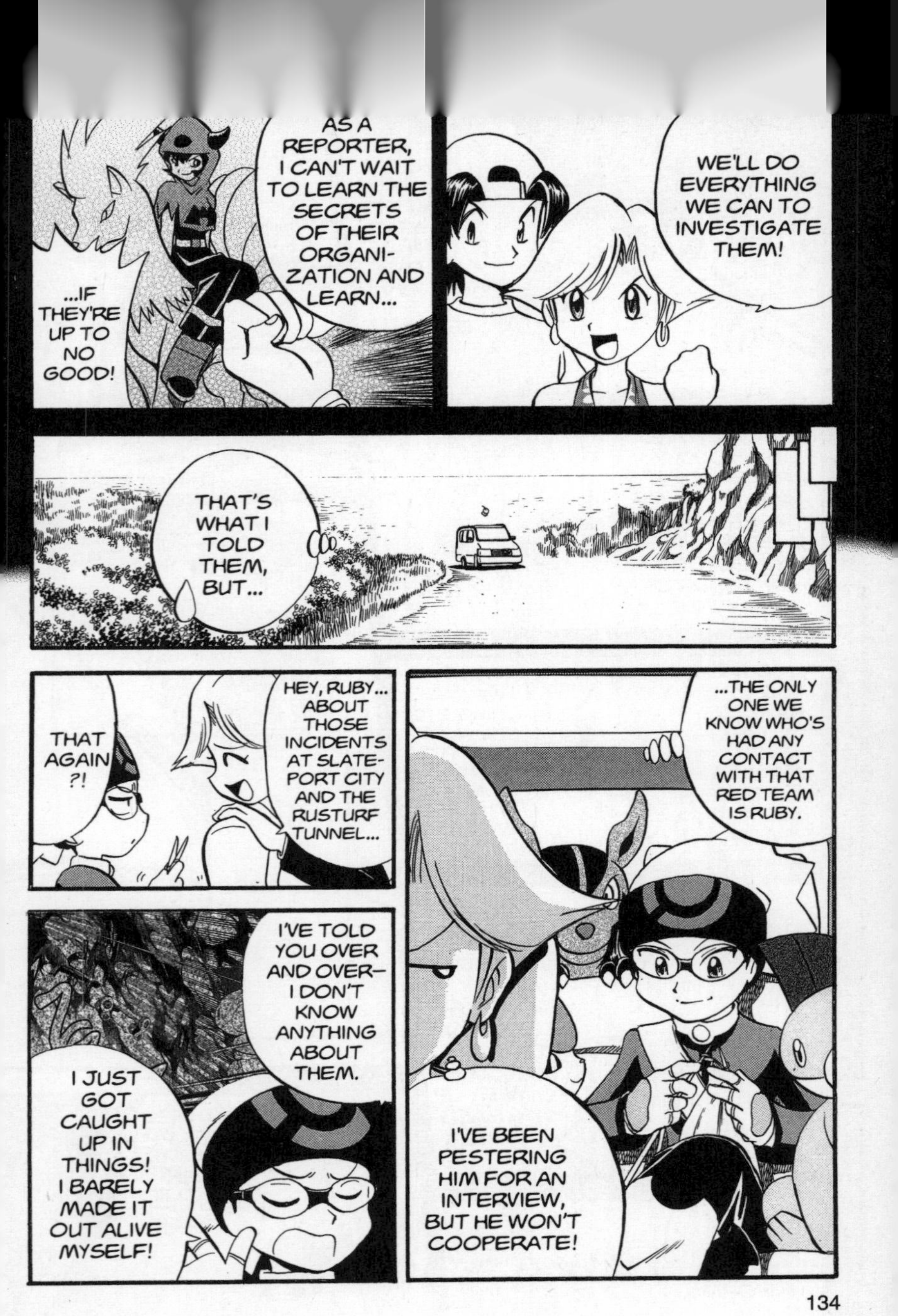
WE'LL DO EVERYTHING WE CAN TO INVESTIGATE THEM!
AS A REPORTER, I CAN'T WAIT TO LEARN THE SECRETS OF THEIR ORGANI-ZATION AND LEARN...
...IF THEY'RE UP TO NO GOOD!
THAT'S WHAT I TOLD THEM, BUT...
...THE ONLY ONE WE KNOW WHO'S HAD ANY CONTACT WITH THAT RED TEAM IS RUBY.
I'VE BEEN PESTERING HIM FOR AN INTERVIEW, BUT HE WON'T COOPERATE!
HEY, RUBY... ABOUT THOSE INCIDENTS AT SLATE-PORT CITY AND THE RUSTURF TUNNEL...
THAT AGAIN?!
I'VE TOLD YOU OVER AND OVER– I DON'T KNOW ANYTHING ABOUT THEM.
I JUST GOT CAUGHT UP IN THINGS! I BARELY MADE IT OUT ALIVE MYSELF!

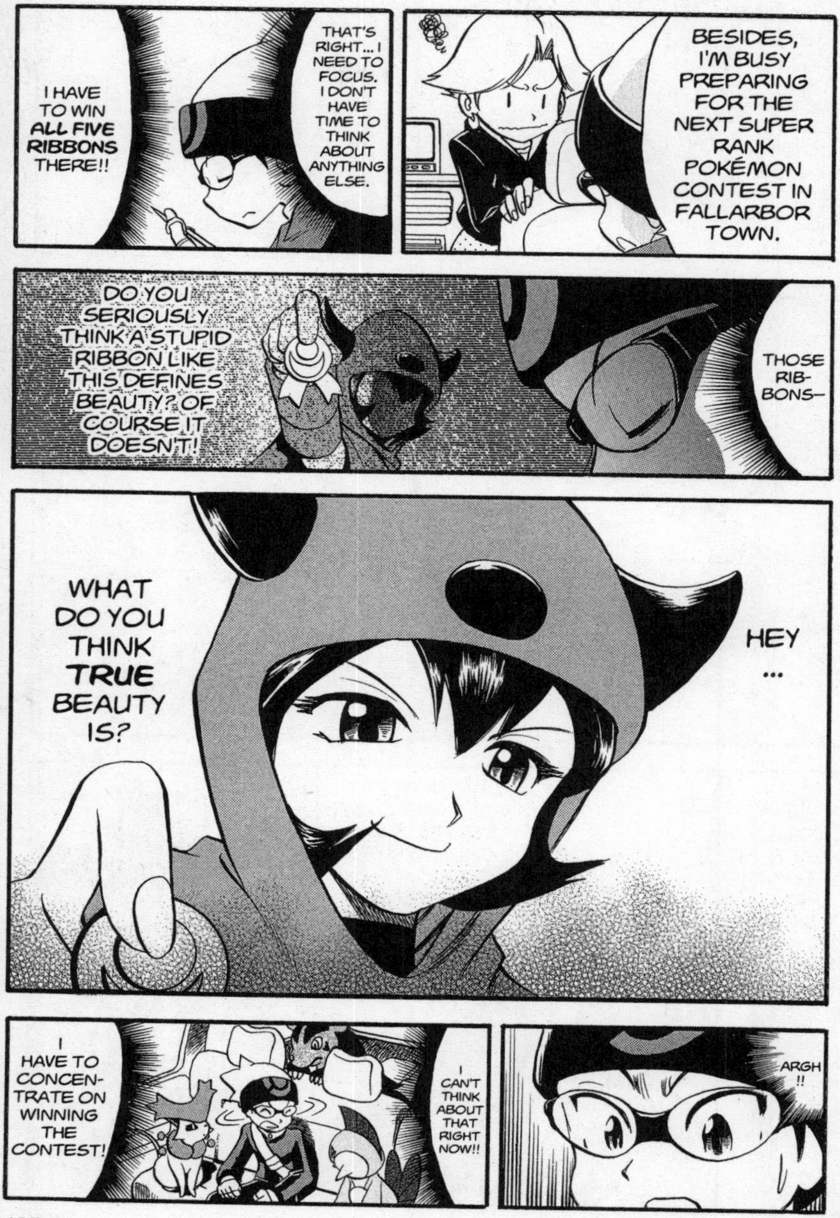
BESIDES, I'M BUSY PREPARING FOR THE NEXT SUPER RANK POKÉMON CONTEST IN FALLARBOR TOWN.
THAT'S RIGHT... I NEED TO FOCUS. I DON'T HAVE TIME TO THINK ABOUT ANYTHING ELSE.
I HAVE TO WIN **ALL FIVE RIBBONS** THERE!!
THOSE RIB-BONS—
DO YOU SERIOUSLY THINK A STUPID RIBBON LIKE THIS DEFINES BEAUTY? OF COURSE IT DOESN'T!
HEY ...
WHAT DO YOU THINK **TRUE** BEAUTY IS?
ARGH!!
I CAN'T THINK ABOUT THAT RIGHT NOW!!
I HAVE TO CONCEN-TRATE ON WINNING THE CONTEST!

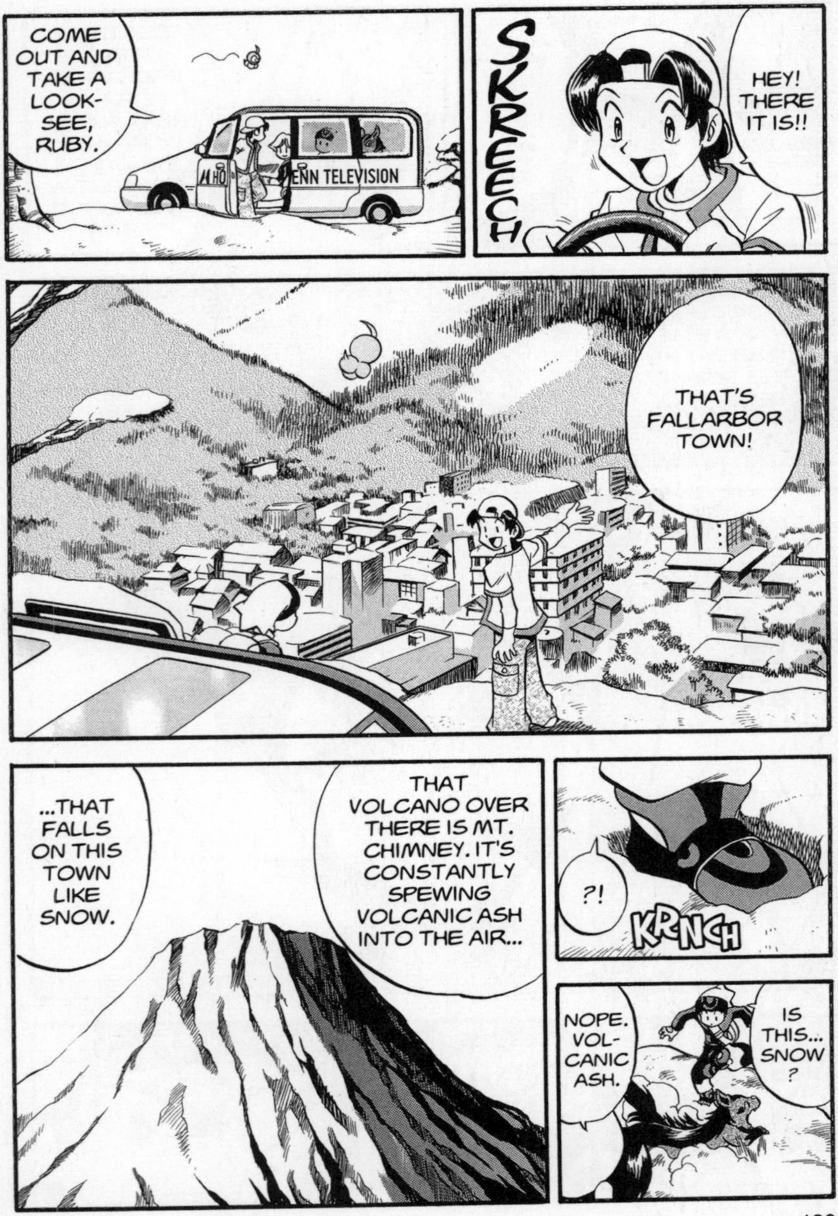
SKREECH
HEY! THERE IT IS!!
COME OUT AND TAKE A LOOK-SEE, RUBY.
THAT'S FALLARBOR TOWN!
?!
KRNCH
IS THIS... SNOW?
NOPE. VOLCANIC ASH.
THAT VOLCANO OVER THERE IS MT. CHIMNEY. IT'S CONSTANTLY SPEWING VOLCANIC ASH INTO THE AIR...
...THAT FALLS ON THIS TOWN LIKE SNOW.

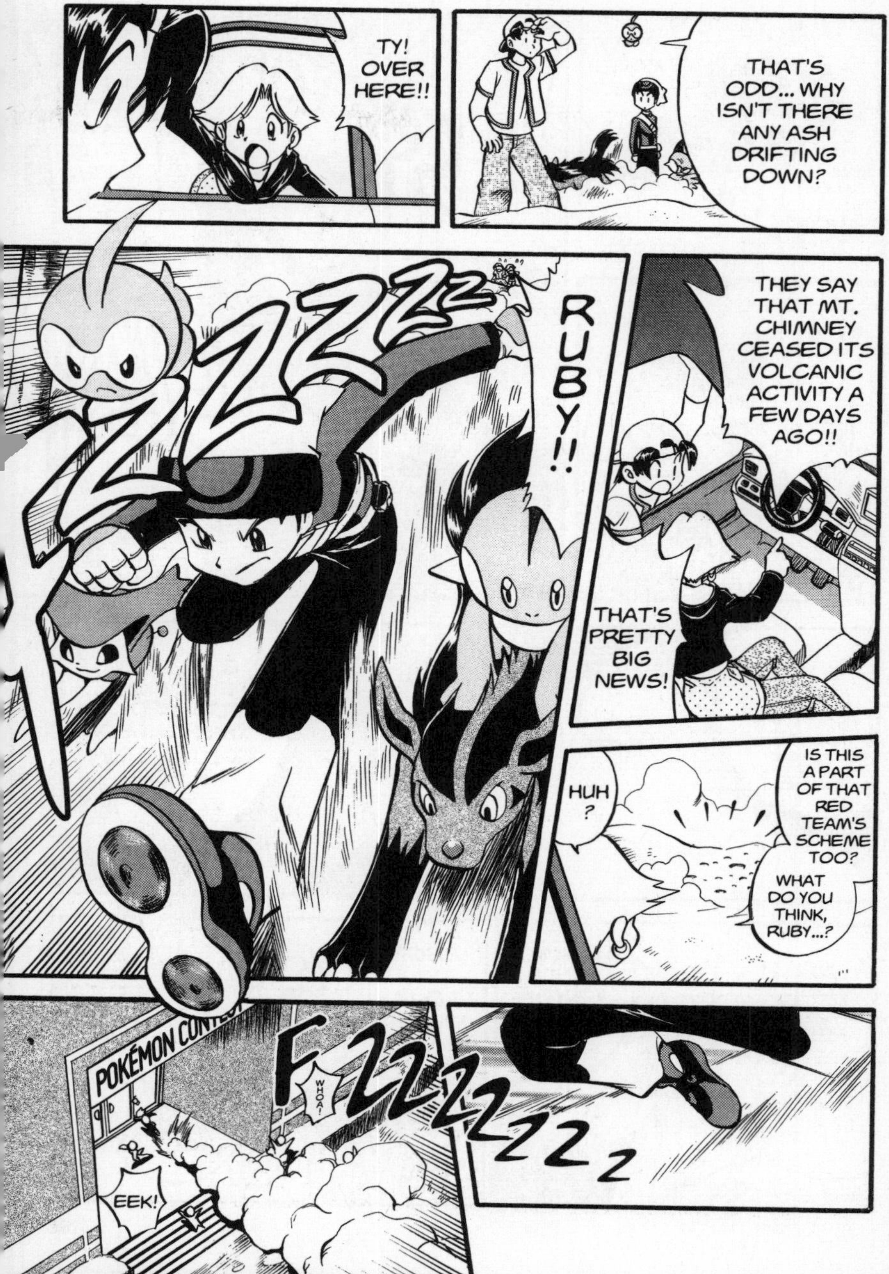
THAT'S ODD... WHY ISN'T THERE ANY ASH DRIFTING DOWN?
TY! OVER HERE!!
THEY SAY THAT MT. CHIMNEY CEASED ITS VOLCANIC ACTIVITY A FEW DAYS AGO!!
THAT'S PRETTY BIG NEWS!
IS THIS A PART OF THAT RED TEAM'S SCHEME TOO?
WHAT DO YOU THINK, RUBY...?
HUH?
RUBY!!
ZZZZZZ
FZZZZZZZ
WHOA!
POKÉMON CONTEST
EEK!

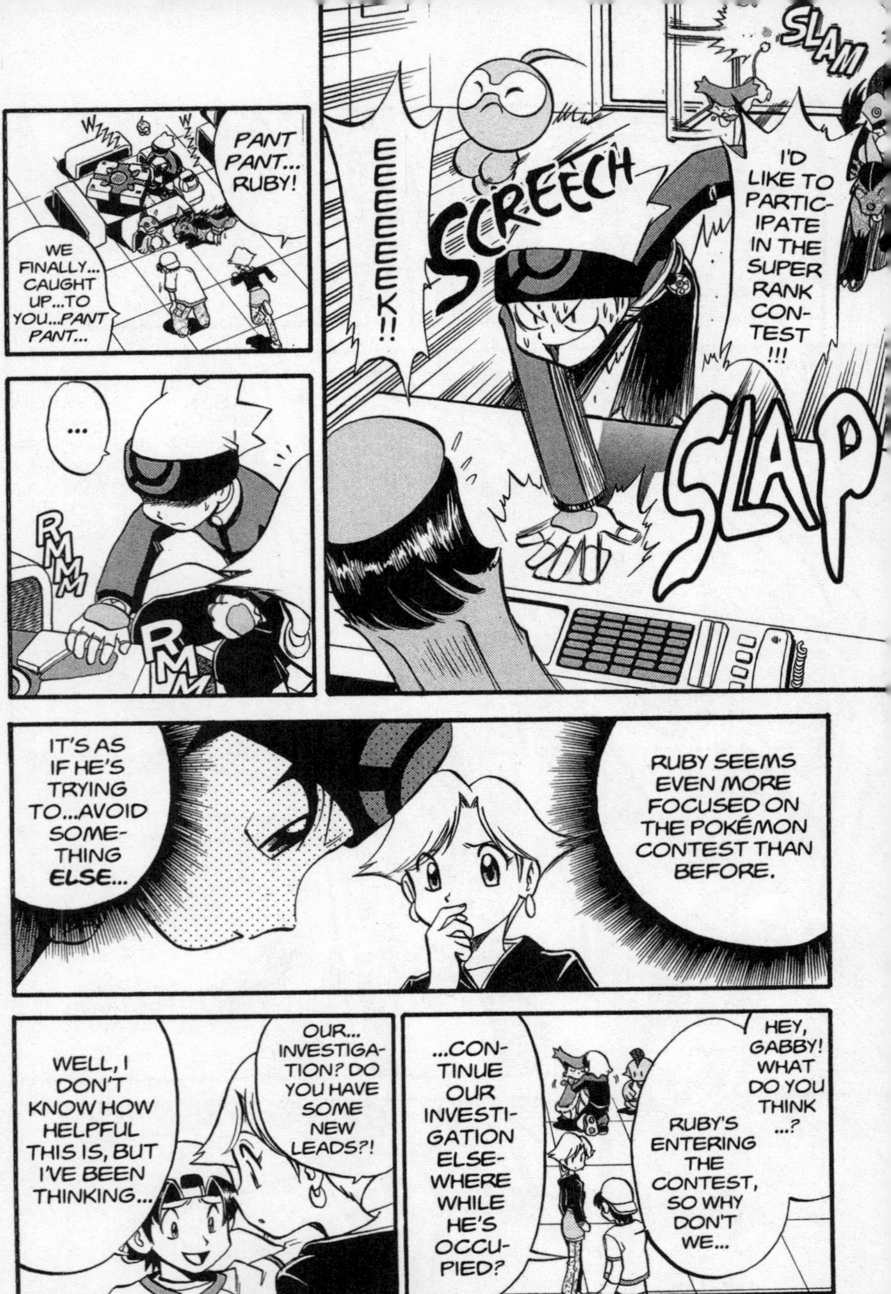
SLAM
EEEEEEEK!!
SCREECH
I'D LIKE TO PARTICIPATE IN THE SUPER RANK CONTEST!!!
SLAP
PANT PANT... RUBY!
WE FINALLY... CAUGHT UP...TO YOU...PANT PANT...
...
RMMM
RMM
RUBY SEEMS EVEN MORE FOCUSED ON THE POKÉMON CONTEST THAN BEFORE.
IT'S AS IF HE'S TRYING TO...AVOID SOMETHING **ELSE**...
HEY, GABBY! WHAT DO YOU THINK ...?
RUBY'S ENTERING THE CONTEST, SO WHY DON'T WE...
...CONTINUE OUR INVESTIGATION ELSEWHERE WHILE HE'S OCCUPIED?
OUR... INVESTIGATION? DO YOU HAVE SOME NEW LEADS?!
WELL, I DON'T KNOW HOW HELPFUL THIS IS, BUT I'VE BEEN THINKING...

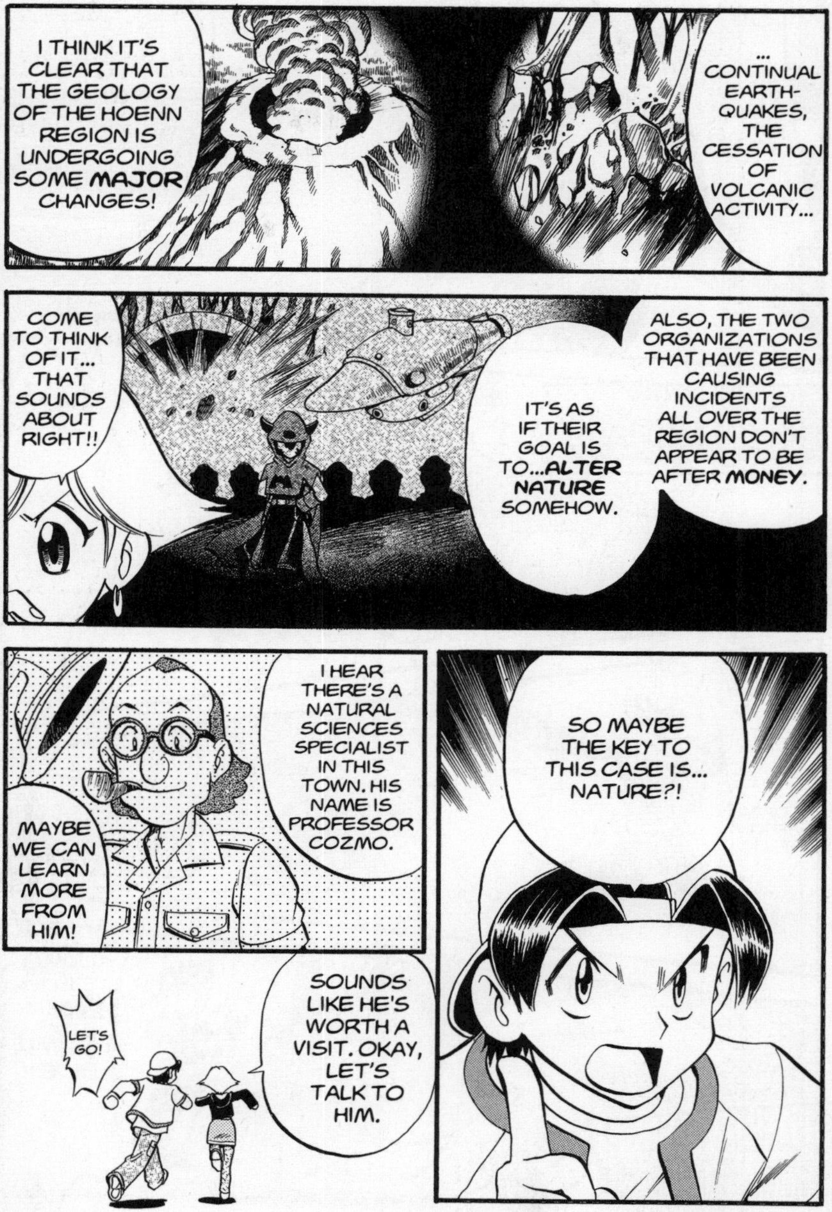
...CONTINUAL EARTH-QUAKES, THE CESSATION OF VOLCANIC ACTIVITY...
I THINK IT'S CLEAR THAT THE GEOLOGY OF THE HOENN REGION IS UNDERGOING SOME **MAJOR** CHANGES!
ALSO, THE TWO ORGANIZATIONS THAT HAVE BEEN CAUSING INCIDENTS ALL OVER THE REGION DON'T APPEAR TO BE AFTER **MONEY**.
IT'S AS IF THEIR GOAL IS TO...**ALTER NATURE** SOMEHOW.
COME TO THINK OF IT... THAT SOUNDS ABOUT RIGHT!!
SO MAYBE THE KEY TO THIS CASE IS... NATURE?!
I HEAR THERE'S A NATURAL SCIENCES SPECIALIST IN THIS TOWN. HIS NAME IS PROFESSOR COZMO.
MAYBE WE CAN LEARN MORE FROM HIM!
SOUNDS LIKE HE'S WORTH A VISIT. OKAY, LET'S TALK TO HIM.
LET'S GO!

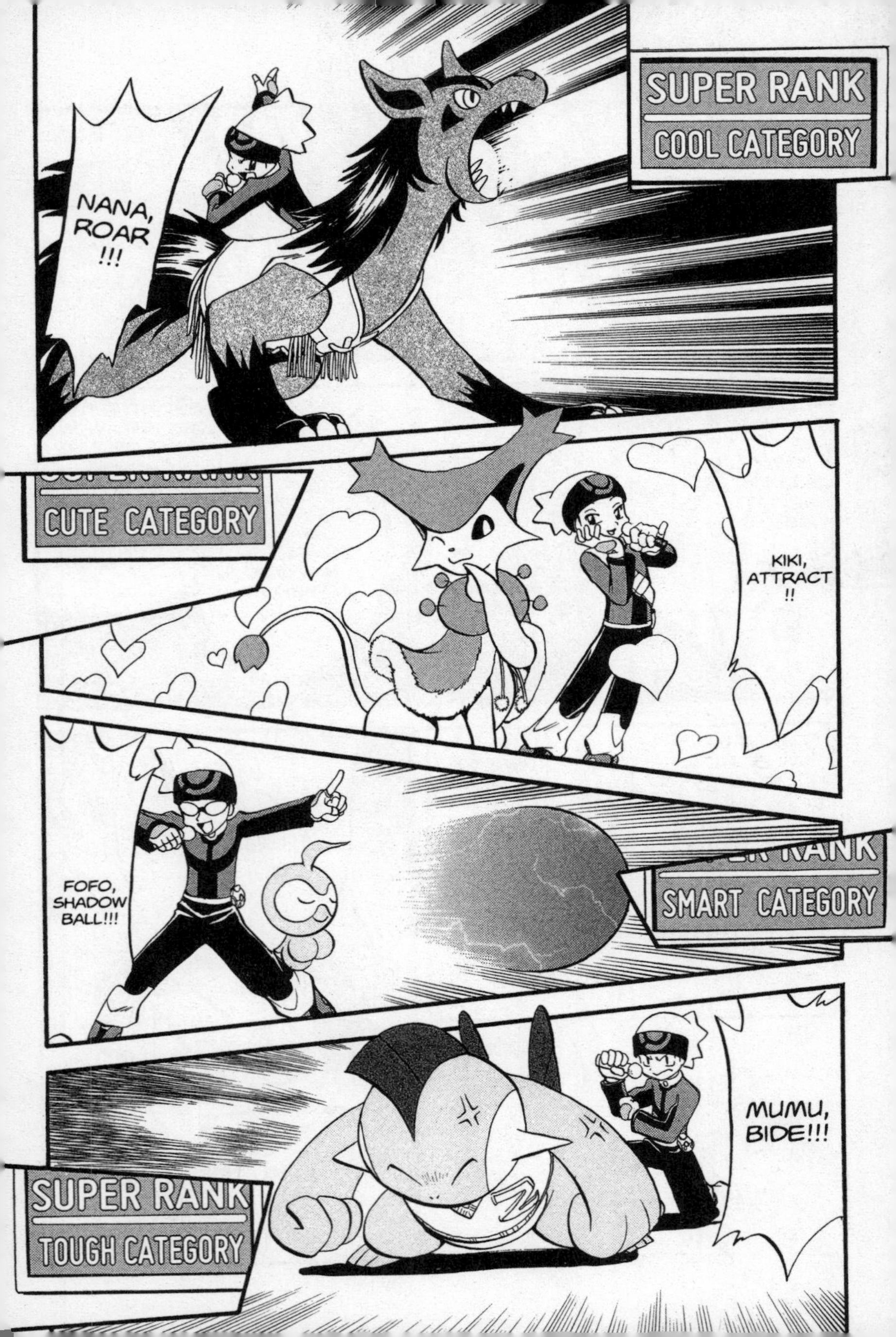
SUPER RANK
COOL CATEGORY
NANA, ROAR!!!
KIKI, ATTRACT!!
CUTE CATEGORY
SMART CATEGORY
FOFO, SHADOW BALL!!!
MUMU, BIDE!!!
SUPER RANK
TOUGH CATEGORY

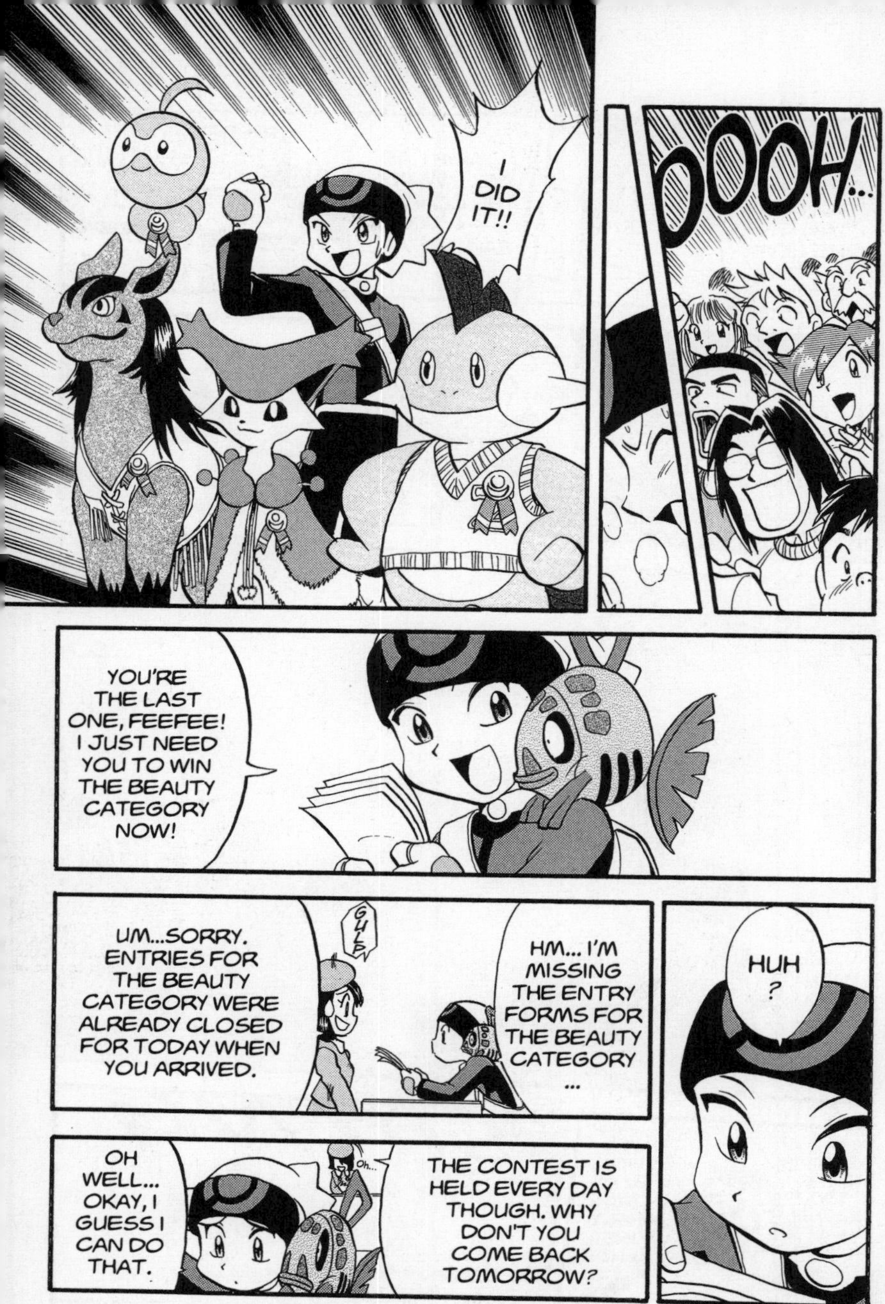
OOOH...
I DID IT!!
YOU'RE THE LAST ONE, FEEFEE! I JUST NEED YOU TO WIN THE BEAUTY CATEGORY NOW!
HUH ?
HM... I'M MISSING THE ENTRY FORMS FOR THE BEAUTY CATEGORY ...
GULP
UM...SORRY. ENTRIES FOR THE BEAUTY CATEGORY WERE ALREADY CLOSED FOR TODAY WHEN YOU ARRIVED.
THE CONTEST IS HELD EVERY DAY THOUGH. WHY DON'T YOU COME BACK TOMORROW?
Oh...
OH WELL... OKAY, I GUESS I CAN DO THAT.

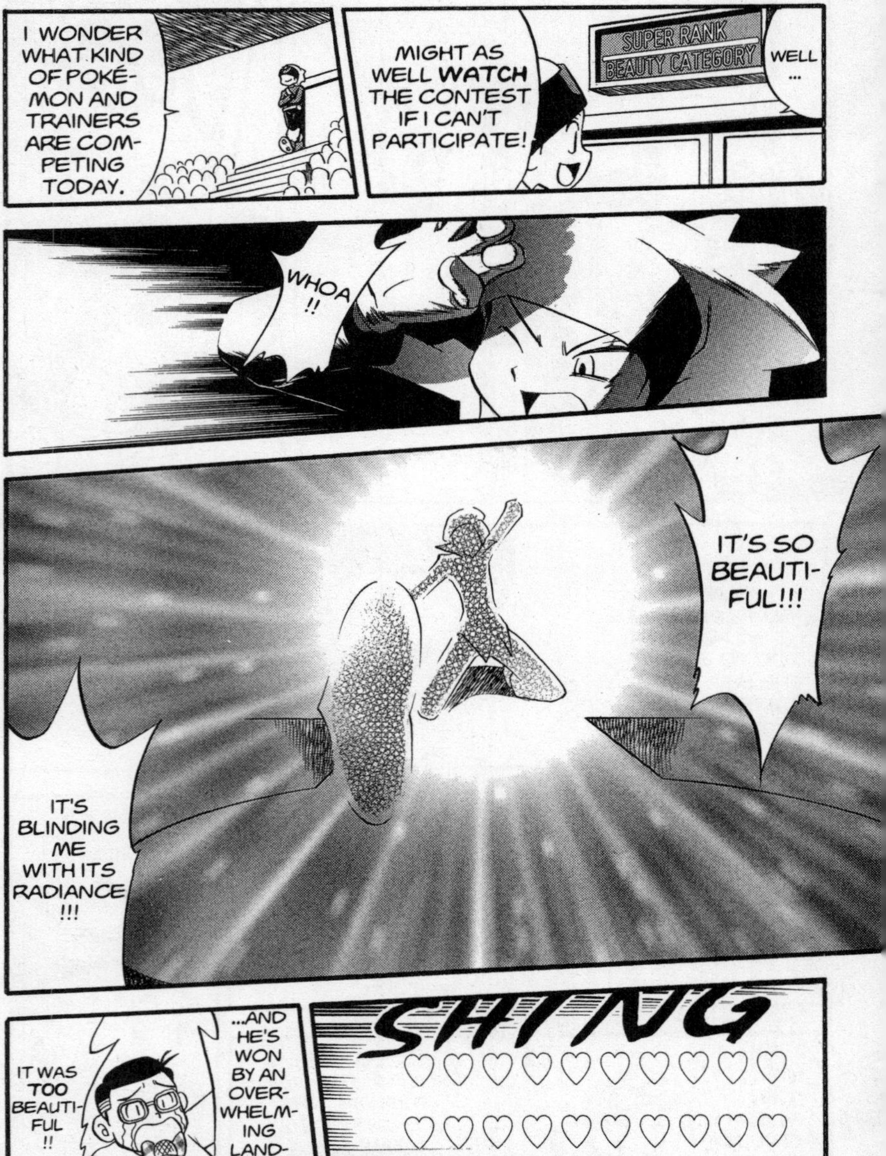
SUPER RANK BEAUTY CATEGORY
WELL ...
MIGHT AS WELL WATCH THE CONTEST IF I CAN'T PARTICIPATE!
I WONDER WHAT KIND OF POKÉMON AND TRAINERS ARE COMPETING TODAY.
WHOA !!
IT'S SO BEAUTIFUL!!!
IT'S BLINDING ME WITH ITS RADIANCE !!!
SHING
...AND HE'S WON BY AN OVERWHELMING LANDSLIDE !!
IT WAS TOO BEAUTIFUL !!

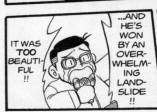

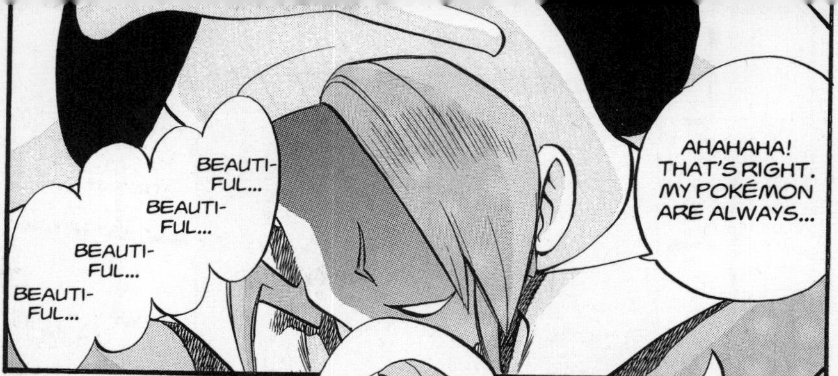
BEAUTI-
FUL...
BEAUTI-
FUL...
BEAUTI-
FUL...
BEAUTI-
FUL...
AHAHAHA!
THAT'S RIGHT.
MY POKÉMON
ARE ALWAYS...

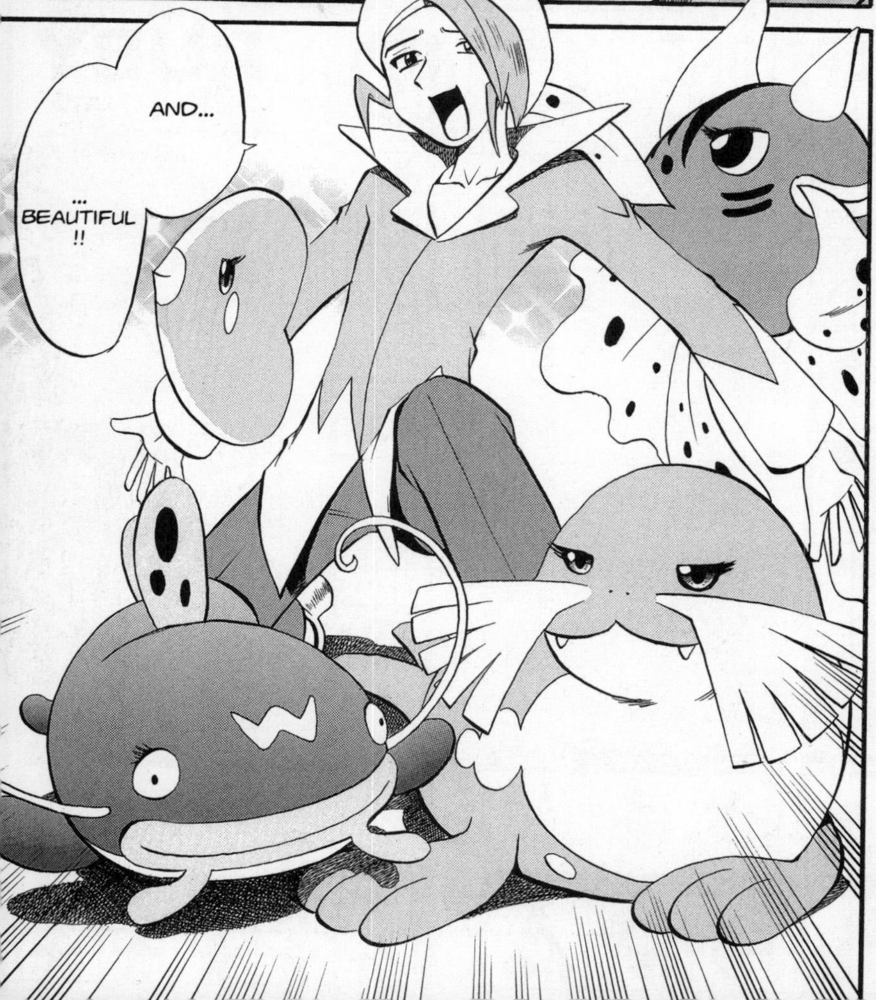
AND...
...
BEAUTIFUL
!!

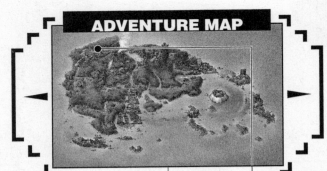

ADVENTURE MAP

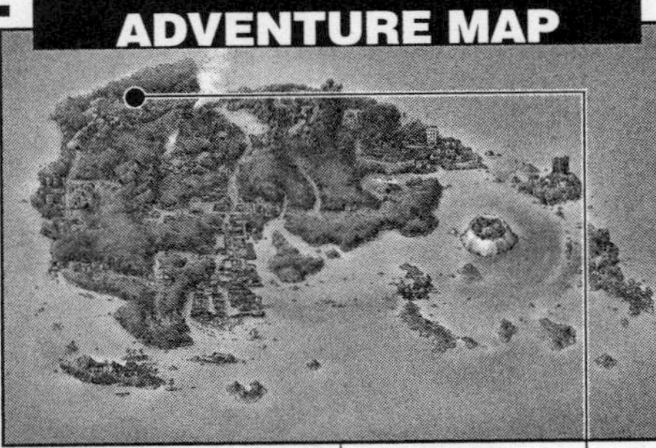

SAPPHIRE

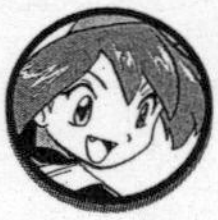

RUBY

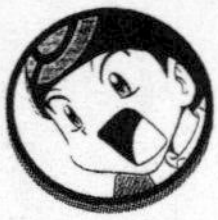

Mt. Chimney → Jagged Pass →

Route 117 → Verdanturf Town → Rusturf Tunnel → Rustboro City → Route 115 → Route 114 → Fallarbor Town

SAPPHIRE

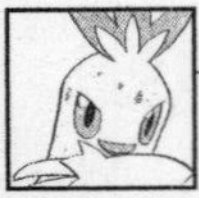

CHIC
Combusken ♀
Lv35

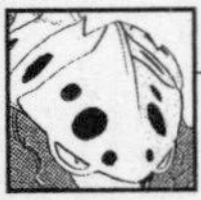

RONO
Lairon ♂
Lv41

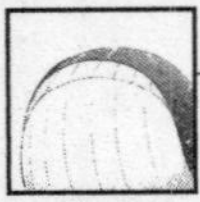

LORRY
Wailord ♂
Lv46

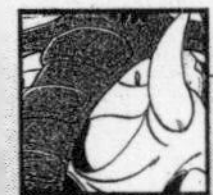

PHADO
Donphan ♂
Lv45

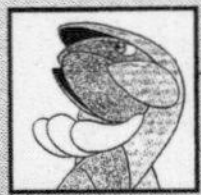

TROPPY
Tropius ♂
Lv44

RUBY

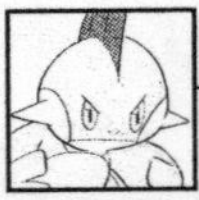

MUMU
Marshtomp ♂

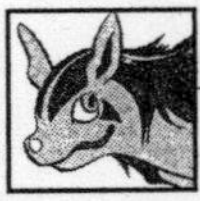

NANA
Mightyena ♀

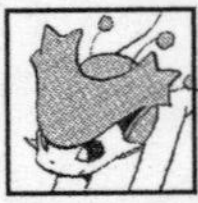

KIKI
Delcatty ♀

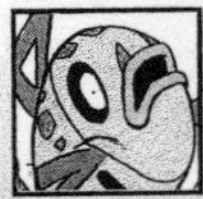

FEEFEE
Feebas ♀

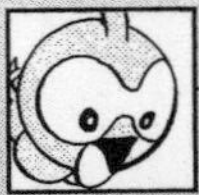

FOFO
Castform ♀

Stone Badge	Knuckle Badge	Dynamo Badge	Heat Badge
Balance Badge	Feather Badge	Mind Badge	Rain Badge

	Cool	Beauty	Cute	Smart	Tough
Normal					
Super					
Hyper					
Master					

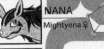

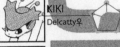

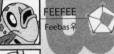

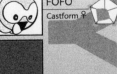

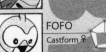

● Chapter 224 ●
I More Than Like You, Luvdisc II

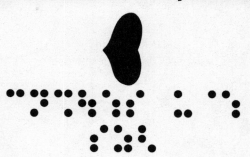

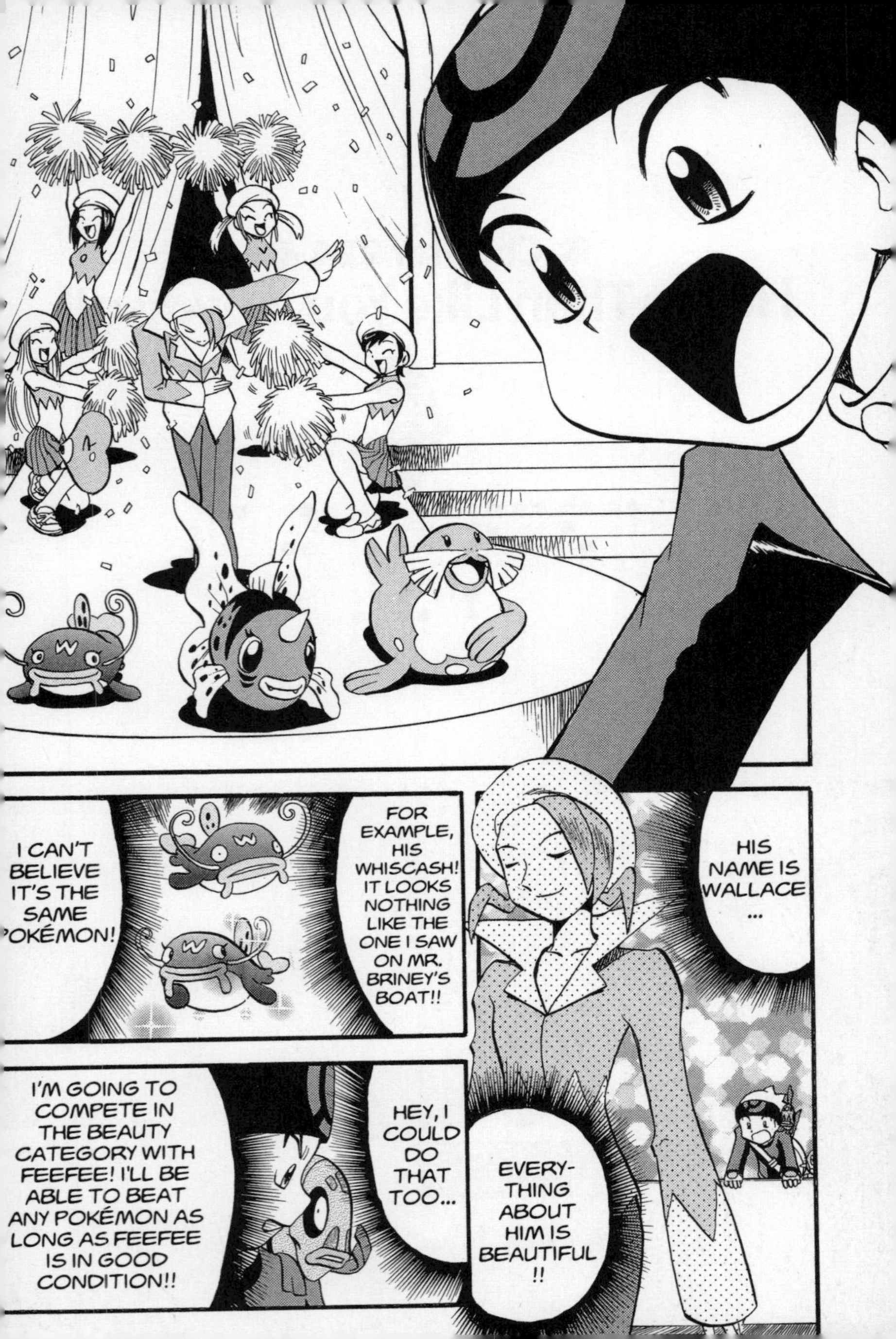
HIS NAME IS WALLACE ...
EVERY-THING ABOUT HIM IS BEAUTIFUL !!
FOR EXAMPLE, HIS WHISCASH! IT LOOKS NOTHING LIKE THE ONE I SAW ON MR. BRINEY'S BOAT!!
I CAN'T BELIEVE IT'S THE SAME POKÉMON!
HEY, I COULD DO THAT TOO...
I'M GOING TO COMPETE IN THE BEAUTY CATEGORY WITH FEEFEE! I'LL BE ABLE TO BEAT ANY POKÉMON AS LONG AS FEEFEE IS IN GOOD CONDITION!!

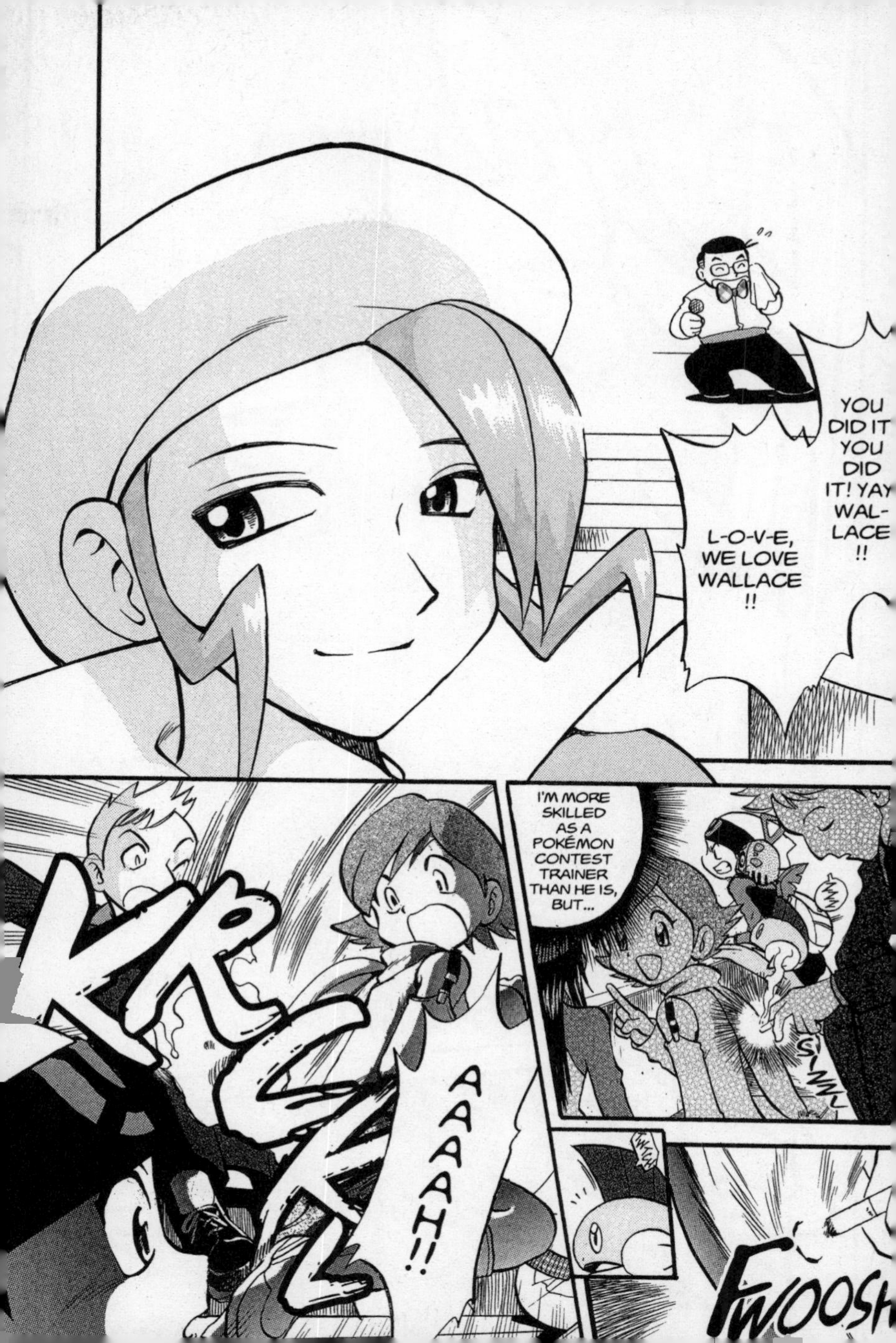
YOU DID IT YOU DID IT! YAY WAL-LACE !!
L-O-V-E, WE LOVE WALLACE !!
I'M MORE SKILLED AS A POKÉMON CONTEST TRAINER THAN HE IS, BUT...
SIZZL
FWOOSH
TWITCH
AAAAAH!!

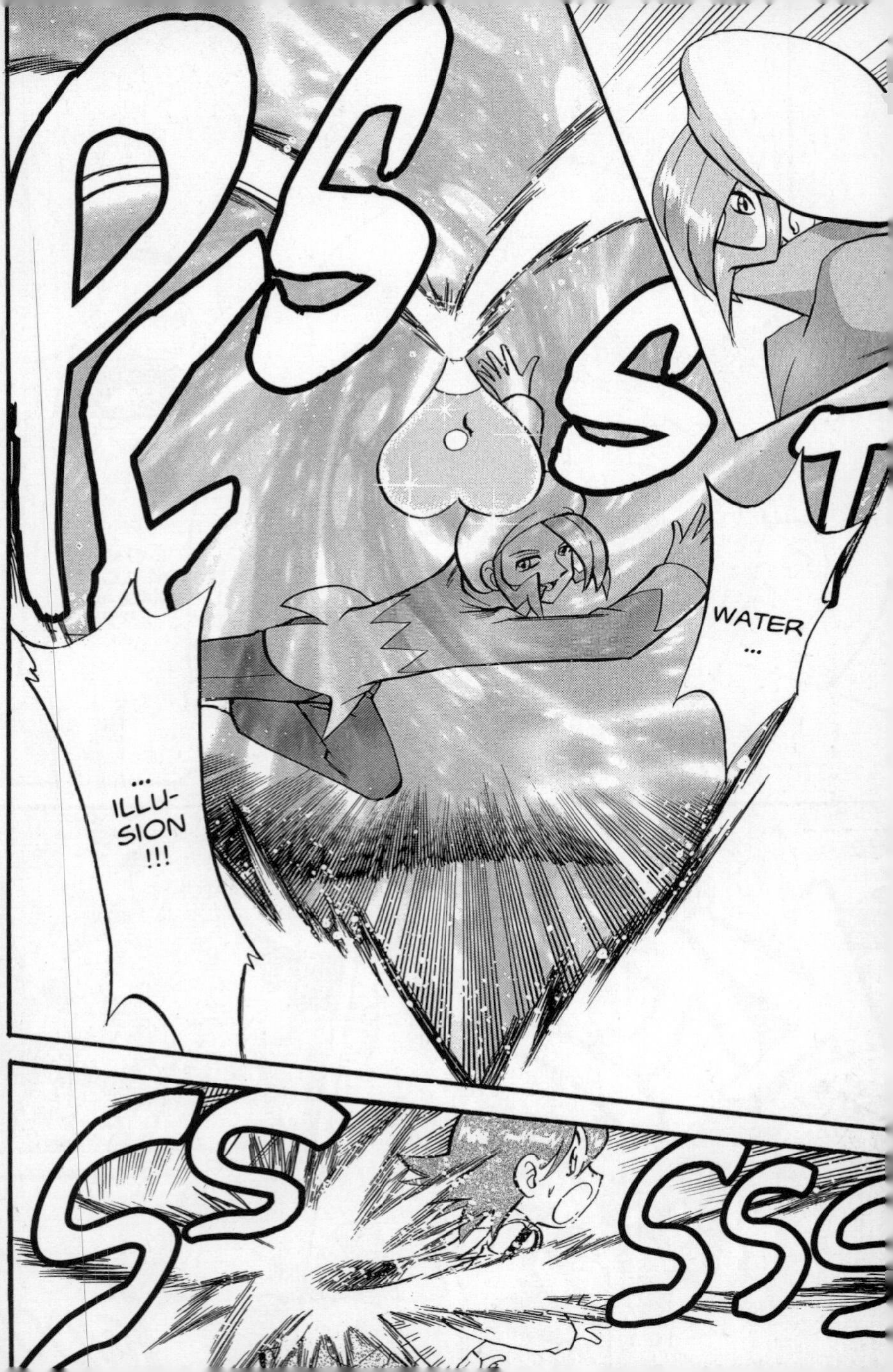
PSST
WATER ...
... ILLUSION !!!
SSSSS

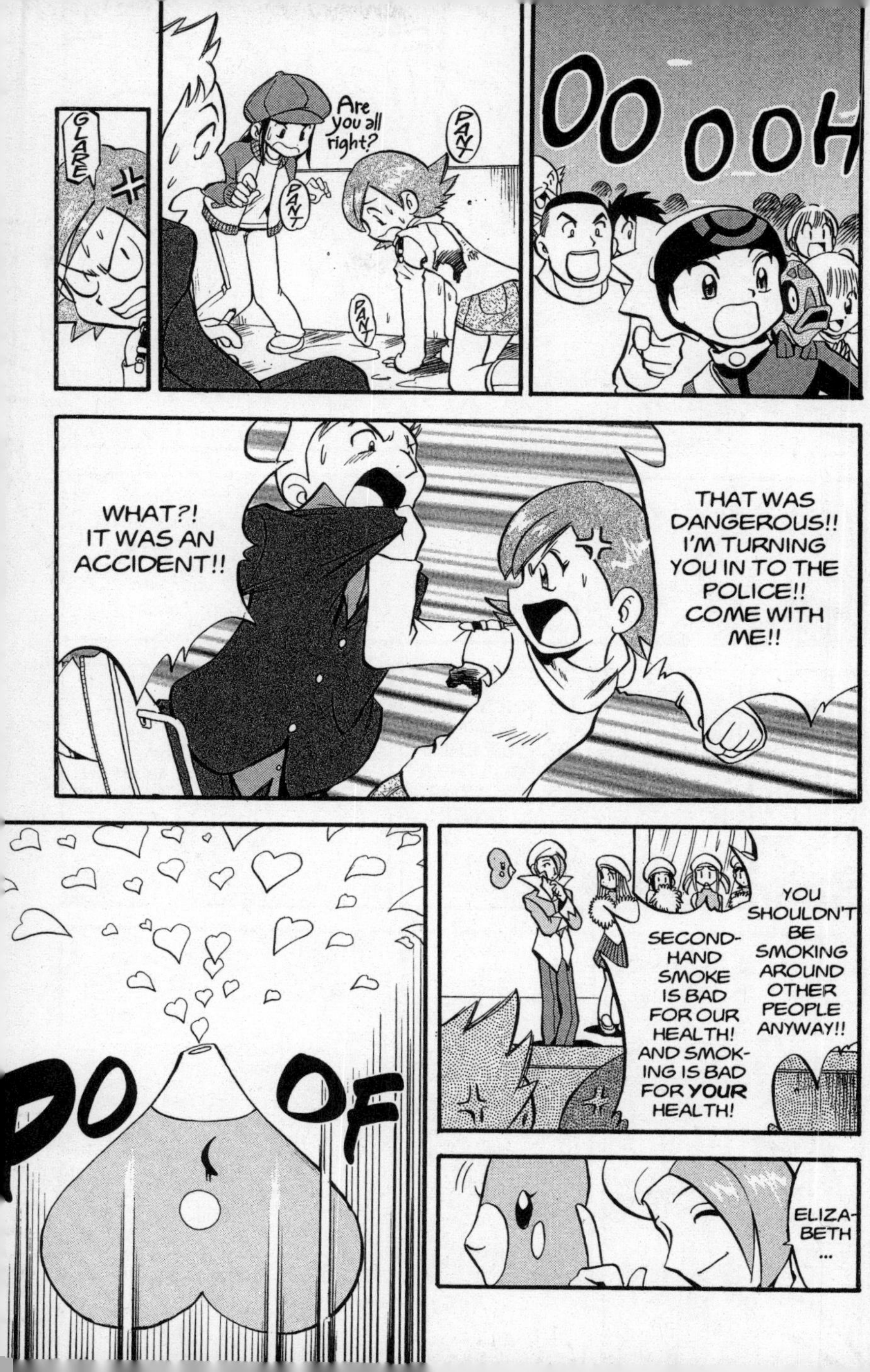
OOOOH
Are you all right?
PANT
PANT
PANT
GLARE
THAT WAS DANGEROUS!! I'M TURNING YOU IN TO THE POLICE!! COME WITH ME!!
WHAT?! IT WAS AN ACCIDENT!!
YOU SHOULDN'T BE SMOKING AROUND OTHER PEOPLE ANYWAY!!
SECOND-HAND SMOKE IS BAD FOR OUR HEALTH! AND SMOK-ING IS BAD FOR **YOUR** HEALTH!
ELIZA-BETH...
POOF

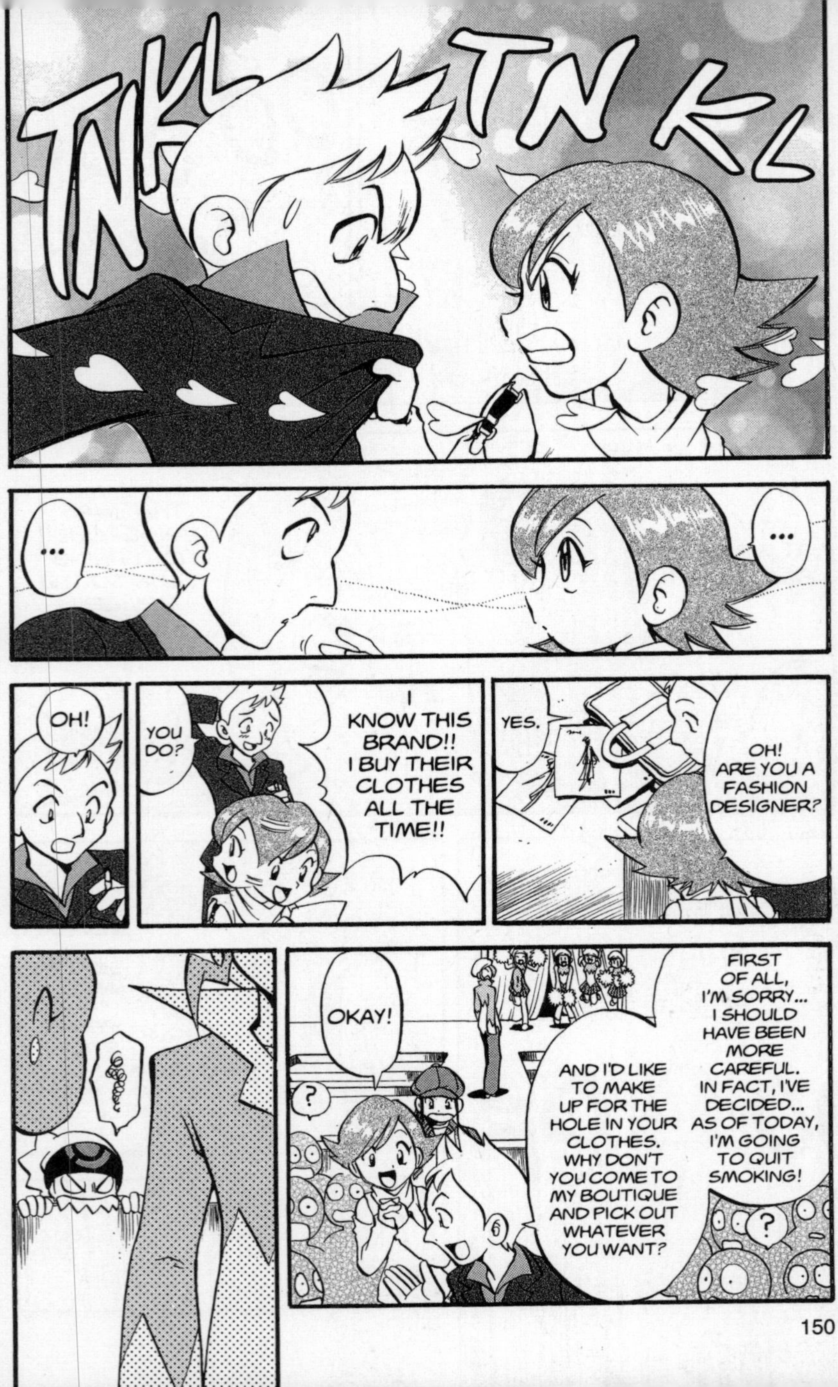
TN KL
TNKL
...
...
OH! ARE YOU A FASHION DESIGNER?
YES.
I KNOW THIS BRAND!! I BUY THEIR CLOTHES ALL THE TIME!!
YOU DO?
OH!
FIRST OF ALL, I'M SORRY... I SHOULD HAVE BEEN MORE CAREFUL. IN FACT, I'VE DECIDED... AS OF TODAY, I'M GOING TO QUIT SMOKING!
AND I'D LIKE TO MAKE UP FOR THE HOLE IN YOUR CLOTHES. WHY DON'T YOU COME TO MY BOUTIQUE AND PICK OUT WHATEVER YOU WANT?
OKAY!
?
?

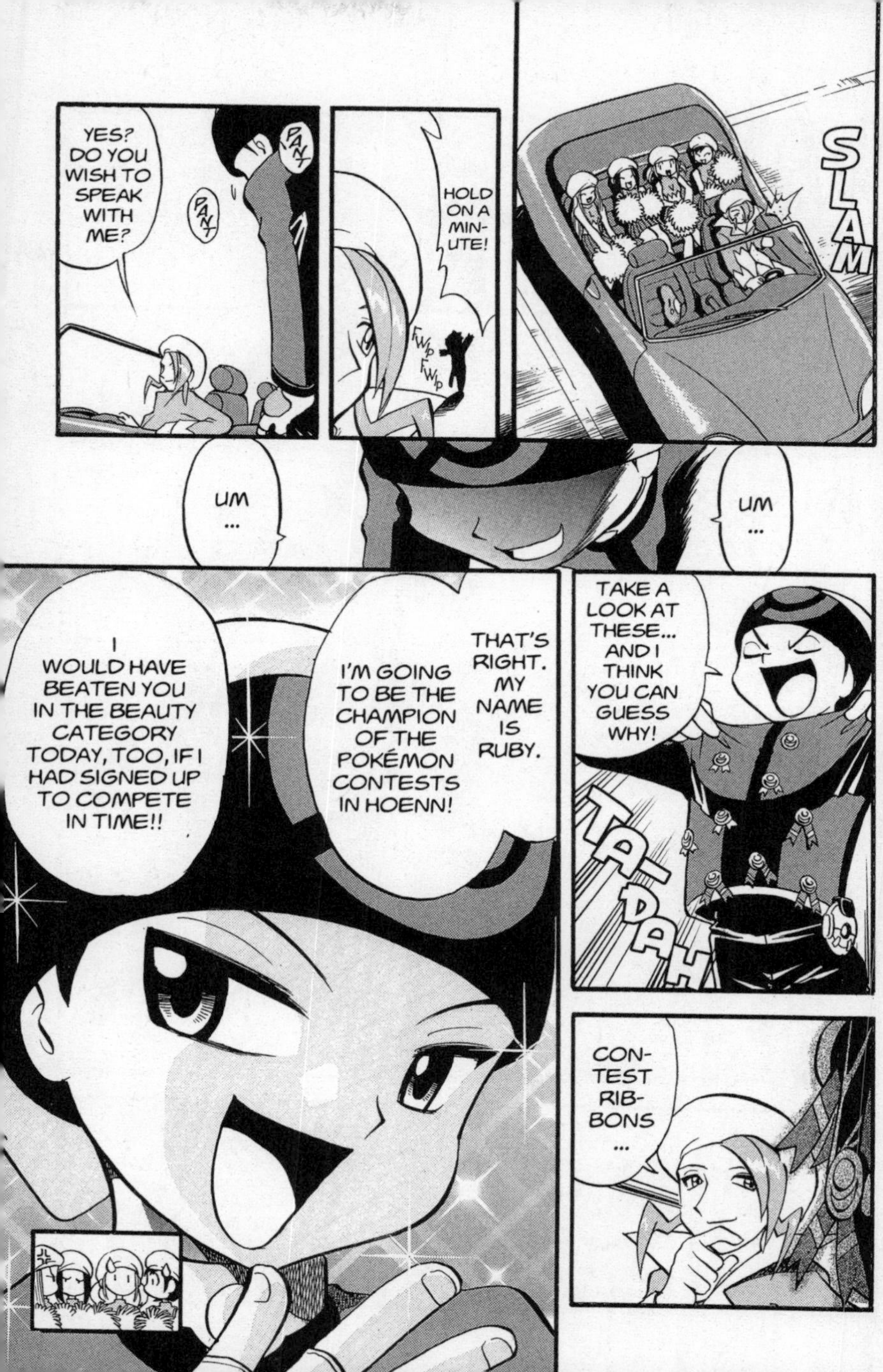
SLAM
HOLD ON A MIN-UTE!
FWIP FWIP
YES? DO YOU WISH TO SPEAK WITH ME?
PANT
PANT
UM ...
UM ...
TAKE A LOOK AT THESE... AND I THINK YOU CAN GUESS WHY!
TA-DAH
CON-TEST RIB-BONS ...
THAT'S RIGHT. MY NAME IS RUBY.
I'M GOING TO BE THE CHAMPION OF THE POKÉMON CONTESTS IN HOENN!
I WOULD HAVE BEATEN YOU IN THE BEAUTY CATEGORY TODAY, TOO, IF I HAD SIGNED UP TO COMPETE IN TIME!!

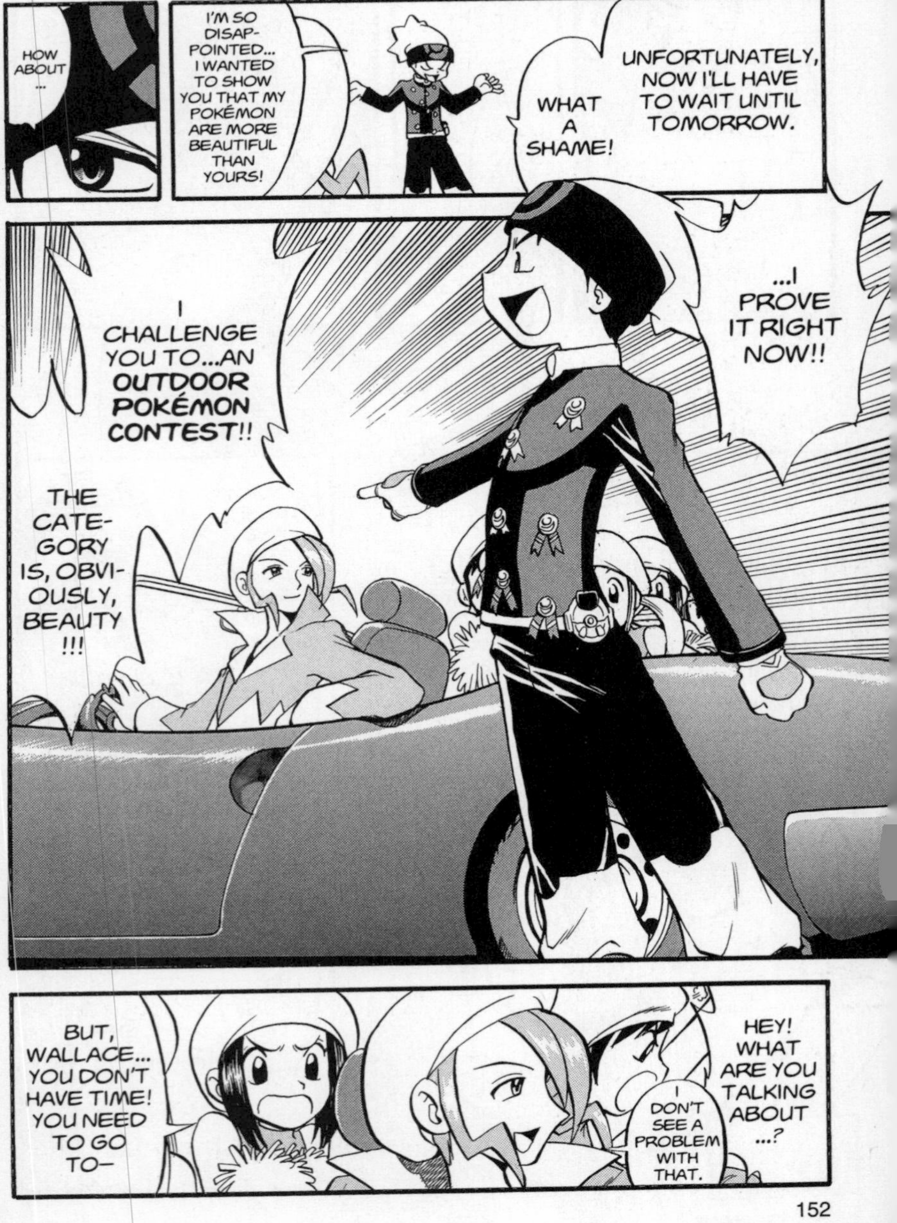
UNFORTUNATELY, NOW I'LL HAVE TO WAIT UNTIL TOMORROW.
WHAT A SHAME!
I'M SO DISAPPOINTED... I WANTED TO SHOW YOU THAT MY POKÉMON ARE MORE BEAUTIFUL THAN YOURS!
HOW ABOUT ...
...I PROVE IT RIGHT NOW!!
I CHALLENGE YOU TO...AN **OUTDOOR POKÉMON CONTEST**!!
THE CATEGORY IS, OBVIOUSLY, BEAUTY!!!
HEY! WHAT ARE YOU TALKING ABOUT ...?
I DON'T SEE A PROBLEM WITH THAT.
BUT, WALLACE... YOU DON'T HAVE TIME! YOU NEED TO GO TO—

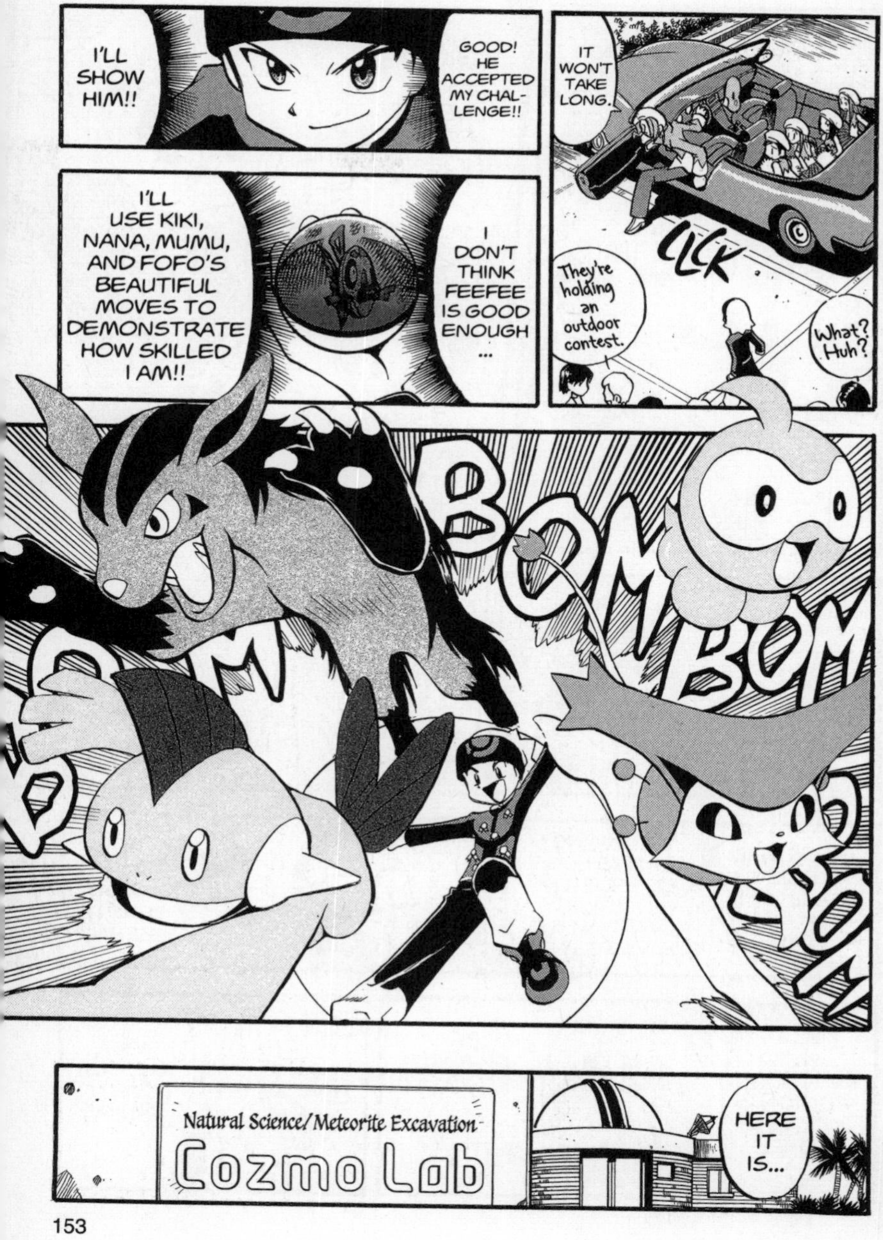
IT WON'T TAKE LONG.
CLICK
They're holding an outdoor contest.
What? Huh?
GOOD! HE ACCEPTED MY CHAL-LENGE!!
I'LL SHOW HIM!!
I DON'T THINK FEEFEE IS GOOD ENOUGH ...
I'LL USE KIKI, NANA, MUMU, AND FOFO'S BEAUTIFUL MOVES TO DEMONSTRATE HOW SKILLED I AM!!
BOM
BOM
HERE IT IS...
Natural Science/Meteorite Excavation
Cozmo Lab

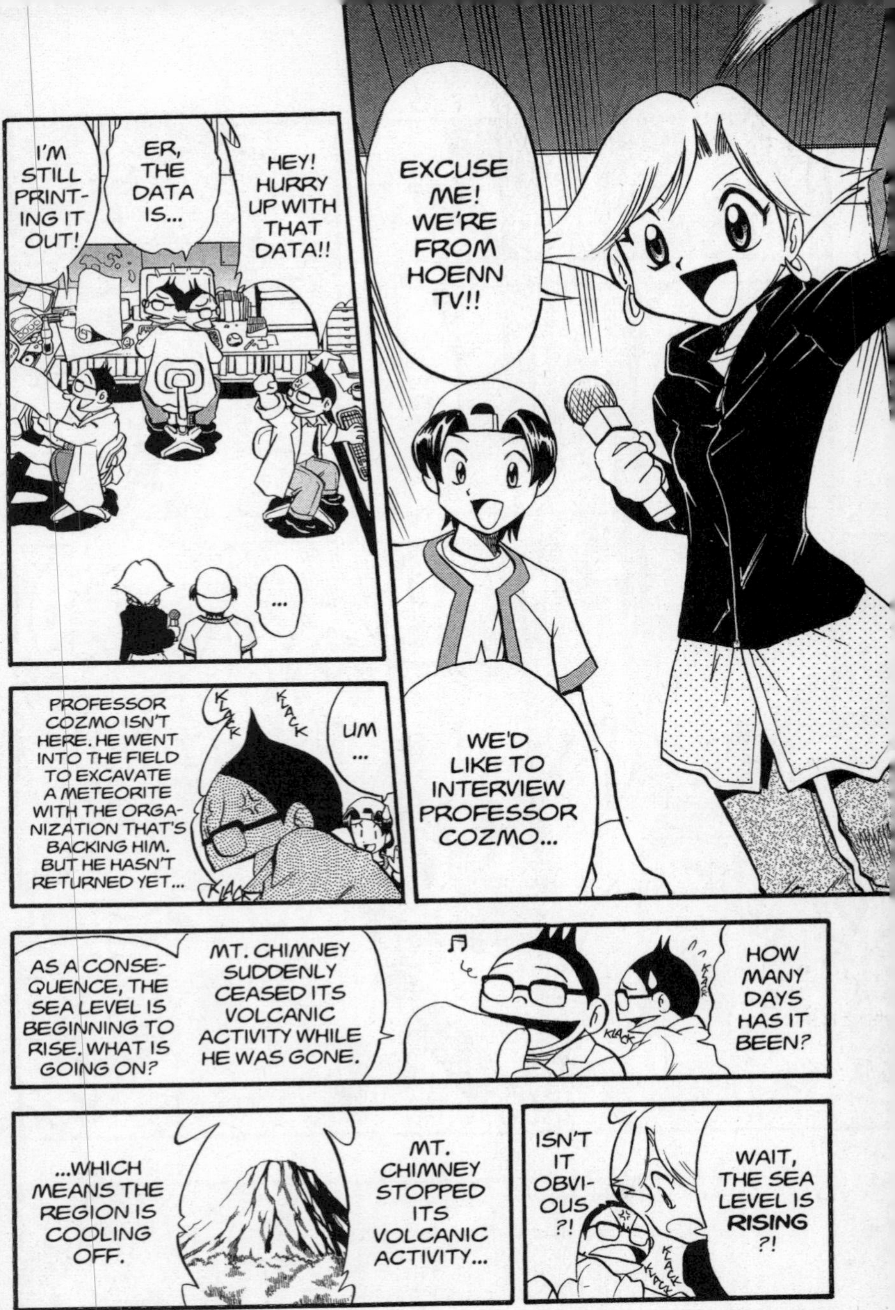
EXCUSE ME! WE'RE FROM HOENN TV!!
WE'D LIKE TO INTERVIEW PROFESSOR COZMO...
HEY! HURRY UP WITH THAT DATA!!
ER, THE DATA IS...
I'M STILL PRINTING IT OUT!
...
UM ...
KLACK
KLACK
PROFESSOR COZMO ISN'T HERE. HE WENT INTO THE FIELD TO EXCAVATE A METEORITE WITH THE ORGANIZATION THAT'S BACKING HIM. BUT HE HASN'T RETURNED YET...
KLACK
HOW MANY DAYS HAS IT BEEN?
KLACK
KLACK
MT. CHIMNEY SUDDENLY CEASED ITS VOLCANIC ACTIVITY WHILE HE WAS GONE.
AS A CONSEQUENCE, THE SEA LEVEL IS BEGINNING TO RISE. WHAT IS GOING ON?
WAIT, THE SEA LEVEL IS **RISING** ?!
ISN'T IT OBVIOUS?!
KLACK
KLACK
MT. CHIMNEY STOPPED ITS VOLCANIC ACTIVITY...
...WHICH MEANS THE REGION IS COOLING OFF.

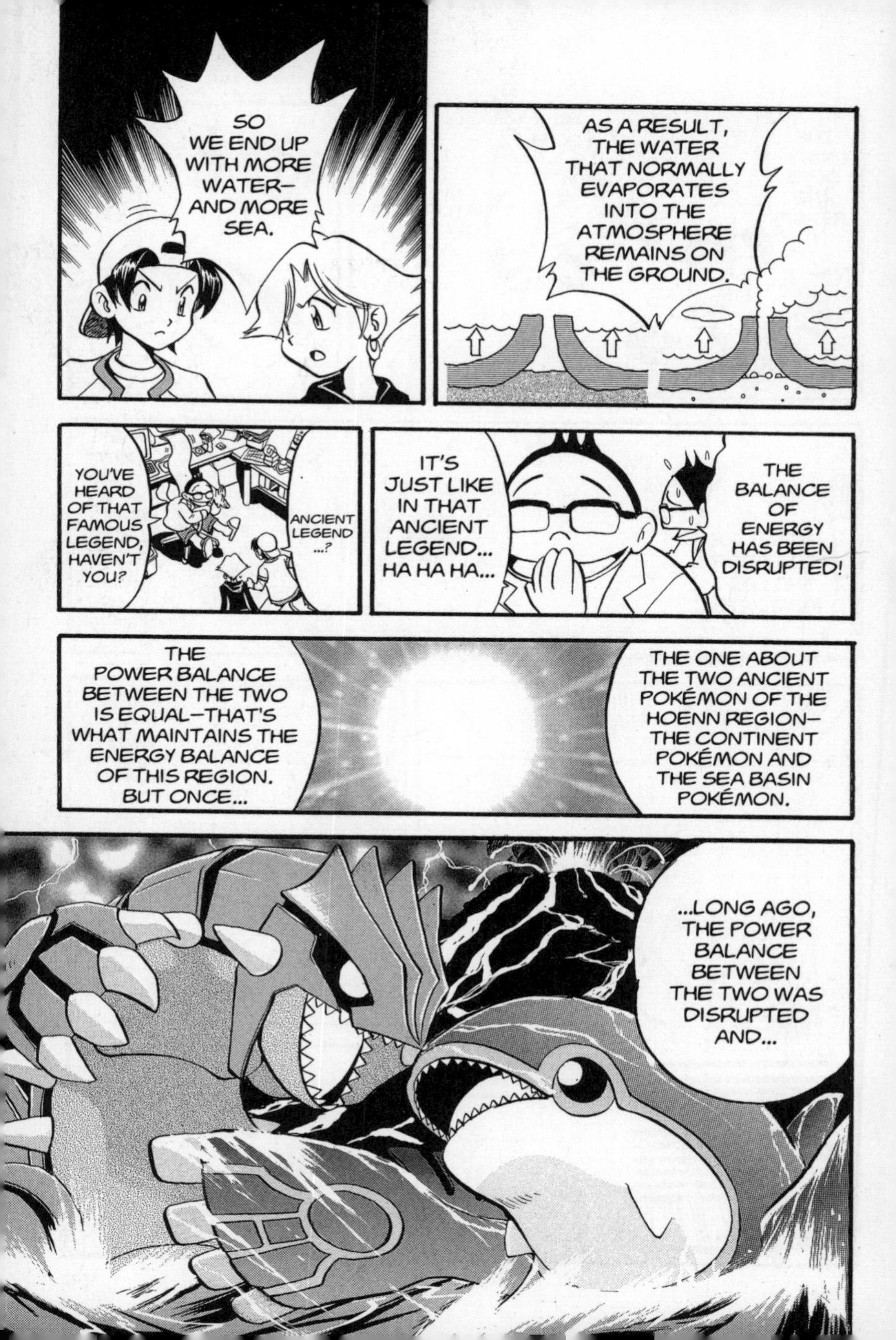
AS A RESULT, THE WATER THAT NORMALLY EVAPORATES INTO THE ATMOSPHERE REMAINS ON THE GROUND.
SO WE END UP WITH MORE WATER— AND MORE SEA.
THE BALANCE OF ENERGY HAS BEEN DISRUPTED!
IT'S JUST LIKE IN THAT ANCIENT LEGEND... HA HA HA...
ANCIENT LEGEND ...?
YOU'VE HEARD OF THAT FAMOUS LEGEND, HAVEN'T YOU?
THE ONE ABOUT THE TWO ANCIENT POKÉMON OF THE HOENN REGION— THE CONTINENT POKÉMON AND THE SEA BASIN POKÉMON.
THE POWER BALANCE BETWEEN THE TWO IS EQUAL—THAT'S WHAT MAINTAINS THE ENERGY BALANCE OF THIS REGION. BUT ONCE...
...LONG AGO, THE POWER BALANCE BETWEEN THE TWO WAS DISRUPTED AND...

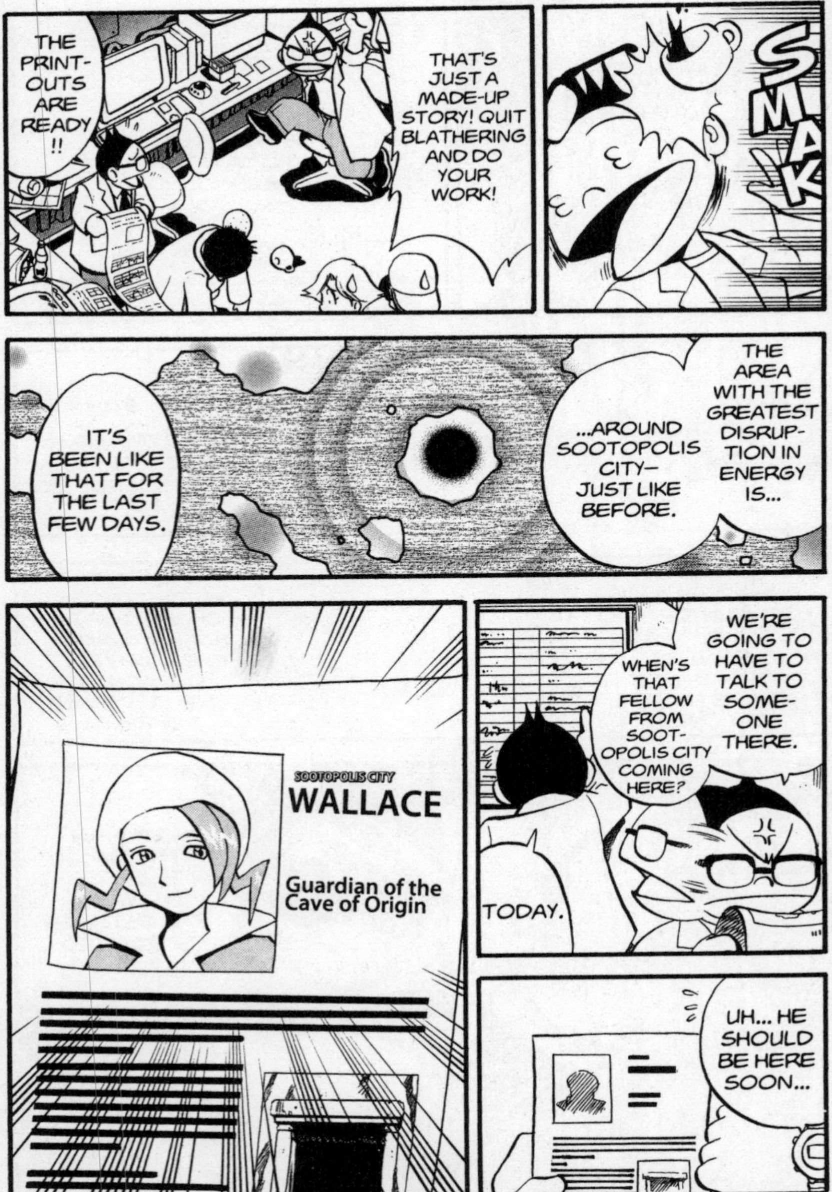
SMAK
THAT'S JUST A MADE-UP STORY! QUIT BLATHERING AND DO YOUR WORK!
THE PRINT-OUTS ARE READY!!
THE AREA WITH THE GREATEST DISRUPTION IN ENERGY IS...
...AROUND SOOTOPOLIS CITY—JUST LIKE BEFORE.
IT'S BEEN LIKE THAT FOR THE LAST FEW DAYS.
WE'RE GOING TO HAVE TO TALK TO SOMEONE THERE.
WHEN'S THAT FELLOW FROM SOOTOPOLIS CITY COMING HERE?
TODAY.
UH... HE SHOULD BE HERE SOON...
SOOTOPOLIS CITY
WALLACE
Guardian of the Cave of Origin

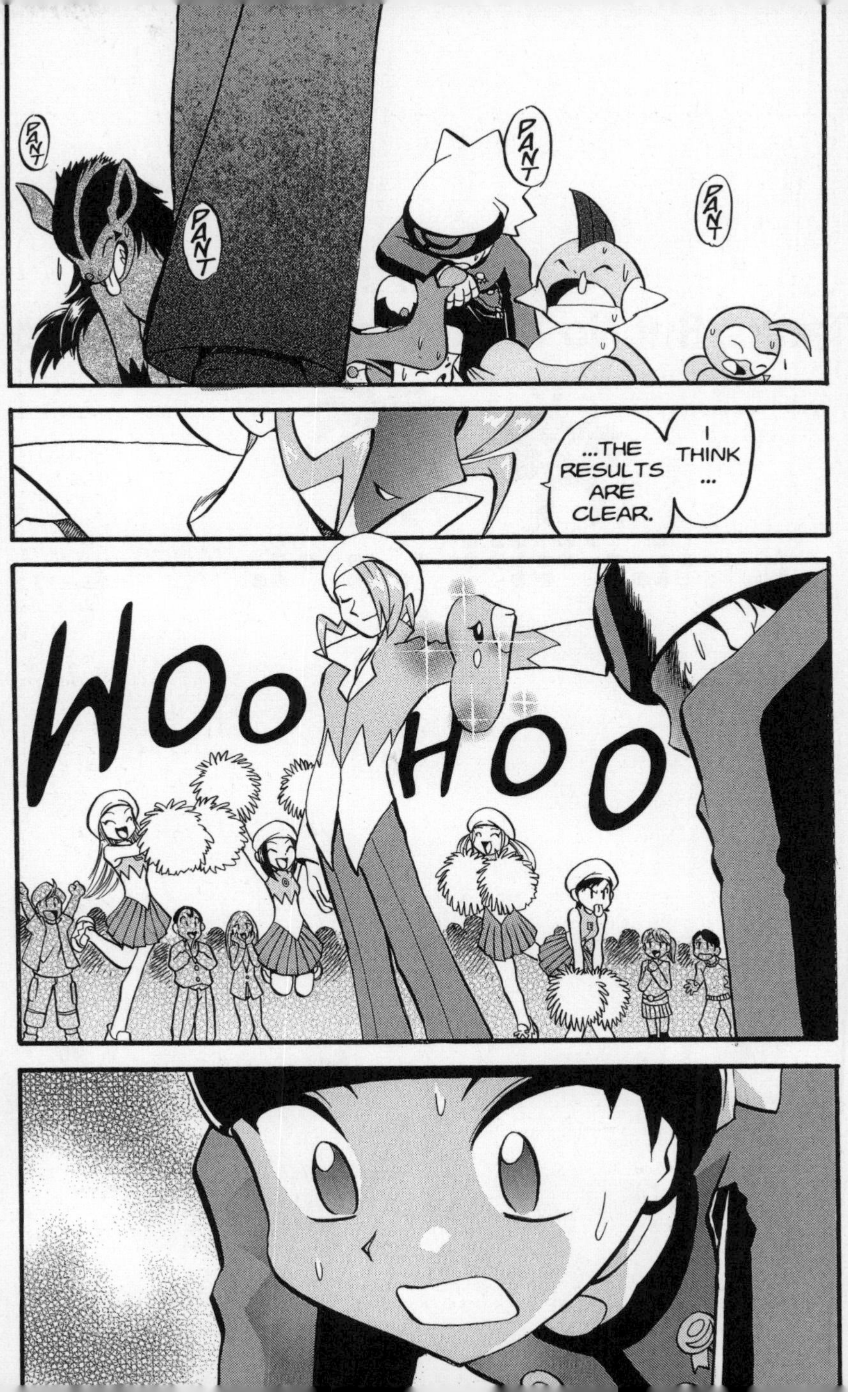
PANT
PANT
PANT
PANT
I THINK ...
...THE RESULTS ARE CLEAR.
WOO HOO

● Chapter 225 ●

Tanks, But No Tanks, Anorith and Lileep

POKéMON ADVENTURES RUBY & SAPPHIRE

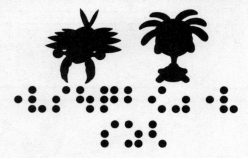

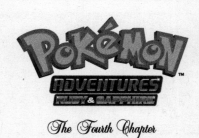

The Fourth Chapter

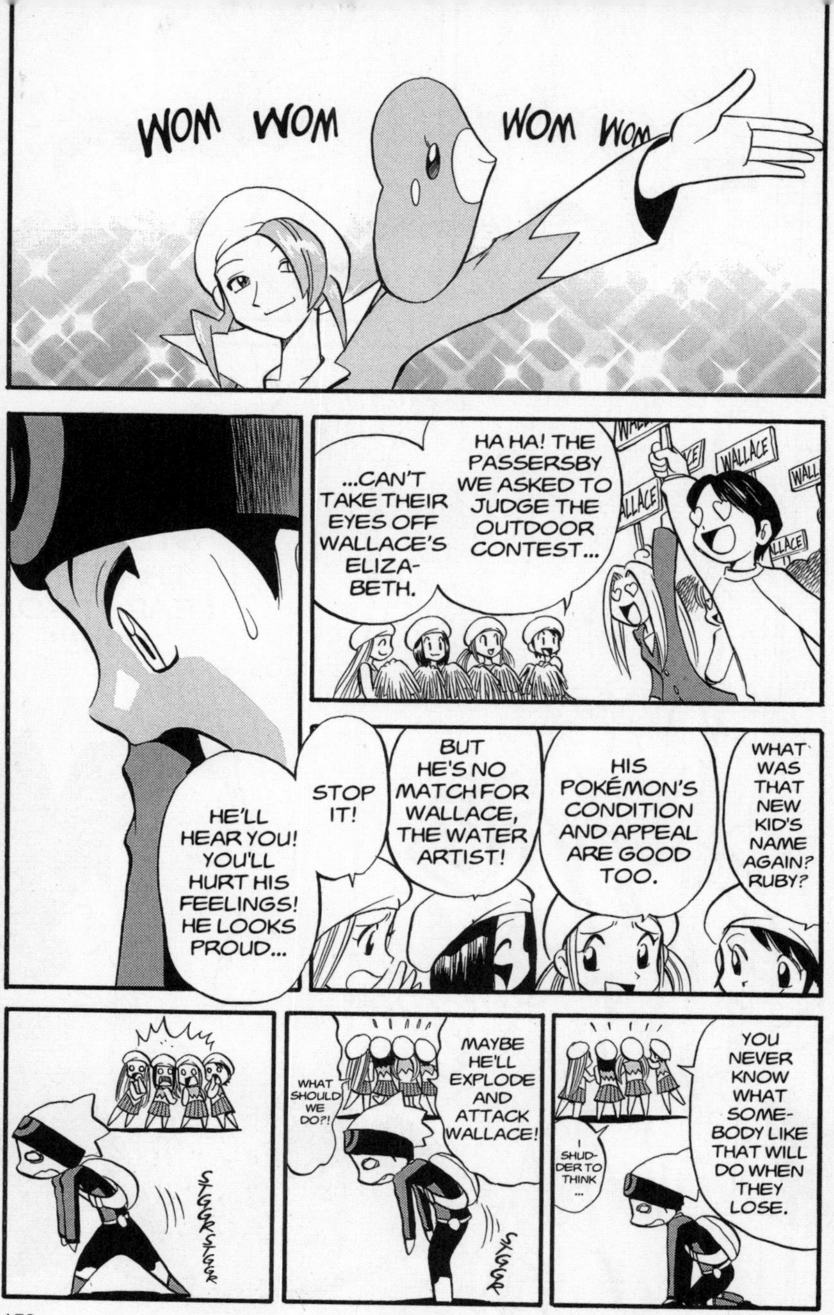
WOM WOM WOM WOM
HA HA! THE PASSERSBY WE ASKED TO JUDGE THE OUTDOOR CONTEST...
...CAN'T TAKE THEIR EYES OFF WALLACE'S ELIZA-BETH.
WALLACE
WALLACE
WHAT WAS THAT NEW KID'S NAME AGAIN? RUBY?
HIS POKÉMON'S CONDITION AND APPEAL ARE GOOD TOO.
BUT HE'S NO MATCH FOR WALLACE, THE WATER ARTIST!
STOP IT!
HE'LL HEAR YOU! YOU'LL HURT HIS FEELINGS! HE LOOKS PROUD...
YOU NEVER KNOW WHAT SOME-BODY LIKE THAT WILL DO WHEN THEY LOSE.
I SHUD-DER TO THINK...
MAYBE HE'LL EXPLODE AND ATTACK WALLACE!
WHAT SHOULD WE DO?!
STGGR
STGGR STGGR

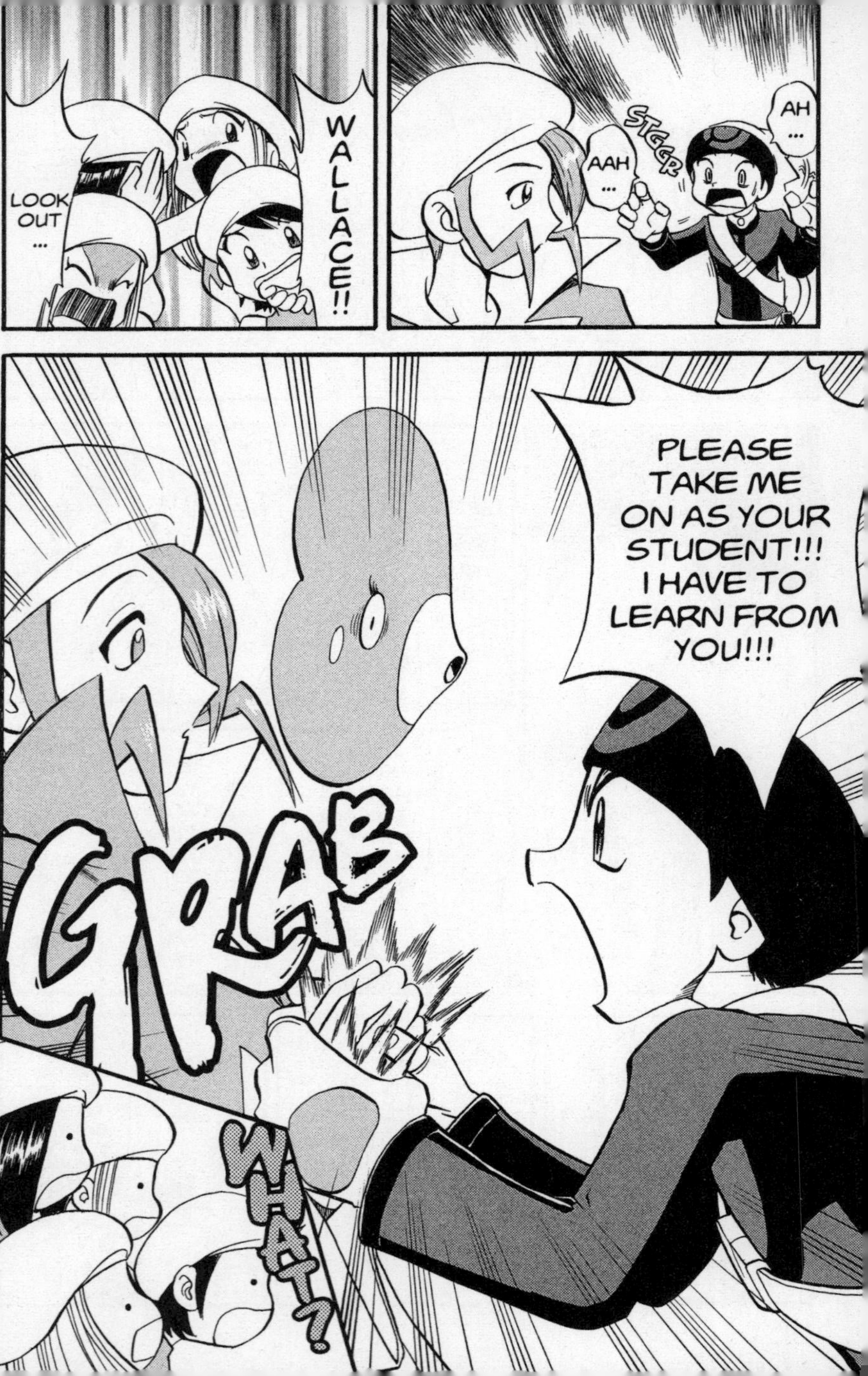
AH ...
STGGR
AAH ...
WALLACE!!
LOOK OUT ...
PLEASE TAKE ME ON AS YOUR STUDENT!!! I HAVE TO LEARN FROM YOU!!!
GRAB
WHAT?!

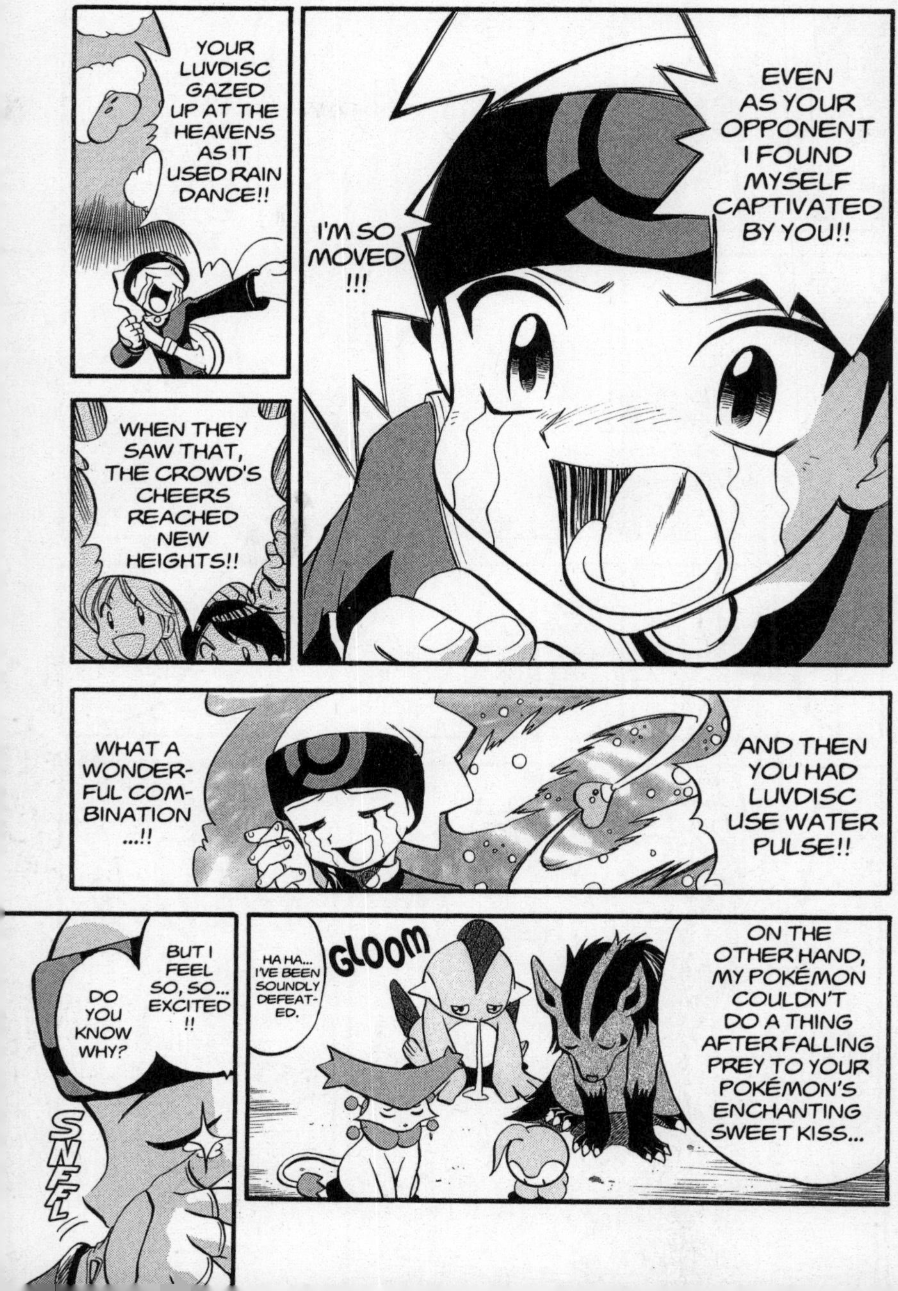
EVEN AS YOUR OPPONENT I FOUND MYSELF CAPTIVATED BY YOU!!
I'M SO MOVED !!!
YOUR LUVDISC GAZED UP AT THE HEAVENS AS IT USED RAIN DANCE!!
WHEN THEY SAW THAT, THE CROWD'S CHEERS REACHED NEW HEIGHTS!!
AND THEN YOU HAD LUVDISC USE WATER PULSE!!
WHAT A WONDER-FUL COM-BINATION ...!!
ON THE OTHER HAND, MY POKÉMON COULDN'T DO A THING AFTER FALLING PREY TO YOUR POKÉMON'S ENCHANTING SWEET KISS...
GLOOM
HA HA... I'VE BEEN SOUNDLY DEFEAT-ED.
BUT I FEEL SO, SO... EXCITED !!
DO YOU KNOW WHY?
SNFFL

EH?

MASTER... MASTER!!

BECAUSE I'VE MET A MASTER POKÉMON CONTEST TRAINER LIKE YOU!

MASTER!!

YOU'LL HAVE TO HONE YOUR SKILLS BY YOURSELF.

I'M SORRY, BUT I DON'T TAKE ON STUDENTS.

WZZZZZZ

I WON'T GIVE UP!!

URROOMM

162

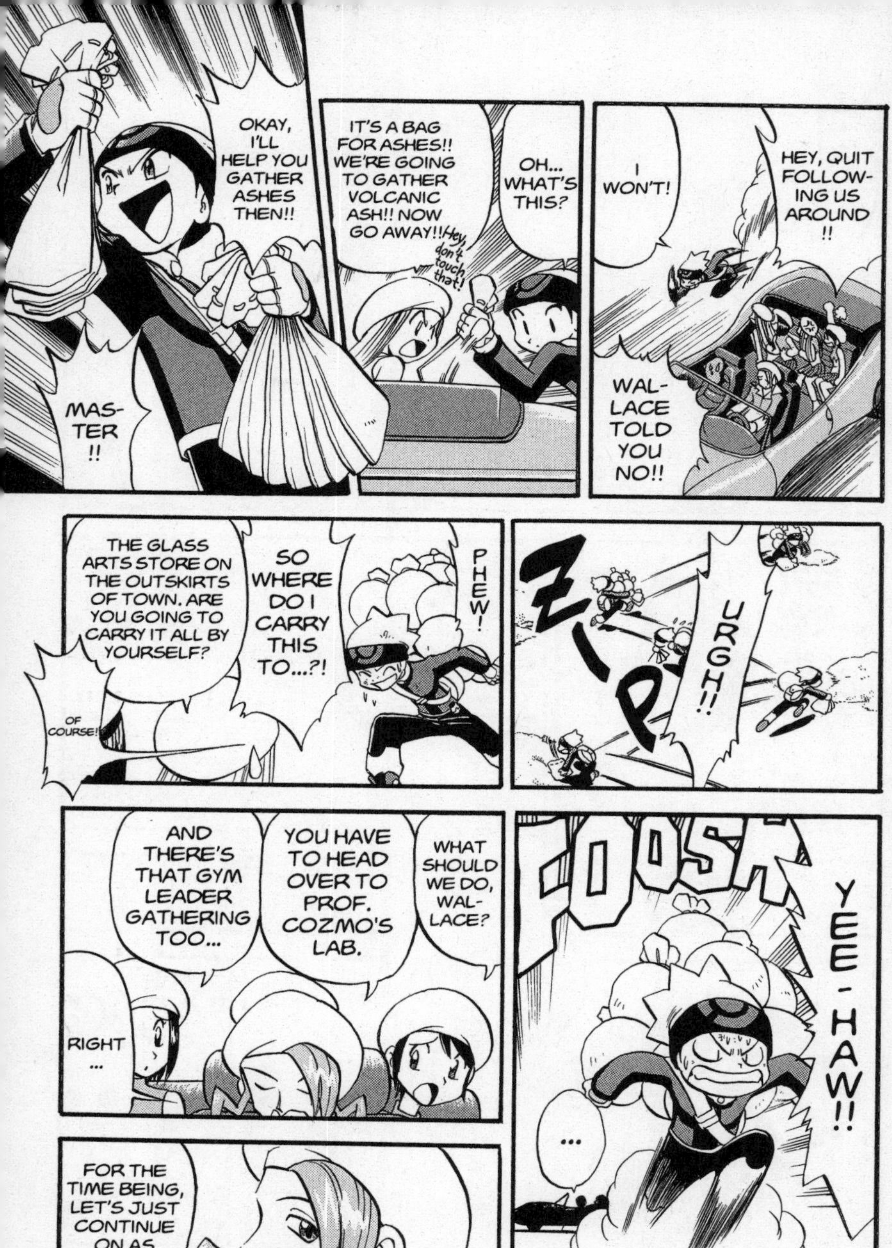

HEY, QUIT FOLLOWING US AROUND!!
I WON'T!
WALLACE TOLD YOU NO!!
OH... WHAT'S THIS?
IT'S A BAG FOR ASHES!! WE'RE GOING TO GATHER VOLCANIC ASH!! NOW GO AWAY!!
Hey, don't touch that!
OKAY, I'LL HELP YOU GATHER ASHES THEN!!
MASTER!!
ZIP
URGH!!
PHEW!
SO WHERE DO I CARRY THIS TO...?!
THE GLASS ARTS STORE ON THE OUTSKIRTS OF TOWN. ARE YOU GOING TO CARRY IT ALL BY YOURSELF?
OF COURSE!
ZOOSH
YEE-HAW!!
...
WHAT SHOULD WE DO, WALLACE?
YOU HAVE TO HEAD OVER TO PROF. COZMO'S LAB.
AND THERE'S THAT GYM LEADER GATHERING TOO...
RIGHT...
FOR THE TIME BEING, LET'S JUST CONTINUE ON AS PLANNED.

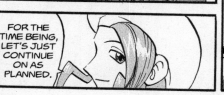

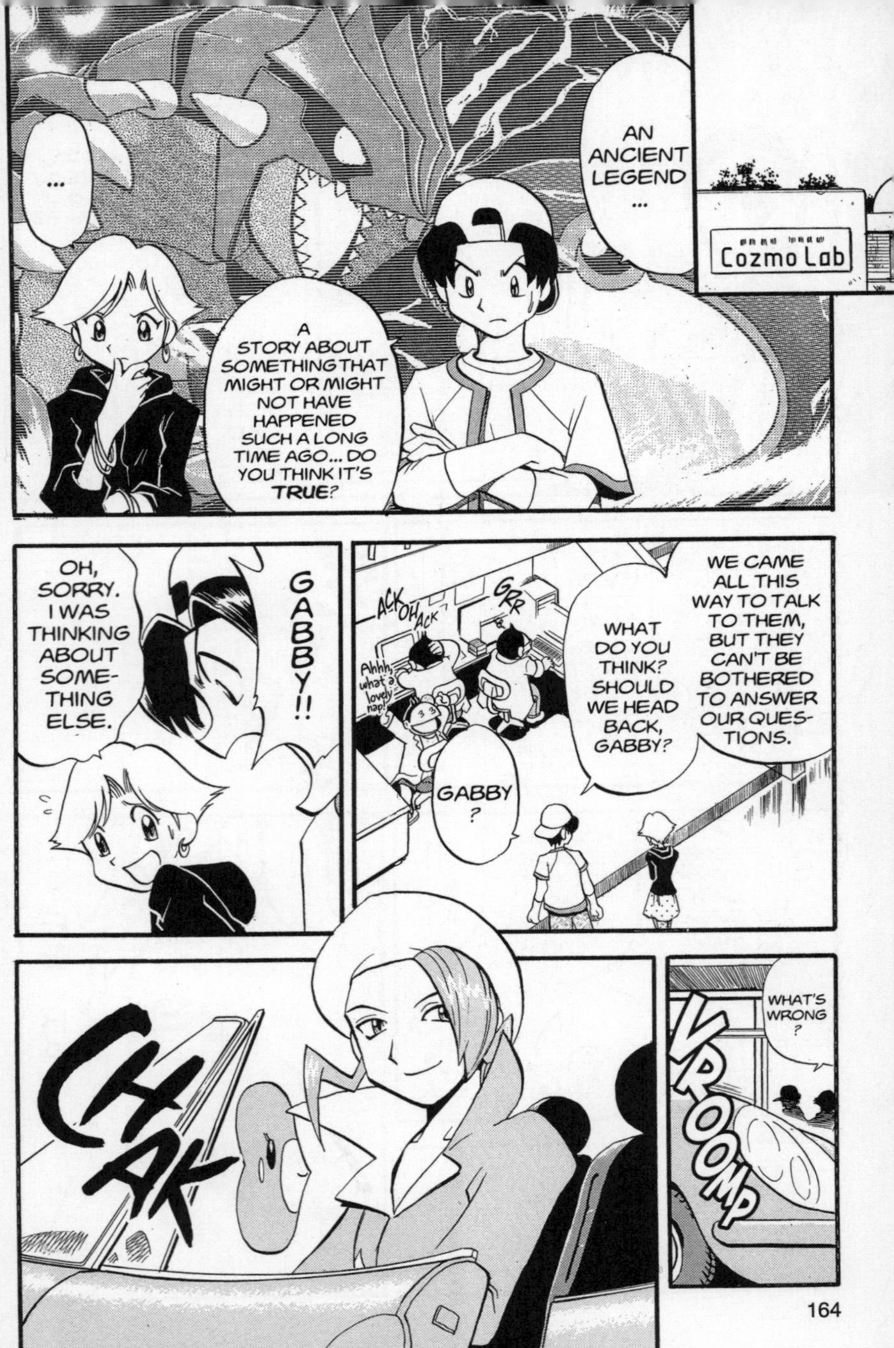
Cozmo Lab
AN ANCIENT LEGEND ...
A STORY ABOUT SOMETHING THAT MIGHT OR MIGHT NOT HAVE HAPPENED SUCH A LONG TIME AGO... DO YOU THINK IT'S TRUE?
...
WE CAME ALL THIS WAY TO TALK TO THEM, BUT THEY CAN'T BE BOTHERED TO ANSWER OUR QUESTIONS.
WHAT DO YOU THINK? SHOULD WE HEAD BACK, GABBY?
GRR
ACK OH ACK
Ahhh, what a lovely nap!
GABBY?
GABBY!!
OH, SORRY. I WAS THINKING ABOUT SOME-THING ELSE.
WHAT'S WRONG?
VROOMP
CHAK

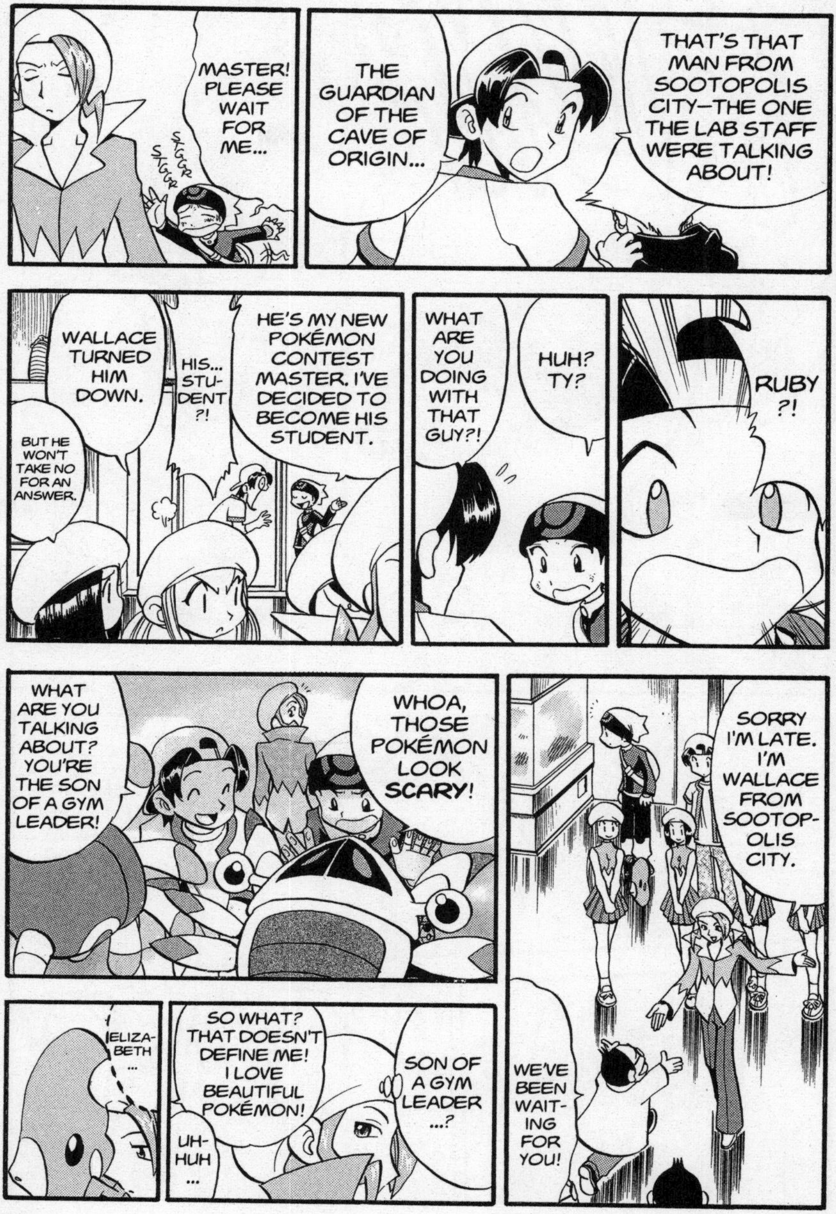
THAT'S THAT MAN FROM SOOTOPOLIS CITY—THE ONE THE LAB STAFF WERE TALKING ABOUT!
THE GUARDIAN OF THE CAVE OF ORIGIN...
MASTER! PLEASE WAIT FOR ME...
STGGR STGGR
RUBY ?!
HUH? TY?
WHAT ARE YOU DOING WITH THAT GUY?!
HE'S MY NEW POKÉMON CONTEST MASTER. I'VE DECIDED TO BECOME HIS STUDENT.
HIS... STUDENT ?!
WALLACE TURNED HIM DOWN.
BUT HE WON'T TAKE NO FOR AN ANSWER.
SORRY I'M LATE. I'M WALLACE FROM SOOTOPOLIS CITY.
WE'VE BEEN WAITING FOR YOU!
WHOA, THOSE POKÉMON LOOK SCARY!
WHAT ARE YOU TALKING ABOUT? YOU'RE THE SON OF A GYM LEADER!
SON OF A GYM LEADER ...?
SO WHAT? THAT DOESN'T DEFINE ME! I LOVE BEAUTIFUL POKÉMON!
UH-HUH ...
ELIZABETH ...

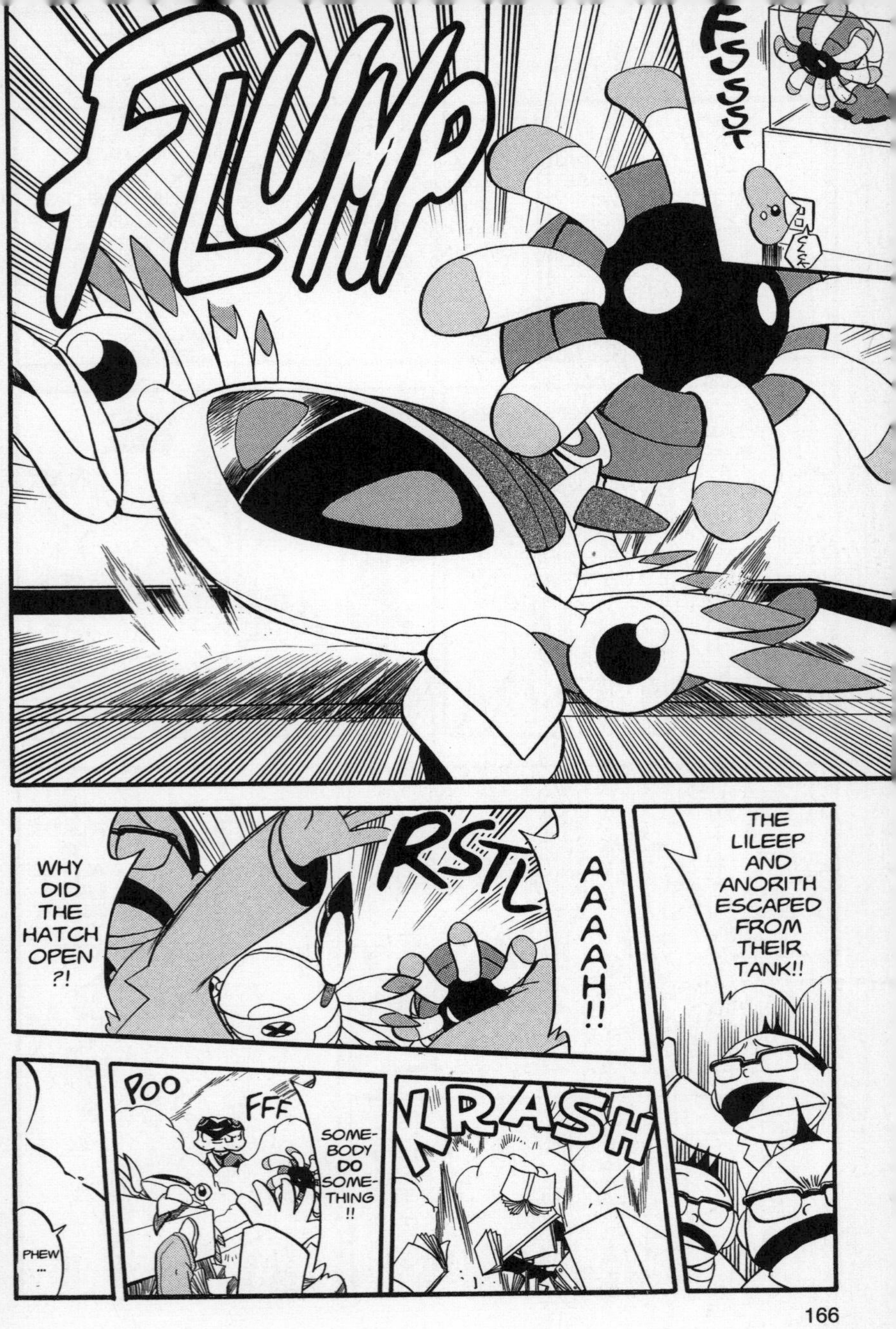
FLUMP
FSSST
THE LILEEP AND ANORITH ESCAPED FROM THEIR TANK!!
RSTL
AAAAAH!!
WHY DID THE HATCH OPEN?!
KRASH
SOME-BODY DO SOME-THING!!
POO FFF
PHEW...

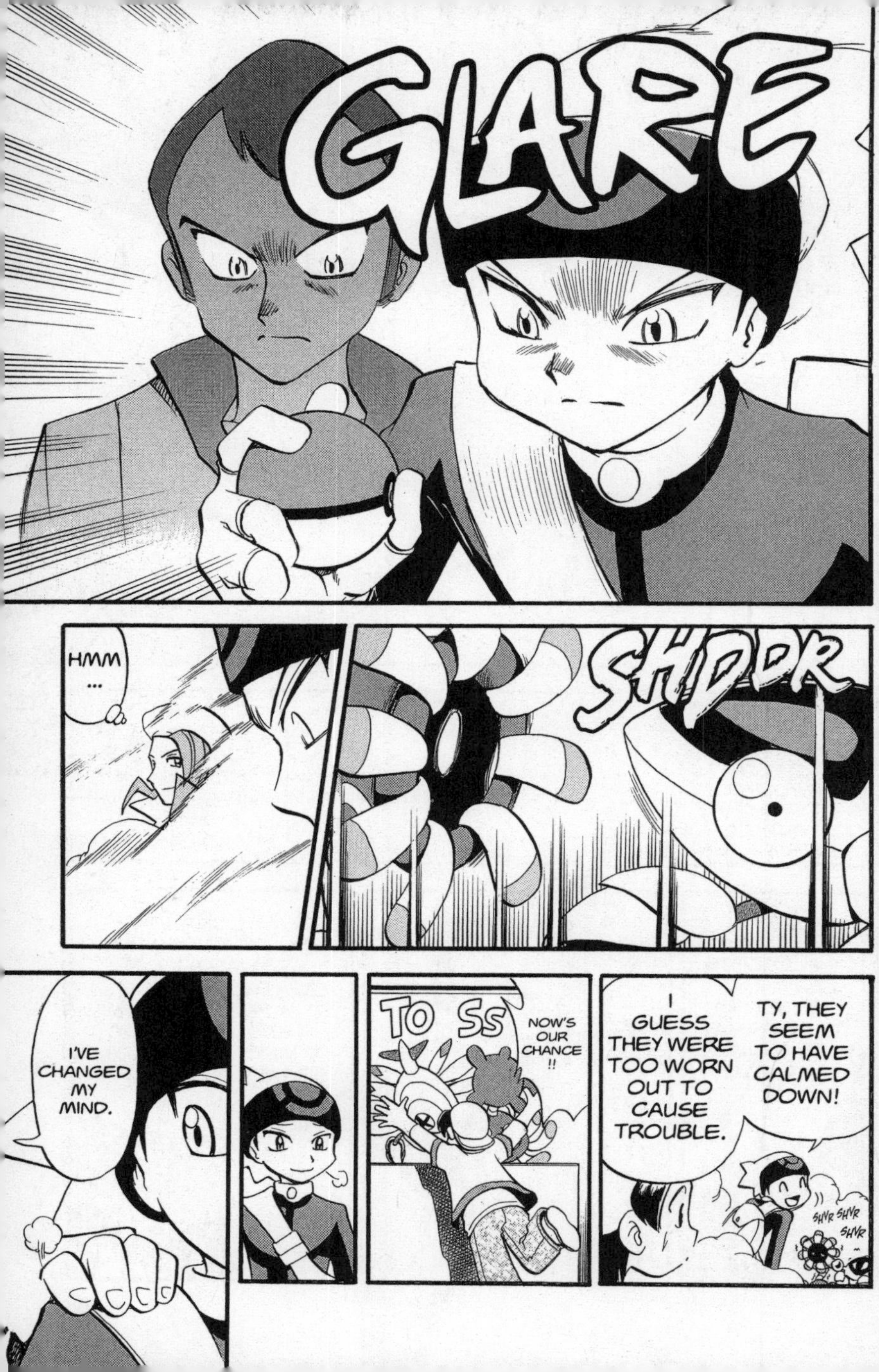
GLARE
SHDDR
HMM...
TY, THEY SEEM TO HAVE CALMED DOWN!
I GUESS THEY WERE TOO WORN OUT TO CAUSE TROUBLE.
SHVR SHVR SHVR
NOW'S OUR CHANCE!!
TOSS
I'VE CHANGED MY MIND.

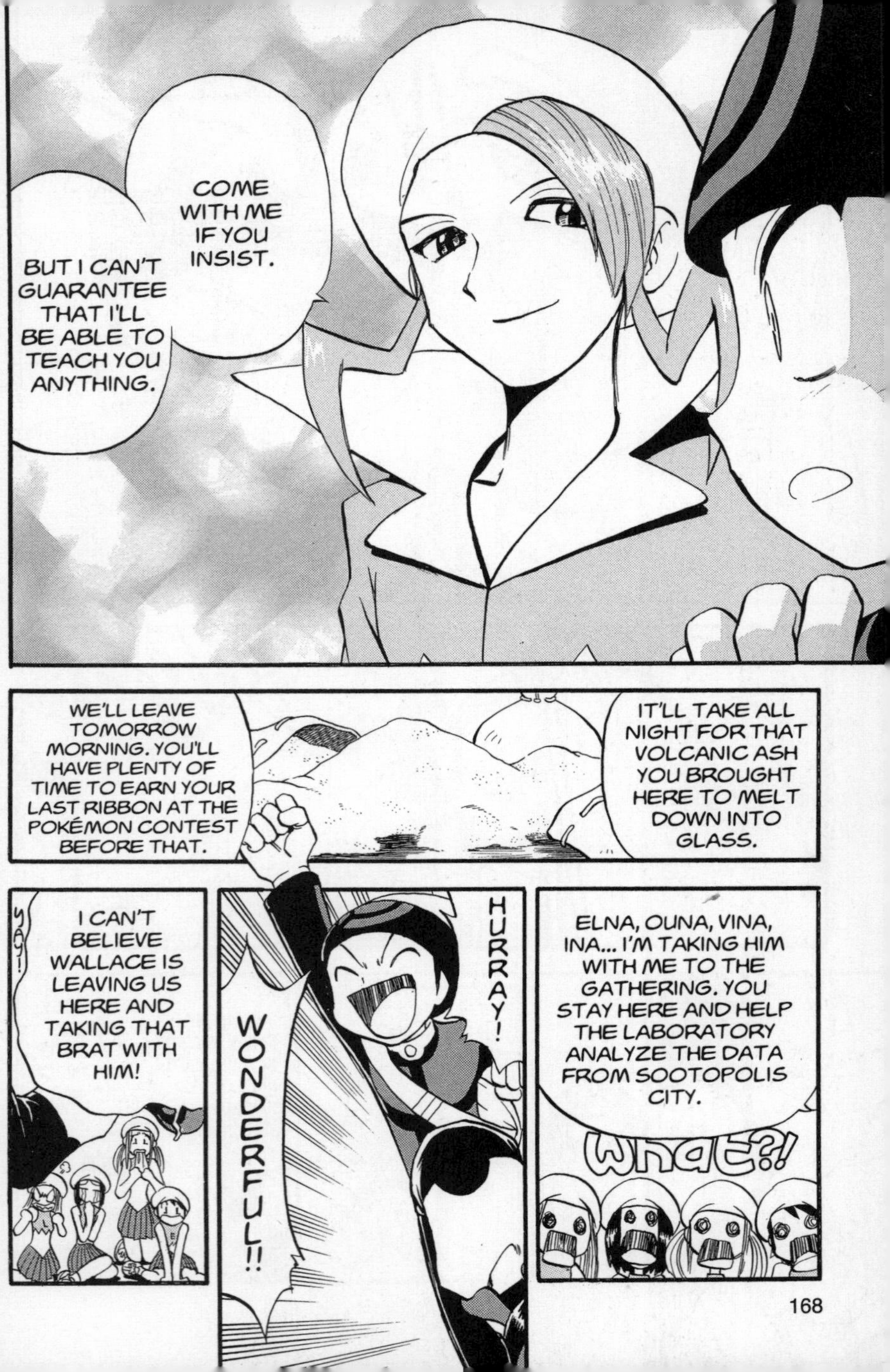
COME WITH ME IF YOU INSIST.
BUT I CAN'T GUARANTEE THAT I'LL BE ABLE TO TEACH YOU ANYTHING.
IT'LL TAKE ALL NIGHT FOR THAT VOLCANIC ASH YOU BROUGHT HERE TO MELT DOWN INTO GLASS.
WE'LL LEAVE TOMORROW MORNING. YOU'LL HAVE PLENTY OF TIME TO EARN YOUR LAST RIBBON AT THE POKÉMON CONTEST BEFORE THAT.
ELNA, OUNA, VINA, INA... I'M TAKING HIM WITH ME TO THE GATHERING. YOU STAY HERE AND HELP THE LABORATORY ANALYZE THE DATA FROM SOOTOPOLIS CITY.
WHAT?!
HURRAY!
WONDERFUL!!
I CAN'T BELIEVE WALLACE IS LEAVING US HERE AND TAKING THAT BRAT WITH HIM!
YAY!

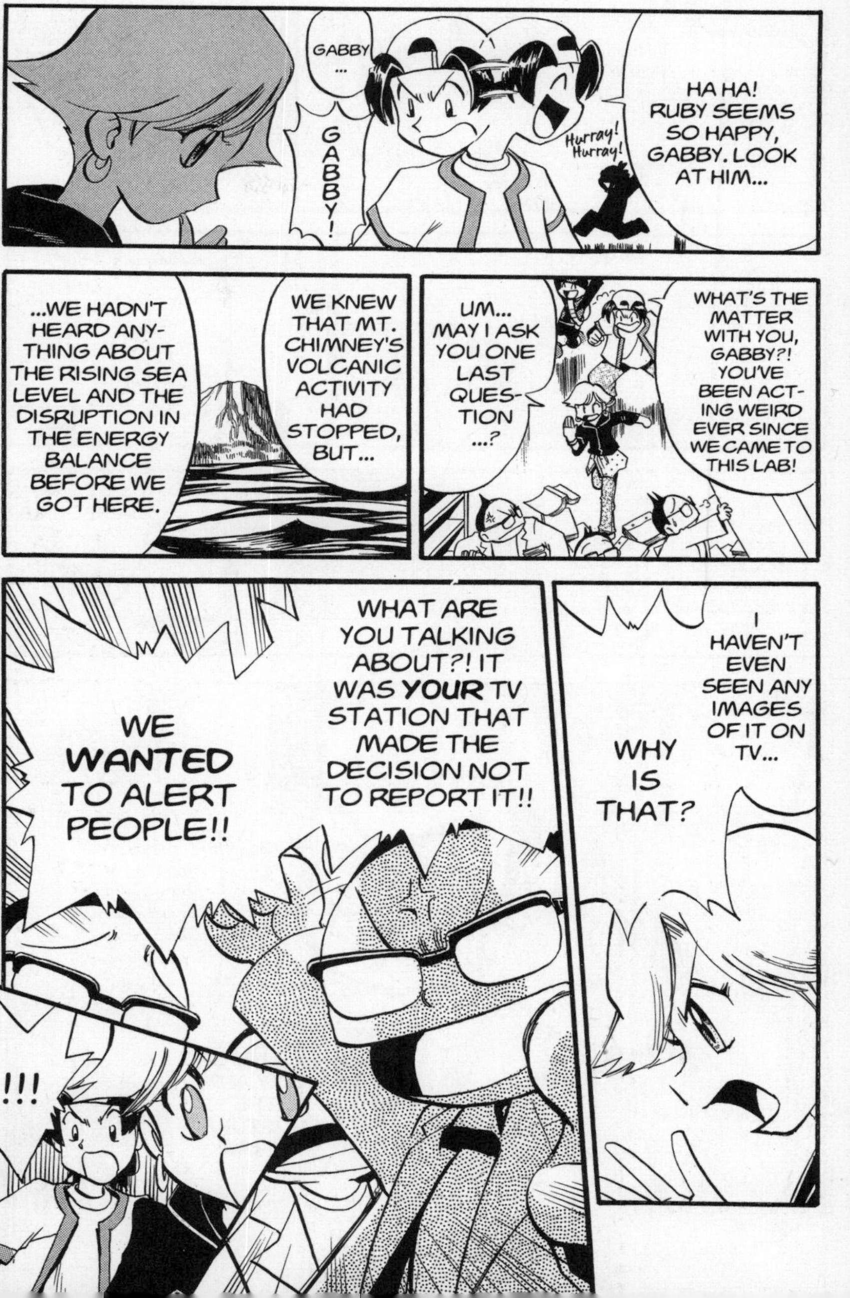
HA HA! RUBY SEEMS SO HAPPY, GABBY. LOOK AT HIM...
Hurray! Hurray!
GABBY!
GABBY ...
WHAT'S THE MATTER WITH YOU, GABBY?! YOU'VE BEEN ACTING WEIRD EVER SINCE WE CAME TO THIS LAB!
UM... MAY I ASK YOU ONE LAST QUESTION ...?
WE KNEW THAT MT. CHIMNEY'S VOLCANIC ACTIVITY HAD STOPPED, BUT...
...WE HADN'T HEARD ANYTHING ABOUT THE RISING SEA LEVEL AND THE DISRUPTION IN THE ENERGY BALANCE BEFORE WE GOT HERE.
I HAVEN'T EVEN SEEN ANY IMAGES OF IT ON TV...
WHY IS THAT?
WHAT ARE YOU TALKING ABOUT?! IT WAS **YOUR** TV STATION THAT MADE THE DECISION NOT TO REPORT IT!!
WE **WANTED** TO ALERT PEOPLE!!
!!!

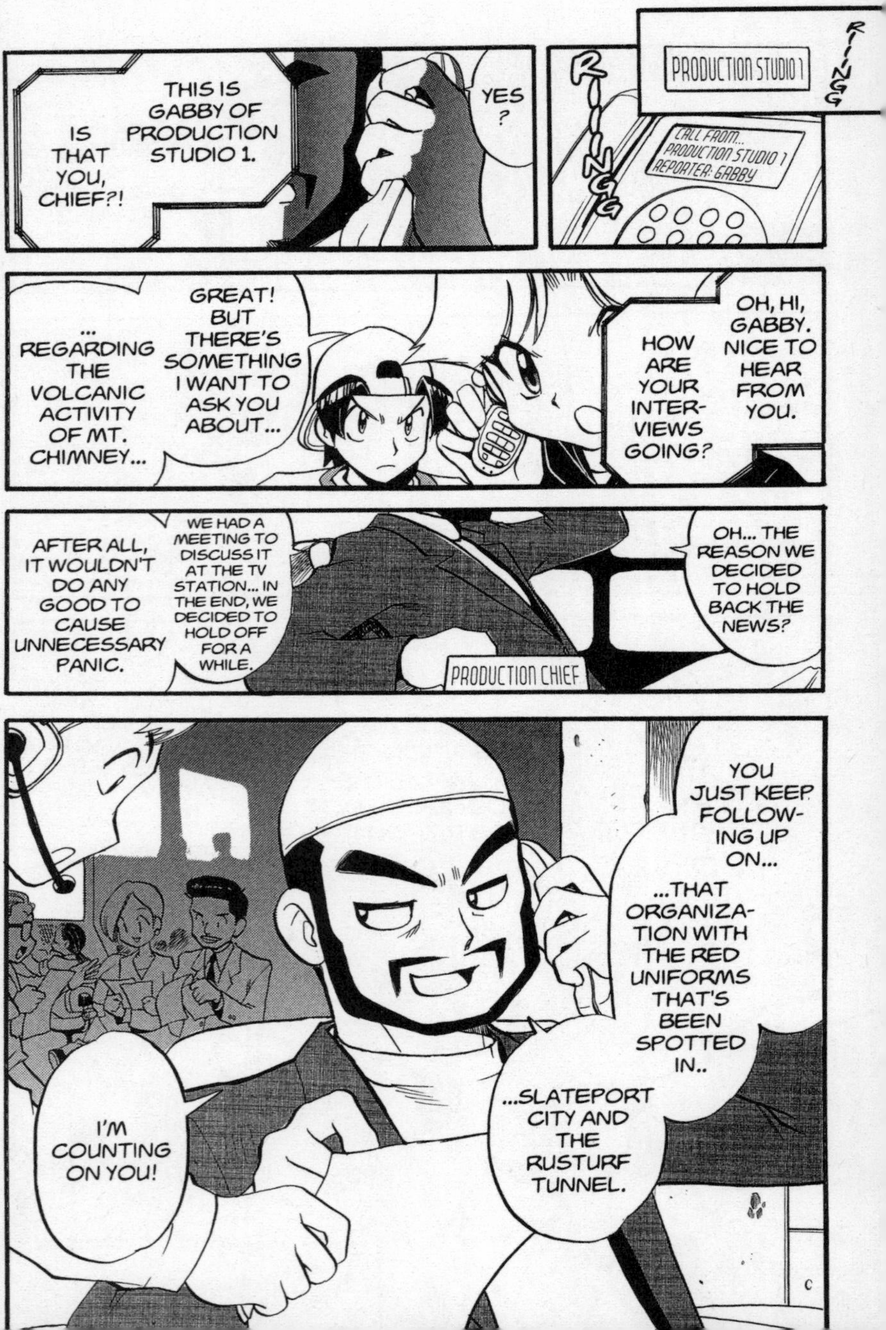
PRODUCTION STUDIO 1
RIIINGG
RIIINGG
CALL FROM... PRODUCTION STUDIO 1 REPORTER: GABBY
YES?
THIS IS GABBY OF PRODUCTION STUDIO 1.
IS THAT YOU, CHIEF?!
OH, HI, GABBY. NICE TO HEAR FROM YOU.
HOW ARE YOUR INTER-VIEWS GOING?
GREAT! BUT THERE'S SOMETHING I WANT TO ASK YOU ABOUT...
...REGARDING THE VOLCANIC ACTIVITY OF MT. CHIMNEY...
PRODUCTION CHIEF
OH... THE REASON WE DECIDED TO HOLD BACK THE NEWS?
WE HAD A MEETING TO DISCUSS IT AT THE TV STATION... IN THE END, WE DECIDED TO HOLD OFF FOR A WHILE.
AFTER ALL, IT WOULDN'T DO ANY GOOD TO CAUSE UNNECESSARY PANIC.
YOU JUST KEEP FOLLOW-ING UP ON...
...THAT ORGANIZA-TION WITH THE RED UNIFORMS THAT'S BEEN SPOTTED IN..
...SLATEPORT CITY AND THE RUSTURF TUNNEL.
I'M COUNTING ON YOU!

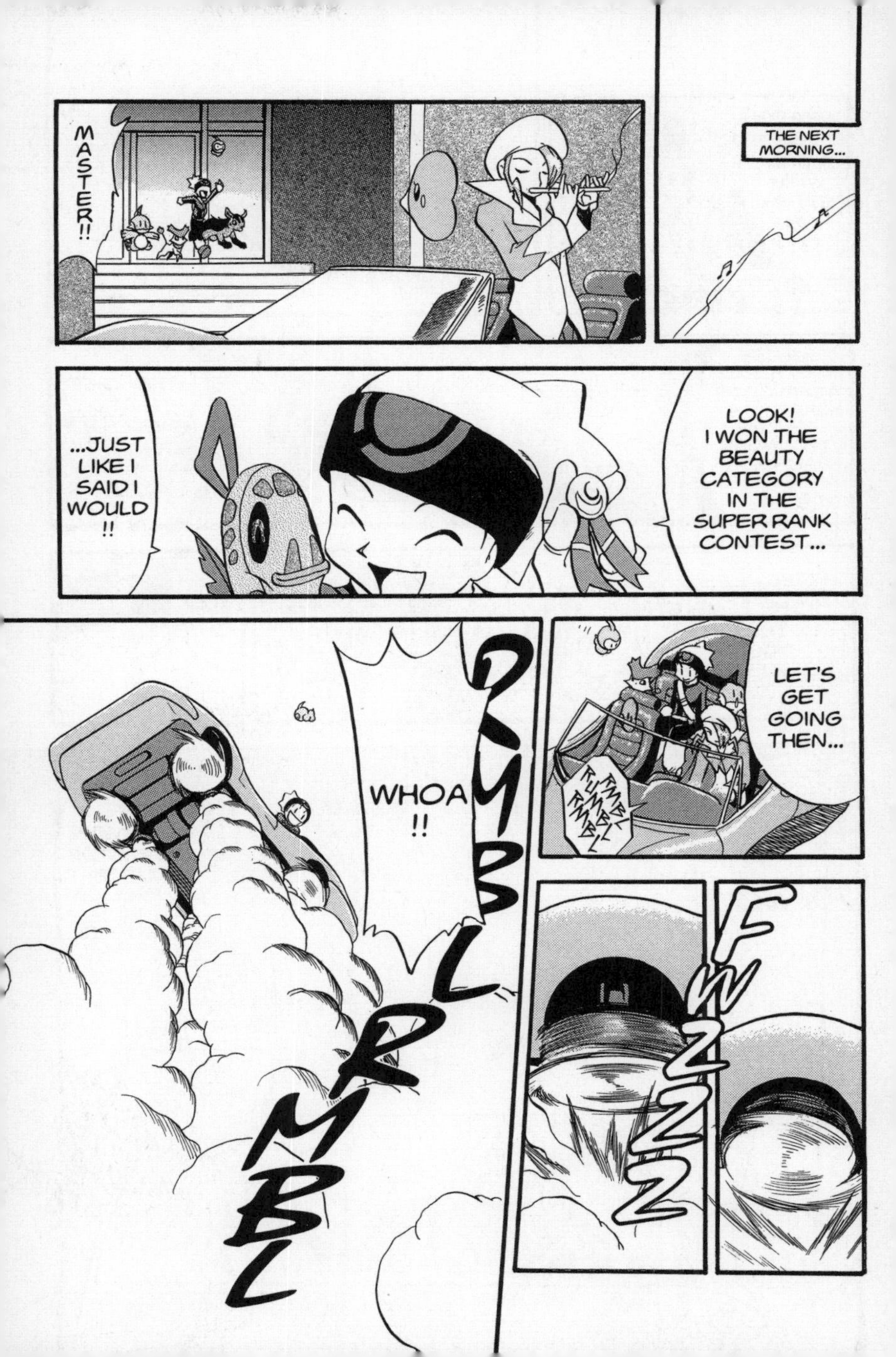
THE NEXT MORNING...
MASTER!!
LOOK! I WON THE BEAUTY CATEGORY IN THE SUPER RANK CONTEST...
...JUST LIKE I SAID I WOULD!!
LET'S GET GOING THEN...
RMBL RUMBL RMBL RMBL
FWZZZZ
WHOA!!
RMBL RMBL

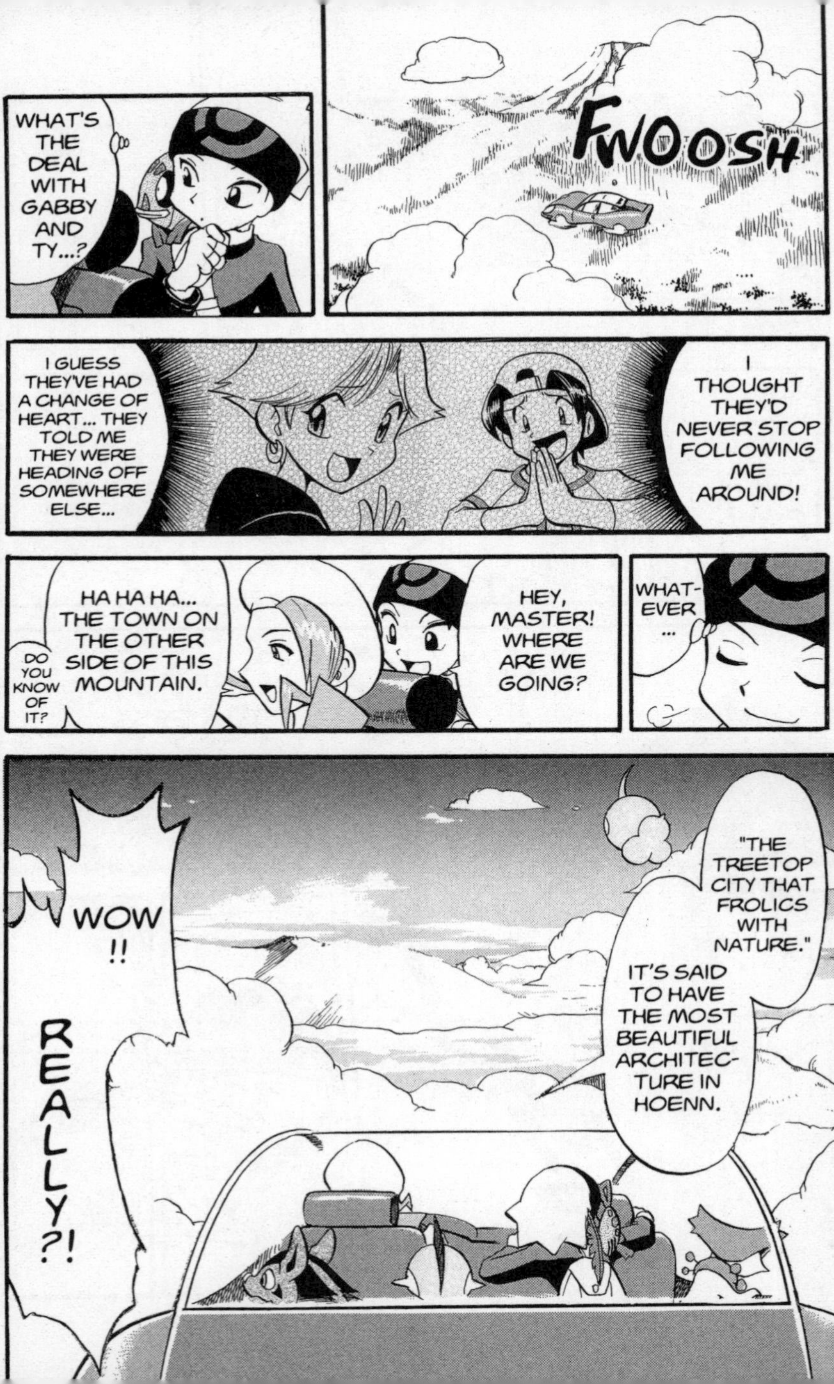
FWOOSH
WHAT'S THE DEAL WITH GABBY AND TY...?
I THOUGHT THEY'D NEVER STOP FOLLOWING ME AROUND!
I GUESS THEY'VE HAD A CHANGE OF HEART... THEY TOLD ME THEY WERE HEADING OFF SOMEWHERE ELSE...
WHAT-EVER...
HEY, MASTER! WHERE ARE WE GOING?
HA HA HA... THE TOWN ON THE OTHER SIDE OF THIS MOUNTAIN.
DO YOU KNOW OF IT?
"THE TREETOP CITY THAT FROLICS WITH NATURE."
IT'S SAID TO HAVE THE MOST BEAUTIFUL ARCHITEC-TURE IN HOENN.
WOW!!
REALLY?!

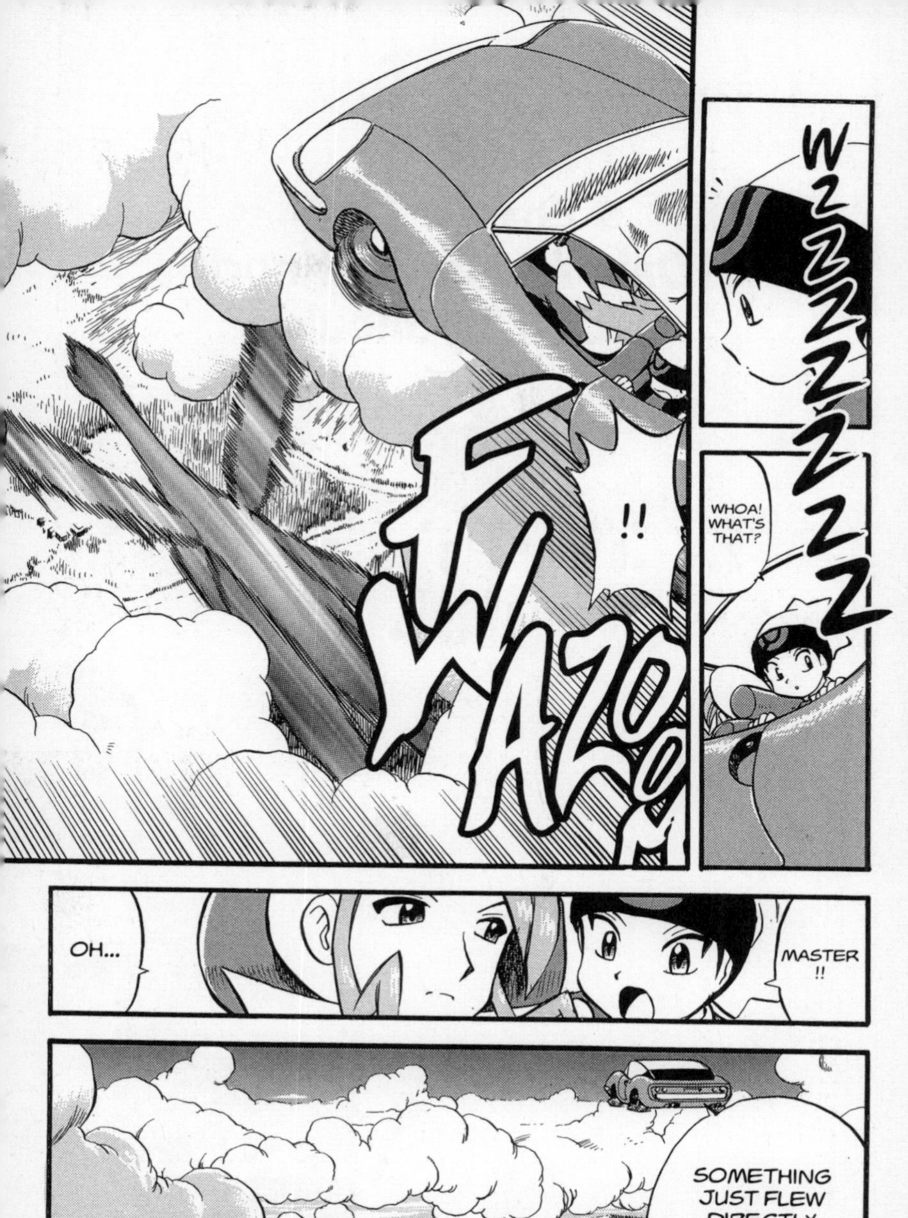
WZZZZZZZZZ
WHOA! WHAT'S THAT?
FWAZOOOM
!!
MASTER !!
OH...
SOMETHING JUST FLEW DIRECTLY UNDER US!!

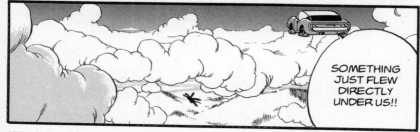

● Chapter 226 ●
I Dare Ya, Altaria...Knock Chic off My Shoulder

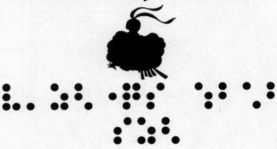

The Fourth Chapter

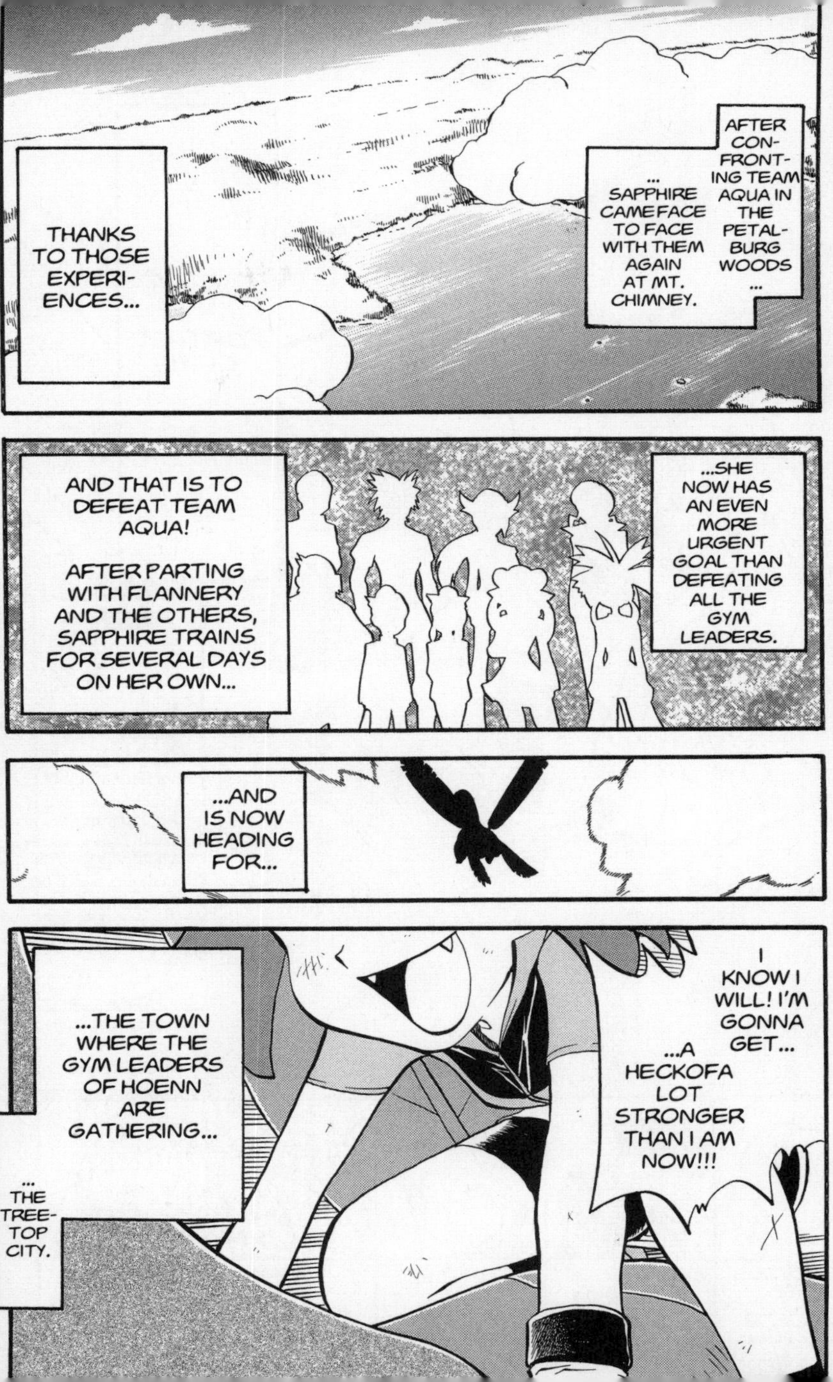
AFTER CON-FRONT-ING TEAM AQUA IN THE PETAL-BURG WOODS...
...SAPPHIRE CAME FACE TO FACE WITH THEM AGAIN AT MT. CHIMNEY.
THANKS TO THOSE EXPERI-ENCES...
...SHE NOW HAS AN EVEN MORE URGENT GOAL THAN DEFEATING ALL THE GYM LEADERS.
AND THAT IS TO DEFEAT TEAM AQUA!
AFTER PARTING WITH FLANNERY AND THE OTHERS, SAPPHIRE TRAINS FOR SEVERAL DAYS ON HER OWN...
...AND IS NOW HEADING FOR...
I KNOW I WILL! I'M GONNA GET...
...A HECKOFA LOT STRONGER THAN I AM NOW!!!
...THE TOWN WHERE THE GYM LEADERS OF HOENN ARE GATHERING...
...THE TREE-TOP CITY.

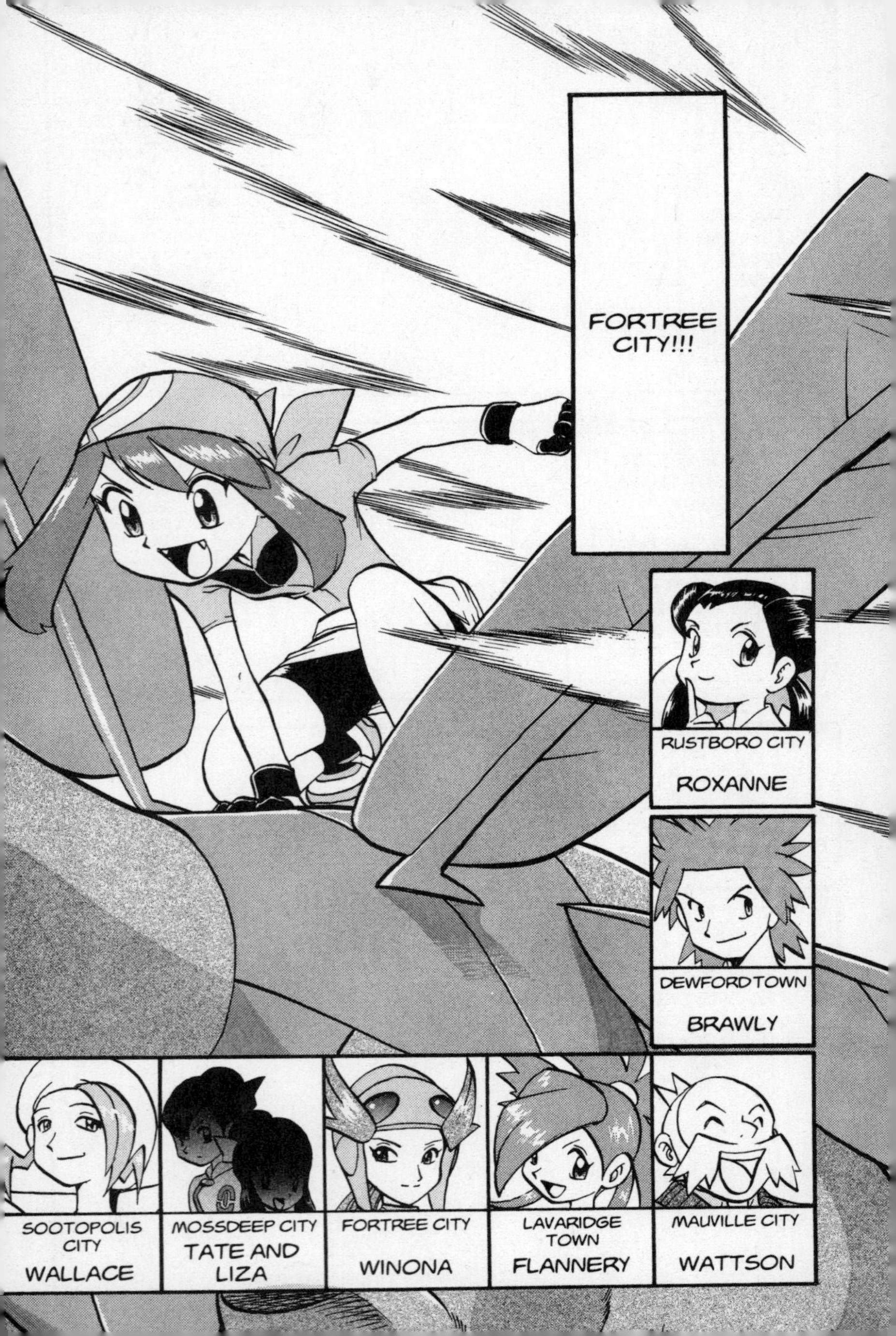
FORTREE CITY!!!
RUSTBORO CITY
ROXANNE
DEWFORD TOWN
BRAWLY
MAUVILLE CITY
WATTSON
LAVARIDGE TOWN
FLANNERY
FORTREE CITY
WINONA
MOSSDEEP CITY
TATE AND LIZA
SOOTOPOLIS CITY
WALLACE

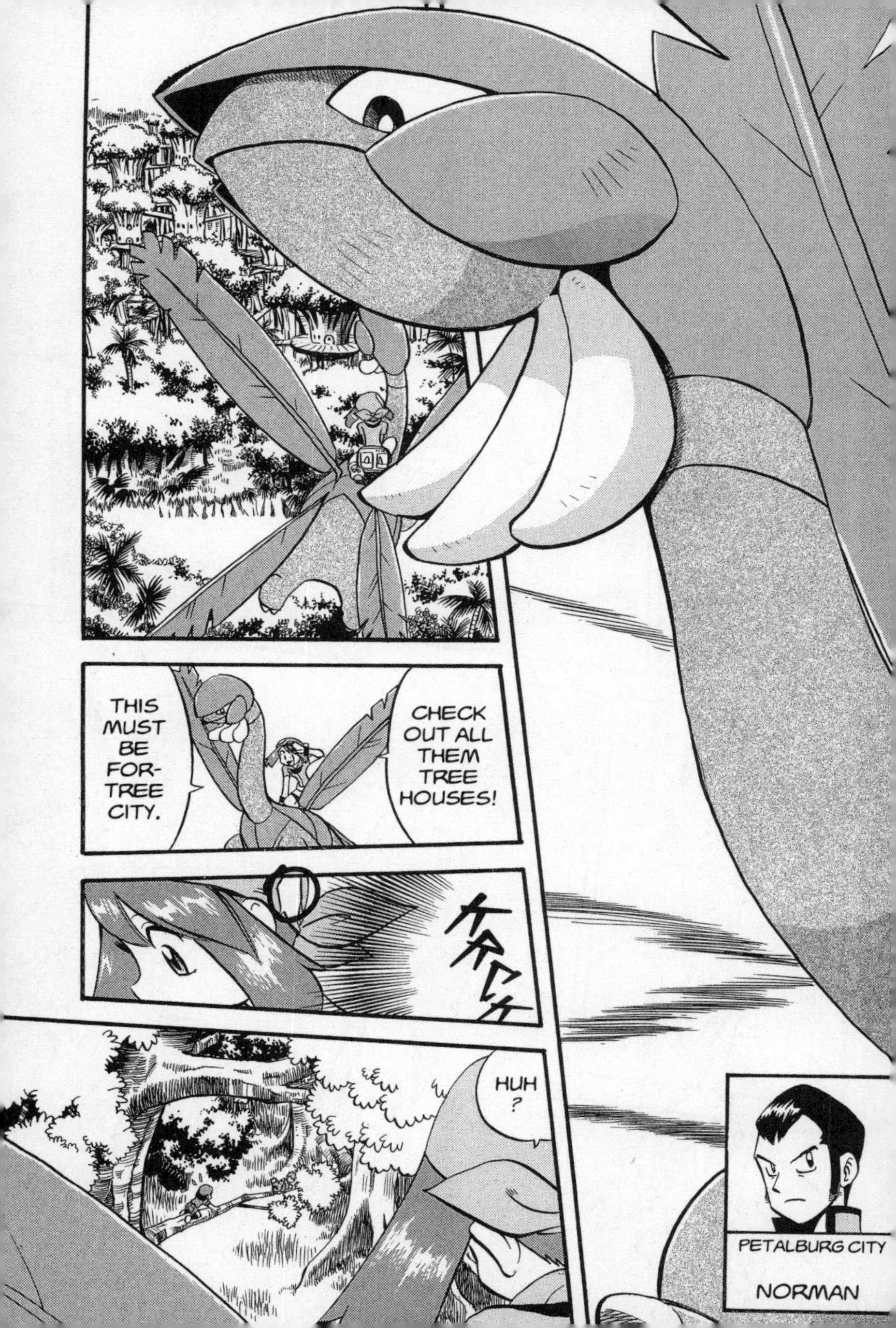
CHECK OUT ALL THEM TREE HOUSES!
THIS MUST BE FOR-TREE CITY.
KRCH
HUH?
PETALBURG CITY
NORMAN

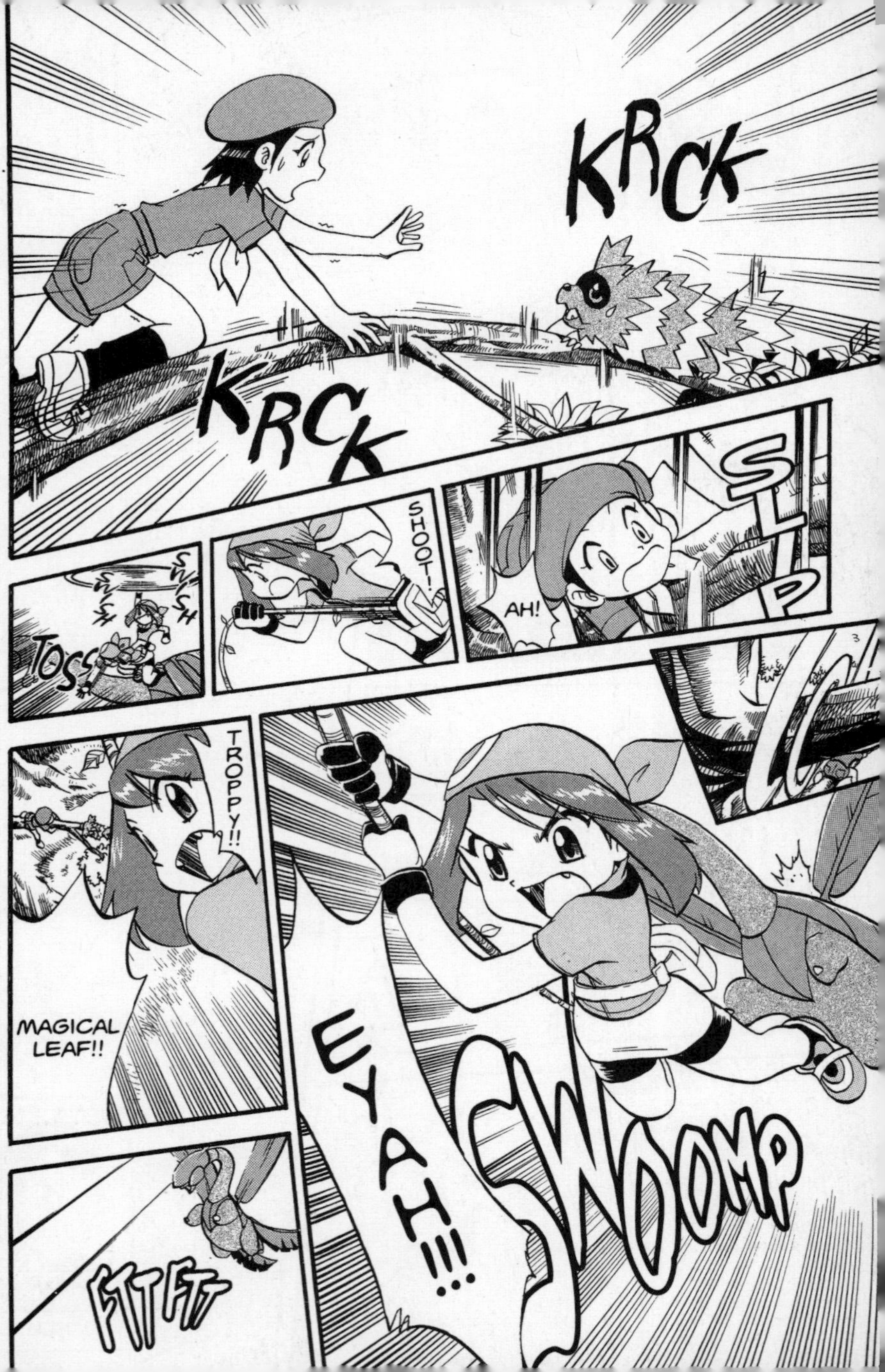
KRCK
KRCK
SLIP
AH!
SHOOT!
SWISH
SWISH
TOSS
EYAH!!!
SWOOMP
TROPPY!!
MAGICAL LEAF!!
FTTFTT

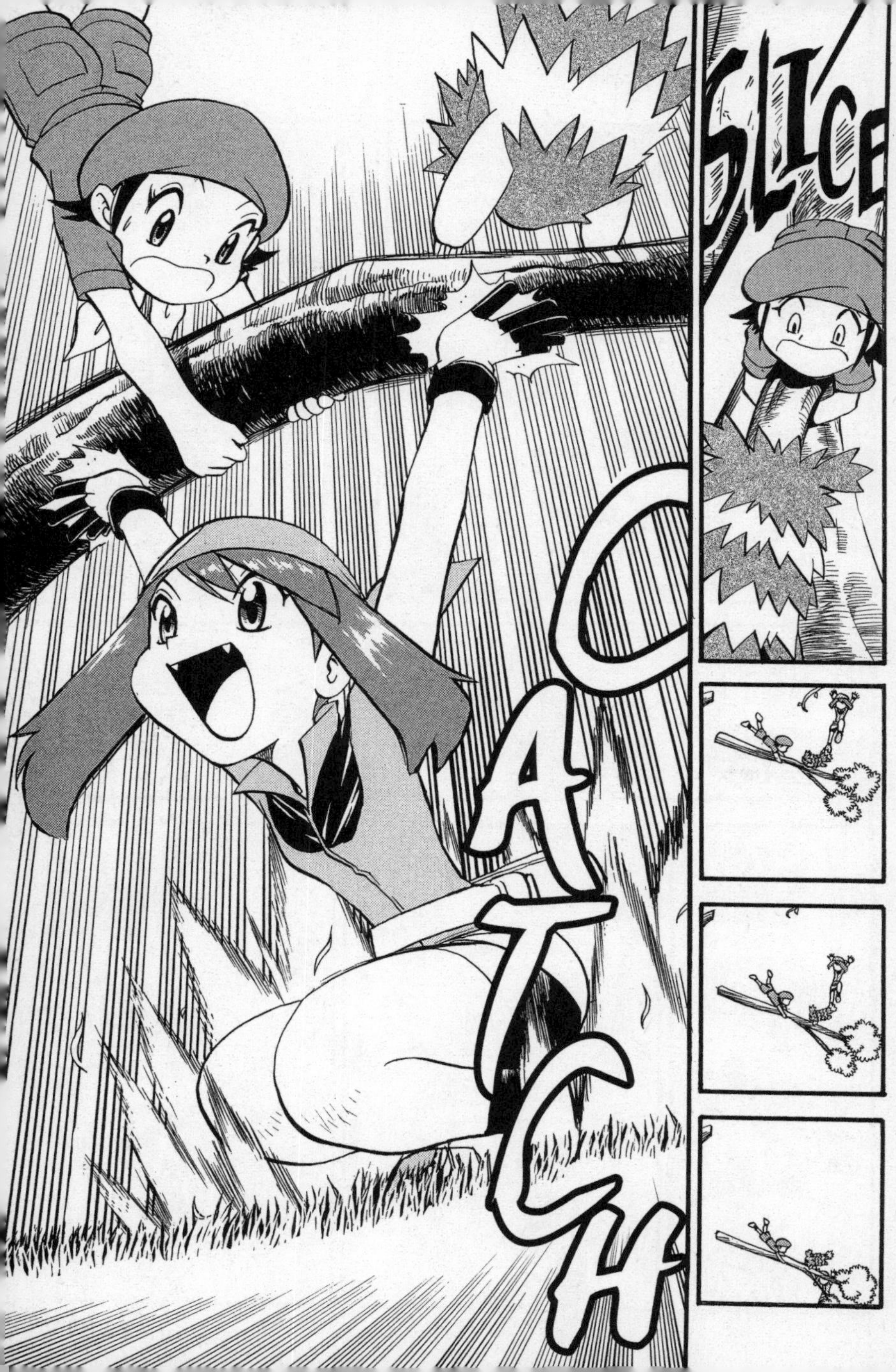
SLICE
CATCH

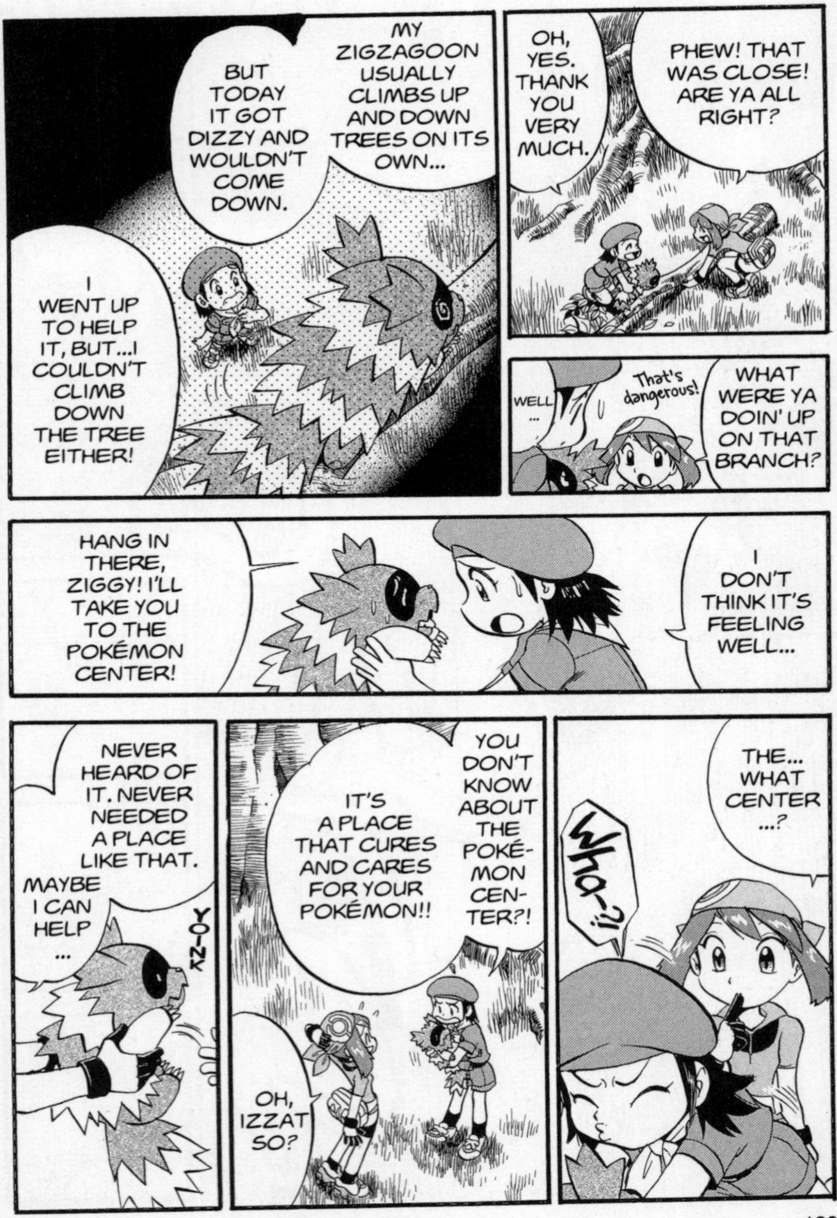
PHEW! THAT WAS CLOSE! ARE YA ALL RIGHT?
OH, YES. THANK YOU VERY MUCH.
WHAT WERE YA DOIN' UP ON THAT BRANCH?
That's dangerous!
WELL...
MY ZIGZAGOON USUALLY CLIMBS UP AND DOWN TREES ON ITS OWN...
BUT TODAY IT GOT DIZZY AND WOULDN'T COME DOWN.
I WENT UP TO HELP IT, BUT...I COULDN'T CLIMB DOWN THE TREE EITHER!
I DON'T THINK IT'S FEELING WELL...
HANG IN THERE, ZIGGY! I'LL TAKE YOU TO THE POKÉMON CENTER!
THE... WHAT CENTER ...?
Wha-?!
YOU DON'T KNOW ABOUT THE POKÉMON CENTER?!
IT'S A PLACE THAT CURES AND CARES FOR YOUR POKÉMON!!
OH, IZZAT SO?
NEVER HEARD OF IT. NEVER NEEDED A PLACE LIKE THAT.
MAYBE I CAN HELP ...
YOINK

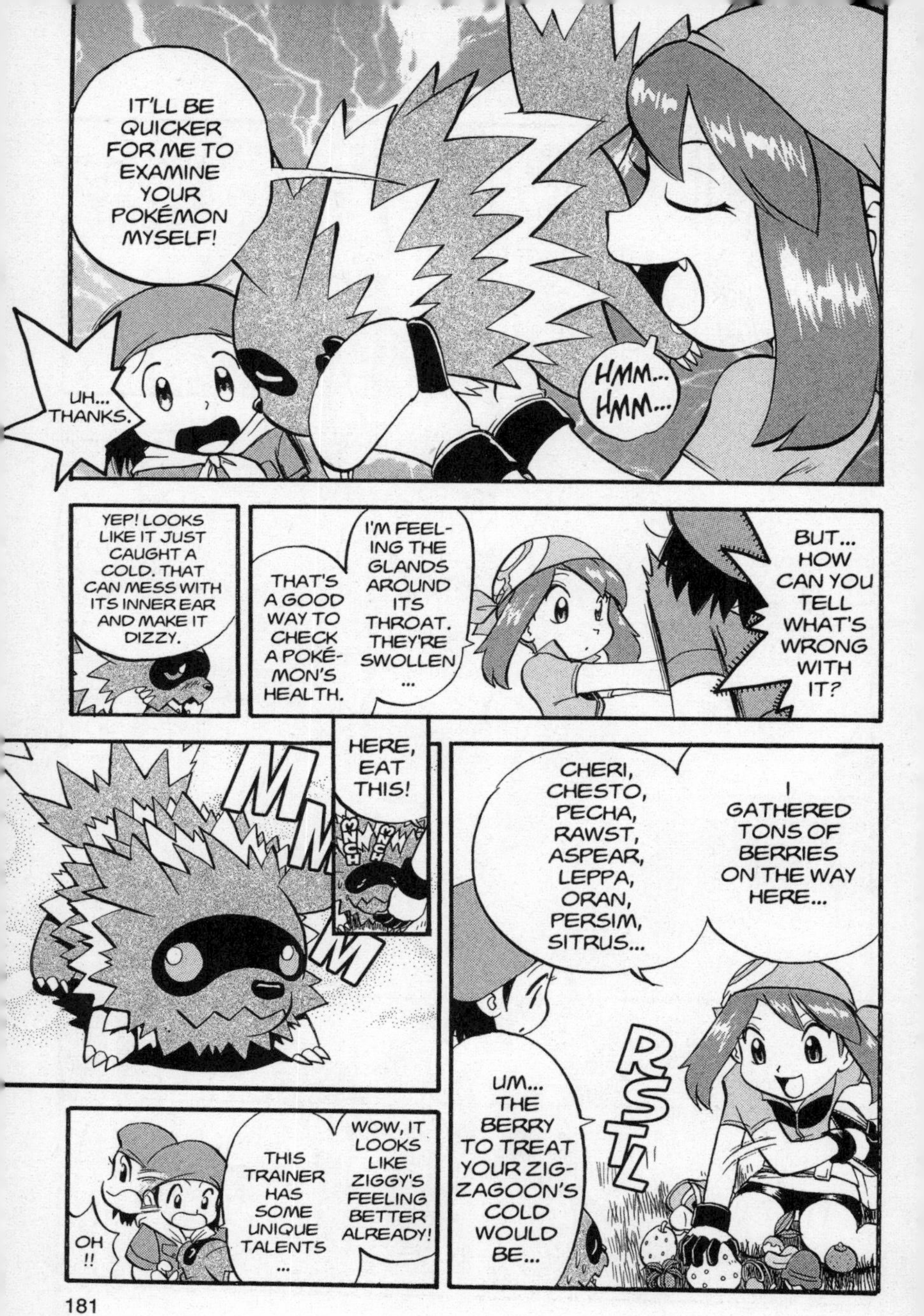
IT'LL BE QUICKER FOR ME TO EXAMINE YOUR POKÉMON MYSELF!
HMM... HMM...
UH... THANKS.
BUT... HOW CAN YOU TELL WHAT'S WRONG WITH IT?
I'M FEEL-ING THE GLANDS AROUND ITS THROAT. THEY'RE SWOLLEN ...
THAT'S A GOOD WAY TO CHECK A POKÉ-MON'S HEALTH.
YEP! LOOKS LIKE IT JUST CAUGHT A COLD. THAT CAN MESS WITH ITS INNER EAR AND MAKE IT DIZZY.
I GATHERED TONS OF BERRIES ON THE WAY HERE...
CHERI, CHESTO, PECHA, RAWST, ASPEAR, LEPPA, ORAN, PERSIM, SITRUS...
RSTL
UM... THE BERRY TO TREAT YOUR ZIG-ZAGOON'S COLD WOULD BE...
HERE, EAT THIS!
MNCH MNCH
MMMM
WOW, IT LOOKS LIKE ZIGGY'S FEELING BETTER ALREADY!
THIS TRAINER HAS SOME UNIQUE TALENTS ...
OH !!

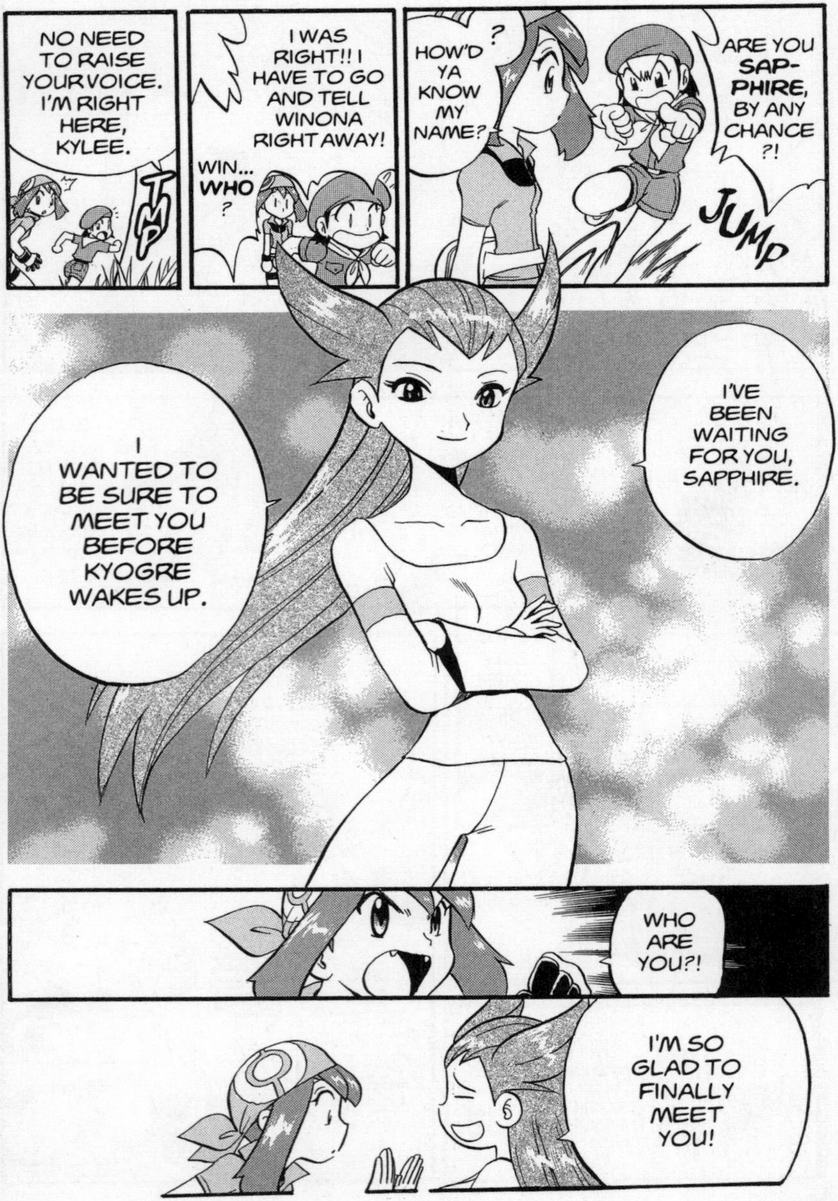

ARE YOU SAPPHIRE, BY ANY CHANCE?!
JUMP
HOW'D YA KNOW MY NAME?
?
I WAS RIGHT!! I HAVE TO GO AND TELL WINONA RIGHT AWAY!
WIN... WHO ?
NO NEED TO RAISE YOUR VOICE. I'M RIGHT HERE, KYLEE.
TMP
I'VE BEEN WAITING FOR YOU, SAPPHIRE.
I WANTED TO BE SURE TO MEET YOU BEFORE KYOGRE WAKES UP.
WHO ARE YOU?!
I'M SO GLAD TO FINALLY MEET YOU!

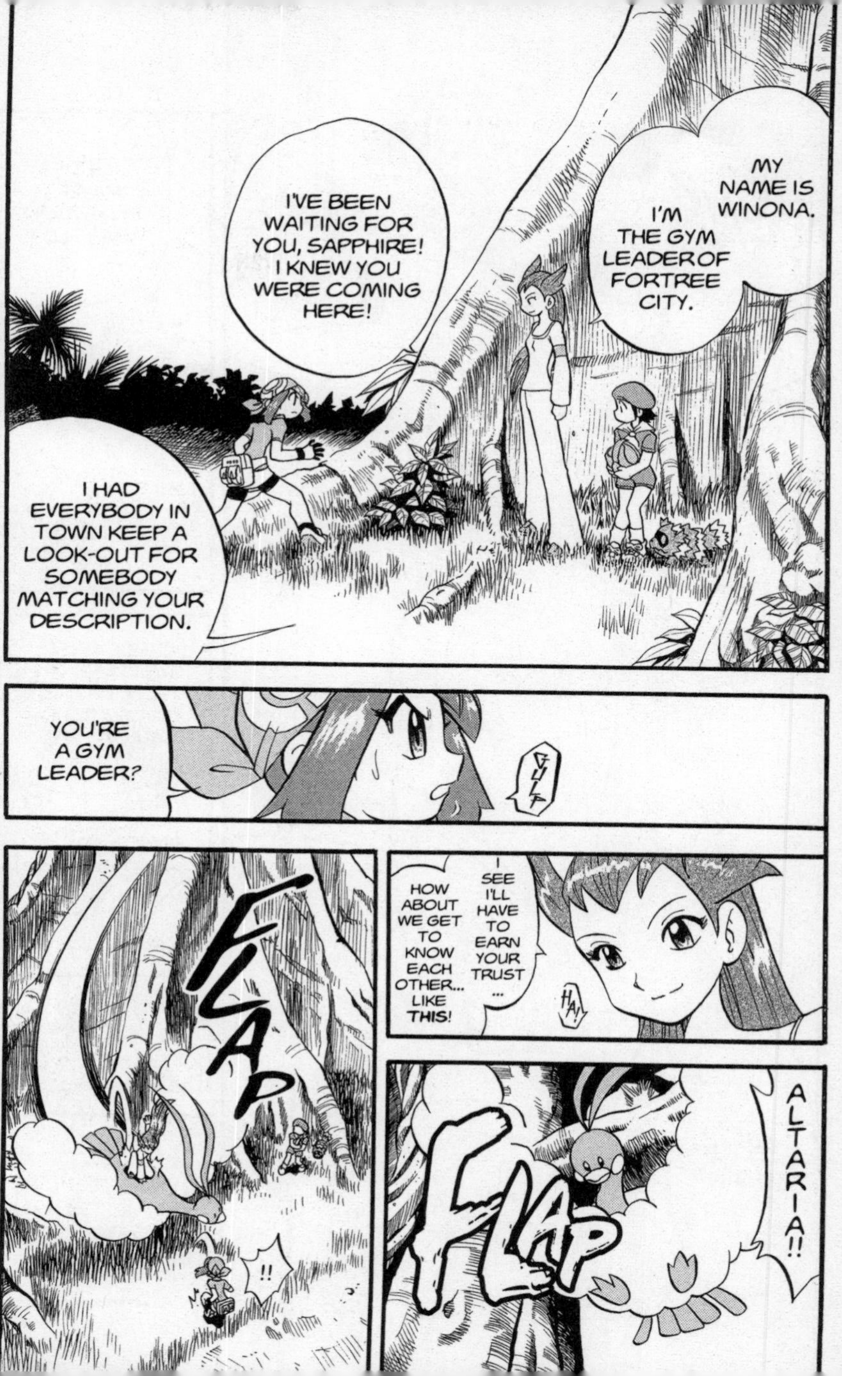
MY NAME IS WINONA.
I'M THE GYM LEADER OF FORTREE CITY.
I'VE BEEN WAITING FOR YOU, SAPPHIRE! I KNEW YOU WERE COMING HERE!
I HAD EVERYBODY IN TOWN KEEP A LOOK-OUT FOR SOMEBODY MATCHING YOUR DESCRIPTION.
GULP
YOU'RE A GYM LEADER?
HA!
I SEE I'LL HAVE TO EARN YOUR TRUST...
HOW ABOUT WE GET TO KNOW EACH OTHER... LIKE THIS!
ALTARIA!!
FLAP
FLAP
!!

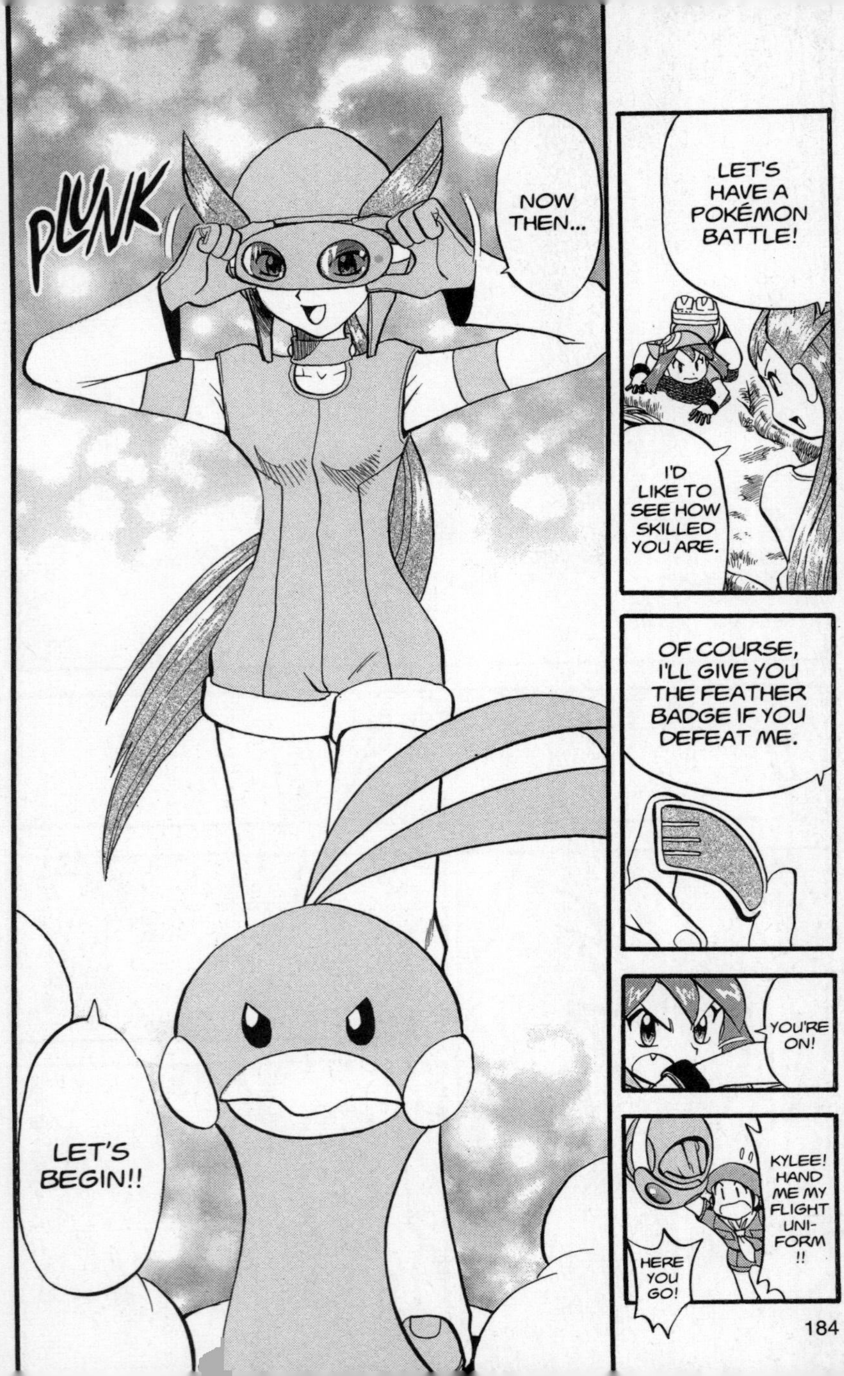
LET'S HAVE A POKÉMON BATTLE!
I'D LIKE TO SEE HOW SKILLED YOU ARE.
OF COURSE, I'LL GIVE YOU THE FEATHER BADGE IF YOU DEFEAT ME.
YOU'RE ON!
KYLEE! HAND ME MY FLIGHT UNI-FORM !!
HERE YOU GO!
PLUNK
NOW THEN...
LET'S BEGIN!!

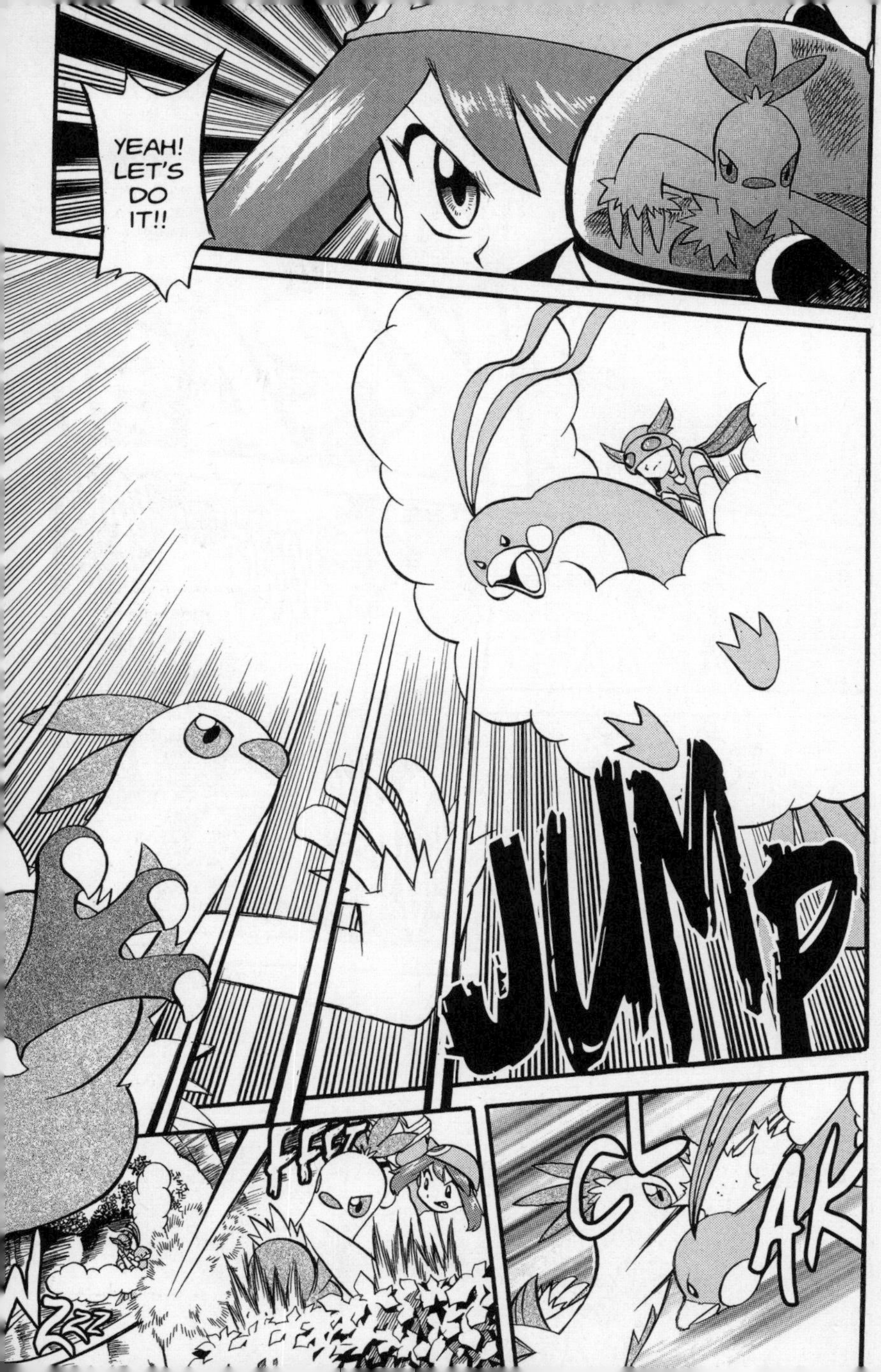
YEAH! LET'S DO IT!!
JUMP
CLAK
FFCT
ZZZ

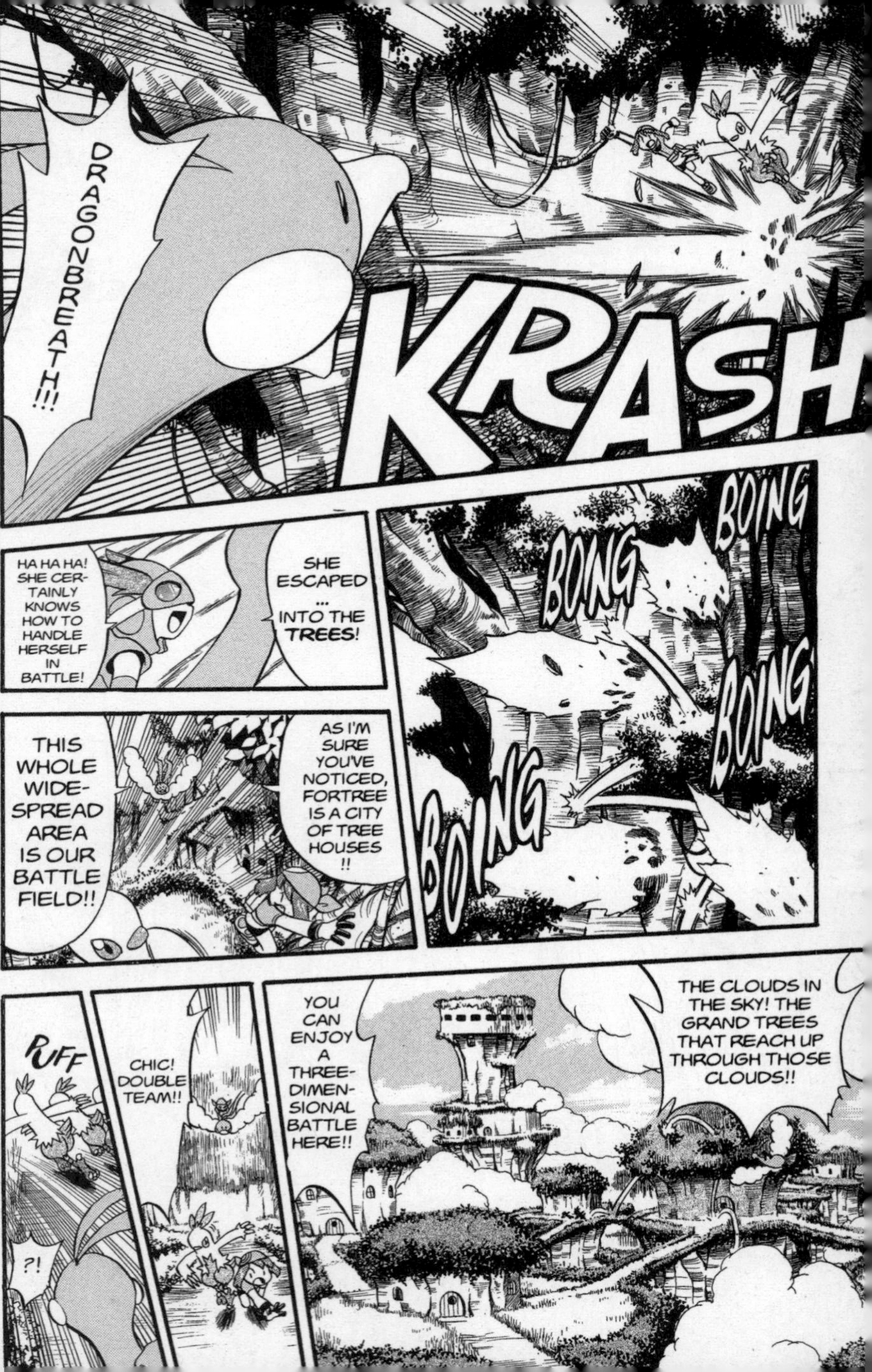
DRAGONBREATH!!!
KRASH
BOING
BOING
BOING
BOING
BOING
SHE ESCAPED ... INTO THE TREES!
HA HA HA! SHE CERTAINLY KNOWS HOW TO HANDLE HERSELF IN BATTLE!
AS I'M SURE YOU'VE NOTICED, FORTREE IS A CITY OF TREE HOUSES !!
THIS WHOLE WIDE-SPREAD AREA IS OUR BATTLE FIELD!!
THE CLOUDS IN THE SKY! THE GRAND TREES THAT REACH UP THROUGH THOSE CLOUDS!!
YOU CAN ENJOY A THREE-DIMENSIONAL BATTLE HERE!!
CHIC! DOUBLE TEAM!!
PUFF
?!

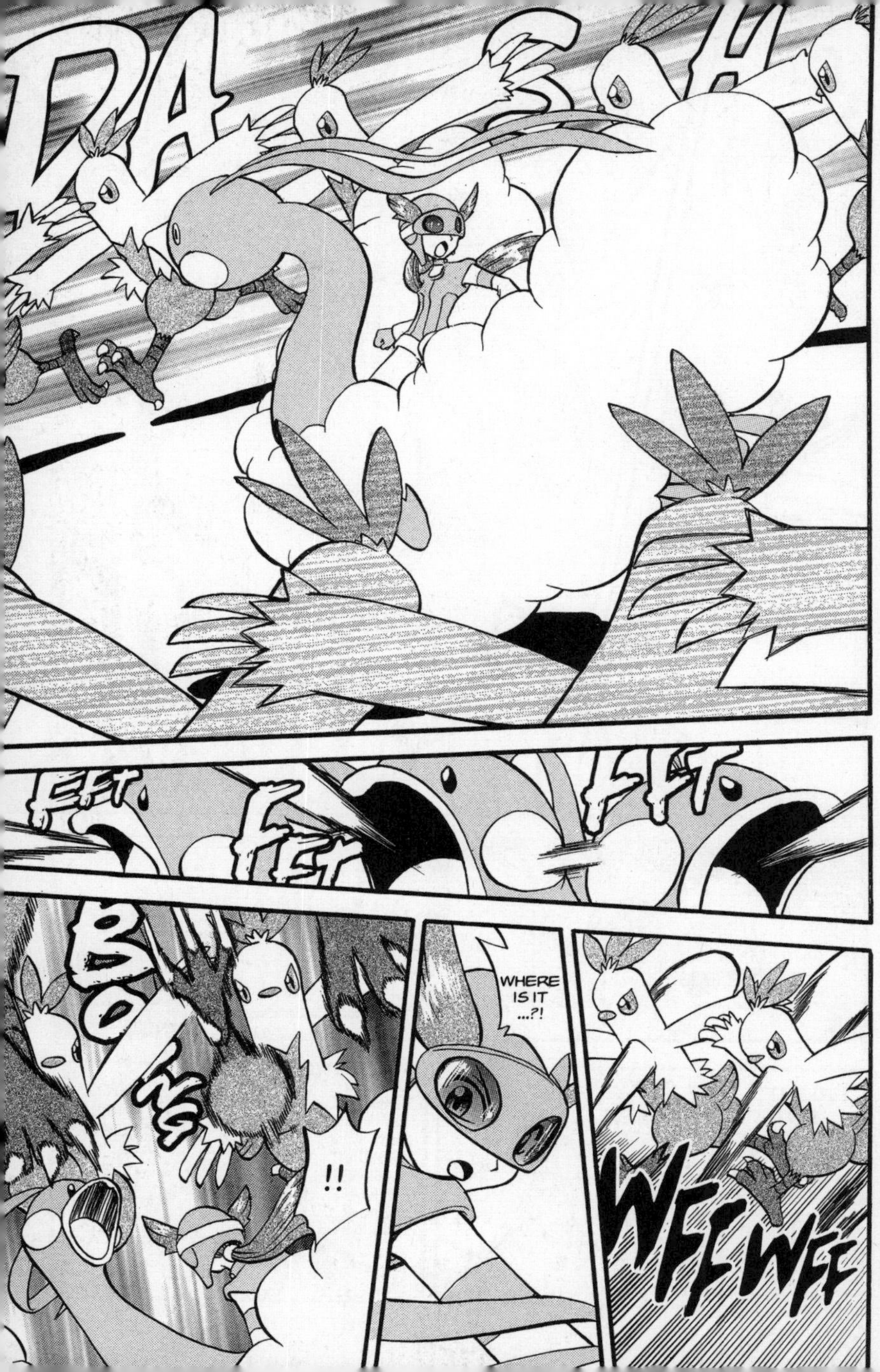
DASH
FFT
FFT
FFT.
WFF WFF
WHERE IS IT ...?!
BOING
!!

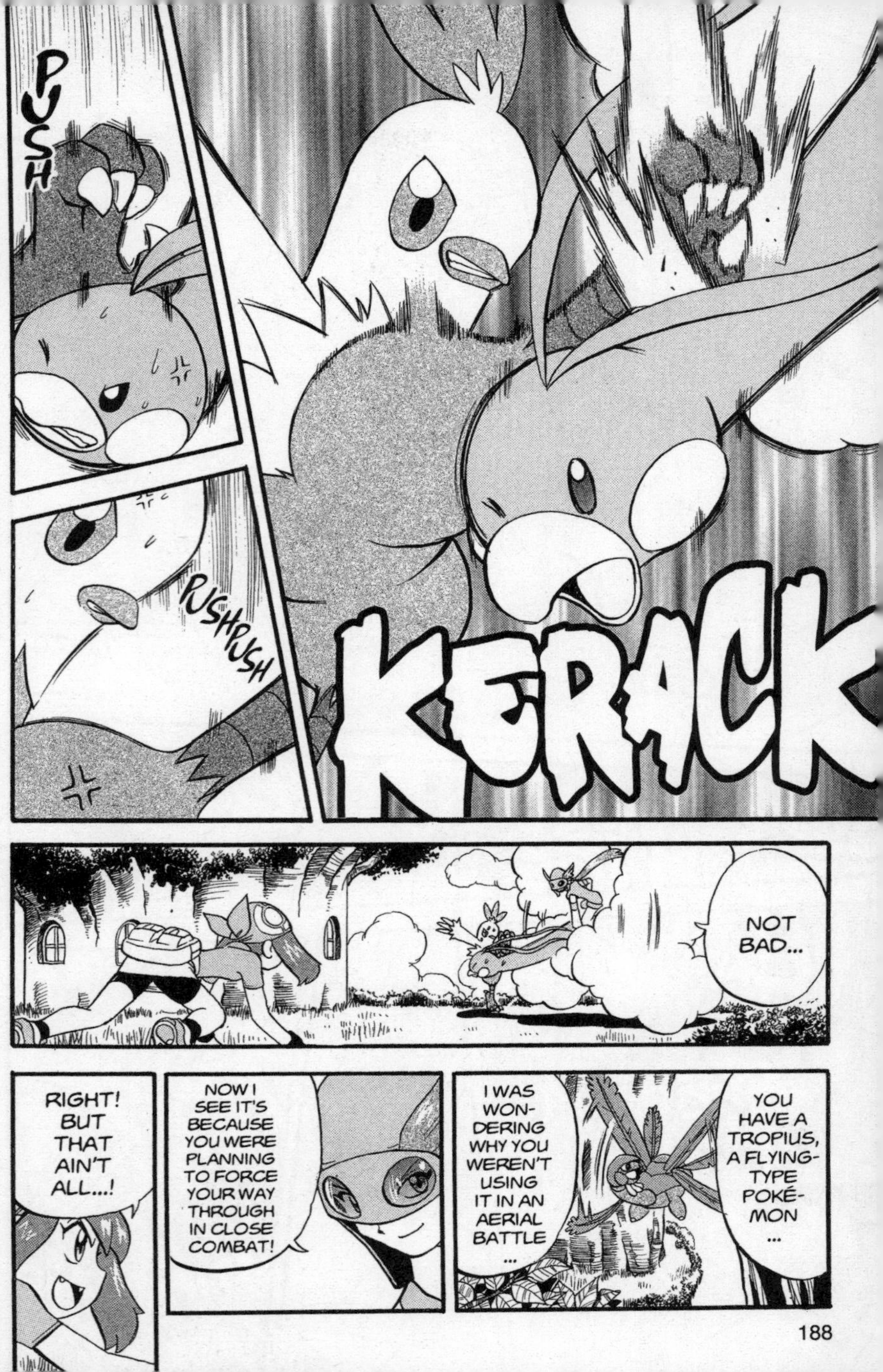
KERACK
PUSH
PUSHPUSH
NOT BAD...
YOU HAVE A TROPIUS, A FLYING-TYPE POKÉMON...
I WAS WONDERING WHY YOU WEREN'T USING IT IN AN AERIAL BATTLE...
NOW I SEE IT'S BECAUSE YOU WERE PLANNING TO FORCE YOUR WAY THROUGH IN CLOSE COMBAT!
RIGHT! BUT THAT AIN'T ALL...!

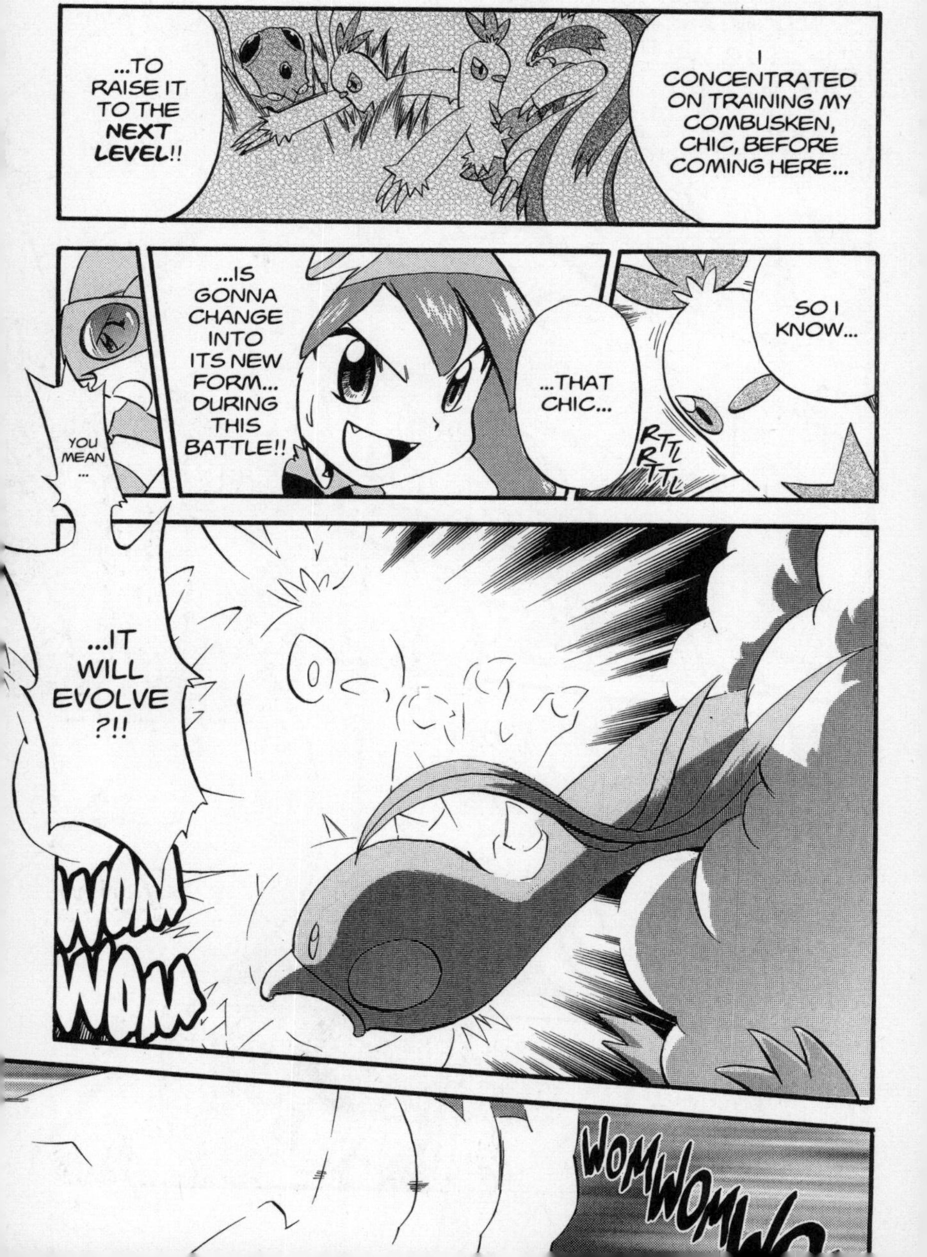
I CONCENTRATED ON TRAINING MY COMBUSKEN, CHIC, BEFORE COMING HERE...
...TO RAISE IT TO THE NEXT LEVEL!!
SO I KNOW...
...THAT CHIC...
RTTL RTTL
...IS GONNA CHANGE INTO ITS NEW FORM... DURING THIS BATTLE!!
YOU MEAN...
...IT WILL EVOLVE?!!
WOM WOM
WOMWOMWO

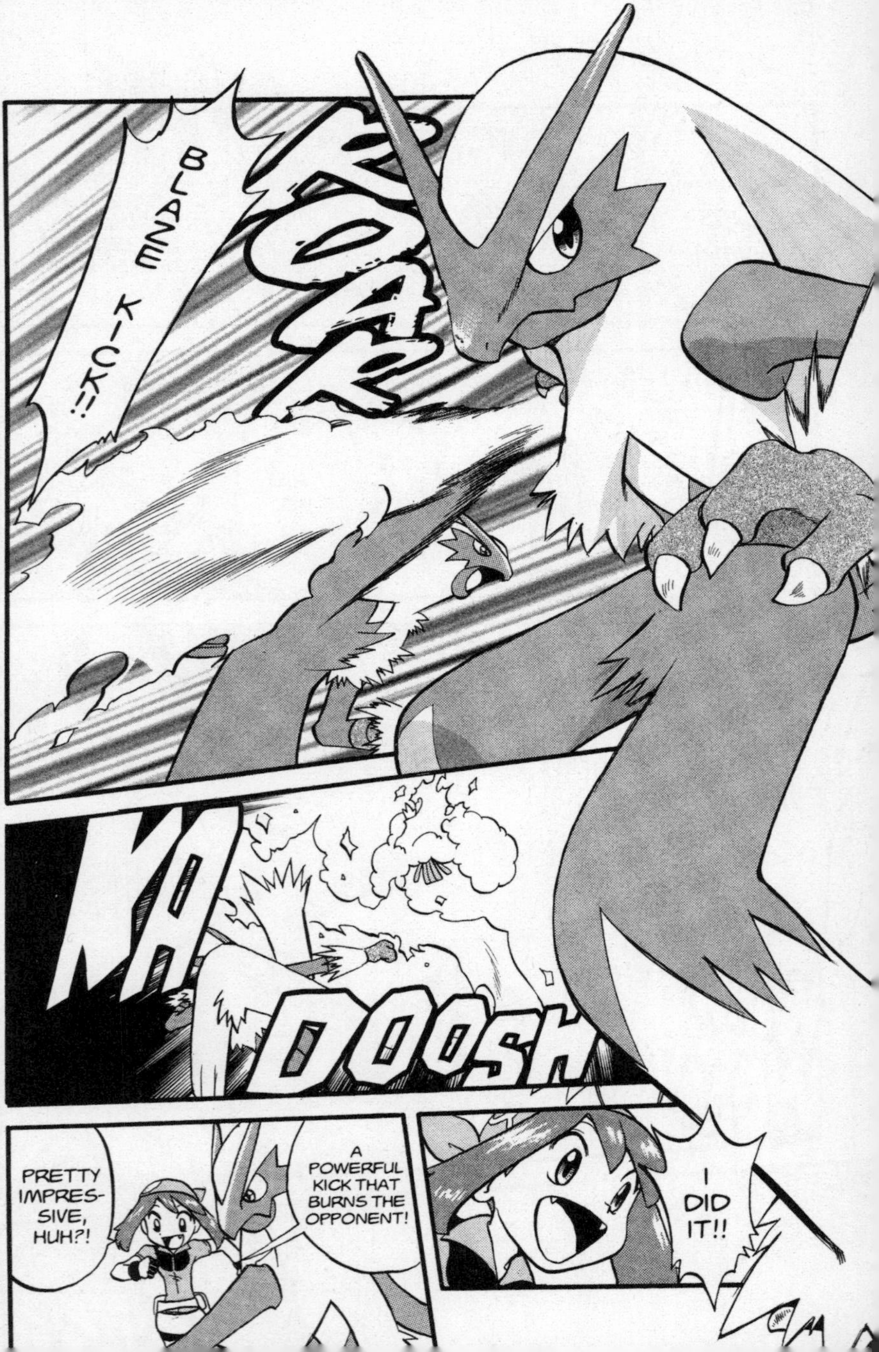
ROAR
BLAZE KICK!!
KA
DOOSH
I DID IT!!
A POWERFUL KICK THAT BURNS THE OPPONENT!
PRETTY IMPRES-SIVE, HUH?!

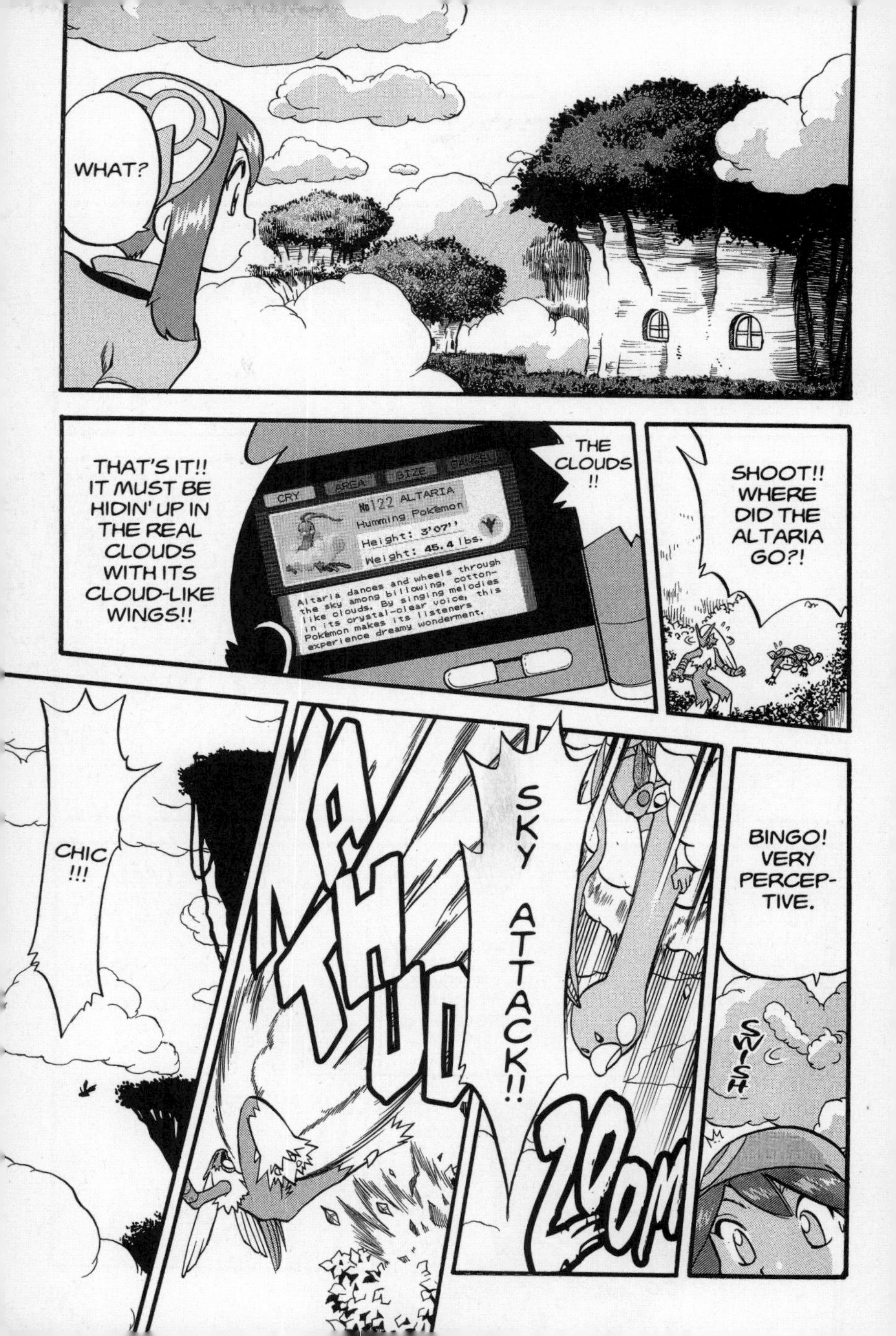
WHAT?
SHOOT!! WHERE DID THE ALTARIA GO?!
THE CLOUDS !!
THAT'S IT!! IT MUST BE HIDIN' UP IN THE REAL CLOUDS WITH ITS CLOUD-LIKE WINGS!!
CRY
AREA
SIZE
CANCEL
No122 ALTARIA
Humming Pokémon
Height: 3'07''
Weight: 45.4 lbs.
Altaria dances and wheels through the sky among billowing, cotton-like clouds. By singing melodies in its crystal-clear voice, this Pokémon makes its listeners experience dreamy wonderment.
BINGO! VERY PERCEP-TIVE.
SWISH
SKY ATTACK!!
ZOOM
CHIC !!!

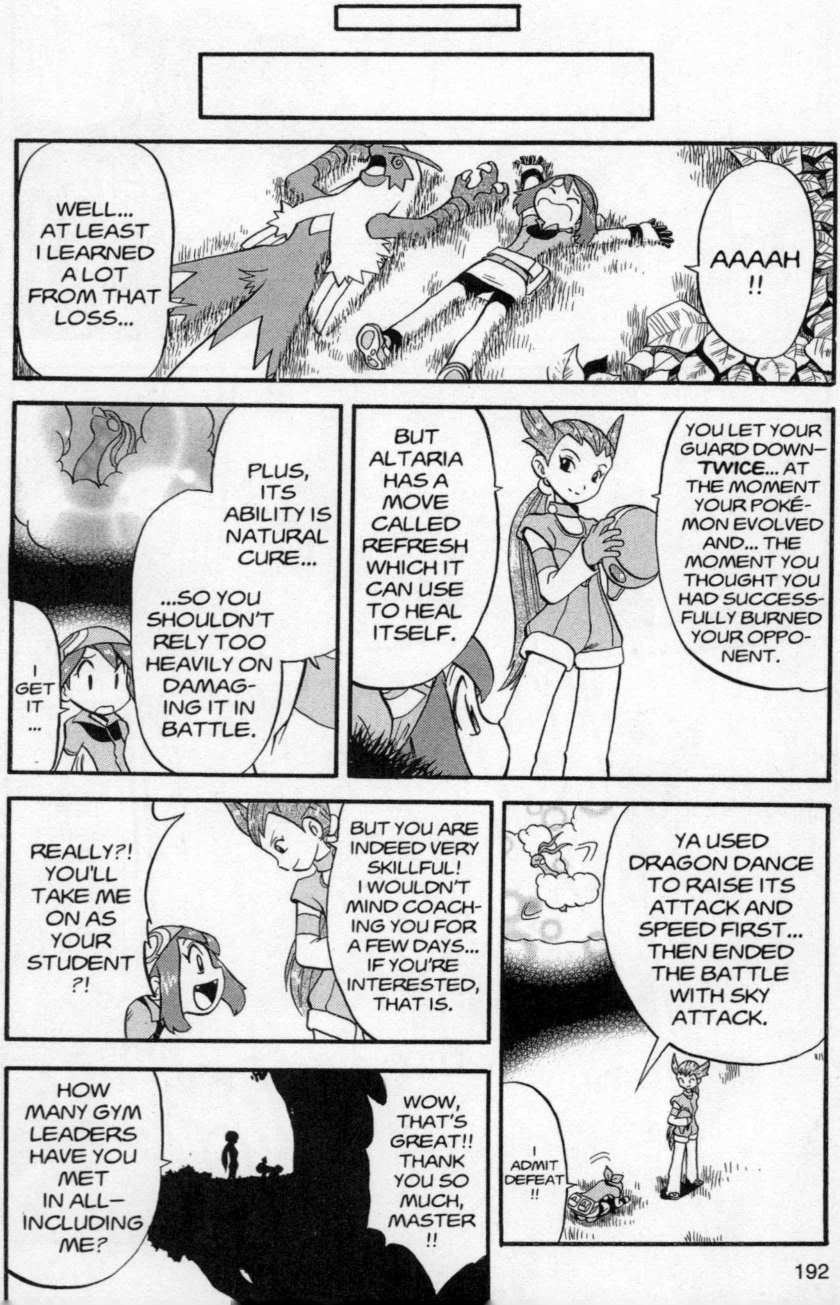
AAAAH !!
WELL... AT LEAST I LEARNED A LOT FROM THAT LOSS...
YOU LET YOUR GUARD DOWN—**TWICE**... AT THE MOMENT YOUR POKÉ-MON EVOLVED AND... THE MOMENT YOU THOUGHT YOU HAD SUCCESS-FULLY BURNED YOUR OPPO-NENT.
BUT ALTARIA HAS A MOVE CALLED REFRESH WHICH IT CAN USE TO HEAL ITSELF.
PLUS, ITS ABILITY IS NATURAL CURE...
...SO YOU SHOULDN'T RELY TOO HEAVILY ON DAMAG-ING IT IN BATTLE.
I GET IT ...
YA USED DRAGON DANCE TO RAISE ITS ATTACK AND SPEED FIRST... THEN ENDED THE BATTLE WITH SKY ATTACK.
I ADMIT DEFEAT !!
BUT YOU ARE INDEED VERY SKILLFUL! I WOULDN'T MIND COACH-ING YOU FOR A FEW DAYS... IF YOU'RE INTERESTED, THAT IS.
REALLY?! YOU'LL TAKE ME ON AS YOUR STUDENT ?!
WOW, THAT'S GREAT!! THANK YOU SO MUCH, MASTER !!
HOW MANY GYM LEADERS HAVE YOU MET IN ALL— INCLUDING ME?

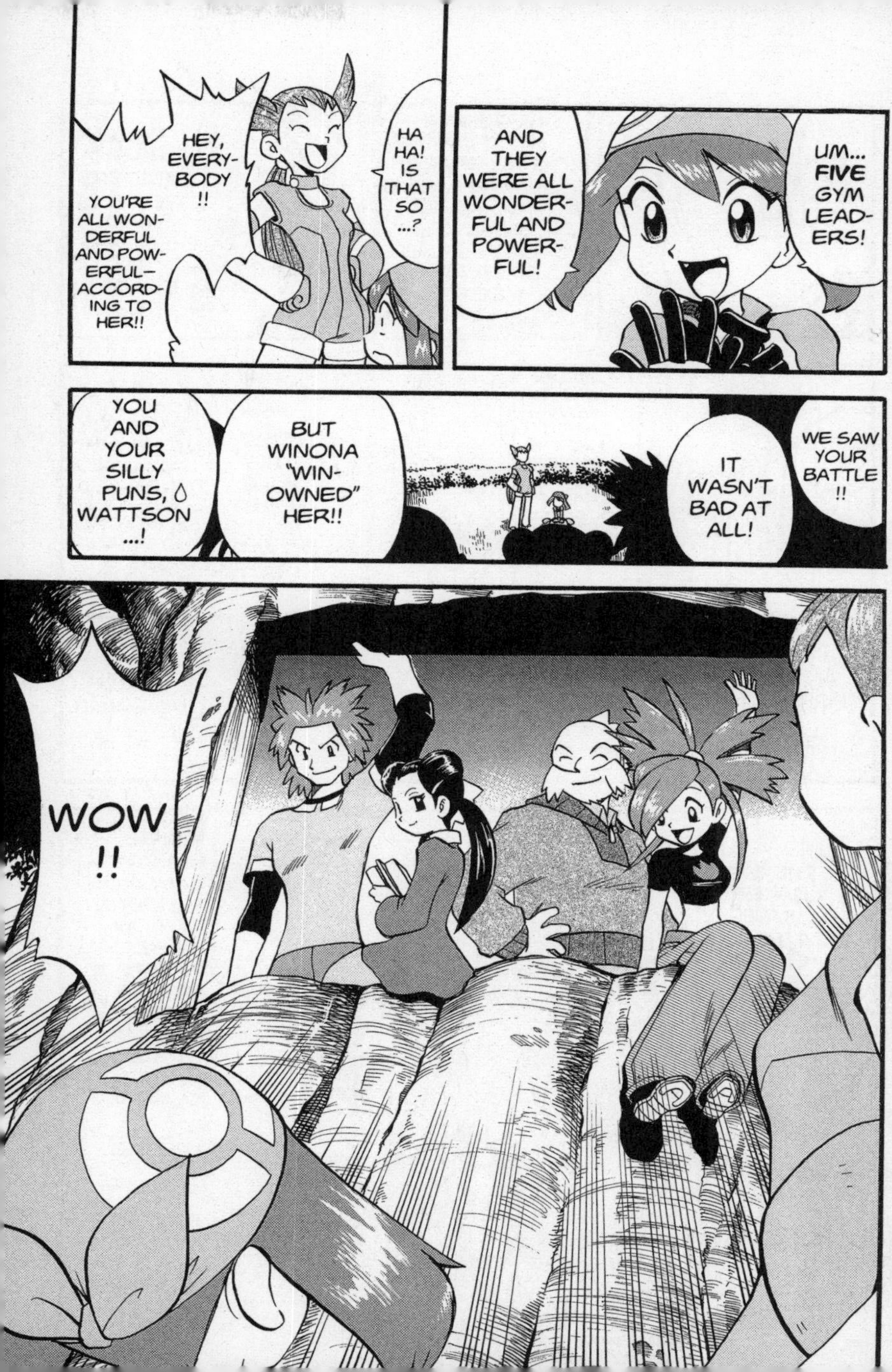
UM... FIVE GYM LEADERS!
AND THEY WERE ALL WONDERFUL AND POWERFUL!
HA HA! IS THAT SO ...?
HEY, EVERYBODY !!
YOU'RE ALL WONDERFUL AND POWERFUL—ACCORDING TO HER!!
WE SAW YOUR BATTLE !!
IT WASN'T BAD AT ALL!
BUT WINONA "WIN-OWNED" HER!!
YOU AND YOUR SILLY PUNS, WATTSON ...!
WOW !!

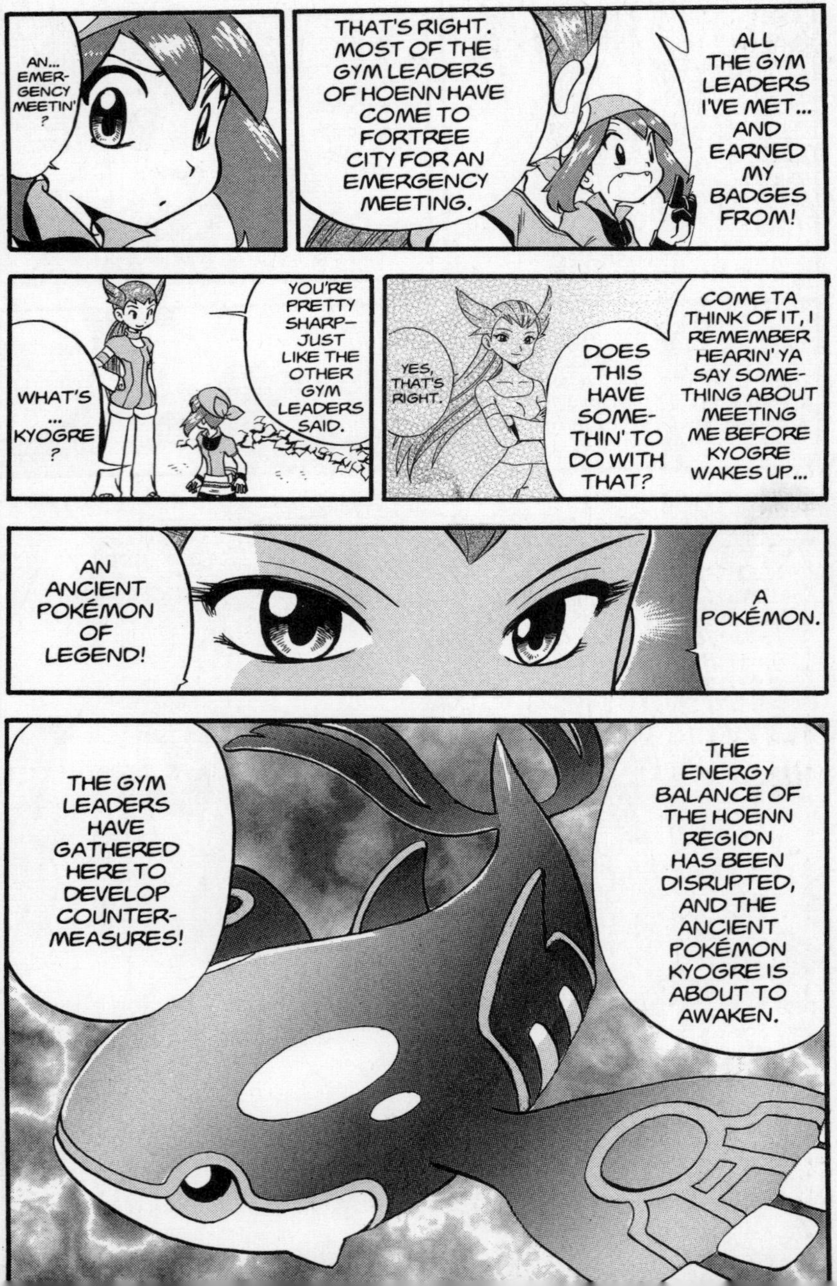
ALL THE GYM LEADERS I'VE MET... AND EARNED MY BADGES FROM!
THAT'S RIGHT. MOST OF THE GYM LEADERS OF HOENN HAVE COME TO FORTREE CITY FOR AN EMERGENCY MEETING.
AN... EMERGENCY MEETIN'?
COME TA THINK OF IT, I REMEMBER HEARIN' YA SAY SOMETHING ABOUT MEETING ME BEFORE KYOGRE WAKES UP...
DOES THIS HAVE SOMETHIN' TO DO WITH THAT?
YES, THAT'S RIGHT.
YOU'RE PRETTY SHARP—JUST LIKE THE OTHER GYM LEADERS SAID.
WHAT'S ... KYOGRE?
A POKÉMON.
AN ANCIENT POKÉMON OF LEGEND!
THE ENERGY BALANCE OF THE HOENN REGION HAS BEEN DISRUPTED, AND THE ANCIENT POKÉMON KYOGRE IS ABOUT TO AWAKEN.
THE GYM LEADERS HAVE GATHERED HERE TO DEVELOP COUNTER-MEASURES!

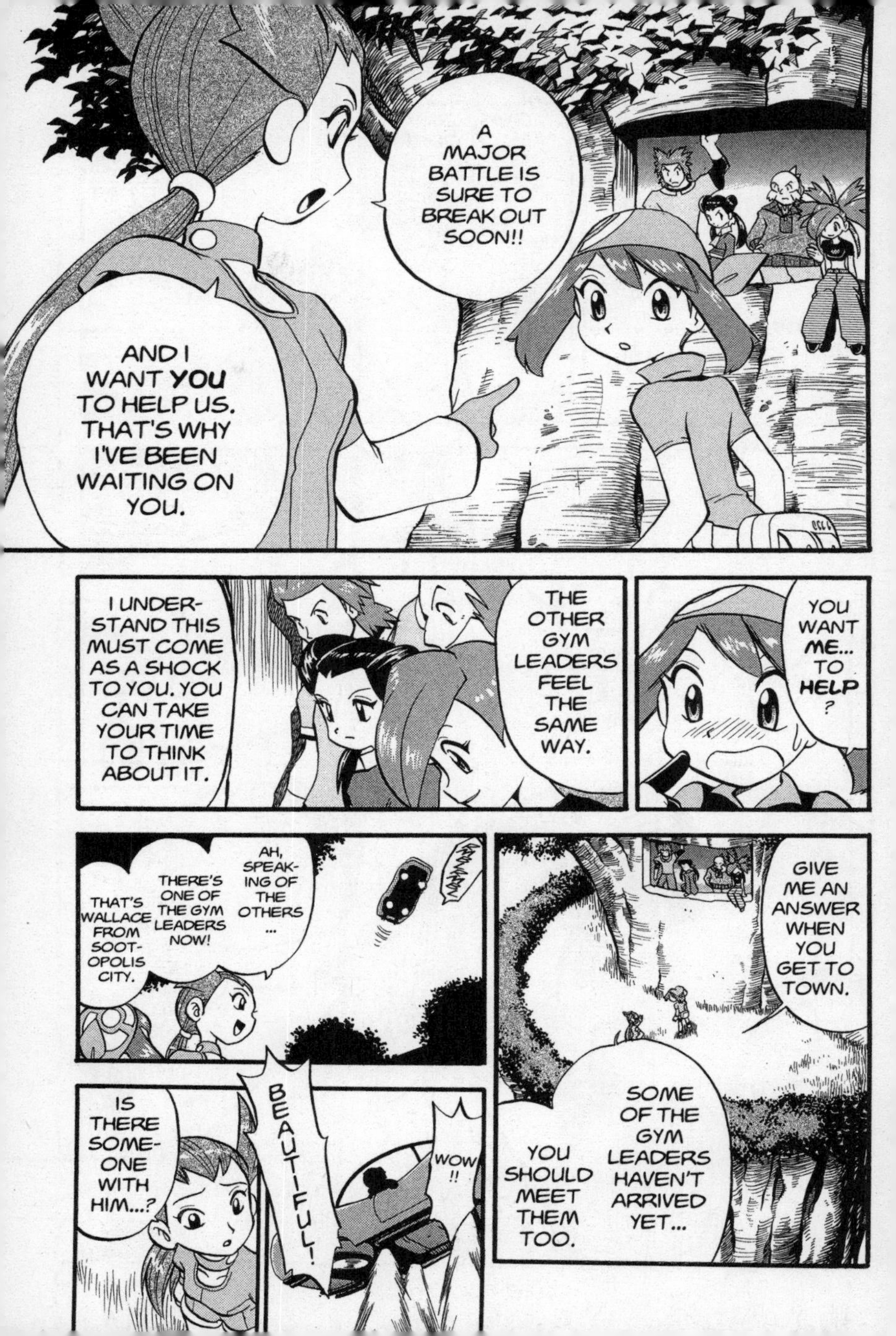
A MAJOR BATTLE IS SURE TO BREAK OUT SOON!!
AND I WANT **YOU** TO HELP US. THAT'S WHY I'VE BEEN WAITING ON YOU.
YOU WANT **ME**... TO **HELP**?
THE OTHER GYM LEADERS FEEL THE SAME WAY.
I UNDERSTAND THIS MUST COME AS A SHOCK TO YOU. YOU CAN TAKE YOUR TIME TO THINK ABOUT IT.
GIVE ME AN ANSWER WHEN YOU GET TO TOWN.
SOME OF THE GYM LEADERS HAVEN'T ARRIVED YET...
YOU SHOULD MEET THEM TOO.
AH, SPEAKING OF THE OTHERS ...
THERE'S ONE OF THE GYM LEADERS NOW!
THAT'S WALLACE FROM SOOTOPOLIS CITY.
WOW !!
BEAUTIFUL!
IS THERE SOMEONE WITH HIM...?

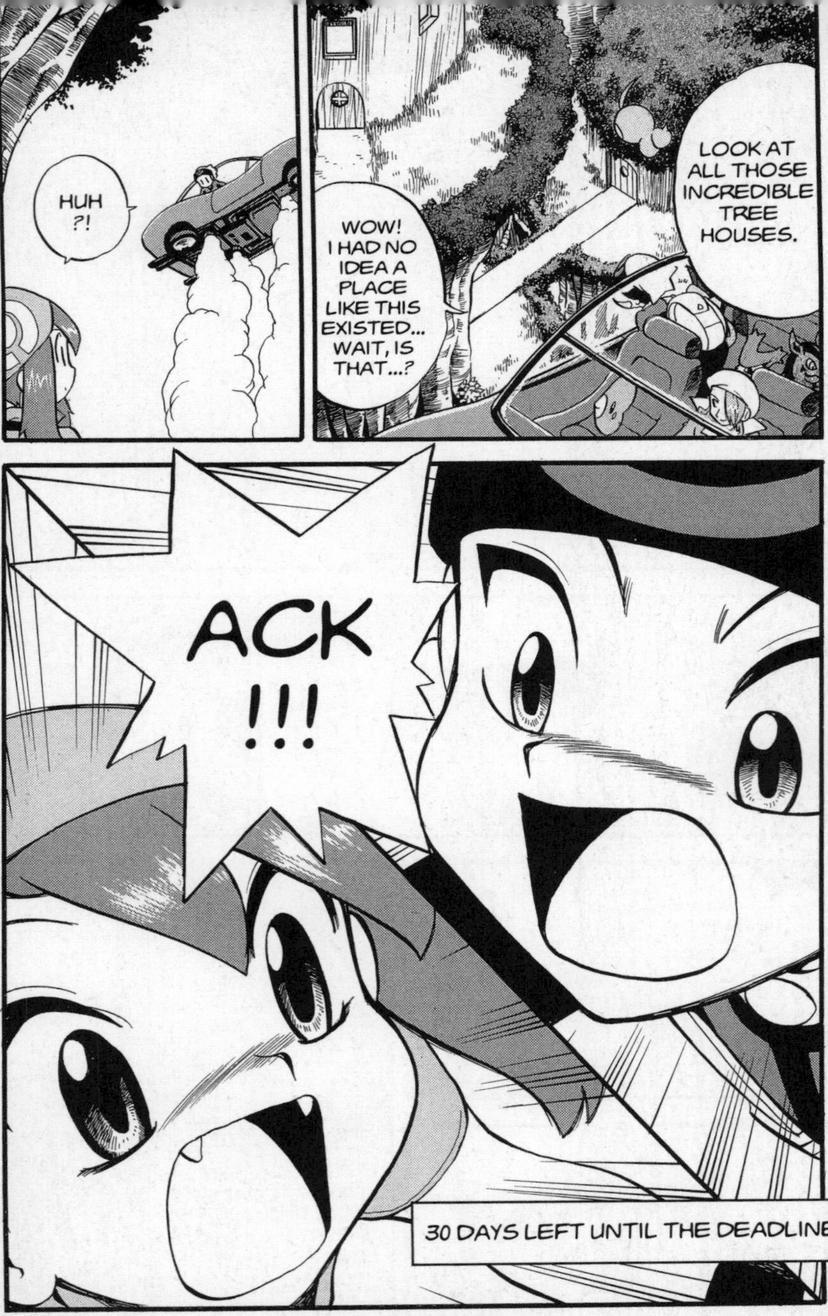
LOOK AT ALL THOSE INCREDIBLE TREE HOUSES.
WOW! I HAD NO IDEA A PLACE LIKE THIS EXISTED... WAIT, IS THAT...?
HUH ?!
ACK !!!
30 DAYS LEFT UNTIL THE DEADLINE!

TO BE CONTINUED...

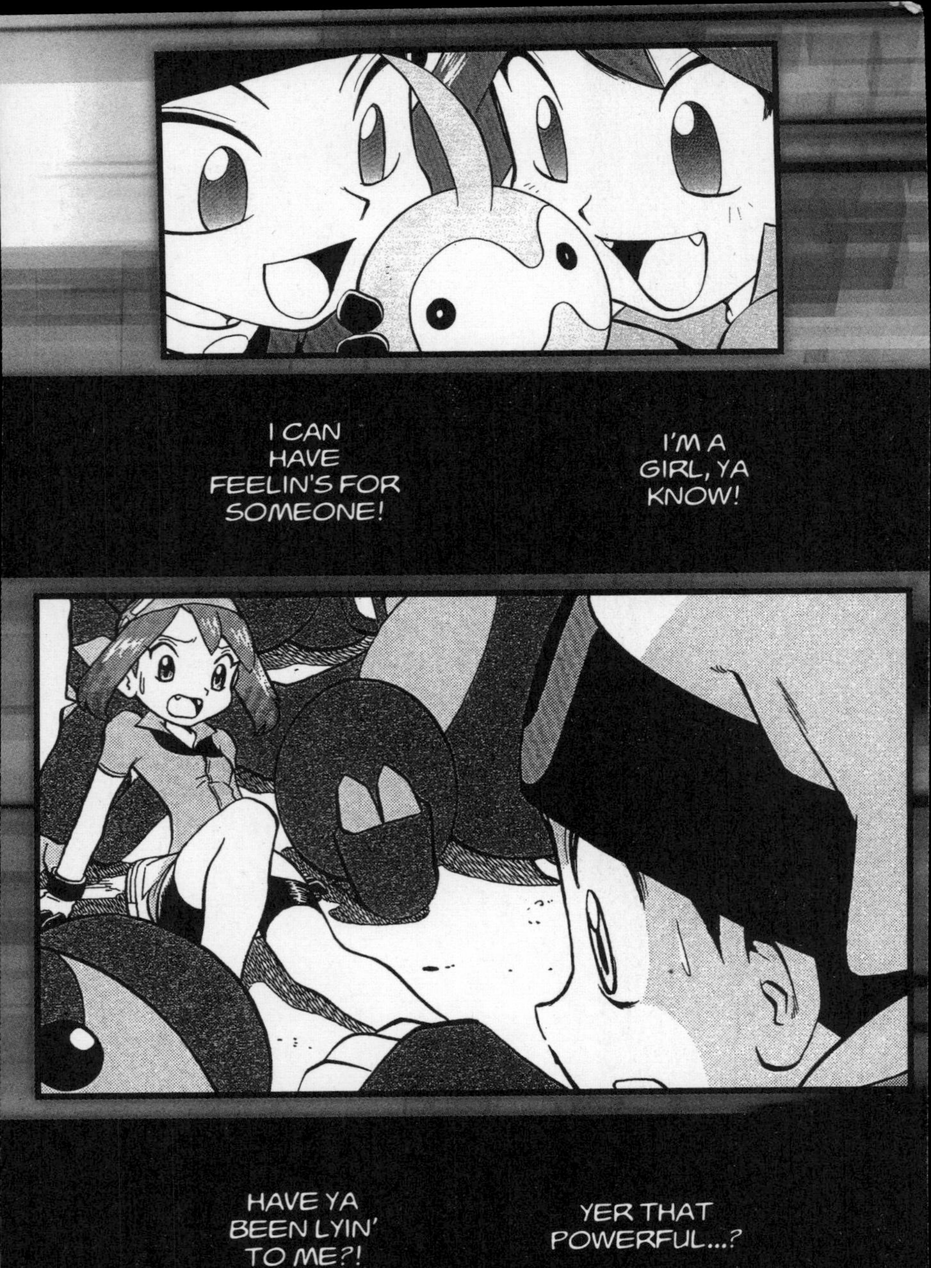
I'M A GIRL, YA KNOW!
I CAN HAVE FEELIN'S FOR SOMEONE!
YER THAT POWERFUL...?
HAVE YA BEEN LYIN' TO ME?!

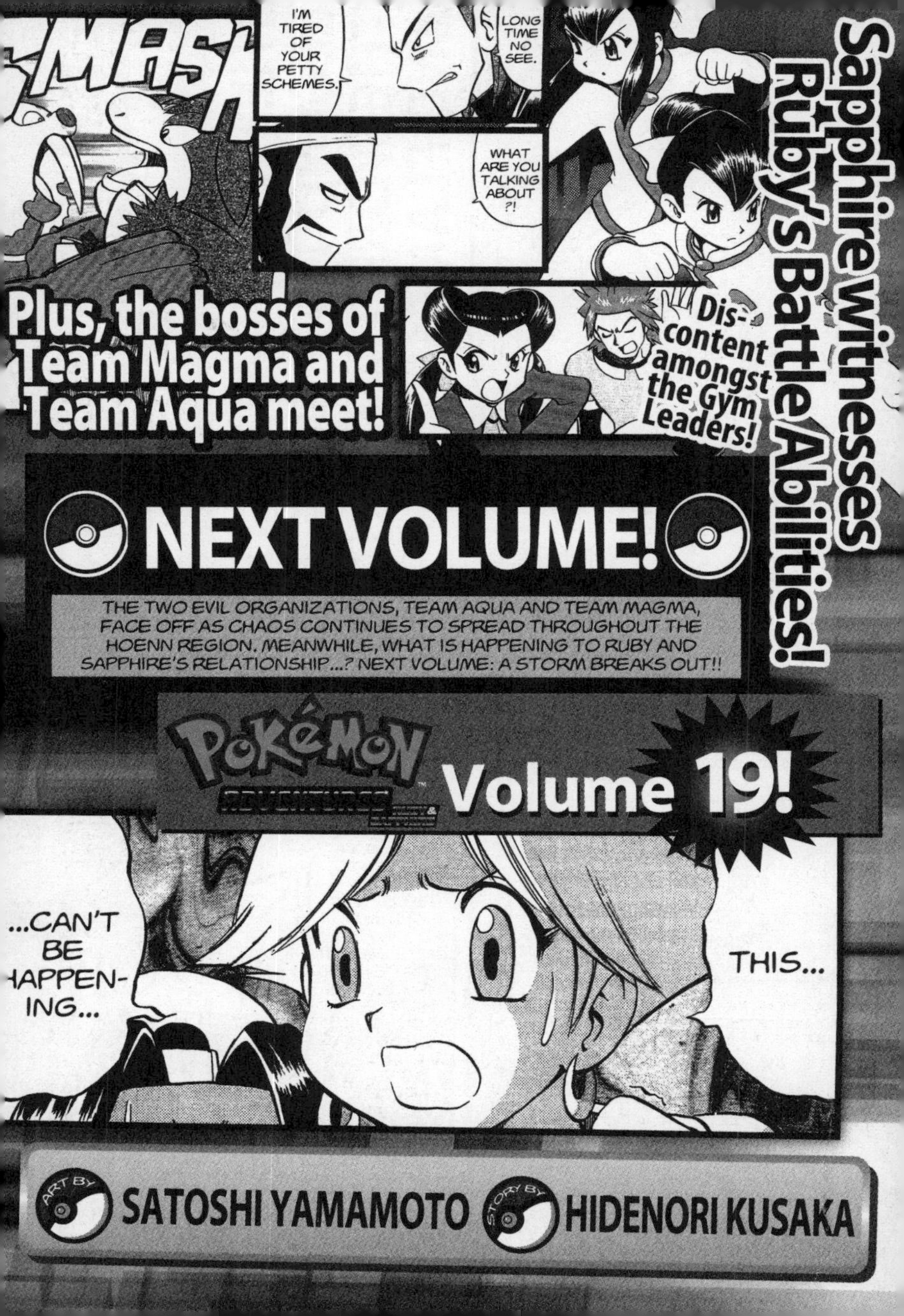

Sapphire Witnesses Ruby's Battle Abilities!
LONG TIME NO SEE.
I'M TIRED OF YOUR PETTY SCHEMES.
WHAT ARE YOU TALKING ABOUT ?!
MASH
Dis-content amongst the Gym Leaders!
Plus, the bosses of Team Magma and Team Aqua meet!
NEXT VOLUME!
THE TWO EVIL ORGANIZATIONS, TEAM AQUA AND TEAM MAGMA, FACE OFF AS CHAOS CONTINUES TO SPREAD THROUGHOUT THE HOENN REGION. MEANWHILE, WHAT IS HAPPENING TO RUBY AND SAPPHIRE'S RELATIONSHIP...? NEXT VOLUME: A STORM BREAKS OUT!!
Pokémon
Volume 19!
THIS...
...CAN'T BE HAPPEN-ING...
ART BY SATOSHI YAMAMOTO
STORY BY HIDENORI KUSAKA

Special Feature: The Conflict Between Land and Sea! The existence of the ancient Legendary Pokémon finally revealed!

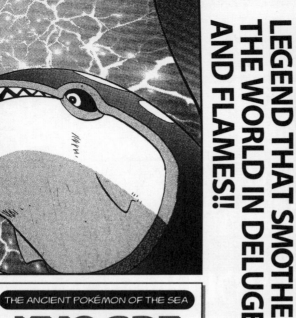

The Hoenn Region

THE ANCIENT LEGENDARY POKÉMON

Team Aqua and Team Magma attempt to awaken them! Legend is about to become reality, as the time for the two Pokémon's awakening draws near...

THE FIERCE BATTLE OF LEGEND THAT SMOTHERED THE WORLD IN DELUGES AND FLAMES!!

ACCORDING TO THE LEGEND PASSED DOWN FOR GENERATIONS IN THE HOENN REGION, IN ANCIENT TIMES, THESE TWO POKÉMON FELL INTO A DEEP SLUMBER AFTER FIGHTING A CEASELESS BATTLE, A COLOSSAL CLASH BETWEEN LAND AND SEA. IF THESE TWO WERE TO APPEAR AGAIN, THE BATTLE WOULD RAGE AGAIN AS FAR AND WIDE AS BEFORE. WHAT WOULD HAPPEN TO THE HOENN REGION THEN...?

!!!

THE ANCIENT POKÉMON OF THE SEA

KYOGRE

THE SEA BASIN POKÉMON CREATES RAIN CLOUDS AND TORRENTIAL DELUGES.

RAIN CLOUDS COVER THE SKIES! THE HEAVY RAIN AND WAVES CREATED BY KYOGRE SWALLOWED UP THE LAND BY FILLING THE SEA UNTIL IT OVERFLOWED ITS BORDERS. AFTER KYOGRE'S BATTLE AGAINST GROUDON, IT FELL INTO A DEEP SLUMBER...

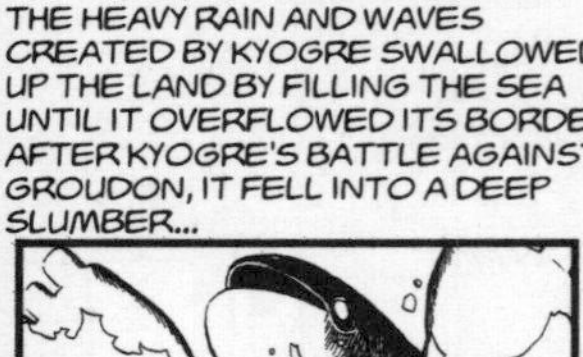

▲IT IS SAID THAT THE RAINS KYOGRE CREATED WERE A BLESSING FOR THE PEOPLE AND THEIR LAND BECAUSE THEY WERE PLAGUED BY DROUGHTS.

The ones who wish to awaken Kyogre are...

...TEAM AQUA!

◀TEAM AQUA'S OBJECTIVE IS TO INCREASE THE AREA OF THE SEA BY AWAKENING KYOGRE.

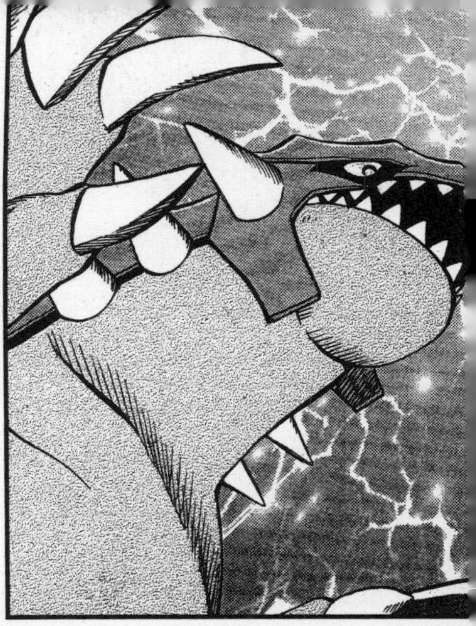

THE ANCIENT POKÉMON OF THE LAND

GROUDON

THE CONTINENT POKÉMON EVAPORATES THE SEA WITH LIGHT AND HEAT.

A POWERFUL HEAT RAY THAT EVAPORATES EVERY LIQUID! GROUDON'S FIRE SCORCHED THE LAND. GROUDON FOUGHT A FIERCE BATTLE AGAINST KYOGRE.

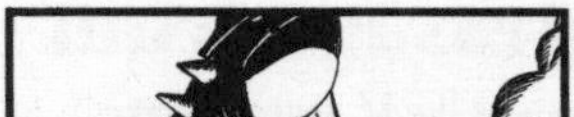

▲ GROUDON'S HEAT SAVED THE PEOPLE FROM FLOODS BY DRYING UP THE LAND.

The ones who wish to awaken Groudon are...

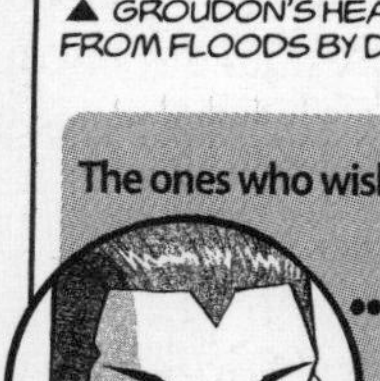

...TEAM MAGMA!

◀ TEAM MAGMA'S OBJECTIVE IS TO INCREASE THE AREA OF THE LAND BY AWAKENING GROUDON.

DID TWO ORBS END THE BATTLE OF THE LEGENDARY POKÉMON?

ACCORDING TO LEGEND, IN ANCIENT TIMES, IT WAS TWO ORBS WITH MYSTICAL POWERS THAT ENDED THE INTERMINABLE BATTLE BETWEEN GROUDON AND KYOGRE. IN OTHER WORDS, THESE TWO ORBS HAVE THE POWER TO CONTROL THESE TWO MIGHTY POKÉMON. BUT WHERE ARE THE ORBS NOW...?

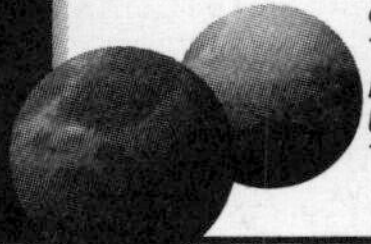

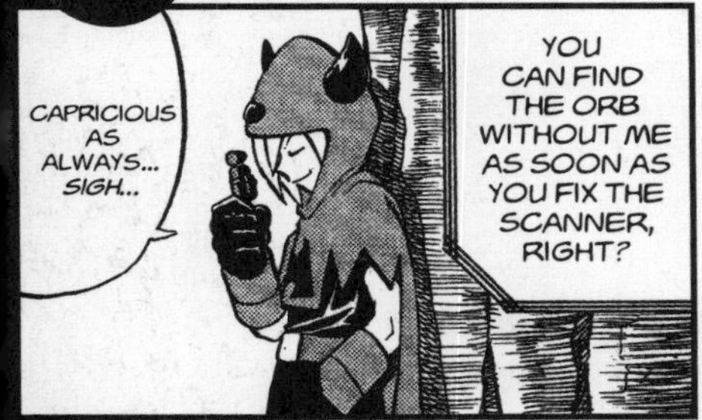
YOU CAN FIND THE ORB WITHOUT ME AS SOON AS YOU FIX THE SCANNER, RIGHT?
CAPRICIOUS AS ALWAYS... SIGH...

▲TEAM MAGMA'S SCANNER TURNED OUT TO BE A DEVICE TO LOCATE THE RED ORB AND THE BLUE ORB!

IT SEEMS THE CHAIRMAN OF THE POKÉMON ASSOCIATION WAS AWARE OF THE EXISTENCE OF THESE TWO LEGENDARY POKÉMON AS WELL.

THE CHAIRMAN OF THE POKÉMON ASSOCIATION PREDICTED THE AWAKENING OF THE ANCIENT POKÉMON AND AGREED TO LET FLANNERY GATHER THE GYM LEADERS OF THE HOENN REGION TO PREPARE FOR THEIR RETURN. BUT DOES THE CHAIRMAN KNOW MORE THAN HE'S LETTING ON...?

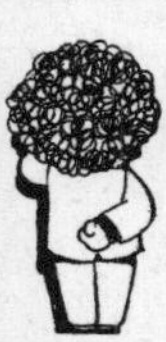

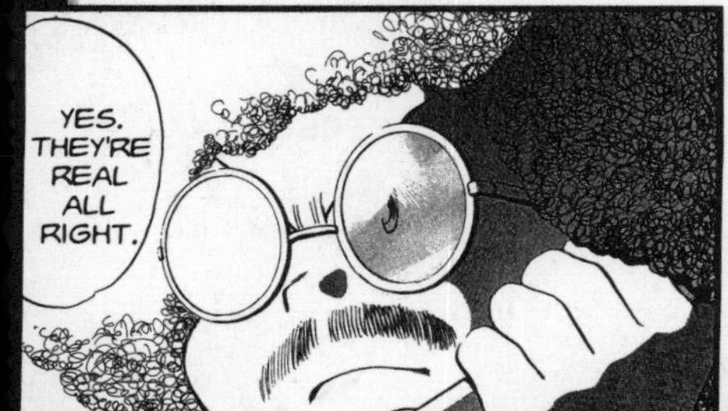
YES. THEY'RE REAL ALL RIGHT.

▲THE HIGHEST AUTHORITY OF THE POKÉMON ASSOCIATION, WHO HANDPICKED THE GYM LEADERS. APPARENTLY THE CHAIRMAN HAS ALREADY DEPLOYED SOME OF THEM ON A SECRET MISSION...

Message from
Hidenori Kusaka

You can play with *Pokémon FireRed* and *Pokémon LeafGreen* in all sorts of ways, so I've been playing these games for a really long time. Communication is an important aspect of these Pokémon games. Unfortunately, at the moment I don't have anybody to play with. But I'll get my chance at large events, which are attended by lots of players. In fact, I'm off to one of them now with my game console!

Message from
Satoshi Yamamoto

It's been four years since I started working on *Pokémon Adventures*. This is the first long series that I've done, and volume 18 marks my ninth volume! I like a lot of the episodes and characters, but I get encouragement by always telling myself, "This latest volume is the best!" (*laugh*)

More Adventures Coming Soon...

Ruby is losing friends by the minute...! Why does Sapphire never want to see his face again? And why has one of his Pokémon run away? Meanwhile, the Hoenn region is on the verge of destruction as two Legendary Pokémon clash in the depths of the ocean—and only Ruby knows how to reach them to intervene!

Then, what will happen when evil Team Aqua and equally evil Team Magma *team up*?!

AVAILABLE NOW!

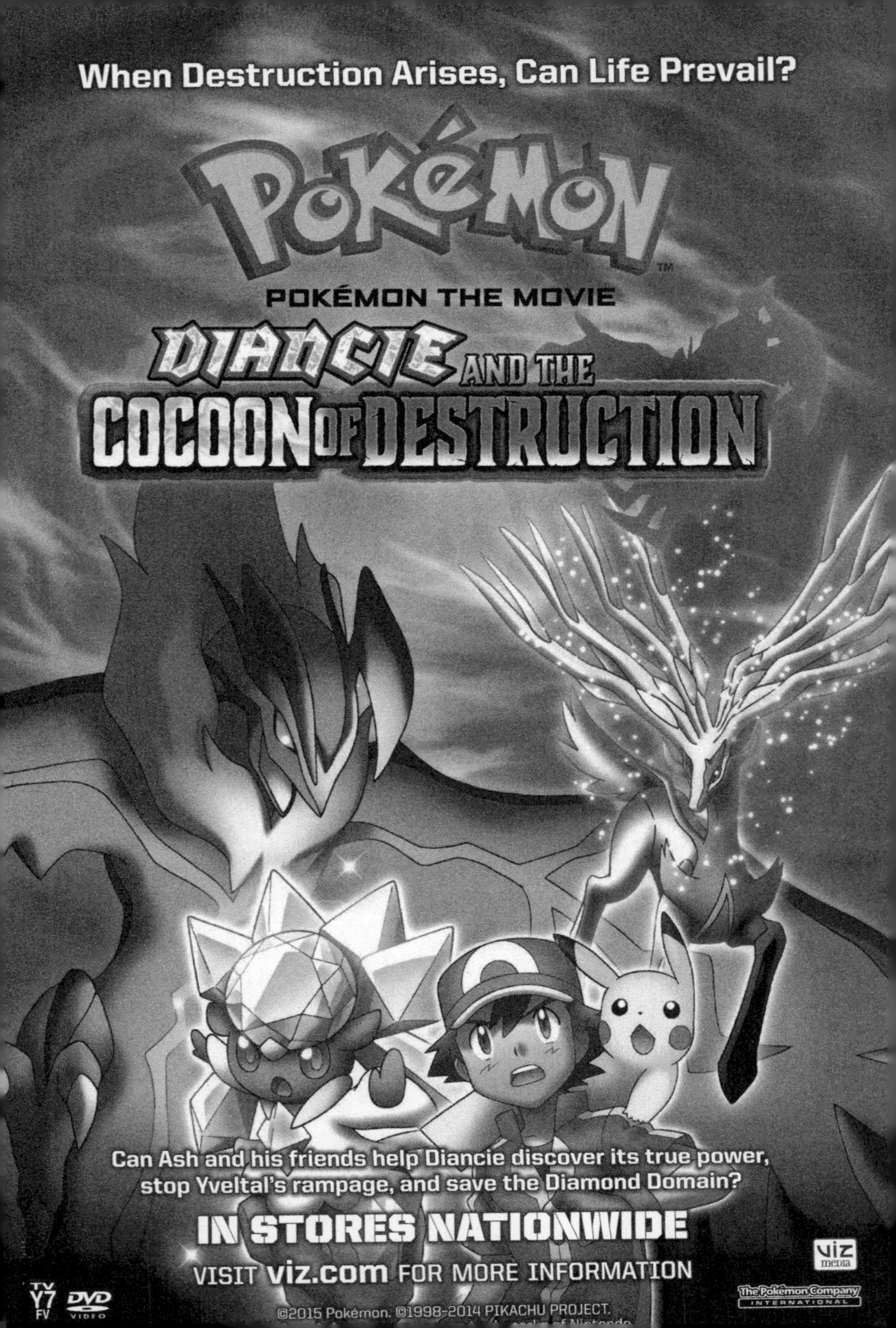
When Destruction Arises, Can Life Prevail?
POKÉMON™
POKÉMON THE MOVIE
DIANCIE AND THE COCOON OF DESTRUCTION
Can Ash and his friends help Diancie discover its true power, stop Yveltal's rampage, and save the Diamond Domain?
IN STORES NATIONWIDE
VISIT viz.com FOR MORE INFORMATION
TV Y7 FV
DVD VIDEO
VIZ media
The Pokémon Company INTERNATIONAL
©2015 Pokémon. ©1998-2014 PIKACHU PROJECT.

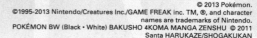

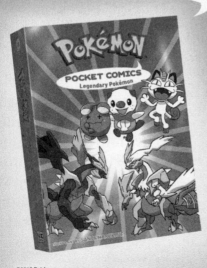

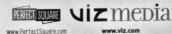